APULEIUS

METAMORPHOSES

I

LCL 44

APULEIUS

METAMORPHOSES

BOOKS I–VI

WITH AN ENGLISH TRANSLATION BY

J. ARTHUR HANSON

HARVARD UNIVERSITY PRESS
CAMBRIDGE, MASSACHUSETTS
LONDON, ENGLAND

First published 1989
Reprinted with corrections 1996

Library of Congress Cataloging-in-Publication Data

Apuleius.
Metamorphoses.
(The Loeb classical library)
Latin and English.
Includes bibliographical references.
CONTENTS: v. 1. Books I–VI—v. 2. Books VII–XI.
I. Hanson, John Arthur. II Title. III. Series.
PA6209.M3H36 1989 873′.01 89–15577
ISBN 0-674-99049-8 (v. 1)
ISBN 0-674-99498-1 (v. 2)

Typeset by Chiron Inc.
Printed in Great Britain by St Edmundsbury Press Ltd,
Bury St Edmunds, Suffolk, on acid-free paper.
Bound by Hunter & Foulis Ltd, Edinburgh, Scotland.

CONTENTS

FOREWORD

JOHN ARTHUR HANSON died suddenly on March 28, 1985, less than a month after his 54th birthday. Two years earlier he had completed his replacement of the Loeb 'Golden Ass' commissioned by my predecessor, but the Library's large backlog of prior commitments prevented immediate publication then and has compelled postponement to the present date.

Had he lived to write a preface he would have stressed that his foremost aim was to bring out the enchanting qualities of his author, which he feared an emphasis on scholarship would obscure. For detailed textual information he expected readers to consult the critical editions in the Teubner or Budé series, and so he limited himself to indicating departures from the text of the tradition and adjusted the Latin spelling to imperial norms. We had agreed that when publication was imminent, he would be allowed, in the process of copy-editing, to submit any additions and changes of opinion he then desired to make.

Haec prius fuere: as it is, these volumes constitute an achievement of Arthur Hanson to which he was unable to give a final polish. In seeing his work through the press I have added a few items to the bibliography, compiled an index (largely adapted from the old volume), and made such changes as I am confident he would have approved, as my own small tribute to a fine scholar and teacher, whose death caused all who knew him a lasting sadness.

December 29, 1988 — G. P. GOOLD
Yale University — General Editor

INTRODUCTION

APULEIUS was born in the Roman province of Africa about A.D. 125, probably in the town of Madauros. The date of his birth, as well as most other facts about his life, are inferred from his *Apology*, which purports to be a speech delivered in his own defence before the proconsul of Africa, and from the *Florida*, a small collection of "purple" passages from his other orations. He studied at Carthage and in Athens, travelled extensively, including at least one visit to Rome, and apparently settled in Carthage. He claims to have been left a comfortable inheritance by his father, who had been a successful local magistrate. By profession he was a lecturer and philosopher, who engaged in a wide variety of scholarly and literary pursuits. According to his own estimation he composed "poems for the baton and the lyre, the slipper and the buskin; also satires and riddles, not to mention various prose histories and speeches praised by orators and dialogues praised by philosophers—and all these in Greek as well as in Latin with twin desire, equal zeal, and like style."[1]

[1] poemata omnigenus apta virgae, lyrae, socco, coturno, item satiras ac griphos, item historias varias rerum nec non orationes laudatas disertis nec non dialogos laudatos philosophis, atque haec et alia eiusdem modi tam graece quam latine, gemino voto, pari studio, simili stilo (*Florida* IX 27–29).

INTRODUCTION

Of these works only a handful have survived, all in Latin and all in prose. *De deo Socratis* ("Socrates' God") is a lecture about *daemones*, the spirits which people the world between transcendent gods and mortal men, mediating between pure divinity and humankind. *De Platone et eius dogmate* ("Plato and his Doctrine") is a philosophical handbook beginning with a biography of Plato and summarising the metaphysical and ethical teachings of the Platonic school of Apuleius' time. *De mundo* ("The Cosmos") is a description of the physical universe and meteorological phenomena, ending with a virtual hymn of praise for the eternal god who controls the world. This last short treatise is an adapted translation of an extant Greek work, *Peri kosmou*, of the first century B.C. or the first century A.D., which circulated under the name of Aristotle.[1] Taken together, these three works reveal the mind of an intelligent dabbler in philosophy, eclectic in his reading but strongly drawn to Plato and contemporary Platonism, and with a special interest in the religious aspect of philosophical teaching.

The *Apology* is a long, playfully learned speech in which the author defends himself against the charge of having employed magic to beguile a wealthy woman much older than himself, a widow named Pudentilla, to marry him. Whether the facts

[1] See the introduction by D. J. Furley to his translation of the work (Loeb Classical Library: Aristotle, *On Sophistical Refutations*, etc. (1955), 333 ff.).

of the case are autobiographical—as they are usually assumed to be—or not, the oration as a whole is a tongue-in-cheek defence of the scholar-philosopher against his boorish contemporaries, with elements of parody of Plato's *Apology*.

The chief claim to fame, in modern times at least, of this "Platonic philosopher from Madauros"[1] is the long fictional narrative known first as *Metamorphoses*, but later called "The Golden Ass". It recounts, in the first person, the story of a certain Greek named Lucius, who, because of his curiosity to learn about magic, is transformed into an ass; in this form he is variously used and misused by robbers, farmhands, mendicant priests, a miller, a gardener, a soldier, and a pair of cooks, until at the end of a year he regains his human form through the intervention of the goddess Isis, whose devotee he then becomes. Both before and after taking on his ass's hide, he hears a large number of tales, some entertaining, some gruesome, which he includes in his narrative so that his reader too may enjoy them.

This same story of Lucius, without any inserted tales and with a strikingly different ending, exists in a Greek version ascribed by the manuscripts to the second-century sophist Lucian, under the title

[1] Philosophus Platonicus Madaurensis, as he is labelled in several of the later manuscripts of his works.

Loukios e onos ("Lucius or The Ass").[1] The ninth-century Byzantine scholar Photius knew yet another Greek version, which he describes as "The *Metamorphoses* of Lucius of Patras, a work in several books." Photius concluded that "Lucius or The Ass" was a condensation of this Greek *Metamorphoses*, and most modern scholars (who deny the work to Lucian) concur. The Greek *Metamorphoses* may also have served as Apuleius' model for *The Golden Ass.*

Critical estimates of Apuleius' book vary greatly, as do opinions about its form and function. At one extreme it has been viewed as an ill-organised collection of scabrous tales loosely hung on the ludicrous story of the Man-turned-Ass, solely for the entertainment of the reader; at the other extreme, as the serious confession of an Apuleius saved from the errors of the flesh by the grace of Isis, and desiring to thank the goddess and convert the reader. It can be, and has been, read as Platonic allegory, psychic autobiography, *Bildungsroman*, and literary parody. It is a complex and carefully wrought work whose ass-man narrator is often ironic and frequently warns the reader against accepting his words at face value.

"Pay attention, reader, and you will find delight."[2]

[1] Translated by M. D. Macleod in the Loeb Classical Library, Lucian, vol. VIII: see his introduction (pp. 47–51) on the question of authorship.

[2] Lector intende: laetaberis (Apul. *Met.* I 1).

INTRODUCTION

TEXT AND TRANSLATION

The text of the *Metamorphoses* has come down to us in approximately 40 manuscripts, of which all the later ones are almost certainly direct descendants of the earliest, produced in the Beneventan monastery of Monte Cassino in the eleventh century: Codex Laurentianus 68,2, known as F. Modern editors, therefore, have rightly seen their task as reproducing a legible text of F, making use of other manuscripts and conjectures only where F is unreadable or patently in error. I have followed the same principle, making use of the excellent editions of Helm, Robertson, and Giarratano-Frassinetti. The purpose of my critical apparatus is practical: to signal those words in the Latin text which the reader may need to regard with suspicion. These include (1) significant emendations of F, whether these are found in later manuscripts or have been proposed by modern scholars, and (2) places where, although I have printed the reading of F, there are strong arguments which might support emendation. Except in a few cases I have made no attempt to show the sources of emendations or to discuss variant readings: such information is readily available in the critical apparatuses of the editions mentioned above, especially that of Robertson.

I have modernised and regularised the Latin spelling throughout, making no attempt to reproduce the orthographic variations of the eleventh-century manuscript. Likewise I have punctuated according to modern English practice, rather than in the continental style still adopted in most Latin texts.

The virtues of Apuleius' style in the *Golden Ass* would be regarded for the most part as faults in contemporary English prose: exaggeration and repetitiveness, archaism and preciosity, sonority and lyricism. A translator, obliged to make orderly sense out of Apuleius' wonderfully ordered sounds and images, too frequently corrects the faults of his Latin author in the interests of a precision and lucidity foreign to his original. I have tried to avoid this insofar as my childhood English teachers and my academic habits would allow. My success has been limited, and all too often a Latin phrase which was intended as boldly inventive has suffered metamorphosis into standard English. In cases of uncertainty as to the sense of a passage I have tried to hedge the translation where possible, but otherwise not to burden the reader with caveats and alternative translations. The notes to the translation are largely limited to explanations of proper names and allusions necessary for a literal understanding of the text.

BIBLIOGRAPHY

The following list is highly selective. The books marked with an asterisk contain extensive bibliographies. In addition, there is a bibliography covering 1938–70 by C. C. Schlam, *Classical World* 64 (1971) 286–309.

Editions

R. Helm, *Apulei Platonici Madaurensis Opera quae supersunt, Vol. I: Metamorphoseon Libri XI*, 3rd ed. with suppl. (Teubner), Leipzig 1955

D. S. Robertson, *Apulée. Les Métamorphoses*, 3 vols. (Budé), Paris 1940–45 (with French translation by P. Vallette)

C. Giarratano, *Apulei Metamorphoseon Libri XI*, 2nd ed. by P. Frassinetti (Corpus Paravianum), Turin 1960

E. Brandt and W. Ehlers, *Apuleius. Der goldene Esel*, 3rd ed., Munich 1980 (with German translation)

English translations

William Adlington, London 1566 (frequently reprinted)

Thomas Taylor, London 1822
H. E. Butler (2 vols.), Oxford 1910
J. Lindsay, New York 1932
R. Graves, London 1950

Commentaries

Book I: * A. Scobie, *Apuleius Metamorphoses (Asinus Aureus) I: A Commentary* (Beiträge zur Klassischen Philologie 54), Meisenheim am Glan 1975

Book III: * R. T. van der Paardt, *L. Apuleius Madaurensis, The Metamorphoses: A Commentary on Book III with Text and Introduction*, Groningen 1971

Book IV: * B. L. Hijmans Jr. and others, *Apuleius Madaurensis, Metamorphoses Book IV 1–27, Text, Introduction and Commentary* (Groningen Commentaries on Apuleius), Groningen 1977

The Cupid and Psyche Story: Louis C. Purser, *The Story of Cupid and Psyche as related by Apuleius* (copious introduction, text, annotations), London 1910 (repr. College Classical Series, New Rochelle, NY 1983)

Pierre Grimal, *Apulée, Métamorphoses (IV. 28–VI. 24) (Le conte d'Amour et Psyche): Edition, introduction et commentaire*, Paris 1963

Books VI and VII: * B. L. Hijmans Jr. and others, *Apuleius Madaurensis, Metamorphoses VI 25–32 and VII* (Groningen Comm.), Groningen 1981

Book VIII: * B. L. Hijmans and others (Groningen Comm.), Groningen 1985

BIBLIOGRAPHY

Book XI: * J. G. Griffiths, *Apuleius of Madauros, The Isis-Book (Metamorphoses Book XI)*, Leiden 1975

Other

A.-J. Festugière, "Lucius and Isis": chapter 5 of *Personal Religion Among the Greeks* (Sather Classical Lectures 26), Berkeley and Los Angeles 1954

A. R. Heiserman, *The Novel Before the Novel*, Chicago 1977

* B. L. Hijmans Jr. and R. Th. van der Paardt (eds.), *Aspects of Apuleius' Golden Ass*, Groningen 1978

A. D. Nock, "The Conversion of Lucius": chapter 9 of *Conversion*, Oxford 1933

W. A. Oldfather, H. V. Canter, B. E. Perry, *Index Apuleianus*, Middletown, CT 1934

B. E. Perry, *The Ancient Romances* (Sather Classical Lectures 37), Berkeley and Los Angeles 1967

C. C. Schlam, *Cupid and Psyche: Apuleius and the Monuments*, University Park, PA 1976

J. H. Tatum, *Apuleius and "The Golden Ass"*, Ithaca, NY 1979

M. L. von Franz, *A Psychological Interpretation of the Golden Ass of Apuleius*, Zürich 1970

P. G. Walsh, *The Roman Novel*, Cambridge 1970

John J. Winkler, *Auctor & Actor: A Narratological Reading of Apuleius's The Golden Ass*, Berkeley and Los Angeles 1985

THE METAMORPHOSES OF APULEIUS

APVLEI MADAVRENSIS METAMORPHOSEON

LIBER I

1 At ego tibi sermone isto Milesio varias fabulas conseram, auresque tuas benivolas lepido susurro permulceam, modo si papyrum Aegyptiam argutia Nilotici calami inscriptam non spreveris inspicere, figuras fortunasque hominum in alias imagines conversas et in se rursum mutuo nexu refectas ut mireris. Exordior. Quis ille? Paucis accipe. Hymettos Attica et Isthmos Ephyrea et Taenaros Spartiaca, glebae felices aeternum libris felicioribus

---

[1] The work opens as if in the middle of a literary discussion.

[2] This is usually taken to refer to so-called "Milesian tales", pornographic stories named for Aristides of Miletus, whose Greek fiction was translated into Latin by the Roman historian Sisenna in the first century B.C. It may also suggest "Asianic" or florid in style, in contrast to the purer "Attic" style sought by some of Apuleius' contemporary writers. Cf. also IV 32 and note.

[3] Papyrus imported from Egypt was a common writing

APULEIUS OF MADAUROS
METAMORPHOSES

BOOK I

1 But[1] I would like to tie together different sorts of tales for you in that Milesian style of yours,[2] and to caress your ears into approval with a pretty whisper, if only you will not begrudge looking at Egyptian papyrus inscribed with the sharpness of a reed from the Nile,[3] so that you may be amazed at men's forms and fortunes transformed into other shapes and then restored again in an interwoven knot. I begin my prologue. Who am I? I will tell you briefly. Attic Hymettos and Ephyrean Isthmos and Spartan Taenaros,[4] fruitful lands preserved for

material in the Greco-Roman world.

[4] The three locations are literally a mountain near Athens (famous for its honey), the Isthmus of Corinth, and the southernmost mountain in the Peloponnesus. Lucius claims to have been a student at Athens (I 24); Mt. Taenarus recurs as the point of departure for Psyche's visit to the underworld in VI 18–20; and Corinth is the scene of Lucius' retransformation and initiation in Book XI.

conditae, mea vetus prosapia est. Ibi linguam Attidem primis pueritiae stipendiis merui. Mox in urbe Latia advena studiorum Quiritium indigenam sermonem aerumnabili labore, nullo magistro praeeunte, aggressus excolui. En ecce praefamur veniam, siquid exotici ac forensis sermonis rudis locutor offendero. Iam haec equidem ipsa vocis immutatio desultoriae scientiae stilo quem accessimus[1] respondet.[2] Fabulam Graecanicam incipimus. Lector intende: laetaberis.

2 Thessaliam—nam et illic originis maternae nostrae fundamenta a Plutarcho illo incluto ac mox Sexto philosopho nepote eius prodita gloriam nobis faciunt—eam Thessaliam ex negotio petebam. Postquam ardua montium et lubrica vallium et roscida caespitum et glebosa camporum emersi, in[3] equo indigena peralbo vehens, iam eo quoque

[1] Should perhaps be emended to *accersimus* "summoned".

[2] F *respondit*, perfect tense.

[3] F *emersi me*. Vallette proposed *emensus emersi in*, to avoid the unusual transitive use of *emergo*.

ever in even more fruitful books, form my ancient stock. There I served my stint with the Attic tongue in the first campaigns of childhood. Soon afterwards, in the city of the Latins, as a newcomer to Roman[1] studies I attacked and cultivated their native speech with laborious difficulty and no teacher to guide me. So, please, I beg your pardon in advance if as a raw speaker of this foreign tongue of the Forum I commit any blunders. Now in fact this very changing of language corresponds to the type of writing we have undertaken, which is like the skill of a rider jumping from one horse to another. We are about to begin a Greekish story. Pay attention, reader, and you will find delight.

2 I was travelling to Thessaly,[2] where the ancestry of my mother's family brings us fame in the persons of the renowned Plutarch and later his nephew, the philosopher Sextus.[3] Thessaly, I say, is where I was heading on business. I had emerged from steep mountain tracks and slippery valley roads, damp places in the meadows and cloddy paths through the fields. I was riding a native-bred pure white horse;

[1] *Quirites* is an archaic and legalistic term for Roman citizens.

[2] A region in northeastern Greece.

[3] The famous essayist Plutarch (*c.* A.D. 45–125) was from Chaeronea in Boeotia. His significance here is doubtless as a philosopher of the Platonic school. His nephew was a teacher of the Roman emperor Marcus Aurelius.

admodum fesso, ut ipse etiam fatigationem sedentariam incessus vegetatione discuterem, in pedes desilio, equi sudorem frontem[1] curiose effrico, aures remulceo, frenos detraho, in gradum lenem sensim proveho, quoad lassitudinis incommodum alvi solitum ac naturale praesidium eliquaret. Ac dum is ientaculum ambulatorium—prata quae praeterit[2]—ore in latus detorto pronus affectat,[3] duobus comitum, qui forte paululum processerant, tertium me facio. Ac dum ausculto quid sermonis agitarent, alter exserto cachinno "Parce" inquit "in verba ista haec tam absurda tamque immania mentiendo."

Isto accepto, sititor alioquin novitatis, "Immo vero" inquam "impertite sermone[4] non quidem curiosum, sed qui velim scire vel cuncta vel certe plurima. Simul iugi quod insurgimus aspritudinem fabularum lepida iucunditas levigabit."

3 At ille qui coeperat "Ne" inquit "istud mendacium tam verum est quam siqui velit dicere magico susurramine amnes agiles reverti, mare pigrum colligari, ventos inanimes exspirare, solem inhiberi, lunam despumari, stellas evelli, diem tolli, noctem teneri."

[1] To avoid the double accusative editors have printed various emendations, all plausible: *sudoram frontem* (the most attractive), *sudorem fronte*, *sudore frontem*, *sudorem fronde*, and *sudorem fronde detergeo frontem.*

[2] F *prataque*, with *praeterit* above the line. The words may be a gloss to explain the clever phrase *ientaculum ambulatorium.*

[3] F *adlectat.*

[4] F *sermones.*

as he too was now quite tired, and in order also to dispel my own weariness from sitting by the stimulation of walking, I jumped down to my feet. I carefully rubbed the sweat from my horse's forehead, caressed his ears, unfastened his bridle, and led him along slowly at a gentle pace, until his belly's customary and natural remedy cleared out the discomfort of his fatigue. While he was eagerly setting upon his walking breakfast—the grass he passed beside—with his head twisted down to one side, I made myself a third to two companions who happened to be a little ahead of me. While I tried to hear what they were talking about, one of them burst out laughing and exclaimed: "Stop telling such ridiculous and monstrous lies."

When I heard that, my thirst for novelty being what it is, I asked, "Please let me share your conversation. Not that I am inquisitive, but I am the sort who wants to know everything, or at least most things. Besides, the charming delight of some stories will smooth out the ruggedness of the hill we are climbing."

3 But the first speaker continued: "Indeed that lie you told is just as true as if someone should assert that by magic mutterings rivers can be reversed, the sea sluggishly shackled, the winds reduced to a dead breathlessness, the sun be halted, the moon drop her dew, the stars made to fall, daylight banished, and the night prolonged."

Tunc ego in verba fidentior "Heus tu," inquam "qui sermonem ieceras priorem, ne pigeat te vel taedeat reliqua pertexere." Et ad alium "Tu vero crassis auribus et obstinato corde respuis quae forsitan vere perhibeantur. Minus hercule calles pravissimis opinionibus ea putari mendacia quae vel auditu nova vel visu rudia vel certe supra captum cogitationis ardua videantur; quae si paulo accuratius exploraris, non modo compertu evidentia,
4 verum etiam factu facilia senties. Ego denique vespera, dum polentae caseatae modico secus offulam grandiorem in convivas aemulus contruncare gestio, mollitie cibi glutinosi faucibus inhaerentis et meacula[1] spiritus distinentis minimo minus interii. Et tamen Athenis proximo[2] et ante Poecilen porticum isto gemino obtutu circulatorem aspexi equestrem spatham praeacutam mucrone infesto devorasse; ac mox eundem invitamento exiguae stipis venatoriam lanceam, qua parte minatur exitium, in ima viscera condidisse. Et ecce pone lan-

[1] F *mea gula.*

[2] Usually emended to *proxime.*

At that point I spoke up more confidently. "You there," I said, "the one who started the story before, don't become disgusted and lose interest in spinning out the rest of your tale. And you," I said to the other one, "with your thick ears and stubborn mind, are rejecting what may be a true report. You are not being very clever, by Hercules,[1] if your wrong-headed opinions make you judge as false what seems new to the ear or unfamiliar to the eye or even too difficult for the intellect to grasp, but which upon a little more careful investigation you will perceive to be not only easy to ascertain, but even sim-
4 ple to perform. In my case, last evening when I was trying to compete with my dinner-companions and devour a disproportionately large bite of cheese pudding, the softness of the sticky food clung to my throat and blocked my breathing-passages, and I very nearly died; yet recently at Athens in front of the Stoa Poikile,[2] I saw with my very own eyes a street performer swallow an extremely sharp cavalry sword with a lethal edge; and later I watched the same fellow, encouraged by a meagre donation, bury a hunting spear all the way down to the bottom of his bowels with the death-dealing end foremost. Then suddenly, above the metal part of

[1] A mild oath, which I have translated literally throughout.

[2] A covered colonnade in the agora at Athens, decorated with paintings.

ceae ferrum, qua bacillum inversi teli ad occipitium per ingluviem subit, puer in mollitiem decorus insurgit inque flexibus tortuosis enervam et exossam saltationem explicat, cum omnium qui aderamus admiratione. Diceres dei medici baculo, quod ramulis semiamputatis nodosum gerit, serpentem generosum lubricis amplexibus inhaerere. Sed iam cedo tu sodes, qui coeperas, fabulam remetire. Ego tibi solus haec pro isto credam, et quod ingressui primum fuerit stabulum prandio participabo. Haec tibi merces deposita est."

5 At ille: "Istud quidem quod polliceris aequi bonique facio, verum quod incohaveram porro exordiar. Sed tibi prius deierabo Solem istum omnividentem[1] deum me vera comperta memorare; nec vos ulterius dubitabitis, si Thessaliam[2] proximam civitatem perveneritis, quod ibidem passim per ora populi sermo iactetur quae palam gesta sunt. Sed ut prius noritis cuiatis sim, [qui sim,][3] Aegiensis. Audite et quo quaestu me teneam: melle vel caseo et huiusce modi cauponarum mercibus per Thessaliam Aetoliam

[1] F *videntem*, corr. Leo.

[2] *Thessaliam* should perhaps be deleted as an explanatory gloss.

[3] This passage has been emended in various ways. Some modern editors supply *Aristomenes sum* before *Aegiensis*, but this is neither necessary nor consonant with Apuleius' usual practice of postponing the introduction of his characters' names.

the spear where the staff of the inverted weapon rose from his throat toward his crown, an effeminately beautiful boy shinnied up and unfolded a dance without muscle or spine, all twists and turns, to the amazement of all of us there. You would have said it was that noble serpent clinging in its slippery embrace to the Physician-God's staff, the one he carries all knotty with half-amputated branches.[1] "But please go on now, you who started the story, and run through it again. Instead of him I will believe you, and I will invite you to share dinner with me at the first inn after we come into town: that is your guaranteed payment."

5 "I consider that a fair and reasonable promise," he replied, "and I shall forthwith continue the story I had started. But first I shall swear to you by the Sun, this all-seeing god, that I am narrating events which I know at first hand to be true; and you will have no further doubts when you arrive at the next town in Thessaly, for the story is circulating there on everyone's lips about what occurred in plain daylight. But first, so that you may know where I am from, I am from Aegium.[2] Hear too how I make my living: I deal in honey and cheese and that sort of innkeepers' merchandise, travelling back and forth

[1] One of Asclepius' attributes was a staff entwined by a snake.

[2] A town in Achaea on the southern shore of the Gulf of Corinth; he travels in the area north of the Gulf.

Boeotiam ultro citro discurrens. Comperto itaque Hypatae, quae civitas cunctae Thessaliae antepollet, caseum recens et sciti saporis admodum commodo pretio distrahi, festinus accucurri id omne praestinaturus. Sed ut fieri assolet, sinistro pede profectum me spes compendii frustrata est. Omne enim pridie Lupus negotiator magnarius coemerat. Ergo igitur inefficaci celeritate fatigatus commodum vespera oriente ad balneas processeram.

6 "Ecce Socratem contubernalem meum conspicio. Humi sedebat scissili palliastro semiamictus, paene alius lurore, ad miseram maciem deformatus, qualia solent Fortunae decermina[1] stipes in triviis erogare. Hunc talem, quamquam necessarium et summe cognitum, tamen dubia mente propius accessi. 'Hem,' inquam 'mi Socrates, quid istud? Quae facies! Quod flagitium! At vero domi tuae iam defletus et conclamatus es, liberis tuis tutores iuridici provincialis decreto dati, uxor persolutis feralibus[2] officiis luctu

[1] F *deterrima.*
[2] F *ferialibus*; *inferialibus* is also possible.

---

[1] Despite the cheese-merchant's assertion, and Byrrhena's remarks in II 19, Hypata seems to have been little more than a small town on the slopes of Mt. Oeta, off the main north-south route through Thessaly.

through Thessaly, Aetolia, and Boeotia. So when I learned that at Hypata, which is the most important city in all Thessaly,[1] some fresh fine-flavoured cheese was being sold at a quite advantageous price, I rushed there in a hurry to buy it all up. But, as usually happens, I started out with my left foot and my hope of profit was frustrated, because a wholesale merchant named Lupus[2] had purchased it all the day before. Therefore, exhausted as a result of my inefficacious haste, I begin to walk toward the baths just as the evening-star was rising.

6 "Suddenly I caught sight of Socrates,[3] an old friend of mine. He was sitting on the ground, half covered by a tattered old cloak, almost unrecognisable in his sallowness, pitiably deformed and shrunken, like those cast-offs of Fortune who are forever begging alms at street corners. Seeing him in such a state, even though he was a very close friend whom I knew well, I approached him with some doubts in my mind.

"'Oh Socrates, my friend,' I said, 'what has happened to you? How terrible you look! What a disgrace! At your home you have already been lamented and ritually addressed as dead, guardians have been appointed for your children by decree of the provincial judge, and your wife, after performing

[2] His name means "wolf" in Latin.

[3] He has the same name as the famous philosopher executed by the Athenians in 399 B.C. See below, X 33 and note.

et maerore diuturno deformata, diffletis paene ad extremam captivitatem oculis suis, domus infortunium novarum nuptiarum gaudiis a suis sibi parentibus hilarare compellitur. At tu hic larvale simulacrum cum summo dedecore nostro viseris.'

"'Aristomene,' inquit 'ne tu fortunarum lubricas ambages et instabiles incursiones et reciprocas vicissitudines ignoras.' Et cum dicto sutili centunculo faciem suam iam dudum punicantem prae pudore obtexit ita ut ab umbilico pube tenus cetera corporis renudaret. Nec denique perpessus ego tam miserum aerumnae spectaculum, iniecta manu ut adsurgat enitor.

7 "At ille, ut erat, capite velato, 'Sine, sine' inquit 'fruatur diutius tropaeo Fortuna quod fixit ipsa.'

"Effeci sequatur, et simul unam e duabus laciniis meis exuo eumque propere vestio dicam an contego, et ilico lavacro trado. Quod unctui, quod tersui, ipse praeministro; sordium enormem eluviem operose effrico; probe curato, ad hospitium lassus ipse fatigatum aegerrime sustinens perduco. Lectulo refoveo, cibo satio, poculo mitigo, fabulis permulceo.

---

[1] His Greek name suggests heroic strength.

all the funeral services, disfiguring herself with long mourning and grief, and nearly weeping her eyes into uselessness, is being pressed by her parents to gladden the family's misfortune with the joys of a new marriage. And you show up here, the image of a ghost, to our utter shame!'

"'Aristomenes,'[1] he answered, 'you just do not know the slippery windings and shifting attacks and alternating reversals of Fortune.' And with that he covered his face, which had long since begun to redden from shame, with his patched cloak, baring the rest of his body from his navel to his loins. I could no longer endure such a pitiable spectacle of suffering, and so I took hold of him and tried to make him stand up.

7 "But he stayed as he was, with his head covered, and answered: 'Let me be! Let Fortune continue to enjoy the trophy she herself has hung up.'

"I made him come along with me, and I took off one of my two garments and hastily clothed him, or should I say covered him up. Then I took him straight to the baths, myself furnished the materials for oiling and drying him, and with effort scraped off his immense crust of filth. When this had been properly attended to, I brought him to an inn, supporting his exhausted body with great difficulty, since I too was tired. I put him to rest on a bed, filled him with food, relaxed him with wine, and soothed him with talk. Then came a willing

Iam allubentia proclivis est sermonis et ioci et scitum etiam[1] cavillum, iam dicacitas timida, cum ille imo de pectore cruciabilem suspiritum ducens, dextra saeviente frontem replaudens, 'Me miserum' infit 'qui dum voluptatem gladiatorii spectaculi famigerabilis consector, in has aerumnas incidi. Nam, ut scis optime, secundum quaestum Macedoniam profectus, dum mense decimo ibidem attentus nummatior revertor, modico prius quam Larissam accederem, per transitum spectaculum obiturus, in quadam avia et lacunosa convalli a vastissimis latronibus obsessus atque omnibus privatus tandem evado. Et utpote ultime affectus ad quandam cauponam Meroen, anum sed admodum scitulam, deverto, eique causas et peregrinationis diuturnae et domuitionis anxiae et spoliationis [diuturnae et dum][2] miserae refero. Quae me nimis[3] quam humane tractare adorta cenae gratae atque gratuitae ac mox urigine percita cubili suo applicat. Et statim miser, ut cum illa acquievi, ab unico congressu annosam ac pestilentem coniunctionem[4] contraho; et ipsas etiam lacinias quas boni latrones

[1] F *et.*

[2] A copyist's erroneous repetition.

[3] An almost certain correction for F's *quae enim his.*

[4] Only one of many suggestions for completing F's *con-*.

inclination for conversation and laughter, and even a clever joke, and then hesitant clowning—when suddenly he drew a pained sob from the depths of his heart and savagely beat his forehead with his hand. 'Woe is me!' he began. 'I was pursuing the pleasure of a famous gladiatorial show when I fell into these tribulations. As you very well know, I had gone to Macedonia on a commercial venture, and after nine months of work there I was on my way back home a more moneyed man. A little before reaching Larissa—where I was going to stop for the show on my way—as I was walking through a desolate and pitted valley, I was set upon by monstrous bandits and stripped of everything I had. I finally escaped and, in my desperate state, stopped at the house of an innkeeper named Meroe,[1] an old but rather attractive woman. I explained to her about my long travels and my anxiety to return home and the miserable robbery. She began treating me terribly kindly with a welcome and generous meal, and then, aroused by lust, she enfolded me in her bed. I was done for immediately, as soon as I slept with her; that one sexual act infected me with a lengthy, disastrous relationship. I even gave her the clothes the good robbers had left me to cover

[1] Her name is perhaps meant to suggest *merum* "strong wine"; but Meroe is the name of a town and region in the upper reaches of the Nile.

contegendo mihi concesserant in eam contuli, operulas etiam quas adhuc vegetus saccariam faciens merebam, quoad me ad istam faciem quam paulo ante vidisti bona uxor et mala Fortuna perduxit.'

8 "'Pol quidem tu dignus' inquam 'es extrema sustinere, siquid est tamen novissimo extremius, qui voluptatem Veneriam et scortum scorteum lari et liberis praetulisti.'

"At ille, digitum a pollice proximum ori suo admovens et in stuporem attonitus, 'Tace, tace' inquit; et circumspiciens tutamenta sermonis, 'Parce' inquit 'in feminam divinam, ne quam tibi lingua intemperante noxam contrahas.'

"'Ain tandem?' inquam. 'Potens illa et regina caupona quid mulieris est?'

"'Saga' inquit 'et divini potens caelum deponere, terram suspendere, fontes durare, montes diluere, manes sublimare, deos infimare,[1] sidera exstinguere, Tartarum ipsum illuminare.'

"'Oro te,' inquam 'aulaeum tragicum dimoveto et siparium scaenicum complicato et cedo verbis communibus.'

"'Vis' inquit 'unum vel alterum, immo plurima eius audire facta? Nam ut se ament efflictim non

[1] F *infirmare* "weaken".

myself with, and even the scant wages I earned as a sack-carrier while I was still vigorous, until my good "wife" and evil Fortune reduced me to that shape you saw a little while ago.'

8 "'By heaven,' I said, 'you deserve to suffer the worst—if indeed there is anything worse than your most recent condition—since you preferred the pleasures of Venus and a leathery old whore to your own hearth and children.'

"But he put his index finger to his lips, shocked and stunned: 'Shhh! Quiet!' he said. Then, after looking around to make sure it was safe to talk, he said, 'Beware of speaking ill of the inspired woman, in case the intemperance of your tongue do you a mischief.'

"'Really?' I retorted. 'What kind of woman is this powerful and royal innkeeper?'

"'A witch,' he replied, 'with supernatural power: she can lower the sky and suspend the earth, solidify fountains and dissolve mountains, raise up ghosts and bring down gods, darken the stars and light up Tartarus[1] itself.'

"'Please,' I said, 'do remove the tragic curtain and fold up the stage drapery, and give it to me in ordinary language.'

"'Do you want to hear,' he answered, 'one or two, or maybe several of her feats? The fact that she makes men fall madly in love with her—not just

[1] The Underworld.

modo incolae, verum etiam Indi vel Aethiopes utrique vel ipsi Anticthones, folia sunt artis et nugae merae. Sed quod in conspectum plurium perpetravit audi.

9 "'Amatorem suum, quod in aliam temerasset, unico verbo mutavit in feram castorem, quod ea bestia captivitati metuens ab insequentibus se praecisione genitalium liberat, ut illi quoque simile, quod Venerem habuit in aliam,[1] proveniret. Cauponem quoque vicinum atque ob id aemulum deformavit in ranam, et nunc senex ille dolium[2] innatans vini sui adventores pristinos in faece summissus officiosis roncis raucus appellat. Alium de foro, quod adversus eam locutus esset, in arietem deformavit, et nunc aries ille causas agit. Eadem amatoris sui uxorem, quod in eam dicacule probrum dixerat, iam in sarcina praegnationis,[3] obsepto utero et repigrato fetu perpetua praegnatione damnavit, et, ut cuncti numerant, iam octo annorum onere misella illa velut elephantum paritura distenditur.

[1] The clause *quod . . . aliam* should perhaps be deleted: it repeats the meaning of *quod in aliam temerasset* above, and may be an explanatory gloss on that somewhat unusual expression.

[2] Often emended to *dolio*.

[3] *praegnationis* should perhaps be deleted as an ancient editor's attempt to clarify the colorful expression *in sarcina* "in the baggage", "with a load".

local inhabitants but also Indians and both kinds of Ethiopians[1] and even Antipodeans[2]—this is only an elementary part of her art, mere trivia. But just listen to what she has accomplished before many witnesses.

9 "'Because one of her lovers had misbehaved himself with another woman, she changed him with one word into a beaver, because when that animal is afraid of being captured it escapes from its pursuers by cutting off its own genitals, and she wanted the same thing to happen to him since he had intercourse with another woman. There was also an innkeeper near her place, and thus a competitor, whom she transformed into a frog; now that old man is swimming in a vat of his own wine, sunken in the dregs, and he calls out hoarsely to his old customers with courteous croaks. She also transformed a lawyer into a ram because he had spoken against her, and now he pleads in the shape of a ram. When a lover's wife, who was carrying the baggage of pregnancy at the time, wittily insulted her, Meroe condemned her to perpetual pregnancy by sealing her womb and delaying the birth; according to everyone's count, the poor woman now has been burdened for eight years and is swollen as if she were going to produce an elephant.

[1] Those dwelling to the East and to the West of the Nile.
[2] Legendary dwellers on the under side of the earth.

10 "'Quae cum subinde ac multi nocerentur,[1] publicitus indignatio percrebruit statutumque ut in eam die altera severissime saxorum iaculationibus vindicaretur. Quod consilium virtutibus cantionum antevertit, et, ut illa Medea unius dieculae a Creone impetratis indutiis totam eius domum filiamque cum ipso sene flammis coronalibus deusserat, sic haec devotionibus sepulcralibus in scrobem procuratis, ut mihi temulenta narravit proxime, cunctos in suis sibi domibus tacita numinum violentia clausit, ut toto biduo non claustra perfringi, non fores evelli, non denique parietes ipsi quiverint perforari, quoad mutua hortatione consone clamitarent quam sanctissime deierantes sese neque ei manus admolituros et, si quis aliud cogitarit, salutare laturos subsidium. Et sic illa propitiata totam civitatem absolvit. At vero coetus illius auctorem nocte intempesta cum tota domo—id est parietibus et ipso solo et omni fundamento—ut erat, clausa, ad centesimum lapidem in aliam civitatem, summo vertice montis exasperati sitam et ob id ad aquas sterilem, trans-

[1] This first clause is difficult, with its ellipsis of a verb before *ac*. Some editors emend by supplying the verb; others change to *a multis notarentur* (or *noscerentur*), "after many people found out about these acts."

---

[1] Medea is the prototype of the dangerous witch. Enraged by her husband Jason's plan to marry the daughter of Creon, king of Corinth, she sent the girl as a

10 "'As these acts kept occurring and many people suffered harm, public indignation grew strong and the townspeople decreed that she should be punished on the following day by the harshest means possible—stoning. But she prevented this plan with the power of her magic spells. Just as the famous Medea, in the one short day's truce gained from Creon, burned up his entire house and daughter and the old man himself with flames from a crown,[1] so Meroe, by performing necromantic rituals in a ditch—as she herself recently told me when she was drunk—shut all the people up in their own homes with the silent strength of supernatural forces. So for two whole days it was impossible to break the locks or tear open the doors or even dig through the walls, until the people, at everyone's unanimous urging, cried out and most solemnly swore that they would not lay hands on her themselves, and furthermore that if anyone should intend otherwise they would come to her defence and rescue. Thus propitiated, she released the entire town. But as for the man who was responsible for the meeting, in the dead of night she took him with his whole house—that is, walls and floor and entire foundation—still locked, and transported them a hundred miles away to another town situated on top of a jagged mountain and therefore

wedding gift a robe and a golden crown which burst into flames when she put them on.

tulit. Et quoniam densa inhabitantium aedificia locum novo hospiti non dabant, ante portam proiecta domo discessit.'

11 "'Mira' inquam 'nec minus saeva, mi Socrates, memoras. Denique mihi quoque non parvam incussisti sollicitudinem, immo vero formidinem, iniecto non scrupulo sed lancea, ne quo numinis ministerio similiter usa sermones istos nostros anus illa cognoscat. Itaque maturius quieti nos reponamus et, somno levata lassitudine, noctis antelucio aufugiamus istinc quam pote[1] longissime.'

"Haec adhuc me suadente, insolita vinolentia ac diuturna fatigatione pertentatus bonus Socrates iam sopitus stertebat altius. Ego vero, adducta fore pessulisque firmatis, grabatulo etiam pone cardinem[2] supposito et probe aggesto, super eum me recipio. Ac primum prae metu aliquantisper vigilo, dein circa tertiam ferme vigiliam paululum coniveo. Commodum quieveram et repente impulsu maiore quam ut latrones crederes ianuae reserantur, immo vero fractis et evulsis funditus cardinibus prosternuntur. Grabatulus, alioquin breviculus et uno pede mutilus ac putris, impetus tanti violentia prosternitur; me quoque evolutum atque excussum

[1] F *puta*.

[2] Or *cardines*, for F's *cardine*.

---

[1] The Latin contains a pun on the literal meaning of *scrupulum* "a piece of gravel."

without water; and since the crowded houses of the natives left no room for the new guest, she dropped the house in front of the town gate and departed.'

11 "'What you tell me is marvellous,' I said, 'but none the less violent, my friend Socrates. You have aroused considerable worry—even fear—in me too. You have hit me with no small concern, but with a spear-thrust of anxiety,[1] that the old woman might learn of our conversation with the help of those same supernatural forces. So let us go to bed early and, after we have relieved our weariness with sleep, let us leave before dawn and get as far away as we can.'

"While I was still giving this advice, the good Socrates, assailed by the effects of unaccustomed imbibing and long exhaustion, had already fallen asleep and was snoring. I shut the door tight, fastened the bolts, and even set my cot behind the door-pivot, pushed it up fast, and lay down on top of it. At first, out of fear, I stayed awake for quite some time. Then about midnight I shut my eyes a bit. I had just fallen asleep when suddenly the doors were opened with a violence far greater than any burglar could have produced. In fact the pivots were broken and torn completely from their sockets, and the doors thrown to the ground. My cot, being low, lame in one foot, and rotten, collapsed from the force of such an assault, and I likewise was rolled out and hurled to the ground. The cot landed upside down

humi recidens in inversum cooperit ac tegit.

12 "Tunc ego sensi naturalitus quosdam affectus in contrarium provenire. Nam ut lacrimae saepicule de gaudio prodeunt, ita et in illo nimio pavore risum nequivi continere, de Aristomene testudo factus. Ac dum infimum[1] deiectus obliquo aspectu quid rei sit, grabatuli sollertia munitus, opperior, video mulieres duas altioris aetatis. Lucernam lucidam gerebat una, spongiam et nudum gladium altera. Hoc habitu Socratem bene quietum circumstetere. Infit illa cum gladio, 'Hic est, soror Panthia, carus Endymion,[2] hic Catamitus meus, qui diebus ac noctibus illusit aetatulam meam, hic qui meis amoribus subterhabitis non solum me diffamat probris, verum etiam fugam instruit. At ego scilicet Ulixi astu deserta vice Calypsonis aeternam solitudinem flebo.' Et porrecta dextera meque Panthiae suae demonstrato, 'At hic bonus' inquit 'consiliator Aristomenes, qui fugae huius auctor fuit et nunc morti

[1] Often emended: e.g. *in imum*, *in fimum* ("into the dung"), *in limum* ("into the mud").

[2] F *enosmion.*

---

[1] Her name means "all-divine" in Greek.

[2] Endymion was a young hunter beloved by the Moon, who put him to sleep in order to embrace him. Ganymede was a Trojan boy beloved by Jupiter and abducted to Mt.

on top of me, covering and hiding me.

12 "At that time I experienced the natural phenomenon in which certain emotions are expressed through their contraries. Just as tears often flow from joy, so also in my excessive fear at that moment I was unable to keep from laughing, as I saw myself turned from Aristomenes into a tortoise. Cast down on the floor under the prudent protection of my cot, I watched out of the corner of my eye to see what was happening. I saw two women of rather advanced age, one carrying a lighted lamp and the other a sponge and a naked sword. Thus equipped they surrounded the soundly sleeping Socrates. The one with the sword began: 'This, sister Panthia,[1] is my darling Endymion, my Ganymede.[2] This is the one who made sport of my tender youth day and night, the one who disdained my love and not only slandered me with his insults but even plotted to escape. Shall I, forsooth, deserted like Calypso[3] by the astuteness of a Ulysses, weep in everlasting loneliness?' Then she stretched out her hand and pointed me out to her friend Panthia. 'And this,' she said, 'is the good counsellor Aristomenes, who advised this escape and now lies near death, stretched out on the

Olympus with the help of an eagle, to become Jupiter's cupbearer.

[3] The goddess who detained Ulysses for seven years on the island of Ogygia.

proximus iam humi prostratus grabatulo succubans iacet et haec omnia conspicit, impune se[1] relaturum meas contumelias putat. Faxo eum sero, immo statim, immo vero iam nunc, ut et praecedentis dicacitatis et instantis curiositatis paeniteat.'

13 "Haec ego ut accepi, sudore frigido miser perfluo, tremore viscera quatior, ut grabatulus etiam succussu meo[2] inquietus super dorsum meum palpitando saltaret. At bona Panthia 'Quin igitur,' inquit 'soror, hunc primum bacchatim discerpimus vel membris eius destinatis virilia desecamus?'

"Ad haec Meroe—sic enim reapse nomen eius tunc fabulis Socratis convenire sentiebam—'Immo' ait 'supersit hic saltem qui miselli huius corpus parvo contumulet humo.' Et capite Socratis in alterum dimoto latus, per iugulum sinistrum capulo tenus gladium totum ei demergit, et sanguinis eruptionem utriculo admoto excipit diligenter, ut nulla stilla compareret usquam. Haec ego meis oculis aspexi. Nam etiam, ne quid demutaret, credo, a victimae religione, immissa dextera per vulnus illud ad viscera penitus cor miseri contubernalis mei Meroe

[1] *se* is an editorial addition. Some emend to *se laturum*.

[2] F *succussus sum eo*.

ground, sprawling under his little cot and watching all this. He thinks he is going to report these insults against me with impunity. Later—no, soon—no, right now—I will make him regret his past raillery and present inquisitiveness.'

13 "When I heard that, my poor body dissolved in cold sweat, and my insides quivered and trembled so that the cot, disturbed by my own shaking, swayed and danced on top of my back. 'Well then, sister,' replied the gentle Panthia, 'why not take him first and tear him limb from limb in a Bacchic frenzy,[1] or at least tie him up and cut off his genitals?'

"Meroe—since I perceived that her name in fact matched Socrates' stories—answered her. 'No,' she said, 'let him at least survive to bury this poor wretch's corpse with a little earth.' And with this she bent Socrates' head to one side and plunged her sword down through the left side of his neck all the way up to the hilt. Then she placed a leather bottle to the wound, carefully collecting the spout of blood so that not a single drop appeared anywhere. I saw all this with my very own eyes. Next, so as not to deviate, I suppose, from the ritual of sacrificing a victim, she inserted her right hand through that wound all the way down to his insides, felt around for my poor comrade's heart, and pulled it out; at

[1] The fate that befell young king Pentheus when he spied on the Bacchic rites of the women of Thebes. See Euripides, *Bacchae* 1043–1152.

bona scrutata protulit, cum ille impetu teli praesecata gula vocem, immo stridorem incertum, per vulnus effunderet et spiritum rebulliret. Quod vulnus qua maxime patebat spongia[1] offulciens, Panthia 'Heus tu,' inquit 'spongia, cave in mari nata per fluvium transeas.' His editis abeunt et una[2] remoto grabatulo varicus super faciem meam residentes vesicam exonerant, quoad me urinae spurcissimae madore perluerent.

14 "Commodum limen evaserant et fores ad pristinum statum integrae resurgunt: cardines ad foramina residunt,[3] ad postes[4] repagula redeunt, ad claustra pessuli recurrunt. At ego, ut eram, etiam nunc humi proiectus, inanimis, nudus et frigidus et lotio perlitus,[5] quasi recens utero matris editus, immo vero semimortuus, verum etiam ipse mihi supervivens et postumus, vel certe destinatae iam cruci candidatus, 'Quid' inquam 'me fiet, ubi iste iugulatus mane paruerit? Cui videbor veri similia dicere perferens[6] vera? "Proclamares saltem suppetiatum, si resistere vir tantus mulieri nequibas. Sub oculis tuis homo iugulatur et siles? Cur autem te simile latrocinium non peremit? Cur saeva cru-

[1] F *quam . . . spongiam.*

[2] *abeunt et una* is one of several proposed restorations for F's *ab una* (with a letter erased between *b* and *u*).

[3] Or *resident.*

[4] F *postes ad.*

[5] Usually emended to *perlutus.*

[6] Regularly emended to *proferens.*

this he emitted a sound from that throat slashed open by the weapon's stroke, or rather poured out an inarticulate squeal through the wound and gurgled forth his life's breath. Panthia staunched the wound at its widest opening with her sponge, saying, 'Listen, o sponge, born in the sea, take care to travel back through a river.' After these words they left him; and both of them removed my cot, spread their feet, and squatted over my face, discharging their bladders until they had drenched me in the liquid of their filthy urine.

14 "No sooner had they crossed the threshold than the doors swung back unharmed into their original position: the pivots settled back in their sockets, the bars returned to the door-posts, and the bolts ran back into the lock. But I stayed where I was, sprawled on the ground, lifeless, naked and cold, and covered with urine, as if I had just come out of my mother's womb. No, it was more like being half-dead but still my own survivor, a posthumous child, or at least a sure candidate for the cross. 'What will become of me,' I said, 'when he is discovered in the morning with his throat cut? Who will think my story is plausible when I tell the truth? "You could at least have called out for help, if a big man like you could not withstand a woman by yourself. A man has his throat cut right in front of your eyes and you keep still? Besides, why didn't such a band of robbers kill you too? Why did their savage cruelty

delitas vel propter indicium sceleris arbitro pepercit? Ergo quoniam evasisti mortem, nunc illo redi."'

"Haec identidem mecum replicabam, et nox ibat in diem. Optimum itaque factu visum est anteluculo furtim evadere et viam licet trepido vestigio capessere. Sumo sarcinulam meam, subdita clavi pessulos reduco; at illae probae et fideles ianuae, quae sua sponte reseratae nocte fuerant, vix tandem et aegerrime tunc clavis suae crebra immissione patefiunt.

"Et 'Heus tu, ubi es?' inquam. 'Valvas stabuli absolve; antelucio volo ire.'

"Ianitor pone stabuli ostium humi cubitans etiam nunc semisomnus, 'Quid? Tu' inquit 'ignoras latronibus infestari vias, qui hoc noctis iter incipis? Nam etsi tu alicuius facinoris tibi conscius scilicet mori cupis, nos cucurbitae caput non habemus ut pro te moriamur.'

"'Non longe' inquam 'lux abest. Et praeterea quid viatori de summa pauperie latrones auferre possunt? An ignoras, inepte, nudum nec a decem palaestritis despoliari posse?'

"Ad haec ille marcidus et semisopitus in alterum latus evolutus, 'Unde autem' inquit 'scio an convec-

spare you as a witness to their crime to inform against them? Therefore, since you escaped death, return to it now!"'

"I kept turning this over and over in my mind as night moved towards day. I decided that the best thing to do was to sneak away just before daybreak and start travelling, even with shaky steps. I picked up my little bag, pushed the key up into the lock, and tried to slide back the bolts. But those good and faithful doors, which had unlocked of their own accord during the night, now opened only with enormous difficulty and a long effort and many insertions of the key.

15 "'Hey you,' I shouted, 'where are you? Open the gates of the inn. I want to leave before daybreak.'

"The porter, who was lying on the ground behind the inn's entrance still half-asleep, answered: 'What? don't you know that the roads are infested with robbers? Do you want to start travelling at this hour of the night? Even if you have some crime on your conscience and are eager to die, I am not enough of a melon-head to die for you.'

"'Daylight is not far off,' I said. 'And besides, what can robbers take away from a traveller who is in total poverty? Or don't you know, you fool, that a naked man cannot be stripped, even by ten professional wrestlers?'

"Then, groggy and half-slumbering, he rolled away on to his other side. 'How do I know,' he asked, 'that you have not slit the throat of that tra-

tore illo tuo, cum quo sero deverteras, iugulato fugae mandes praesidium?'

"Illud horae memini me terra dehiscente ima Tartara inque his canem Cerberum prorsus esurientem mei prospexisse. Ac recordabar profecto bonam Meroen non misericordia iugulo meo pepercisse, sed
16 saevitia cruci me reservasse. In cubiculum itaque reversus de genere tumultuario mortis mecum deliberabam. Sed cum nullum aliud telum mortiferum Fortuna quam solum mihi grabatulum sumministraret, 'Iam iam, grabatule,' inquam 'animo meo carissime, qui mecum tot aerumnas exanclasti conscius et arbiter quae nocte gesta sunt, quem solum in meo reatu testem innocentiae citare possum, tu mihi ad inferos festinanti sumministra telum salutare.' Et cum dicto restim qua erat intextus aggredior expedire, ac tigillo, quod fenestrae subditum altrinsecus prominebat, iniecta atque obdita parte funiculi et altera firmiter in nodum coacta, ascenso grabatulo ad exitium sublimatus et immisso[1] capite laqueum induo. Sed dum pede altero fulcimentum quo sustinebar repello, ut ponderis deductu restis ad ingluviem astricta spiritus officia[2] discluderet, repente putris alioquin et vetus funis dirumpitur,

[1] F *misso.*
[2] Or *officium*, for F's *officio.*

---

[1] The three-headed dog who stood guard at the entrance to the Underworld.

velling companion you came in with yesterday evening, and are running away to protect yourself?'

"I remember that at that moment I saw the earth gape open and beheld the pit of Tartarus with the dog Cerberus there,[1] ready to devour me. And I was thinking that the gentle Meroe had indeed spared my throat not out of mercy, but in her cruelty had
16 reserved me for the cross. And so I went back into the bedroom and started thinking about a quick form of death. But since Fortune provided me with no other death-dealing weapon than my little cot, I turned to it. 'The time is now, my little cot,' I said, 'my heart's dearest cot, you who have endured so many tribulations with me, you who know and can judge what happened last night, you who are the only witness I can summon in my trial to testify to my innocence. I am in haste to die: supply me with the weapon that will save me.' With these words I set to work unravelling the rope which was laced into the cot-frame. Then I tossed one end of the rope over a little beam which projected into the room underneath the window and fastened it. I tied the other end securely in a noose, climbed up on to the cot, raised myself high enough for the death-drop, and fitted my head through the noose. With one foot I pushed away the support which was holding me up, so that the rope would be squeezed tight against my throat by the pull of my weight and shut off the function of breathing. Then suddenly the rope,

atque ego de alto recidens Socratem—nam iuxta me iacebat—superruo cumque eo in terram devolvor.

17 "Et ecce in ipso momento ianitor introrumpit exserte clamitans 'Ubi es tu, qui alta nocte immodice festinabas et nunc stertis involutus?'

"Ad haec, nescio an casu nostro an illius absono clamore experrectus, Socrates exsurgit prior et 'Non'[1] inquit 'immerito stabularios hos omnes hospites detestantur. Nam iste curiosus dum importune irrumpit—credo studio rapiendi aliquid—clamore vasto marcidum alioquin me altissimo somno excussit.'

"Emergo laetus atque alacer insperato gaudio perfusus, et 'Ecce, ianitor fidelissime, comes et pater meus[2] et frater meus, quem nocte ebrius occisum a me calumniabaris.' Et cum dicto Socratem deosculabar amplexus.

"At ille, odore alioquin spurcissimi umoris percussus quo me lamiae illae infecerant, vehementer aspernatur. 'Apage te,' inquit 'foetorem extremae latrinae;' et causas coepit huius odoris comiter inquirere.

"At ego miser, afficto ex tempore absurdo ioco, in alium sermonem intentionem eius denuo derivo, et

[1] F *nc*.

[2] Most editors delete *et pater meus*, thereby reducing Aristomenes' exuberance.

being rotten and old, broke and I fell. I crashed down on top of Socrates, who was lying next to me, and tumbled with him on to the ground.

17 "Suddenly at that very moment the porter broke in, shouting at the top of his lungs. 'Where are you?' he yelled. 'You were in such an enormous hurry in the middle of the night, and here you are wrapped up in your covers snoring.'

"At this, having been awakened either by our fall or by that fellow's discordant yelling, Socrates stood up first. 'It's no wonder,' he said, 'that guests loathe all these innkeepers. Now this inquisitive fellow bursts rudely into the room, wanting to steal something, I suppose, and with his monstrous shouting he shook me out of a very sound sleep, weakened as I was.'

"I emerged happily and briskly, drenched with unexpected joy. 'Look, my trusty porter,' I said, 'here is my friend and father and brother, whom in your drunkenness last night you slanderously accused me of having murdered.' At once I embraced Socrates and began kissing him. He was stunned by the stench of that filthy liquid those she-monsters had soaked me in, and he shoved me violently away. 'Off with you,' he said, 'you stink like a cheap latrine.' And he began to enquire good-humouredly into the reasons for my smell.

"Miserably I invented some silly joke on the spur of the moment and channelled his attention to

iniecta dextra 'Quin imus' inquam 'et itineris matutini gratiam capimus?' Sumo sarcinulam et, pretio mansionis stabulario persoluto, capessimus viam.

18 "Aliquantum processeramus et iam iubaris exortu cuncta collustrantur. Et ego curiose sedulo arbitrabar iugulum comitis, qua parte gladium delapsum videram; et mecum 'Vesane,' aio 'qui poculis et vino sepultus extrema somniasti. Ecce Socrates integer, sanus, incolumis. Ubi vulnus, spongia? Ubi postremum cicatrix tam alta, tam recens?' Et ad illum 'Non'[1] inquam 'immerito medici fidi cibo et crapula distentos saeva et gravia somniare autumant. Mihi denique, quod poculis vesperi minus temperavi, nox acerba diras et truces imagines obtulit, ut adhuc me credam cruore humano aspersum atque impiatum.'

"Ad haec ille surridens 'At tu' inquit 'non sanguine sed lotio perfusus es. Verum tamen et ipse per somnium iugulari visus sum mihi. Nam et iugulum istum dolui[2] et cor ipsum mihi avelli putavi; et nunc etiam spiritu deficior et genua quatior et gradu titubo et aliquid cibatus refovendo spiritu desidero.'

"'En' inquam 'paratum tibi adest ientaculum.' Et

[1] F *ne*.

[2] Should perhaps be emended to *dolari*, "I thought my neck had been pierced."

another subject of conversation. Then I took hold of him and said, 'Why don't we go and take advantage of travelling in the early morning?' I picked up my little bag and paid the charge for our stay at the inn, and we set out.

18 "We had already gone some distance before the sun rose and illuminated everything. Inquisitively, carefully, I inspected the area of my friend's neck where I had seen the sword plunged in. 'You are crazy,' I said to myself. 'You were buried in your wine-cups and you had a very bad nightmare. Look, Socrates is whole and hearty and without a scratch. Where is the wound? The sponge? And finally where is that scar, so deep and so fresh?' I turned to him. 'Good doctors are quite right,' I said, 'when they assert that people swollen with food and drink have violent and oppressive dreams. Take me now. I overindulged in the cups yesterday evening and a rough night brought me such awful, violent visions that I still imagine myself spattered and polluted with human blood.'

"At this he grinned. 'It is not blood,' he answered, 'that you have been soaked with, it is piss! But I had a dream too: I dreamed that my throat had been cut; I felt a pain here on my neck and I even thought my heart had been torn out; and I am still out of breath now, my knees are shaking and I am staggering, and I need something to eat to restore my wind.'

"'Here,' I said, 'breakfast is all ready for you,' and

cum dicto manticam meam umero exuo, caseum cum pane propere ei porrigo, et 'Iuxta platanum istam residamus' aio.

19 "Quo facto et ipse aliquid indidem sumo, eumque avide essitantem aspiciens, aliquanto intentiore macie atque pallore buxeo deficientem[1] video. Sic denique eum vitalis color turbaverat ut mihi prae metu, nocturnas etiam Furias illas imaginanti, frustulum panis quod primum sumpseram, quamvis admodum modicum, mediis faucibus inhaereret ac neque deorsum demeare neque sursum remeare posset. Nam et brevitas ipsa commeantium metum mihi cumulabat. Quis enim de duobus comitum alterum sine alterius noxa peremptum crederet? Verum ille, ut satis detruncaverat cibum, sitire impatienter coeperat. Nam et optimi casei bonam partem avide devoraverat, et haud ita longe radices platani lenis fluvius in speciem placidae paludis ignavus ibat, argento vel vitro aemulus in colorem. 'En' inquam 'explere latice fontis lacteo.' Assurgit et, oppertus paululum planiorem ripae marginem, complicitus in genua appronat se avidus affectans poculum. Necdum satis extremis labiis summum

[1] The same letters may also be divided and punctuated to read *aspiciens aliquanto intentior, e macie . . . deficientem* ("I observed him a little more intently . . .").

---

[1] A reminiscence of Plato, *Phaedrus* 229a.

at once I took my sack off my shoulder and quickly handed him some bread and cheese. 'Let's sit down next to that plane tree,' I said.[1]

19 "After that I took something from the sack for myself too, and observed him greedily devouring his food. I saw him weakening with a rather more drawn emaciation and a pallor like boxwood. His deadly complexion had so distorted him that I recalled the picture of those Furies[2] of the night before; my fright made the first bite of bread I had taken stick in the middle of my throat, even though it was not a very large one, and I could not get it to go down or come up. The very absence of other travellers along the road added to my fear. Who would ever believe that one of two companions was murdered without the other being guilty? Socrates, however, when he had polished off enough food, began to feel unbearably thirsty, since he had greedily bolted down a good share of a fine cheese. Not far from the plane-tree's roots a gentle stream lazily flowed along in the likeness of a quiet pool, rivalling the colour of silver or glass. 'Here,' I said to him, 'quench your thirst with the milky waters of this spring.' He got up, and after a short search for a level enough spot along the edge of the bank, he crouched down on his knees and bent greedily forward to drink. He had not quite touched the water's

[2] Snake-haired female figures from the Underworld, whose function was to exact vengeance.

aquae rorem attigerat, et iugulo eius vulnus dehiscit in profundum patorem et illa spongia de eo repente devolvitur eamque parvus admodum comitatur cruor. Denique corpus exanimatum in flumen paene cernuat, nisi ego altero eius pede retento vix et aegre ad ripam superiorem attraxi, ubi defletum pro tempore comitem misellum arenosa humo in amnis vicinia sempiterna contexi. Ipse[1] trepidus et eximie metuens mihi per diversas et avias solitudines aufugi, et quasi conscius mihi caedis humanae relicta patria et lare ultroneum exilium amplexus, nunc Aetoliam novo contracto matrimonio colo."

20 Haec Aristomenes. At ille comes eius, qui statim initio obstinata incredulitate sermonem eius respuebat, "Nihil" inquit "hac fabula fabulosius, nihil isto mendacio absurdius." Et ad me conversus, "Tu autem," inquit "vir ut habitus et habitudo demonstrat ornatus, accedis huic fabulae?"

"Ego vero" inquam "nihil impossibile arbitror, sed utcumque fata decreverint, ita cuncta mortalibus provenire. Nam et mihi et tibi et cunctis hominibus multa usu venire mira et paene infecta, quae tamen ignaro relata fidem perdant. Sed ego

[1] Or perhaps *At ipse.* F has a *t* erased at the end of *contexi.*

surface with the edge of his lips, when the wound in his throat gaped open with a deep hole and the sponge suddenly rolled out of it, accompanied by just a trickle of blood. Then his lifeless body nearly pitched forward into the river, except that I was just able to catch hold of one of his feet and with great effort drag him higher up on to the bank. There I mourned my poor friend as much as circumstances would allow and covered him over with sandy soil to remain forever beside the river. As for me, trembling and terrified for my life, I fled through remote and trackless wildernesses, and like a man with murder on his conscience, I abandoned my country and my home and embraced voluntary exile. I now live in Aetolia and have remarried."

20 So ended Aristomenes' story. But his companion, who in stubborn disbelief had rejected his tale from the very start, remarked, "That is the most fabulous fable, the most ridiculous lie that I have ever heard." Then he turned to me. "Now you are a cultured fellow," he said, "as your clothes and manners show. Do you go along with that story?"

"Well," I said, "I consider nothing to be impossible. However the fates decide, that is the way everything turns out for mortal men. I and you and all human beings actually experience many strange and almost unparallelled events which are disbelieved when reported to someone who is ignorant of them. But as for Aristomenes, not only do I

huic et credo hercules et gratas gratias memini, quod lepidae fabulae festivitate nos avocavit, asperam denique ac prolixam viam sine labore ac taedio evasi. Quod beneficium etiam illum vectorem meum credo laetari, sine fatigatione sui me usque ad istam civitatis portam non dorso illius sed meis auribus pervecto."

21 Is finis nobis et sermonis et itineris communis fuit. Nam comites uterque ad villulam proximam laevorsum abierunt. Ego vero quod primum ingressui[1] stabulum conspicatus sum accessi, et de quadam anu caupona ilico percontor. "Estne" inquam "Hypata haec civitas?" Annuit. "Nostine Milonem quendam e primoribus?" Arrisit, et "Vere" inquit "primus istic perhibetur Milo, qui extra pomerium et urbem totam colit." "Remoto" inquam "ioco, parens optima, dic oro et cuiatis sit et quibus deversetur aedibus." "Videsne" inquit "extremas fenestras, quae foris urbem prospiciunt, et altrinsecus fores proximum respicientes angiportum? Inibi iste Milo deversatur, ampliter nummatus et longe opulentus, verum extremae avaritiae et sordis infimae infamis homo. Faenus denique copiosum sub arrabone auri et argenti crebriter exercens, exiguo lare inclusus et aerugini semper intentus, cum uxore etiam calamitatis suae comite habet,[2] neque

[1] F *ingressus.*

[2] F *uxorem . . . comitem habeat.*

believe him, by Hercules, but I am also extremely grateful to him for diverting us with a charming and delightful story. I have come out of this rough long stretch of road without either toil or boredom. I think my conveyor is happy over that favour too: without tiring him I have ridden all the way to this city gate here, not on his back, but on my own ears."

21 This was the end of both our conversation and our shared journey. My two companions turned off to the left towards a nearby farmhouse, while I went up to the first inn I spotted after entering the town and immediately made inquiries of an old lady who was the innkeeper. "Is this town Hypata?" I asked. She nodded. "Do you know someone named Milo, one of the foremost citizens?" "Foremost is the right word for your Milo," she replied, "since he lives outside the city-limits and the whole town." "Joking aside," I answered, "good mother, please tell me what his background is and what house he lives in." "Do you see those windows at the end there, looking out on the city, and the door on the other side with a back view of the alley nearby? There is where your friend Milo lives, a man with heaps of money and abundant substance, but notorious for his utter miserliness and sordid squalor. He is constantly lending at high interest, with gold and silver as security, but he keeps himself shut up in a tiny house, worrying about every speck of copper-rust. He lives with a wife, his companion in adversity,

praeter unicam pascit ancillulam, et habitu mendicantis semper incedit."

Ad haec ego risum subicio. "Benigne" inquam "et prospicue Demeas meus in me consuluit, qui peregrinaturum tali viro conciliavit, in cuius hospi-
22 tio nec fumi nec nidoris nebulam vererer." Et cum dicto modico secus progressus ostium accedo et ianuam firmiter oppessulatam pulsare vocaliter incipio. Tandem adulescentula quaedam procedens, "Heus tu," inquit "qui tam fortiter fores verberasti, sub qua specie mutuari cupis? An tu solus ignoras praeter aurum argentumque nullum nos pignus admittere?" "Meliora" inquam "ominare, et potius responde an intra aedes erum tuum offenderim." "Plane," inquit "sed quae causa quaestionis huius?" "Litteras ei a Corinthio Demea scriptas ad eum reddo." "Dum annuntio" inquit "hic ibidem me opperimino." Et cum dicto rursum foribus oppessulatis intro capessit.[1] Modico deinde regressa patefactis aedibus, "Rogat te" inquit.

Intuli me eumque accubantem[2] exiguo admodum grabatulo et commodum cenare incipientem invenio. Assidebat pedes uxor et mensa vacua posita, cuius monstratu "En" inquit "hospitium."

[1] F *capessum.*

[2] Or *accumbentem*, for F's *accumbantem.*

maintains no servants except one little maid, and always goes about dressed like a beggar."

I responded to this with a laugh. "My friend Demeas," I said, "certainly acted kindly and providently on my behalf by giving me a letter of introduction to a man like that as I started on my travels: under his roof I have no need to fear either smoke
22 from the fireplace or cooking fumes." With this observation I walked on a little farther and reached the entrance. The door was firmly bolted, and I began to knock and call vociferously. At long last a girl came out. "Well!" she said. "You certainly have been giving the door a mighty beating. What kind of security do you offer for the loan you want? Or are you the only person unaware that we never accept any guarantee but gold and silver?" "Give me a better omen than that," I said, "and tell me instead if I might find your master at home." "Certainly," she answered, "but what is the reason for your question?" "I have a letter for him from Demeas at Corinth." "Wait for me right here," she said, "while I announce you." With that she bolted the door again and made off inside the house. She returned shortly, opened the door, and announced, "He asks you to come in."

I went in and found him reclining on a very tiny cot, just beginning his supper. His wife was sitting at his feet, and there was an empty table set up, to which he pointed and said, "Welcome!" "Thank

"Bene" ego, et ilico ei litteras Demeae trado. Quibus properiter lectis, "Amo" inquit "meum Demean, qui
23 mihi tantum conciliavit hospitem." Et cum dicto iubet uxorem decedere, utque in eius locum assidam iubet, meque etiam nunc verecundia cunctantem arrepta lacinia detrahens, "Asside" inquit "istic. Nam prae metu latronum nulla sessibula ac ne[1] sufficientem supellectilem parare nobis licet." Feci.

Et sic "Ego te" inquit "etiam de ista corporis speciosa habitudine deque hac virginali prorsus verecundia generosa stirpe proditum et recte conicerem, sed et meus Demeas eadem litteris pronuntiat. Ergo brevitatem gurgustioli nostri ne spernas peto. Erit tibi adiacens en[2] ecce illud cubiculum honestum receptaculum. Fac libenter deverseris in nostro. Nam et maiorem domum dignatione tua feceris, et tibi specimen gloriosum arrogaris, si contentus lare parvulo Thesei illius cognominis patris tui virtutes aemulaveris, qui non est aspernatus Hecales[3] anus hospitium tenue."

Et vocata ancillula, "Photis," inquit "sarcinulas hospitis susceptas cum fide conde in illud cubicu-

[1] F *escsibula anne.*
[2] F *et.*
[3] F *ales* with space for three letters in front.

you," I answered, and immediately handed him Demeas' letter. He read it hastily and then said, "I am grateful to my friend Demeas for introducing
23 such an important guest to me." And with that he told his wife to get up and invited me to sit down in her place. I still hesitated out of modesty, but he grasped the hem of my tunic and pulled me towards him. "Sit here beside me," he said. "The fear of robbers prevents us from acquiring chairs or even sufficient furniture." I sat down and he continued.

"In itself your attractive personal appearance and your quite virginal modesty would lead me to conjecture, and quite rightly, that you come of a noble family; but my friend Demeas also proclaims this in his letter. I beg you, therefore, not to spurn the meagreness of our little hovel. You can have that adjoining bedroom right over there, as a decent little retreat. I hope you will be pleased to stay with us. Not only will you make our house greater by the honour of your presence, but you will lay claim to a token of great repute if you are content with a tiny hearth, in emulation of the virtues of your father's namesake Theseus, who did not disdain the meagre hospitality of old Hecale."

Then he summoned the maid. "Photis,"[1] he said, "pick up our guest's bags and see that they are

[1] Her name, otherwise unparallelled, suggests the Greek word for light (φῶς), just as Lucius' name suggests the Latin (*lux*).

lum, ac simul ex promptuario oleum unctui et lintea tersui et cetera hoc eidem usui profers[1] ociter, et hospitem meum produc ad proximas balneas; satis arduo itinere atque prolixo fatigatus est."

24 His ego auditis, mores atque parsimoniam ratiocinans Milonis volensque me artius ei conciliare, "Nihil" inquam "rerum istarum, quae itineris ubique nos comitantur, indigemus. Sed et balneas facile percontabimur. Plane quod est mihi summe praecipuum, equo, qui me strenue pervexit, faenum atque hordeum acceptis istis nummulis tu, Photis, emito."

His actis et rebus meis in illo cubiculo conditis, pergens ipse ad balneas, ut prius aliquid nobis cibatui prospicerem, forum cuppedinis[2] peto inque eo piscatum opiparem expositum video, et percontato pretio, quod centum nummis indicaret, aspernatus viginti denarios[3] praestinavi. Inde me commodum egredientem continatur Pythias condiscipulus apud Athenas Atticas meus, qui me post aliquantum[4] multum temporis amanter agnitum[5] invadit, amplexusque ac comiter deosculatus, "Mi Luci," ait

[1] Often emended to *profer* or *proferas*; but cf. apparent imperatives in *-fers* at II 6 and VI 13.

[2] F *cupidinis*; but Apuleius probably used the archaic word *cuppedo* "dainty" here, as well as in chap. 25 and II 2.

[3] Usually emended to *denariis* or *denarium*.

[4] Should perhaps be emended to *aliquam*.

[5] Should perhaps be transposed to *agnitum amanter*, to construe the adverb with *invadit*.

safely placed in that bedroom. Also bring some rubbing oil out of the storeroom and drying-towels and whatever else he needs, right away. Then take my guest to the nearest baths. He has had quite a difficult and extensive journey and he is tired."

24 When I heard this I realised Milo's character and stinginess, but since I wished to get further into his good graces, I said to him, "I do not need any of those supplies; they accompany me everywhere on my travels. And I can easily ask directions to the baths. What I am really most especially concerned about is my horse, who has conveyed me here so vigorously. Photis! Here, take these coins and buy him some hay and barley."

After this was arranged and my belongings put in my room, I set out by myself for the baths. But first, since I wanted to procure something for our supper, I headed for the provision-market. I saw some elegant fish on display there, and when I asked the price and was told they cost a hundred sesterces, I refused and bought them for twenty denarii.[1] Just as I was leaving I came upon Pythias,[2] who had been a fellow-student of mine at Athens in Attica. With a loving gleam of recognition after such a long time, he rushed up to me and hugged me and kissed me affectionately. "My friend Lucius,"

[1] 100 sesterces was equal to 25 denarii. I make no attempt to give modern equivalents for prices.

[2] His name suggests the oracle of Apollo at Delphi.

"sat pol diu est quod intervisimus te, at hercules exinde cum a Clytio[1] magistro digressi sumus. Quae autem tibi causa peregrinationis huius?" "Crastino die scies" inquam. "Sed quid istud? Voti gaudeo. Nam et lixas et virgas et habitum prorsus magistratui congruentem in te video." "Annonam curamus" ait "et aedilem gerimus, et si quid obsonare cupis utique commodabimus." Abnuebam, quippe qui iam cenae affatim piscatum prospexeramus. Sed enim Pythias, visa sportula succussisque in aspectum planiorem piscibus, "At has quisquilias quanti parasti?" "Vix" inquam "piscatori extorsimus accipere viginti denarium."

Quo audito, statim arrepta dextera postliminio me in forum cuppedinis[2] reducens, "Et a quo" inquit "istorum nugamenta haec comparasti?" Demonstro seniculum—in angulo sedebat—quem confestim pro aedilitatis imperio voce asperrima increpans, "Iam iam" inquit "nec amicis quidem nostris vel omnino ullis hospitibus parcitis, quod tam magnis pretiis pisces frivolos indicatis et florem Thessalicae

[1] *a Clytio* is an almost certain restoration of the proper name concealed in F's *adstio.*

[2] F *cupidinis.*

he said, "by heaven,[1] it has been a long time since I last saw you. Yes, by Hercules, it was when we took leave of our teacher Clytius.[2] What brings you here in your travels?" "You will find out tomorrow," I replied. "But what's this? Congratulations! I see you have attendants and the rods of office and the dress of a magistrate." "I am administrator of food supplies," he said, "and market inspector, and if you wish to do any shopping I am at your service." "No thanks," I replied, since I had already provided quite enough fish for supper. But Pythias saw my basket and shook the fish up so that he could see them more clearly. "How much did you pay for this rubbish?" he asked. "I just managed to twist a fishmonger's arm to take twenty denarii for them," I answered.

25 When he heard this, he instantly grabbed my hand and led me back to the provision-market. "And from which of these merchants," he asked, "did you buy that junk?" I pointed to a little old man who was sitting in a corner, and Pythias immediately began to berate him in an extremely harsh tone befitting the authority of his office as inspector. "So now!" he shouted. "You do not even spare my friends, or indeed any visitors to this place. You mark up worthless fish at high prices, and you are reducing this flower of Thessalian terri-

[1] *Pol* is a mild oath, a shortened form of "By Pollux."

[2] His name comes from the Greek word "renowned."

regionis ad instar solitudinis et scopuli edulium caritate deducitis? Sed non impune. Iam enim faxo scias quem ad modum sub meo magisterio mali debeant coerceri." Et profusa in medium sportula iubet officialem suum insuper pisces inscendere ac pedibus suis totos obterere. Qua contentus morum severitudine meus Pythias ac mihi ut abirem suadens, "Sufficit mihi, o[1] Luci," inquit "seniculi tanta haec contumelia."

His actis consternatus ac prorsus obstupidus, ad balneas me refero, prudentis condiscipuli valido consilio et nummis simul privatus et cena, lautusque ad hospitium Milonis ac dehinc cubiculum me reporto.

26 Et ecce Photis ancilla "Rogat te" inquit "hospes." At ego iam inde Milonis abstinentiae cognitor excusavi comiter, quod viae vexationem non cibo sed somno censerem diluendam. Isto accepto pergit ipse et iniecta dextera clementer me trahere adoritur. Ac dum cunctor, dum modeste renitor, "Non prius" inquit "discedam quam me sequaris." Et dictum iure iurando secutus iam obstinationi suae me ingratis oboedientem perducit ad illum suum grabatulum, et residenti "Quam salve agit" inquit "Demeas noster? Quid uxor? Quid liberi? Quid ver-

[1] The *o*, written above the line in F, should perhaps be deleted.

tory to the semblance of a deserted, barren cliff by the costliness of your wares. But you will not get away with it, because now I am going to show you how rogues are going to be checked while I am magistrate." Then he emptied the basket out on to the open pavement and ordered his assistant to trample on the fish and crush them to a pulp with his feet. Content with this display of stern morality, my friend Pythias advised me to be off, saying, "I am satisfied, Lucius, just to have abused the old fellow that way."

Speechless and utterly dumbfounded at these events, I went on to the baths, having been robbed of both money and supper by the authoritative counsel of my wise fellow-student. When I had bathed, I returned to Milo's house and then went to my room.

26 Suddenly the maid Photis appeared. "Your host," she said, "invites you to join him." But since I was already acquainted with Milo's parsimony, I excused myself politely on the grounds that I thought the hardship of my trip needed to be dispelled by sleep, not food. When he heard this, Milo came himself and took hold of me and gently began to pull me along. When I hesitated and resisted discreetly, he asserted, "I will not leave until you come with me," and capped this with an oath. He was so stubborn that I had to obey him against my will, and he led me to that little cot of his and sat me down. "How is our friend Demeas' health? How is his wife? The children? The ser-

naculi?" Narro singula. Percontatur accuratius causas etiam peregrinationis meae. Quas ubi probe pertuli,[1] iam et de patria nostra et eius primoribus ac denique de ipso praeside scrupulosissime explorans, ubi me post itineris tam saevi vexationem sensit fabularum quoque serie fatigatum in verba media somnolentum desinere ac nequicquam, defectum iam, incerta verborum salebra balbuttire, tandem patitur cubitum concederem. Evasi aliquando rancidi senis loquax et famelicum convivium, somno non cibo gravatus, cenatus solis fabulis, et in cubiculum reversus optatae me quieti reddidi.

[1] Usually emended to *protuli.*

vants?" I answered each of his questions. He inquired more closely about the reasons for my journey, and when I had carefully explained all, he began a detailed investigation about my home-town, its leading citizens, and finally even the governor himself. When he noticed that after the hardship of my cruel journey I had become further exhausted by this uninterrupted flow of talk, and I would sleepily stop in the middle of a sentence, and that I was now so far gone that I was uselessly muttering inarticulate and jerky noises, he finally let me go off to bed. At long last I escaped the nauseating old man's talkative, famished banquet. Stuffed with drowsiness instead of food, having dined on nothing but talk, I went back to my room and surrendered to the sleep that I yearned for.

LIBER II

1 Ut primum nocte discussa sol novus diem fecit, et somno simul emersus et lectulo, anxius alioquin et nimis cupidus cognoscendi quae rara miraque sunt, reputansque me media Thessaliae loca tenere, quo[1] artis magicae nativa cantamina totius orbis consono ore celebrentur, fabulamque illam optimi comitis Aristomenis de situ civitatis huius exortam, suspensus alioquin et voto simul et studio, curiose singula considerabam. Nec fuit in illa civitate quod aspiciens id esse crederem quod esset, sed omnia prorsus ferali murmure in aliam effigiem translata, ut et lapides quos offenderem de homine duratos, et aves quas audirem indidem plumatas, et arbores quae pomerium ambirent similiter foliatas, et fontanos latices de corporibus humanis fluxos crederem; iam statuas et imagines incessuras, parietes locuturos, boves et id genus pecua dicturas praesagium, de ipso vero caelo et iubaris orbe subito

[1] Some editors emend to *qua* to avoid what may seem an abnormal use of *quo* meaning "where".

BOOK II

1 As soon as night had been scattered and a new sun brought day, I emerged from sleep and bed alike. With my anxiety and my excessive passion to learn the rare and the marvellous, considering that I was staying in the middle of Thessaly, the native land of those spells of the magic art which are unanimously praised throughout the entire world, and recalling that the story told by my excellent comrade Aristomenes had originated at the site of this very city, I was on tenterhooks of desire and impatience alike, and I began to examine each and every object with curiosity. Nothing I looked at in that city seemed to me to be what it was; but I believed that absolutely everything had been transformed into another shape by some deadly mumbo-jumbo: the rocks I hit upon were petrified human beings, the birds I heard were feathered humans, the trees that surrounded the city wall were humans with leaves, and the liquid in the fountains had flowed from human bodies. Soon the statues and pictures would begin to walk, the walls to speak, the oxen and other animals of that sort to prophesy; and from the sky itself and the sun's orb there would

venturum oraculum.

2 Sic attonitus, immo vero cruciabili desiderio stupidus, nullo quidem initio vel omnino vestigio cupidinis meae reperto, cuncta circumibam tamen.[1] Dum in luxum[2] nepotalem similis ostiatim singula pererro, repente me nescius forum cuppedinis[3] intuli. Et ecce mulierem quampiam frequenti stipatam famulitione ibidem gradientem accelerato vestigio comprehendo. Aurum in gemmis et in tunicis, ibi inflexum, hic intextum, matronam profecto confitebatur. Huius adhaerebat lateri senex iam gravis in annis, qui, ut primum me conspexit, "Est," inquit "hercules, est[4] Lucius," et offert osculum, et statim incertum quidnam in aurem mulieris obganniit. "Quin" inquit "etiam ipse parentem tuam accedis et salutas?" "Vereor" inquam "ignotae mihi feminae," et statim rubore suffusus deiecto[5] capite restiti.

At illa, optutum in me conversa, "En" inquit "sanctissimae Salviae matris generosa probitas. Sed et cetera corporis exsecrabiliter ad [regulam

[1] *tamen* in this position is strange: the text may be corrupt and the clause-division wrong. Frassinetti's conjecture is attractive: *circumibam. Tandem, dum . . .*

[2] F *luxu.* Editors, unnecessarily disturbed by the phrase *in luxum nepotalem similis*, have proposed numerous emendations and additions.

[3] F *cupidinis.*

[4] F has one letter erased between *hercules* and *Lucius*; some editors do not print a second *est.*

[5] F *reiecto.*

suddenly come an oracle.

2 I was in such a state of shock, or rather so dumbfounded by my torturous longing, that, although I found no trace or vestige whatever of what I longed to see, I continued to circulate anyway. As I wandered from doorway to doorway, like a man bent on prodigal extravagance, suddenly without knowing it I stumbled upon the provision-market. There I saw a woman walking in the company of a large domestic staff. I quickened my pace and caught up with her. The gold entwined in her jewellery and woven in her clothes marked her surely as the wife of an important man. An old man weighed down with years was clinging to her side. The moment he caught sight of me he exclaimed, "By Hercules, it's Lucius!" He kissed me, and then immediately muttered something indistinct in the woman's ear. "Why don't you go up yourself and greet your aunt?" he said to me. "I am embarrassed in front of a woman whom I do not know," I answered, suddenly blushing; and I just stood there looking at the ground.

Then she turned and stared at me. "He inherited that well-bred behaviour," she said, "from his pure and virtuous mother Salvia.[1] And his physical

[1] A not uncommon Roman name. There is no evidence to connect it with the Plutarch and Sextus mentioned in I 2, and Apuleius may have chosen it here for its healthful sound.

qua diligenter aliquid affingunt] amussim[1] congruentia: inenormis proceritas, suculenta gracilitas, rubor temperatus, flavum et inaffectatum capillitium, oculi caesii quidem, sed vigiles et in aspectu micantes, prorsus aquilini, os quoquoversum floridum, speciosus et immeditatus incessus."

3 Et adiecit, "Ego te, o Luci, meis istis manibus educavi—quidni?—parentis tuae non modo sanguinis, verum alimoniarum etiam socia. Nam et familia Plutarchi ambae prognatae sumus, et eandem nutricem simul bibimus, et in nexu germanitatis una coaluimus. Nec aliud nos quam dignitas discernit, quod illa clarissimas, ego privatas nuptias fecerimus. Ego sum Byrrhena illa, cuius forte saepicule nomen inter tuos educatores frequentatum retines. Accede itaque hospitium fiducia, immo vero iam tuum proprium larem."

Ad haec ego, iam sermonis ipsius mora rubore digesto, "Absit," inquam "parens, ut Milonem hospitem sine ulla querela deseram. Sed plane quod officiis integris potest effici curabo sedulo. Quotiens itineris huius ratio nascetur, numquam erit ut non apud te devertar."

[1] F has only *sim* of *amussim.* The bracketed words are almost certainly a gloss explaining the meaning of *amussim* as "a ruler with which people fashion something carefully."

---

[1] See I 2 and the note there.

appearance is a damnably precise fit too: he is tall but not abnormal, slim but with sap in him, and of a rosy complexion; he has blond hair worn without affectation, wide-awake light-blue eyes with flashing glance just like an eagle's, a face with a bloom in every part, and an attractive and unaffected walk."

3 She went on: "Lucius, I raised you with these very hands of mine; naturally, since not only am I a close relative of your mother, but I was even reared with her. We are both descendants of Plutarch's family,[1] we were suckled together by the same wet-nurse, and we grew up together in the close bond of sisterhood. The only difference between us is our social position, since she married a man of high office and I a private citizen. I am that Byrrhena[2] whose name I suppose you remember hearing mentioned fairly frequently among those who raised you. Come and entrust yourself to my hospitality —or rather, come to your own hearth and home."

I answered her, now that my blushes had had time to disperse while she was speaking. "Please, dear aunt," I said, "I ought not to desert my host Milo without grounds for complaint. But I will try very hard to do what I can without failing my obligations. Whenever I have reason to come this way, I will never fail to stay with you."

[2] This name, if correctly preserved in the manuscript tradition, is otherwise unattested. It may mean "red-haired" or "ruddy".

Dum hunc et huius modi sermonem altercamur, paucis admodum confectis passibus ad domum Byrrhenae pervenimus.

4 Atria longe pulcherrima columnis quadrifariam per singulos angulos stantibus attolerabant statuas,[1] palmaris deae facies, quae pinnis explicitis sine gressu pilae volubilis instabile vestigium plantis roscidis delibantes[2] nec ut maneant inhaerent et iam[3] volare creduntur. Ecce lapis Parius in Dianam factus tenet libratam totius loci medietatem, signum perfecte luculentum, veste reflatum, procursu vegetum, introeuntibus obvium et maiestate numinis venerabile. Canes utrimquesecus deae latera muniunt, qui canes et ipsi lapis erant. His oculi minantur, aures rigent, nares hiant, ora saeviunt, et, sicunde de proximo latratus ingruerit, eum putabis de faucibus lapidis exire; et—in quo summum specimen operae fabrilis egregius ille signifex prodidit—sublatis canibus in pectus arduis pedes imi resistunt, currunt priores.

[1] *statuas* has perhaps been added by a literal-minded commentator or editor to explain the following phrase, *palmaris deae facies.* Compare *simulacrum* near the end of this chapter.

[2] F *decitantes.* Other emendations have been proposed.

[3] F *etiam.*

---

[1] The large reception-hall in a Roman house, often, as here, open to the sky at the centre.

[2] The statue-group represents the myth of Actaeon, who

While exchanging this sort of talk we had walked a short distance and now arrived at Byrrhena's house.

4 The atrium[1] was particularly beautiful. Columns were erected in each of its four corners, and on these stood statues, likenesses of the palm-bearing goddess; their wings were outspread, but, instead of moving, their dewy feet barely touched the slippery surface of a rolling sphere; they were not positioned as though stationary, but you would think them to be in flight. Next I saw a piece of Parian marble made into the likeness of Diana,[2] occupying in balance the center of the whole area. It was an absolutely brilliant statue, robe blowing in the wind, vividly running forward, coming to meet you as you entered, awesome with the sublimity of godhead. There were gods protecting both flanks of the goddess, and the dogs were marble too. Their eyes threatened, their ears stiffened, their nostrils flared, and their mouths opened savagely, so that if the sound of barking burst in from next door you would think it had come from the marble's jaws. Furthermore that superb sculptor displayed the greatest proof of his craftsmanship by making the dogs rear up with their breasts raised high, so that their front feet seemed to run, while their hind feet thrust at

saw the virgin goddess Diana bathing naked, and was punished by being transformed into a stag and killed by his own hunting-dogs.

Pone tergum deae saxum insurgit in speluncae modum, muscis et herbis et foliis et virgulis et sicubi pampinis et arbusculis alibi de lapide florentibus. Splendet intus umbra signi de nitore lapidis. Sub extrema saxi margine poma et uvae faberrime politae dependent, quas ars aemula naturae veritati similes explicuit. Putes ad cibum inde quaedam, cum mustulentus autumnus maturum colorem afflaverit, posse decerpi, et si fontem, qui deae vestigio discurrens in lenem vibratur undam, pronus aspexeris, credes illos ut rure[1] pendentes racemos inter cetera veritatis nec agitationis officio carere. Inter medias frondes lapidis Actaeon simulacrum,[2] curioso optutu in deam versum[3] proiectus, iam in cervum ferinus et in saxo simul et in fonte loturam Dianam opperiens visitur.

5 Dum haec identidem rimabundus eximie delector, "Tua sunt" ait Byrrhena "cuncta quae vides." Et cum dicto ceteros omnes sermone secreto decedere praecipit. Quibus dispulsis omnibus, "Per hanc" inquit "deam, o Luci carissime, ut anxie tibi

[1] F's *rure* has caused much editorial consternation, although it is just possible in the sense "in the country", "in nature". Wiman's *pure* is the most attractive emendation; a sample list of others follows: *vere*, *vite*, *rore*, *rupe*.

[2] *simulacrum* is possibly a gloss: cf. *statuas* above.

[3] F *sum*.

the ground. Behind the goddess's back the rock rose in the form of a cave, with moss, grass, leaves, bushes, and here vines and there little trees all blossoming out of the stone. In the interior the statue's shadow glistened with the marble's sheen. Up under the very edge of the rock hung apples and the most skilfully polished grapes, which art, rivalling nature, displayed to resemble reality. You would think that some of them could be plucked for eating, when wine-gathering Autumn breathes ripe colour upon them; and if you bent down and looked in the pool that runs along by the goddess's feet shimmering in a gentle wave, you would think that the bunches of grapes hanging there, as if in the country, possessed the quality of movement, among all other aspects of reality. In the middle of the marble foliage the image of Actaeon could be seen, both in stone and in the spring's reflection, leaning towards the goddess with an inquisitive stare, in the very act of changing into a stag and waiting for Diana to step into the bath.

5 I was staring again and again at the statuary enjoying myself enormously, when Byrrhena spoke. "Everything you see," she said, "belongs to you." And with that she ordered everyone else to leave so that we might talk in private. When all had been dismissed she began. "My dearest Lucius," she said, "I swear by this goddess[1] that I am very

[1] Diana, one of whose forms is Hecate, goddess of witchcraft. See also XI 2 and 5.

metuo et ut pote pignori meo longe provisum cupio, cave tibi, sed cave fortiter a malis artibus et facinorosis illecebris Pamphiles illius, quae cum Milone isto, quem dicis hospitem, nupta est. Maga primi nominis et omnis carminis sepulcralis magistra creditur, quae surculis et lapillis et id genus frivolis inhalatis omnem istam lucem mundi sideralis imis Tartari et in vetustum Chaos summergere novit. Nam simul quemque conspexerit speciosae formae iuvenem, venustate eius sumitur et ilico in eum et oculum et animum detorquet. Serit blanditias, invadit spiritum, amoris profundi pedicis aeternis alligat. Tunc minus morigeros et viles fastidio in saxa et in pecua et quodvis animal puncto reformat, alios vero prorsus exstinguit. Haec tibi trepido et cavenda censeo. Nam et illa urit[1] perpetuum, et tu per aetatem et pulchritudinem capax eius es." Haec mecum Byrrhena satis anxia.

6 At ego curiosus alioquin, ut primum artis magicae semper optatum nomen audivi, tantum a cautela Pamphiles afui ut etiam ultro gestirem tali magisterio me volens ampla cum mercede tradere et prorsus in ipsum barathrum saltu concito praecipi-

[1] Frequently emended to *uritur*; *prurit* ("itches") and *surit* ("is in heat") have also been suggested.

---

[1] Her name means "universally amorous", "Mrs. Loveall".

worried and afraid for you, and I want you to be forewarned far in advance, as if you were my own son. Be careful! I mean watch out carefully for the evil arts and criminal seductions of that woman Pamphile,[1] who is the wife of that Milo you say is your host. She is considered to be a witch of the first order and an expert in every variety of sepulchral incantation, and by breathing on twigs and pebbles and stuff of that sort she can drown all the light of the starry heavens in the depths of hell and plunge it into primeval Chaos. No sooner does she catch sight of some young man of attractive appearance than she is consumed by his charm and immediately directs her eye and her desire at him. She sows her seductions, attacks his soul, and binds him with the everlasting shackles of passionate love. If any do not respond and become cheap in her eyes by their show of repugnance, she transforms them on the spot into rocks or sheep or any other sort of animal; some, however, she completely annihilates. That is why I am afraid for you. I advise you to be on your guard, because she is always on fire, and you are quite young and handsome enough to suit her." Byrrhena told me all this with great concern.

6 But in my curiosity, as soon as I heard that forever desirable name of magic, far from being cautious of Pamphile, I yearned to turn myself over to an apprenticeship of that sort willingly and voluntarily, with all its high costs, and plunge right to the bottom of the pit with one quick leap. Out of my

tare. Festinus denique et vecors animi manu eius velut catena quadam memet expedio et, "Salve" propere addito, ad Milonis hospitium perniciter evolo. Ac dum amenti similis celero vestigium, "Age," inquam "o Luci, evigila et tecum esto. Habes exoptatam occasionem et voto diutino poteris fabulis miris[1] explere pectus. Aufers[2] formidines pueriles, comminus cum re ipsa naviter congredere, et a nexu quidem venerio hospitis tuae tempera et probi Milonis genialem torum religiosus suspice, verum enimvero[3] Photis famula petatur enixe. Nam et forma scitula et moribus ludicra et prorsus argutula est. Vesperi quoque cum somno concederes, et in cubiculum te deduxit comiter et blande lectulo collocavit et satis amanter cooperuit et osculato tuo capite quam invita discederet vultu prodidit, denique saepe retrorsa respiciens substitit. Quod bonum felix et faustum itaque, licet salutare non erit, Photis illa temptetur."

7 Haec mecum ipse disputans fores Milonis accedo et, quod aiunt, pedibus in sententiam meam vado. Nec tamen domi Milonem vel uxorem eius offendo, sed tantum caram meam Photidem. Suis parabat

[1] F *miseris.*
[2] Usually emended to *aufer*, but cf. I 23 and VI 13.
[3] F *enim puero.*

---

[1] Compare the priest's words at XI 29.

mind with impatience, I extricated myself from Byrrhena's grasp as from a chain, added a quick "Farewell," and flew rapidly back to Milo's lodgings. While speeding along like a madman I talked to myself. "Come on, Lucius," I said, "stay alert and keep in control of yourself. You have the opportunity you have been waiting for. You can have your heart's fill of marvellous stories, as you have always wanted. Lay aside childish fears and come to grips with the situation bravely, in hand to hand combat. Avoid any amorous connection with your hostess and scrupulously honour Milo's marriage-bed; instead Photis the maid should be strenuously wooed. After all she is pretty to look at, playful in disposition, and as sharp as a needle. Last night when you were about to fall asleep, she led you graciously into the bedroom, arranged you seductively in bed, and tucked you in quite lovingly. After she kissed you on the head, her expression betrayed how unwilling she was to leave, and she stopped and looked back several times. So now may this be good, favorable, and auspicious—even if it will not be salutary: let Photis be assailed."[1]

7 While debating with myself I arrived at Milo's front door, and, as they say, I made my decision with my feet.[2] I did not find either Milo or his wife at home, but only my dear Photis. She was fixing pork

[2] Roman senators voted by walking to one side or the other of the senate-house.

viscus[1] fartim concisum et pulpam frustatim consectam, † ambacupascuae †[2] iurulenta et, quod naribus iam inde hariolabar, tuccetum perquam sapidissimum. Ipsa linea tunica mundule amicta et russea[3] fasceola praenitente altiuscule sub ipsas papillas succinctula, illud cibarium vasculum floridis palmulis rotabat in circulum, et in orbis flexibus crebra succutiens et simul membra sua leniter illubricans, lumbis sensim vibrantibus, spinam mobilem quatiens placide decenter undabat. Isto aspectu defixus obstupui et mirabundus steti; steterunt et membra quae iacebant ante. Et tandem ad illam "Quam pulchre quamque festive," inquam "Photis mea, ollulam istam cum natibus intorques! Quam mellitum pulmentum apparas! Felix et certius[4] beatus, cui permiseris illuc digitum intingere."

Tunc illa, lepida alioquin et dicacula puella, "Discede," inquit "miselle, quam procul a meo foculo, discede. Nam si te vel modice meus igniculus afflaverit, ureris intime nec ullus exstinguet

[1] F *viscum.*

[2] The correct reading behind F's corrupt *ambacupascuae* is probably irrecoverable.

[3] F *rursus se a.*

[4] Perhaps *certo* should be inserted before *certius*; but it is tempting to emend *certius* to *ter* ("thrice"), parallelling the priest's characterisation of Lucius in XI 16 as *felix et ter beatus.*

innards cut up for stuffing and meat sliced into pieces . . . juicy and, as I had already divined with my nostrils, an utterly delicious sausage.[1] She herself was neatly dressed in a linen tunic and had a dainty, bright red band tied up under her breasts. She was turning the cooking pot round and round with her flower-like hands, and she kept shaking it with a circular motion, at the same time smoothly sliding her own body, gently wiggling her hips, softly shaking her supple spine, beautifully rippling. I was transfixed by the sight, utterly stunned. I stood in amazement, as did a part of me which had been lying limp before. Finally I spoke. "How gorgeously, my Photis," I said, "and how delightfully you twist your little pot with your buttocks! What a delicious stew you are cooking! A man would be lucky—surely even blessed—if you would let him dip his finger in there."

Then she, with her wit and her ready tongue, retorted: "Get away, poor boy; get as far away as you can from my oven, because if my little flame should blow against you even slightly, you will burn deep inside and no one will be able to extinguish your fire

[1] The translation of the various items of food is very uncertain.

ardorem tuum nisi ego, quae dulce condiens et ollam et lectulum suave quatere novi."

8 Haec dicens in me respexit et risit. Nec tamen ego prius inde discessi quam diligenter omnem eius explorassem habitudinem. Vel quid ego de ceteris aio, cum semper mihi unica cura fuerit caput capillumque sedulo et publice prius intueri et domi postea perfrui, sitque iudicii huius apud me certa et statuta ratio[1]: vel quod praecipua pars ista corporis in aperto et perspicuo posita prima nostris luminibus occurrit, et quod in ceteris membris floridae vestis hilaris color, hoc in capite nitor nativus operatur; denique pleraeque indolem gratiamque suam probaturae lacinias omnes exuunt, amicula dimovent, nudam pulchritudinem suam praebere se gestiunt, magis de cutis roseo rubore quam de vestis aureo colore placiturae. At vero—quod nefas dicere, nec quod[2] sit ullum huius rei tam dirum exemplum!—si cuiuslibet eximiae pulcherrimaeque feminae caput capillo spoliaveris et faciem nativa specie nudaveris, licet illa caelo deiecta, mari edita, fluctibus educata, licet inquam Venus ipsa fuerit, licet omni Gratiarum choro stipata et toto Cupidi-

[1] F *ratione*.

[2] Should perhaps be emended to *neque*.

except me. I can season things deliciously, and I know how to shake a pot and a bed to your equal delight."

8 As she spoke she looked around at me and laughed. But I did not move away until I had carefully scrutinised every aspect of her appearance. Yet why should I mention anything else, since my exclusive concern has always been with a person's head and hair, to examine it intently first in public and enjoy it later at home? The reasoning behind this preference of mine is deliberate and well-considered: namely, as the dominant part of the body openly located for clear visibility, it is the first thing to meet our eyes. Secondly, what the cheerful colour of flowery clothing does for the rest of the body, its own natural lustre does for the head. Finally, when most women want to prove their own real loveliness, they take off all their garments, remove their clothes: they wish to show their beauty naked, knowing that they will be better liked for the rosy blush of their skin than for the golden colour of their dress. However—though it is forbidden to mention this and I hope that such a horrible illustration of this point will never occur—if you were to strip the hair from the head of the most extraordinary and beautiful woman and rob her face of its natural decoration, even if she were descended from heaven, born out of the sea, and raised by the waves, even, I say, if she were Venus herself, surrounded by the whole chorus of Graces and accompanied by the

num populo comitata et balteo suo cincta, cinnama fraglans et balsama rorans, calva processerit, placere non poterit nec Vulcano suo.

9 Quid cum capillis color gratus et nitor splendidus illucet, et contra solis aciem vegetus fulgurat vel placidus renitet, aut[1] in contrariam gratiam variat aspectum, et nunc aurum coruscans in lenem mellis deprimitur umbram, nunc corvina nigredine caerulus columbarum collis[2] flosculos aemulatur, vel cum guttis Arabicis obunctus et pectinis arguti dente tenui discriminatus et pone versum coactus amatoris oculis occurrens ad instar speculi reddit imaginem gratiorem? Quid cum frequenti subole spissus cumulat verticem, vel prolixa serie porrectus dorsa permanat? Tanta denique est capillamenti dignitas ut quamvis auro veste gemmis omnique cetero mundo exornata mulier incedat, tamen, nisi capillum distinxerit, ornata non possit audire.

Sed in mea Photide non operosus sed inordinatus

[1] F *at*.

[2] Various emendations have been suggested to avoid the simple ablative plural without preposition.

---

[1] The one that Hera borrowed in order to seduce Zeus in Homer's *Iliad* (XIV 215ff.): "On it are figured all beguilements, and loveliness | is figured upon it, and

entire throng of Cupids, wearing her famous girdle,[1] breathing cinnamon, and sprinkling balsam—if she came forth bald she could not attract even her husband Vulcan.[2]

9 But think what it is like when hair shines with its own lovely colour and brilliant light, and when it flashes lively against the sunbeams or gently reflects them; or when it shifts its appearance to produce opposite charms, now glistening gold compressed into the smooth shadows of honey, now with raven-blackness imitating the dark blue flowerets on pigeons' necks; or when it is anointed with Arabian oils and parted with a sharp comb's fine tooth and gathered at the back so as to meet the lover's eyes and, like a mirror, reflect an image more pleasing than reality; or when, compact with all its tresses, it crowns the top of her head or, let out in a long train, it flows down over her back. In short, the significance of a woman's coiffure is so great that, no matter how finely attired she may be when she steps out in her gold, robes, jewels, and all her other finery, unless she has embellished her hair she cannot be called well-dressed.

In my Photis' case, her coiffure was not elaborate,

passion of sex is there, and the whispered | endearment that steals the heart away even from the thoughtful" (tr. R. Lattimore).

[2] The Greek Hephaestus, god of fire and metallurgy. On Venus' marital relations, see V 29–30 and note.

ornatus addebat gratiam. Uberes enim crines leniter emissos[1] et cervice dependulos ac dein per colla dispositos sensimque sinuato patagio residentes paulisper ad finem conglobatos in summum verticem nodus astrinxerat.

10 Nec diutius quivi tantum cruciatum voluptatis eximiae sustinere, sed pronus in eam, qua fine summum cacumen capillus ascendit, mellitissimum illud savium impressi. Tum illa cervicem intorsit et ad me conversa limis et morsicantibus oculis, "Heus tu, scolastice," ait "dulce et amarum gustulum carpis. Cave ne nimia mellis dulcedine diutinam bilis amaritudinem contrahas."

"Quid istic" inquam "est, mea festivitas, cum sim paratus vel uno saviolo interim recreatus super istum ignem porrectus assari?" Et cum dicto artius eam complexus coepi saviari. Iamque aemula libidine in amoris parilitatem congermanescenti mecum, iam patentis oris inhalatu cinnameo et occursantis linguae illisu nectareo prona cupidine allibescenti, "Pereo," inquam "immo iam dudum perii, nisi tu propitiaris."

Ad haec illa rursum me deosculato, "Bono animo

[1] Should perhaps be emended to *remissos*.

but its casualness gave her added charm. Her luxuriant tresses were softly loosened to hang down over her neck, then they spread over her shoulders and momentarily rested upon the slightly curved border of her tunic; they were then gathered in a mass at the end and fastened in a knot to the crown of her head.

10 I could no longer endure the excruciating torture of such intense pleasure, but rushed toward her and planted that most delicious of kisses on the spot where her hair rose toward the top of her head. Then she twisted her neck and turned toward me with a sidelong glance of those biting eyes. "Well, well, my schoolboy," she said, "that is a bittersweet appetiser you are sampling. Be careful not to catch a chronic case of bitter indigestion from eating too sweet honey."

"How so, my merry one?" I replied. "I am prepared, if you will revive me now with one little kiss, to be stretched out over your fire and barbecued." And with that I held her tight and began to kiss her. Her ardour now began to rival my own, and she grew with me to an equal intensity of passion. Her mouth was open now, her breath like cinnamon and her tongue darting against mine with a touch like nectar, her passion unrestrained in her desire for me.

"I am dying," I said. "No, I am already dead unless you have mercy."

After another long kiss she answered, "Cheer up!

esto" inquit. "Nam ego tibi mutua voluntate mancipata sum, nec voluptas nostra differetur ulterius, sed prima face cubiculum tuum adero. Abi ergo ac te compara: tota enim nocte tecum fortiter et ex animo proeliabor."

11 His et talibus obgannitis sermonibus inter nos discessum est. Commodum meridies accesserat et mittit mihi Byrrhena xeniola, porcum opimum[1] et quinque gallinulas et vini cadum in aetate pretiosi. Tunc ego vocata Photide, "Ecce" inquam "Veneris hortator et armiger Liber advenit ultro. Vinum istud hodie sorbamus omne, quod nobis restinguat pudoris ignaviam et alacrem vigorem libidinis incutiat. Hac enim sitarchia navigium Veneris indiget sola, ut in nocte pervigili et oleo lucerna et vino calix abundet."

Diem ceterum lavacro ac dein cenae dedimus. Nam Milonis boni concinnaticiam mensulam rogatus accubueram, quam pote tutus ab uxoris eius aspectu, Byrrhenae monitorum memor, et perinde in eius faciem oculos meos ac si in Avernum lacum formidans deieceram. Sed assidue respiciens praeministrantem Photidem inibi recreabar animi, cum ecce iam vespera lucernam intuens Pamphile, "Quam largus" inquit "imber aderit crastino," et percontanti marito qui comperisset istud, respondit

[1] F *optimum*.

Because I want what you want, I have become your slave, and our pleasure will not be postponed much longer. When the first lights are lit I will come to your bedroom. So go away now and prepare your forces, because all night long I will make war on you bravely and with all my heart."

11 After this bantering conversation we separated. It had just turned noon when Byrrhena sent me some tokens of her friendship: a plump pig, five chickens, and a keg of expensive vintge wine. I summoned Photis. "Look," I said, "Venus' prompter and arms-bearer, Bacchus, has come too. We should drink up all this wine today, to extinguish modesty's faint-heartedness and force our desire to remain eager and strong. The only provisioning the ship of Venus needs is enough oil in the lamp and enough wine in the cup to last a sleepless night."

We devoted the rest of the day to bathing, and then supper. I had been invited to noble Milo's elegant little table and taken a place as protected as possible from his wife's gaze, mindful of Byrrhena's warnings. When I cast my eyes upon her face, I was as fearful as if I were looking into Lake Avernus.[1] But I kept turning round to look at Photis serving, and this renewed my spirits. Evening had come now, and Pamphile was staring at the lamp. "A huge rainstorm is coming tomorrow," she remarked. When her husband asked her how she knew that,

[1] The site of one of the entrances to the Underworld, near the Bay of Naples.

sibi lucernam praedicere. Quod dictum ipsius Milo risu secutus, "Grandem" inquit "ista in lucerna[1] Sibyllam pascimus, quae cuncta caeli negotia et solem ipsum de specula candelabri contuetur."

12 Ad haec ego subiciens "Sunt" aio "prima huiusce divinationis experimenta. Nec mirum, licet modicum istum igniculum et manibus humanis laboratum, memorem tamen illius maioris et caelestis ignis velut sui parentis, quid is sit[2] editurus in aetheris vertice, divino praesagio et ipsum scire et nobis enuntiare. Nam et Corinthi nunc apud nos passim Chaldaeus quidam hospes miris totam civitatem responsis turbulentat, et arcana fatorum stipibus emerendis edicit in vulgum, qui dies copulas nuptiarum affirmet, qui fundamenta moenium perpetuet, qui negotiatori commodus, qui viatori celebris, qui navigiis opportunus. Mihi denique proventum huius peregrinationis inquirenti multa

[1] F probably read *istam lucerno*, later changed to *lucerne*: one may choose among *istam lucernam*, *istam in lucerna* and *ista in lucerna*, and interpret the Sibyl as residing in the lamp, being in the form of a lamp, or being the lamp itself.

[2] Or possibly *quid is esset*, for F's *quis esset*.

she replied that the lamp had forecast it to her. Milo retorted, with a laugh: "That is a mighty Sibyl[1] we are feeding there in that lamp. She scans all heaven's affairs, and the sun too, from the observatory on top of her lamp-stand."

12 At this I interrupted. This is my first experience," I said, "of this sort of divination. There is nothing strange about it. Even though that tiny flame of yours is small and made by human hands, it still retains consciousness of that greater heavenly fire, as if of its own parent; thus by divine presentiment it can itself know and announce to us what the latter is about to enact in the summit of the sky. At Corinth where I live, there is a Chaldaean[2] visitor right now throwing the whole city everywhere into an uproar with his marvellous oracular responses, collecting donations for his public announcements of fate's secrets. He tells what day will make marriage-bonds strong or wall-foundations lasting, which day is advantageous for the businessman, illustrious for the traveller, or seasonable for sailing. When I asked him about the outcome of this trip of mine, he gave several strange

[1] An inspired prophetess. The most famous Sibyl in the Roman world resided at Cumae on the Bay of Naples. In this chapter Apuleius is probably thinking of Book VI of Virgil's *Aeneid*.

[2] The Chaldaeans were famous for their astrological lore, and the word could be used alone to mean "astrologer".

respondit et oppido mira et satis varia: nunc enim gloriam satis floridam, nunc historiam magnam et incredundam fabulam et libros me futurum."

13 Ad haec renidens Milo "Qua" inquit "corporis habitudine praeditus quove nomine nuncupatus hic iste Chaldaeus est?" "Procerus" inquam "et suffusculus, Diophanes nomine." "Ipse est" ait "nec ullus alius. Nam et hic apud nos multa multis similiter effatus, non parvas stipes, immo vero mercedes opimas[1] iam consecutus, Fortunam scaevam, an saevam verius dixerim, miser incidit.

"Nam die quadam cum frequentis populi circulo consaeptus coronae circumstantium fata donaret, Cerdo quidam nomine negotiator accessit eum, diem commodum peregrinationi cupiens. Quem cum electum destinasset ille, iam deposita crumina, iam profusis nummulis, iam dinumeratis centum denarium quos mercedem divinationis auferret, ecce quidam de nobilibus adulescentulus a tergo arrepens eum lacinia prehendit et conversum amplexus exosculatur artissime. At ille ubi primum consaviatus eum iuxtim se ut assidat effecit, attonitus et repentinae

[1] F *optimas.*

---

[1] His name is compounded of "Zeus" and "enlightening".
[2] His name suggests "profit".

and quite contradictory responses: on the one hand my reputation will really flourish, but on the other I will become a long story, an unbelievable tale, a book in several volumes."

13 Here Milo asked with a smile, "What does this Chaldaean friend of yours look like, and what name does he go by?" "He is tall," I responded, "and rather swarthy, and his name is Diophanes."[1] "That's the one," he said, "and none other. You see, he has also been here in our town, making the same sort of revelations to numerous people. He had already taken in, not just small contributions, but fat profits, when, poor fellow, he met with an awkward—or should I rather say, a cruel turn of Fortune.

"One day, you see, he was surrounded by a crowded circle of citizenry and handing out their fates to the audience gathered around him, when he was approached by a salesman named Cerdo[2] who wanted a suitable day to start travelling. Diophanes chose it and assigned it to him. The salesman had just put down his purse, poured out his coins, and counted out a hundred denarii as payment for the divination, when suddenly a young gentleman came sneaking up from behind, grabbed the Chaldaean by the cloak and swung him around, kissing and hugging him tightly. The latter, after he returned the kiss and made the young man sit down beside him, was so astonished and dumb-

visionis stupore et praesentis negotii quod gerebat oblitus,[1] infit ad eum, 'Quam olim equidem exoptatus nobis advenis?' Respondit ad haec ille alius 'Commodum vespera oriente. Sed vicissim tu quoque, frater, mihi memora quem ad modum exinde, ut de Euboea insula festinus enavigasti, et maris et viae confeceris iter.'

14 "Ad haec Diophanes ille Chaldaeus egregius, mente viduus necdum suus, 'Hostes' inquit 'et omnes inimici nostri tam diram, immo vero Ulixeam peregrinationem incidant. Nam et navis ipsa qua[2] vehebamur, variis turbinibus procellarum quassata, utroque regimine amisso aegre ad ulterioris ripae marginem detrusa, praeceps demersa est; et nos omnibus amissis vix enatavimus. Quodcumque vel ignotorum miseratione vel amicorum benevolentia contraximus, id omne latrocinalis invasit manus, quorum audaciae repugnans etiam Arignotus[3] unicus frater meus sub istis oculis miser iugulatus est.'

"Haec eo adhuc narrante maesto, Cerdo ille negotiator, correptis nummulis suis quos divinationis mercedi destinaverat, protinus aufugit. Ac dehinc tunc demum Diophanes expergitus sensit impru-

[1] Those troubled by the unusual word-order of this compound participial phrase have a choice of several remedies: remove the first *et*, remove the second *et*, or transpose *attonitus* after the first *et* or after *stupore*.

[2] F omits *qua*.

[3] F *arisnotus*.

founded by this sudden appearance that he forgot the business he was then about. 'I have been so hoping you would come,' he said to the youth. 'How long ago did you get here?' 'Yesterday at nightfall,' the other replied. 'But now it is your turn, my dear brother. Tell me, after you sailed away from the island of Euboea in such a hurry, how was the rest of your trip, both by sea and on the road?'

14 "Then Diophanes, our excellent Chaldaean, not yet back to his senses, thoughtlessly answered: 'I wish all our foes and enemies would encounter such a dreadful, really Odyssean voyage. First, the ship we were sailing on was battered by storm-blasts from every direction, lost both its rudders, and was with difficulty beached on the farther shore, where it sank straight to the bottom. We lost all our belongings and barely managed to swim ashore. Whatever we then collected out of strangers' pity or friends' kindness was all stolen by a band of robbers, and Arignotus,[1] my only brother, who was trying to put up a defence against their bold attack, had his throat slit before my very eyes, poor wretch.'

"While he was still woefully recounting this tale, Cerdo the salesman snatched up the coins he had intended as payment for his prophecy and fled at full speed. It was only then that Diophanes finally woke up and discovered the catastrophe caused by

[1] If correctly restored, the name means "well-known".

dentiae suae labem, cum etiam nos omnes circumsecus astantes in clarum cachinnum videret effusos.

"Sed tibi plane, Luci domine, soli omnium Chaldaeus ille vera dixerit, sisque felix et iter dexterum porrigas."

15 Haec Milone diutine sermocinante tacitus ingemescebam, mihique non mediocriter suscensebam, quod ultro inducta serie inopportunarum fabularum partem bonam vesperae eiusque gratissimum fructum amitterem. Et tandem denique devorato pudore ad Milonem aio, "Ferat suam Diophanes ille Fortunam et spolia populorum rursum conferat mari pariter ac terrae. Mihi vero fatigationis hesternae etiam nunc saucio da veniam, maturius concedam cubitum." Et cum dicto facesso et cubiculum meum contendo, atque illic deprehendo epularum dispositiones satis concinnas. Nam et pueris extra limen—credo, ut arbitrio nocturni gannitus ablegarentur—humi quam procul distratum fuerat. Et grabatulum meum astitit mensula cenae totius honestas reliquias tolerans, et calices boni, iam infuso latice semipleni, solam temperiem sustinentes, et lagoena iuxta orificio caesim deasceato patescens facilis hauritu—prorsus gladiatoriae Veneris antecenia.

his carelessness, when he saw all of us who were standing around dissolved in loud laughter.

"But I really hope, master Lucius, that the Chaldaean has told the truth to you, if to no one else. May you be fortunate and your voyage continue fair."

5 As Milo kept chattering on and on, I was silently groaning and becoming not a little angry with myself for having voluntarily brought on this series of untimely tales and losing a good part of the evening and its most agreeable fruit. So finally I swallowed my good manners and said to Milo, "Let Diophanes suffer his own Fortune. Let him gather folks' loot again and consign it to sea and land alike. As for me, I am still suffering from yesterday's exhaustion; so forgive me if I retire to bed a little early." And with that I left and headed for my room. There I discovered quite elegant arrangements for a banquet. A place had been laid out for the slaves on the ground outside the door, as far away as possible, to dispatch them out of hearing-range of our nocturnal chatter, I suppose. In front of my cot stood a little table displaying some fine leftovers from the whole supper, and good-sized cups already half full of poured wine awaiting only tempering,[1] and next to them a flask with its mouth hewed down to make it open and easy to draw from—exactly the right appetisers before Venus' gladiatorial games.

[1] The Romans usually added water to their wine before drinking it.

16 Commodum cubueram et ecce Photis mea, iam domina cubitum reddita, laeta[1] proximat, rosa serta[2] et rosa soluta in sinu tuberante. Ac me pressim deosculato et corollis revincto ac flore persperso, arripit poculum ac desuper aqua calida iniecta porrigit bibam; idque modico[3] prius quam totum exsorberem clementer invadit, ac relictum pullulatim[4] labellis minuens meque respiciens sorbillat dulciter. Sequens et tertium inter nos vicissim et frequens alternat poculum, cum ego iam vino madens, nec animo tantum verum etiam corpore ipso ad libidinem inquies[5] alioquin et petulans, et iam saucius paulisper, inguinum fine lacinia remota impatientiam Veneris Photidi meae monstrans, "Miserere" inquam "et subveni maturius. Nam, ut vides, proelio quod nobis sine fetiali officio indixeras iam proximante vehementer intentus, ubi primam sagittam saevi Cupidinis in ima praecordia mea delapsam excepi, arcum meum et ipse vigorate tetendi et oppido formido ne nervus rigoris nimietate rumpatur. Sed ut mihi morem plenius gesseris, in effusum

[1] F *lacta.* [2] F *rosae.* [3] F *modicum.*

[4] Most editors have not been able to accept F's unusual adverb (which recurs in V 20) and have emended to the seemingly more conventional *paullulatim* "little by little".

[5] F *inquiens. Inquies* would seem an almost certain correction, but the long compound phrase *nec . . . paulisper* is unusual enough in word-order to suggest the possibility of some additional corruption.

16 I had just reclined[1] when suddenly Photis, who had already put her mistress to bed, entered gaily with rose wreaths and loose roses swelling in the fold of her gown. She kissed me close and bound me with garlands and showered me with blossoms. Then she snatched up a cup, poured hot water into it, and handed it to me to drink. Shortly before I had swallowed it all, she gently laid hold of the cup and sweetly sipped the rest like a little bird, making it disappear between her lips while looking round at me. A second and a third cup passed swiftly back and forth between us. I was now under the influence of the wine; I was naturally both mentally and physically restless and eager with desire, and I had been feeling the wound for some time: I removed my clothes as far as my loins and showed Photis my impatience for Venus. "Have pity," I said, "and come quickly to my rescue. As you see, now that the battle you challenged me to without the sanction of a herald is approaching, I am taut with expectation. When I felt cruel Cupid's first arrow plunge into the depths of my heart, I vigorously stretched my own bow, and I am terribly afraid that the string is going to break from too much tension. But humour me even more: unloose

[1] Romans reclined at formal meals.

laxa crinem et capillo fluenter undante redde[1] complexus amabiles."

17 Nec mora cum, omnibus illis cibariis vasculis raptim remotis, laciniis cunctis suis renudata crinibusque dissolutis ad hilarem lasciviam, in speciem Veneris quae marinos fluctus subit pulchre reformata, paulisper etiam glabellum feminal rosea palmula potius obumbrans de industria quam tegens verecundia, "Proeliare" inquit "et fortiter proeliare, nec enim tibi cedam nec terga vertam. Comminus in aspectum, si vir es, derige, et grassare naviter et occide moriturus. Hodierna pugna non habet missionem."

Haec simul dicens inscenso grabatulo, super me sensim residens ac crebra subsiliens lubricisque gestibus mobilem spinam quatiens, pendulae Veneris fructu me satiavit, usque dum lassis animis et marcidis artibus defatigati simul ambo corruimus inter mutuos amplexus animas anhelantes. His et huius modi colluctationibus ad confinia lucis usque pervigiles egimus, poculis interdum lassitudinem refoventes et libidinem incitantes et voluptatem integrantes. Ad cuius noctis exemplar similes astruximus alias plusculas.

18 Forte quadam die de me magno opere Byrrhena contendit apud eam cenulae[2] interessem, et, cum

[1] I print Wiman's attractive suggestion for F's *fluenter undanter ede*. Another, but far less euphonic solution is *fluente undanter ede*.

[2] Or possibly *cenulae ut*, for F's *cenulaeve*.

your tresses and let them flow, and embrace me lovingly with your hair rippling like waves."

17 Without a moment's delay she whipped away all the dinner dishes, stripped herself of all her clothes, and let down her hair. With joyous wantonness she beautifully transformed herself into the picture of Venus rising from the ocean waves. For a time she even held one rosy little hand in front of her smooth-shaven pubes, purposely shadowing it rather than modestly hiding it. "Fight," she said, "and fight fiercely, since I will not give way and I will not turn my back. Close in and make a frontal assault, if you are a real man. Attack zealously and slay, as you are about to die. Today's battle admits no quarter."

As she said this she mounted the couch and sat slowly down on top of me, then bounced repeatedly up and down while wiggling her supple spine with sinuous movements, as she satiated me with the pleasures of Venus on a swing, until our spirits were flagging and our limbs had grown slack, and we both collapsed exhausted at the same time, caressing each other and panting out our life's breath. In combats like these we spent the whole night awake until just before dawn, from time to time using the wine to relieve our weariness, excite our passion, and renew our pleasure. With that night as blueprint we built many others like it.

18 One day, by chance, Byrrhena urged me very strongly to come to supper at her house, and

impendio excusarem, negavit veniam. Ergo igitur Photis erat adeunda deque nutu eius consilium velut auspicium petendum. Quae quamquam invita quod a se ungue latius digrederer, tamen comiter amatoriae militiae brevem commeatum indulsit. Sed "Heus tu" inquit "cave regrediare cena maturius. Nam vesana factio nobilissimorum iuvenum pacem publicam infestat.[1] Passim trucidatos per medias plateas videbis iacere, nec praesidis auxilia longinqua levare civitatem tanta clade possunt. Tibi vero fortunae splendor insidias, contemptus etiam peregrinationis poterit afferre."

"Fac sine cura" inquam "sis, Photis mea. Nam praeter quod epulis alienis voluptates meas anteferrem, metum etiam istum tibi demam maturata regressione. Nec tamen incomitatus ibo. Nam gladiolo solito cinctus altrinsecus ipse salutis meae praesidia gestabo."

Sic paratus cenae me committo.

19 Frequens ibi numerus epulonum, et utpote apud primatem feminam flos ipse civitatis. Mensae[2] opipares citro et ebore nitentes, lecti aureis vestibus intecti, ampli calices variae quidem gratiae sed pretiositatis unius: hic vitrum fabre sigillatum,

[1] F *infecta*.

[2] F *civitatisae*. The first noun in this sentence must be supplied by conjecture, and *mensae* is very likely. More than a single word, however, may have been lost.

although I tried hard to make my excuses she would not let me off. Therefore I had to approach Photis and consult her will as if I were taking auspices. Although she was unwilling for me to go more than a hair's breadth away from her, nevertheless she kindly granted me a short leave from amatory combat-duty. She warned me, however. "Now take care," she said, "and come back early from supper, because an insane gang of young aristocrats has been disturbing the public peace. You will see people lying murdered everywhere right out in the street, and the governor's troops are too far away to relieve the town of all this slaughter. Envy of your fine fortune, as well as contempt for you as a foreign visitor, could cause you to be ambushed."

"Please don't worry, darling Photis," I replied. "Besides the fact that I prefer my own pleasures to other people's banquets, I shall relieve your fear by returning early. And besides I will not be going without company: for with my dagger buckled at my side as usual I shall be carrying the protection of my own safety."

Thus prepared I ventured out to supper.

19 There was a large company of dinner-guests, and since she was one of the first ladies of the town, the very flower of society was there. There were luxuriant tables gleaming with citron-wood and ivory, couches draped with golden cloth, generous cups of varied appeal but alike in costliness—here skilfully moulded glass, there flawless crystal, else-

ibi crystallum impunctum, argentum alibi clarum et aurum fulgurans et sucinum mire cavatum et lapides ut bibas; et quidquid fieri non potest ibi est. Diribitores plusculi splendide amicti fercula copiosa scitule sumministrare, pueri calamistrati pulchre indusiati gemmas formatas in pocula vini vetusti frequenter offerre. Iam illatis luminibus epularis sermo percrebuit, iam risus affluens et ioci liberales et cavillus hinc inde.

Tum[1] infit ad me Byrrhena, "Quam commode versaris in nostra patria? Quod sciam, templis et lavacris et ceteris operibus longe cunctas civitates antecellimus, utensilium praeterea pollemus affatim. Certe libertas otioso,[2] et negotioso quidem advenae Romana frequentia, modesto vero hospiti quies villatica. Omni denique provinciae voluptarii secessus sumus."

20 Ad haec ego subiciens, "Vera memoras, nec usquam gentium magis me liberum quam hic fuisse credidi. Sed oppido formido caecas et inevitabiles latebras magicae disciplinae. Nam ne mortuorum quidem sepulchra tuta dicuntur, sed et[3] bustis et rogis reliquiae quaedam et cadaverum praesegmina ad exitiabiles viventium fortunas petuntur; et cantatrices anus in ipso momento choragii funeris[4] praepeti celeritate alienam sepulturam antevertunt."

[1] Perhaps *inde, cum* should be read, continuing the sentence in a typical Apuleian pattern.

[2] F *otiosa*. [3] Usually emended to *ex*.

[4] Usually emended to *funebris*.

where shining silver and glistening gold and marvellously hollowed-out amber and precious stones made to drink from—in short, everything impossible was there. Several brilliantly robed waiters elegantly served heaped platters; curly-haired boys in beautiful clothes continually offered vintage wine in gems shaped into cups. Soon lamps were brought in and the table-talk increased, with plentiful laughter and free wit and banter on every side.

Byrrhena turned to me then and asked, "How do you like your stay here in our home town? To my knowledge we are far ahead of all other cities with our temples, our baths, and our other public buildings, and besides we are amply provided with the necessities of life. Indeed we offer freedom for the man of leisure, the bustle of Rome for the travelling businessman, and resort-like restfulness for the tourist of modest means. In short, we are the pleasure-seeker's retreat for the entire province."

20 "What you say is true," I responded. "I think I have never been freer anywhere in the world than here. But I am terribly frightened by the dark and unavoidable lairs of magical science. They say that not even the tombs of the dead are safe, but at graves and pyres they hunt for remnants and cuttings of corpses to bring mortal harm to the living. Even at the very moment when the funeral is being staged, old witches with the speed of wings arrive before the family and forestall the burial."

His meis addidit alius, "Immo vero istic nec viventibus quidem ullis parcitur. Et nescio qui simile passus ore undique omnifariam deformato truncatus est."

Inter haec convivium totum in licentiosos cachinnos effunditur, omniumque ora et optutus in unum quempiam angulo secubantem conferuntur. Qui cunctorum obstinatione confusus indigna murmurabundus[1] cum vellet exsurgere, "Immo, mi Thelyphron," Byrrhena inquit "et subsiste paulisper et more tuae urbanitatis fabulam illam tuam remetire, ut et filius meus iste Lucius lepidi sermonis tui perfruatur comitate."

At ille "Tu quidem, domina," ait "in officio manes sanctae tuae bonitatis, sed ferenda non est quorundam insolentia." Sic ille commotus. Sed instantia Byrrhenae, quae eum adiuratione suae salutis ingratis cogebat effari, perfecit ut vellet.

21 Ac sic aggeratis in cumulum stragulis, et effultus in cubitum suberectusque in torum porrigit dexteram, et ad instar oratorum conformat articulum, duobusque infimis conclusis digitis ceteros eminus porrigens[2] et infesto pollice clementer surrigens

[1] F *murmurabundas.* The minimal correction printed here still leaves a very difficult text, and further corruption is likely.

[2] *eminus porrigens*: the original reading of F is hard to determine here, and editors vary greatly on what, if anything, needs to be changed in this difficult sentence.

Someone else added to my remarks: "Yes, but here they do not even spare the living. There was a man who had an experience of that kind; his face was completely mutilated and disfigured."

At these words the whole party dissolved into unrestrained laughter, and all faces turned staring toward one man reclining by himself in the corner. Upset by the general interest in him, he muttered some complaints and tried to get up to leave, but Byrrhena said, "Don't, my friend Thelyphron.[1] Stay a little while and tell us your story once again with your usual kindness, so that my son Lucius here may share the pleasure of your charming talk too."

"You, my lady," he answered, "are always true to your own virtuous kindness. But some people's insolence is intolerable." He was extremely upset, but Byrrhena persisted. Swearing by her own life, she pressed him to speak out despite his reluctance and finally won his consent.

21 And so Thelyphron piled the covers in a heap and propped himself on his elbow, sitting half upright on the couch. He extended his right arm, shaping his fingers to resemble an orator's: having bent his two lowest fingers in, he stretched the others out at long range and poised his thumb to strike, gently rising

[1] The name means "female-minded". Apuleius plays on it in the first sentence of chap. 23.

infit Thelyphron:

"Pupillus ego Mileto profectus ad spectaculum Olympicum, cum haec etiam loca provinciae famigerabilis adire cuperem, peragrata cuncta Thessalia fuscis avibus Larissam accessi. Ac dum singula pererrans tenuato admodum viatico paupertati meae fomenta conquiro, conspicor medio foro procerum quendam senem. Insistebat lapidem claraque voce praedicabat, siqui mortuum servare vellet, de pretio liceretur. Et ad quempiam praetereuntium 'Quid hoc' inquam 'comperior? Hicine mortui solent aufugere?'

"'Tace' respondit ille. 'Nam oppido puer et satis peregrinus es, meritoque ignoras Thessaliae te consistere, ubi sagae mulieres ora mortuorum passim demorsicant, eaque sunt illis artis magicae supplementa.'

22 "Contra ego 'Et quae, tu' inquam 'dic sodes, custodela ista feralis?'

"'Iam primum' respondit ille 'perpetem noctem eximie vigilandum est exsertis et inconivis oculis semper in cadaver intentis, nec acies usquam devertenda, immo ne obliquanda quidem, quippe cum

---

[1] The difficulties of this sentence arise from the fact that Apuleius is using military metaphors to describe a standard rhetorical pose. "At long range" (*eminus*) etymologically suggests "out of the hand."

[2] Also the home of Milesian tales; see I 1.

as he began.[1]

"When I was still a minor I set out from Miletus[2] to see the Olympic games.[3] Since I also wanted to visit this area of the celebrated province, I travelled through the whole of Thessaly and, under dark omens, arrived at Larissa.[4] Since my travel-allowance had worn quite thin, I wandered all over town trying to find some remedy for my poverty. I caught sight of a tall old man in the middle of the forum, who was standing up on a rock and proclaiming in a loud voice that anyone willing to guard a dead man should bid for the job. I said to a passerby, 'What is this I hear? Do dead men usually run away around here?'

"'Quiet!' he answered. 'You are terribly young and very much a stranger, and naturally you do not understand that you are in Thessaly, where witches are always taking bites out of corpses' faces to get supplies for their magic art.'

22 "'But please tell me,' I countered, 'what guarding of the dead do you require?'

"'First of all,' he replied, 'you must stay perfectly wide awake all night long, with straining unblinking eyes concentrated continuously on the corpse. You must never look around you, or even look aside,

[3] The famous contests held every four years at Olympia, in the northwestern part of the Peloponnese.

[4] Socrates' troubles also began in the vicinity of Larissa (I 7).

deterrimae versipelles in quodvis animal ore converso latenter arrepant, ut ipsos etiam oculos Solis et Iustitiae facile frustrentur. Nam et aves et rursum canes et mures, immo vero etiam muscas, induunt. Tunc diris cantaminibus somno custodes obruunt. Nec satis quisquam definire poterit quantas latebras nequissimae mulieres pro libidine sua comminiscuntur. Nec tamen huius tam exitiabilis operae merces amplior quam quaterni vel seni ferme offeruntur aurei. Ehem et—quod paene praeterieram—siqui non integrum corpus mane restituerit, quidquid inde decerptum deminutumque fuerit, id omne de facie sua desecto sarcire compellitur.'

23 "His cognitis animum meum commasculo et ilico accedens praeconem, 'Clamare' inquam 'iam desine. Adest custos paratus. Cedo praemium.' 'Mille' inquit 'nummum deponentur tibi. Sed heus, iuvenis, cave diligenter principum civitatis filii cadaver a malis Harpyis probe custodias.' 'Ineptias' inquam 'mihi narras et nugas meras. Vides hominem ferreum et insomnem, certe perspicaciorem ipso Lynceo vel Argo, et oculeum totum.'

"Vix finieram et ilico me perducit ad domum

[1] Their name means "snatchers". They were rapacious creatures, half bird, half woman.

[2] Lynceus was one of the Argonauts, famous for his keen sight, while Argus was a giant with eyes all over his body.

because those horrible creatures can change their skins and creep in secretly with their looks transformed into any sort of animal at all. They could easily cheat even the Sun's eyes, or Justice's. They put on the form of birds, and again dogs, and mice—yes, and even flies. Then with their dreadful spells they overwhelm watchmen with sleep. No one can even count the number of subterfuges these evil women contrive on behalf of their lust. And yet, as pay for such dangerous work no more than four or maybe six pieces of gold are offered. Oh yes, and I had almost forgotten to mention that if someone fails to deliver the body unscathed in the morning, he is forced to patch any part that has been plucked off or reduced in size with a piece sliced from his own face.'

23 "After I heard this I manfully screwed up my courage, went straight up to the crier, and said, 'Stop your announcing now. your watchman is here and ready. Let's have the price.' 'A thousand sesterces,' he said, 'will be held in deposit for you. But look out now, young man. Be careful. The corpse belongs to the son of one of the city's first families: guard it well from those wicked Harpies.'[1] 'A paltry matter,' I said, 'a mere trifle. You see before you a man of iron, sleepless, more keen-sighted indeed than Lynceus himself or Argus,[2] and every bit of him an eye.'

"I had scarcely finished talking when he led me

quampiam, cuius ipsis foribus obsaeptis per quandam brevem posticulam intro vocat me et, conclave quoddam reserans[1] obseratis luminibus umbrosum, demonstrat matronam flebilem fusca veste contectam. Quam propter assistens, 'Hic' inquit 'auctoratus ad custodiam mariti tui fidenter accessit.' At illa, crinibus antependulis hinc inde dimotis etiam in maerore luculentam proferens faciem meque respectans, 'Vide oro' inquit 'quam expergite munus obeas.' 'Sine cura sis' inquam. 'Modo corollarium idoneum compara.'

24 "Sic[2] placito consurrexit[3] et ad aliud me cubiculum inducit. ibi corpus splendentibus linteis coopertum introductis quibusdam septem testibus manu revelat, et diutine insuper fleto[4] obtestata fidem praesentium singula demonstrat anxie, verba concepta de industria quodam tabulis praenotante. 'Ecce' inquit 'nasus integer, incolumes oculi, salvae aures, illibatae labiae, mentum solidum. Vos in hanc rem, boni Quirites, testimonium perhibetote.' Et cum dicto consignatis illis tabulis facessit.

[1] *reserans* is a conjectural addition. Some change is needed: simplest would be to add *-que* to *matronam*, but it seems more likely that a participle has fallen out after *quoddam* or *umbrosum*, with the meaning "opening", "revealing", or "entering".

[2] F *comparas. Ic.*

[3] F *ocin surrexit*; *hoc insurrexit* or *ocius surrexit* are also possible.

[4] F *usu perfleto.*

quickly off to a house whose entrance was bolted shut. He invited me in through a tiny back door, and when we had entered a darkened room with tightly barred windows, he pointed out a weeping woman wrapped in a black robe. He approached her and spoke. 'Here is a man,' he said, 'who has contracted to guard your husband faithfully.' She moved her hair, which was hanging down in front, to both sides, revealing a face beautiful even in grief. Looking at me she said, 'Please be sure to do your duty as vigilantly as possible.' 'Don't worry,' I answered. 'Just get a suitable tip ready.'

24 "Our agreement concluded, she rose and led me into another room where the body lay, covered with shining linen. She had seven witnesses brought in, uncovered the corpse with her own hand, and after weeping over it at length and administering a solemn oath to those present, she anxiously pointed out each individual item while someone assiduously wrote down a formal inventory on a tablet. 'Look,' she said, 'nose whole, eyes unharmed, ears sound, lips untouched, chin solid. Ye citizens good and true, furnish witness unto this fact.' As soon as she finished, the tablets were sealed and she started to leave.

"At ego 'Iube,' inquam 'domina, cuncta quae sunt usui necessaria nobis exhiberi.' 'At quae' inquit 'ista sunt?' 'Lucerna' aio 'praegrandis, et oleum ad lucem luci sufficiens, et calida cum oenophoris et calice, cenarumque reliquiis discus ornatus.' Tunc illa capite quassanti 'Abi,' inquit 'fatue, qui in domo funesta cenas et partes requiris, in qua totiugis iam diebus ne fumus quidem visus est ullus. An istic comissatum te venisse credis? Quin sumis potius loco congruentes luctus et lacrimas?' Haec simul dicens respexit ancillulam et 'Myrrhine,' inquit 'lucernam et oleum trade confestim et incluso custode cubiculo protinus facesse.'

25 "Sic desolatus ad cadaveris solacium, perfrictis oculis et obarmatis ad vigilias, animum meum permulcebam cantationibus, cum ecce crepusculum et nox provecta et nox altior et dein concubia altiora et iam nox intempesta. Mihique oppido formido cumulatior quidem, cum repente introrepens mustela contra me constitit optutumque acerrimum in me destituit, ut tantillula animalis prae nimia sui fiducia mihi turbarit animum. Denique sic ad illam 'Quin abis,' inquam 'impurata bestia, teque ad tui similes musculos[1] recondis, antequam nostri vim praesentariam experiaris? Quin abis?'

[1] F *mosculos.* Some editors prefer other corrections, of which Helm's *in hortulos* is the best paleographically, giving the meaning "go off to your own kind in the gardens."

"I spoke up. 'My lady, please have someone furnish all the equipment I will need.' 'What equipment is that?' she asked. 'A very big lamp,' I answered, 'and enough oil to keep a light until daylight, and hot water with jugs of wine and a drinking cup, and a platter decked out with leftovers from dinner.' At that she shook her head and said, 'Get away, stupid! This is a house in mourning: you are asking for dinners and leftovers and there has not even been a puff of smoke seen in the house for days on end. Do you think you came here for a party? Why don't you adapt yourself to the place instead, and put on mourning and tears?' While she spoke she turned to a maid and gave orders: 'Myrrhine, hand over the lamp and oil quickly, lock the watchman inside the room, and go away at once.'

"Thus left alone to console a corpse, I rubbed my eyes and armed them for their guard duty. I beguiled my spirit with songs as dusk came, then late evening, then deeper dark, then even deeper sleeptime, and finally the dead of night. Fear really began to pile up on me, when suddenly a weasel slunk in, stopped in front of me, and fixed me with a very piercing stare. It had too much self-confidence for such a tiny creature, and this upset me. Finally I said to it, 'Go away, you filthy beast. Hide yourself away with your kin the mice before I make you feel my strength, and quickly too. Go away!'

"Terga vertit et cubiculo protinus exterminatur. Nec mora cum me somnus profundus in imum barathrum repente demergit, ut ne deus quidem Delphicus ipse facile discerneret duobus[1] nobis iacentibus, quis esset magis mortuus. Sic inanimis et indigens alio custode paene ibi non eram.

26 "Commodum noctis indutias cantus perstrepebat cristatae cohortis. Tandem expergitus et nimio pavore perterritus cadaver accurro, et admoto lumine revelataque eius facie rimabar singula, quae cuncta convenerant. Ecce uxor misella flens cum hesternis testibus introrumpit anxia, et statim corpori superruens multumque ac diu deosculata sub arbitrio luminis recognoscit omnia, et conversa Philodespotum requirit actorem. Ei praecipit bono custodi redderet sine mora praemium. Et oblato statim, 'Summas' inquit 'tibi, iuvenis, gratias agimus, et hercules ob sedulum istud ministerium inter ceteros familiares dehinc numerabimus.'

"Ad haec ego insperato lucro diffusus in gaudium, et in aureos refulgentes, quod identidem manu mea ventilabam, attonitus, 'Immo,' inquam 'domina, de famulis tuis unum putato, et quotiens

[1] Perhaps *ex* or *de* should be supplied before *duobus*.

---

[1] Apollo.

[2] The name means "fond of one's master."

"It turned its back and immediately left the confines of the room. Instantly deep slumber plunged me swiftly down to the bottom of the abyss. Even the god of Delphi[1] could not easily have decided which of the two of us lying there was more dead. I was so lifeless and so much in need of another guardian for myself that I was practically not there.

26 "The clarion of the crested cohort was just sounding a truce to night when I finally woke up and in great panic ran terrified to the corpse. I moved a light up close, uncovered his face, and carefully scrutinised it item by item: they all tallied. Then his poor little weeping wife broke into the room with the witnesses from the previous day. She was worried, and she fell at once upon the corpse, kissed it long and passionately, and inspected every detail with a lamp as arbiter. Then she turned aside and called for her steward Philodespotus,[2] instructing him to pay the good guardian his reward without delay. He immediately gave me the money, and she added her thanks. 'We are extremely grateful to you, young man,' she said, 'and by Hercules in return for this diligent service of yours, from now on we will count you as one of our close friends.'

"I was dissolved in joy at this unexpected income and astonished at those shining gold coins, which I jangled over and over again in my hand. 'No, my lady,' I answered her, 'consider me rather one of your servants, and as often as you need my services

operam nostram desiderabis, fidenter impera.'

"Vix effatum me statim familiares, omen[1] nefarium exsecrati, raptis cuiusque modi telis insequuntur: pugnis ille malas offendere, scapulas alius cubitis impingere, palmis infestis hic latera suffodere, calcibus insultare, capillos distrahere, vestem discindere. Sic in modum superbi iuvenis Aoni vel musici vatis Piplei[2] laceratus atque discerptus domo proturbor.

27 "Ac dum in proxima platea refovens animum infausti atque improvidi sermonis mei sero reminiscor dignumque me pluribus etiam verberibus fuisse merito consentio, ecce iam ultimum defletus atque conclamatus processerat mortuus, rituque patrio, utpote unus de optimatibus, pompa funeris publici ductabatur per forum. Occurrit atratus[3] quidam maestus in lacrimis genialem canitiem revellens senex, et manibus ambabus invadens torum, voce contenta quidem sed assiduis singultibus impedita, 'Per fidem vestram,' inquit 'Quirites, per pietatem publicam, perempto civi subsistite et extremum

[1] An almost certain correction for the manuscripts' *omne*, *omnem*, or *omnes*.

[2] One can forgive the scribes for jumbling the learned allusions in these proper names: F has *adoni vel mustejuatis pipletis.* Modern scholarship just may have restored the correct text.

[3] F *adhsatus.*

call on me with confidence.'

"No sooner had I pronounced the words when the members of the household, cursing my abominable omen, began attacking me with any weapons they could lay their hands on. One pounded my jaws with his fists, another punched my shoulders with his elbows, a third violently dug at my ribs with the flat of his palms; they jumped on me and kicked me with their feet, pulled my hair, and ripped my clothes. Thus I was tumbled out of the house, torn and mangled just like the haughty Aonian youth or the Pierian bard.[1]

27 "While I was recovering my strength in the street next to the house, I recalled—too late—my ill-omened and careless remark and agreed that I fully deserved even more of a beating than I had got. Just then the dead man came forth from his house, mourned and hailed for the last time; with hereditary rites befitting a leading citizen he was being carried through the forum in a public funeral procession. A sorrowing old man in black came rushing up, weeping and tearing at his handsome white hair. He laid hold of the bier with both hands and cried out, in a voice that was intense but broken by frequent sobs. 'For your honour's sake, noble citizens,' he said, 'as a public duty help your murdered fellow-citizen and exact stern vengeance on

[1] Allusions to Pentheus (see note at I 13) and Orpheus, both of whom were torn apart by frenzied Maenads.

facinus in nefariam scelestamque istam feminam severiter vindicate. Haec enim nec ullus alius miserum adulescentem, sororis meae filium, in adulteri gratiam et ob praedam hereditariam exstinxit veneno.'

"Sic ille senior lamentabiles questus singulis instrepebat. Saevire vulgus interdum et facti verisimilitudine ad criminis credulitatem impelli. Conclamant ignem, requirunt saxa, parvulos[1] ad exitium mulieris hortantur. Emeditatis ad haec illa fletibus quamque sanctissime poterat adiurans cuncta numina, tantum scelus abnuebat.

28 "Ergo igitur senex ille: 'Veritatis arbitrium in divinam providentiam reponamus. Zatchlas[2] adest Aegyptius propheta primarius, qui mecum iam dudum grandi praemio pepigit reducere paulisper ab inferis spiritum corpusque istud postliminio mortis animare.' Et cum dicto iuvenem quempiam linteis amiculis iniectum pedesque palmeis baxeis inductum et adusque deraso capite producit in medium. Huius diu manus deosculatus et ipsa

[1] Many editors prefer to emend away the picture of children being used to stone a woman.

[2] Given scribes' usual trouble with proper names, this one may well be wrong; but no convincing emendation has been proposed.

this wicked and criminal woman for the worst of crimes. For she herself, and no one else, poisoned this poor young man, my sister's son, to gratify her lover and steal the inheritance.'

"The old man kept shouting these mournful complaints to each and all, and the crowd began to grow enraged. The plausibility of the deed led them to believe the accusation. They began shouting for fire, searching for stones, urging youngsters to kill the woman. With tears contrived for the occasion, and swearing by all the gods as reverently as anyone could, she denied she had committed the terrible crime.

28 "Consequently the old man spoke up again. 'Let us put the judgement of the truth,' he said, 'into the hands of divine Providence. There is a man here named Zatchlas,[1] an Egyptian prophet of the first rank, who has already contracted with me for a great price to bring my nephew's spirit back from the dead for a brief time and reanimate his body as it was before his death.'[2] At this point he introduced a young man dressed in long linen robes and wearing sandals woven from palm leaves. His head was completely shaven. The old man kissed his hands at

[1] This exotic name, if correctly transmitted, has not been satisfactorily explained.

[2] *Postliminium* was the process in Roman law by which citizens who had been war-captives or exiles regained their rights upon their return.

genua contingens, 'Miserere,' ait 'sacerdos, miserere. Per caelestia sidera, per inferna numina, per naturalia elementa, per nocturna silentia et adyta Coptitica,[1] et per incrementa Nilotica et arcana Memphitica et sistra Phariaca, da brevem solis usuram et in aeternum conditis oculis modicam lucem infunde. Non obnitimur[2] nec terrae rem suam denegamus, sed ad ultionis solacium exiguum vitae spatium deprecamur.'

"Propheta sic propitiatus herbulam quampiam ob os corporis et aliam pectori eius imponit. Tunc orientem obversus, incrementa Solis augusti tacitus imprecatus, venerabilis scaenae facie studia praesentium ad miraculum tantum certatim arrexit.

29 "Immitto me turbae socium et pone ipsum lectulum editiorem quendam lapidem insistens cuncta curiosis oculis arbitrabar. Iam tumore pectus extolli, iam salubris[3] vena pulsari, iam spiritu

[1] F *adepcaco* (or *adepaco*) *o eptitica.* The emendation adopted here is obviously far from certain, although attractive in both sense and sound.

[2] Most editors want to supply an object for *obnitimur*: e.g. *necessitati*, *fato*, *neci*, *Libitinae* ("necessity", "fate", "death", "the goddess of undertakers").

[3] Usually emended to *salebris* "with jolts". Some specific artery is probably meant.

length and even touched his knees. 'Mercy, priest, mercy!' he begged. 'In the name of the stars of heaven and the spirits of hell, in the name of the elements of nature and the silences of night and the sanctuaries of Coptus, in the name of the Nile's risings and Memphis' mysteries and Pharus' rattles[1]: grant a short borrowing of the sun and pour a little light into eyes closed for eternity. We make no resistance, nor do we deny the Earth her property; we beg only for a tiny period of life to furnish the consolation of revenge.'

"The prophet, propitiated by this prayer, placed a certain little herb on the corpse's mouth and another on its chest. Then he turned to the east and silently invoked the rising power of the majestic Sun. With the visual effect of this holy spectacle he roused the audience to eager expectation of a great miracle.

29 "I pushed my way in to join the crowd and, standing on a rather high rock right behind the bier, I watched everything with eyes full of curiosity. Now his chest rose with a swell; now his health-giving

[1] The Egyptian necromancer is decked out like a priest of Isis, wearing no skin or cloth made from animal-hair, and fully shaven. The old man adjures him in Isiac, or at least Egyptianate, phrases. Coptus is in upper Egypt, Memphis is at the head of the Nile delta, and Pharus is an island off Alexandria (site of the renowned lighthouse). The *sistrum* was a rattle used in Isiac rites (see XI 4 for a description).

corpus impleri. Et assurgit cadaver, et profatur adulescens: 'Quid, oro, me post Lethaea pocula iam Stygiis paludibus innatantem ad momentariae vitae reducitis officia? Desine iam, precor, desine, ac me in meam quietem permitte.'

"Haec audita vox de corpore, sed aliquanto propheta commotior 'Quin refers' ait 'populo singula tuaeque mortis illuminas arcana? An non putas devotionibus meis posse Diras invocari, posse tibi membra lassa torqueri?'

"Suscipit ille de lectulo et imo cum gemitu[1] populum sic adorat: 'Malis novae nuptae peremptus artibus et addictus noxio poculo, torum tepentem adultero mancipavi.'

"Tunc uxor egregia capit praesentem audaciam et mente sacrilega coarguenti marito resistens altercat. Populus aestuat, diversa tendentes, hi pessimam feminam viventem statim cum corpore mariti sepeliendam, alii mendacio cadaveris fidem non habendam.

30 "Sed hanc cunctationem sequens adulescentis sermo distinxit. Nam rursus altius ingemescens, 'Dabo,' inquit 'dabo vobis intemeratae veritatis documenta perlucida, et quod prorsus alius nemo cognorit vel ominarit[2] indicabo.' Tunc digito me

[1] F *congestu*; the emendation is far from certain.

[2] Robertson's convincing emendation of F's *cognominarit.*

artery pulsated; now his body was filled with breath; and the corpse rose, and the young man spoke. 'Why,' he asked, 'when after Lethe's draughts I was already swimming in the Stygian pool, why are you bringing me back to the functions of life for but a moment? Stop now, I beg you. Stop and let me go back to my rest.'

"Those were the corpse's words, but the prophet answered rather heatedly. 'No,' he said. 'Tell the people everything and throw some light on the secret of your death. Or do you not believe that I can invoke the Furies with my curses and have your weary body tortured?'

"The corpse replied from his couch and with a deep moan addressed the crowd. 'I was murdered,' he said, 'by the evil arts of my new bride and sacrificed to her poisoned cup, ceding my still warm bed to an adulterer.'

"At this his fine wife showed daring presence of mind and blasphemously began to defend herself by wrangling with her husband as he accused her. The mob seethed, torn in opposite directions. Some said that the horrible woman ought to be buried alive immediately with the body of her husband, others that the lies of a corpse ought not to be trusted.

30 "But their doubt was removed by the young man's next utterance. Once more he groaned deeply. 'I shall give you proofs,' he said, 'clear proofs of inviolate truth. I shall inform you of something which absolutely no one else could know or even

demonstrans: 'Nam cum corporis mei custos hic sagacissimus exsertam mihi teneret vigiliam, cantatrices anus exuviis meis imminentes atque ob id reformatae frustra saepius cum industriam sedulam eius fallere nequivissent, postremum iniecta somni nebula eoque in profundam quietem sepulto, me nomine ciere non prius desierunt quam dum hebetes artus et membra frigida pigris conatibus ad artis magicae nituntur obsequia. Hic utpote vivus quidem, sed tantum[1] sopore mortuus, quod eodem mecum vocabulo nuncupatur, ad suum nomen ignarus exsurgit, et, in exanimis umbrae modum ultroneus gradiens, quamquam foribus cubiculi diligenter occlusis, per quoddam foramen prosectis naso prius ac mox auribus vicariam pro me lanienam suscitavit.[2] Utque fallaciae reliqua convenirent, ceram in modum prosectarum formatam aurium ei applicant examussim nasoque ipsius similem comparant. Et nunc assistit miser hic, praemium non industriae sed debilitationis consecutus.'

"His dictis perterritus temptare Fortunam[3] aggredior. Iniecta manu nasum prehendo: sequitur;

[1] Many editors find this phrase troublesome and try to make it less so by emending *tantum*.

[2] Often emended to *sustinuit*. This common Apuleian word is also regularly emended out of the text in XI 29.

[3] All modern editors change to *formam*.

divine.' Then he pointed his finger at me. 'You see, while this very keen-witted watchman was maintaining his intensive vigil over my body, some old witches tried to get at my remains. They had transmuted themselves for the purpose, but to no avail, since in several attempts they were unable to elude his unremitting attentiveness. Finally they threw a cloud of sleep over him and buried him in deep slumber. Then they began calling my name, and kept it up until my sluggish joints and chilly limbs were struggling with slow effort to obey the commands of their magic art. Since, however, the watchman was alive in fact, but only dead asleep, because he had the same name as mine, he unwittingly arose at the sound of his name and walked mechanically like a lifeless ghost. Although the doors to the chamber had been carefully bolted, there was a hole through which he had first his nose and then his ears sliced off; he brought on himself the butchery intended for me. Then, to put the proper finishing touch on their trick, they shaped some wax into ears like the amputated ones and fastened them on him in a perfect fit, and made him a wax nose like his own. And now the poor wretch is standing here, having earned the reward, not of hard work, but of mutilation.'

"I was terrified at his words and started to test Fortune.[1] I put my hand up and grasped my nose: it

[1] The text is usually emended to give "to test my appearance."

aures pertracto: deruunt. Ac dum directis digitis et detortis nutibus praesentium denotor, dum risus ebullit, inter pedes circumstantium frigido sudore defluens evado. Nec postea debilis ac sic ridiculus Lari me patrio reddere potui, sed capillis hinc inde laterum deiectis aurium vulnera celavi, nasi vero dedecus linteolo isto pressim agglutinato decenter obtexi."

31 Cum primum Thelyphron hanc fabulam posuit, compotores vino madidi rursum cachinnum integrant. Dumque bibere solitarias[1] postulant, sic ad me Byrrhena: "Sollemnis" inquit "dies a primis cunabulis huius urbis conditus crastinus advenit, quo die soli mortalium sanctissimum deum Risum hilaro atque gaudiali ritu propitiamus. Hunc tua praesentia nobis efficies gratiorem. Atque utinam aliquid de proprio lepore laetificum honorando deo comminiscaris, quo magis pleniusque tanto numini litemus."

"Bene," inquam "et fiet ut iubes. Et vellem hercules materiam repperire aliquam quam deus tantus affluenter indueret."

[1] The manuscript reading should be accepted, even if the phrase is difficult. At any rate, the intrusion of the god Risus in the dative (*bibere solita Risui*, a commonly printed emendation) is gratuitous and unidiomatic.

---

[1] No such official cult of Laughter is known from the ancient world, although Carnival-like holidays were common, such as the Roman Saturnalia.

came away; I rubbed my ears: they fell off. The crowd were pointing their fingers at me and twisting their heads round to nod at me, and laughter broke out. Dripping with cold sweat, I escaped through the legs of the surrounding mob. I could never afterwards return to my ancestral home so maimed and so ludicrous, but I have let my hair grow long on both sides to hide the scars of my ears, and I have tightly attached this linen bandage for decency's sake to conceal the shame of my nose."

31 As soon as Thelyphron finished this story, the banqueters, soused in their wine, renewed their uproarious laughter. While they were asking for their individual drinks Byrrhena spoke to me. "Tomorrow there comes a holiday," she said, "founded during this city's infancy. On that day we alone in the world seek to propitiate the most sacred god Laughter with merry and joyful ritual.[1] By your presence you will make this a happier occasion for us. And I hope you will invent something cheerful from your own wit to honour the god with, to help us appease this powerful deity better and more thoroughly."

"Thanks," I said. "I accept your invitation. And by Hercules I wish I could find some material that so mighty a god could wear in flowing folds."[2]

[2] Gods' statues were often dressed on their holidays. The Latin also suggests "some raw material which so mighty a god could turn into an extravaganza."

Post haec monitu famuli mei, qui noctis admonebat, iam et ipse crapula distentus protinus exsurgo et appellata propere Byrrhena titubante vestigio domuitionem capesso.

32 Sed cum primam plateam vadimus,[1] vento repentino lumen quo nitebamur exstinguitur, ut vix improvidae noctis caligine liberati, digitis pedum detunsis ob lapides, hospitium defessi rediremus. Dumque iam iunctim proximamus, ecce tres quidam vegetes[2] et vastulis corporibus fores nostras ex summis viribus irruentes, ac ne praesentia quidem nostra tantillum conterriti, sed magis cum aemulatione virium crebrius insultantes, ut nobis—ac mihi potissimum—non immerito latrones esse et quidem saevissimi viderentur. Statim denique gladium, quem veste mea contectum ad hos usus extuleram, sinu liberatum arripio; nec cunctatus medios latrones involo ac singulis, ut quemque colluctantem offenderam, altissime demergo, quoad tandem ante ipsa vestigia mea vastis et crebris perforati vulneribus spiritus efflaverint.

Sic proeliatus, iam tumultu eo Photide suscitata, patefactis aedibus anhelans et sudore perlutus

[1] Should perhaps be emended to *invadimus.*

[2] An unusual third-declension form, which should perhaps be emended to *vegetis* or *vegetos.*

After that I received a warning signal from my servant reminding me of the time of night. I was bloated with drink myself, and so I immediately got to my feet, bid a hasty farewell to Byrrhena, and set my homeward course with staggering steps.

32 When we reached the first square a sudden wind blew out the light on which we were relying. With difficulty we extricated ourselves from the blackness of improvident Night, and, smashing our toes against stones, we reached our lodgings in a state of exhaustion. As we were approaching arm in arm, we saw three robust fellows with pretty enormous bodies shoving against our doors with all their might. They were not the least bit frightened by our presence, but went on kicking at the doors all the more rapidly in a contest of force. We thought—I most of all—not unreasonably that they were robbers, and very bloodthirsty ones at that. At once I snatched the sword free from the folds of my robe, where I had hidden it for just such a contingency. Unhesitatingly I flew into the midst of the robbers, and as I came at each one in combat I plunged my sword into him to its full depth, until at long last, punctured with multiple gaping wounds, they gasped out their breath at my feet.

The battle was over. Photis had been awakened by the uproar and had opened the door. I crept inside panting and bathed in sweat, and immediately—as befitted a man exhausted in

irrepo, meque statim, utpote pugna trium latronum in vicem Geryoneae caedis fatigatum, lecto simul et somno tradidi.

battle against three thieves in the manner of the slaughter of Geryon[1]—I surrendered simultaneously to bed and sleep.

[1] A three-bodied giant, slain by Hercules in one of his twelve labors.

LIBER III

1 Commodum punicantibus phaleris Aurora roseum quatiens lacertum caelum inequitabat, et me securae quieti revulsum nox diei reddidit. Aestus invadit animum vesperni[1] recordatione facinoris. Complicitis denique pedibus ac palmulis in alternas digitorum vicissitudines super genua conexis, sic grabatum cossim insidens ubertim flebam, iam forum et iudicia, iam sententiam, ipsum denique carnificem imaginabundus. "An mihi quisquam tam mitis tamque benivolus iudex obtinget, qui me trinae caedis cruore perlitum et tot civium sanguine delibutum innocentem pronuntiare poterit? Hanc illam mihi gloriosam peregrinationem fore Chaldaeus Diophanes obstinate praedicabat."

Haec identidem mecum replicans fortunas meas eiulabam. Quati fores interdum et frequenti
2 clamore ianuae nostrae perstrepi. Nec mora cum,

[1] Often emended to the more familiar *vespertini.*

BOOK III

1 No sooner had Aurora begun to ride with crimson caparisons across the sky, shaking her rosy arm,[1] than I was torn from carefree sleep, and night returned me to day. Anguish flooded my mind as I recalled the evening's escapade. I enfolded my feet and joined my hands together with fingers interlocked over my knees, and as I sat squatting on my cot I wept profusely, already picturing to myself the forum and the trial, the sentence, even the executioner himself. "Could I," I thought, "find any juror merciful and kindly enough to be able to pronounce me innocent, besmeared as I am with the gore of a triple slaughter and steeped in the blood of so many citizens? Yes, this is the fame my journey will bring me, as Diophanes the Chaldaean firmly foretold."[2]

I kept repeating these thoughts to myself and bewailing my misfortunes. Meanwhile the doors had begun to shake, and a mass of people were
2 shouting and knocking at the gate. Suddenly the

[1] Aurora is the dawn. This is one of several parodies of the epic daybreaks of Homer and Vergil.

[2] Related in II 12.

magna irruptione patefactis aedibus, magistratibus eorumque ministris et turbae miscellaneae frequentia[1] cuncta completa, statimque lictores duo de iussu magistratuum immissa manu trahere me sane non retinentem occipiunt. Ac dum primum angiportum insistimus, statim civitas omnis in publicum effusa mira densitate nos insequitur. Et quamquam capite in terram, immo ad ipsos inferos, iam deiecto maestus incederem, obliquato tamen aspectu rem admirationis maximae conspicio. Nam inter tot milia populi circumsedentis[2] nemo prorsum qui non risu dirumperetur aderat. Tandem perratis plateis omnibus, et in modum eorum quibus lustralibus piamentis minas portentorum hostiis circumforaneis expiant circumductus angulatim, forum eiusque tribunal astituor.

Iamque sublimo suggestu magistratibus residentibus, iam praecone publico silentium clamante, repente cuncti consona voce flagitant, propter coetus multitudinem, quae pressurae nimia densitate periclitaretur, iudicium tantum theatro redderetur. Nec mora cum passim populus procurrens caveae consaeptum mira celeritate complevit. Aditus etiam et tectum omne fartim stipaverant. Plerique

[1] *frequentia* not in F.

[2] Those who question the appropriateness of the verb may choose among a dozen conjectures, e.g. *circumfluentis*, *circumfrementis*, *circumferentis*.

house was forced open and a great crowd burst in. The whole place was filled with officials and their assistants and a miscellaneous swarm of folk; instantly on the officials' orders two lictors arrested me and began to drag me away, while I offered absolutely no resistance. The moment we set foot in the alleyway, the whole city poured out on to the streets and began to follow us in an incredible throng. Although I was walking along gloomily with my head bent towards the ground—or rather towards Hell itself—out of the corner of my eye I caught sight of something extremely bewildering: among all the thousands of people sitting around there was not a single one who was not bursting with laughter. Finally, after we had wandered through every street and I had been led around into every corner—like those purificatory processions when they carry sacrificial animals all round the town to expiate threatening portents—I was brought into the forum and stationed in front of the tribunal.

The magistrates had already taken their seats on the lofty dais and the town crier was calling for silence, when suddenly everybody with one voice demanded, because of the size of the gathering and the resultant danger of being crushed from overcrowding, that such an important trial be held in the theatre. Instantly people running from every direction filled up the entire enclosure of the auditorium with amazing speed. They even crammed and stuffed the entrances and filled the roof. Several

columnis implexi, alii statuis dependuli, nonnulli per fenestras et lacunaria semiconspicui, miro tamen omnes studio visendi pericula salutis[1] neglegebant. Tunc me per proscaenium medium velut quandam victimam publica ministeria producunt et orchestrae mediae sistunt.

3 Sic rursum praeconis amplo boatu citatus, accusator quidam senior exsurgit et, ad dicendi spatium vasculo quodam in vicem coli graciliter fistulato ac per hoc guttatim defluo infusa aqua, populum sic adorat:

"Neque parva res ac praecipue pacem civitatis cunctae respiciens et exemplo serio profutura tractatur, Quirites sanctissimi. Quare magis congruit sedulo singulos atque universos vos pro dignitate publica providere ne nefarius homicida tot caedium[2] lanienam, quam cruenter exercuit, impune commiserit. Nec me putetis privatis simultatibus instinctum odio proprio saevire. Sum namque nocturnae custodiae praefectus, nec in hodiernum credo quemquam pervigilem diligentiam meam culpare posse.

"Rem denique ipsam et quae nocte gesta sunt cum fide perferam.[3] Nam cum fere iam tertia vigilia

[1] F *salutaris*. [2] F *tota aedium*.
[3] Usually emended to *proferam*.

---

[1] A water-clock (clepsydra) was regularly used in Greek and Roman court proceedings.
[2] See note at I 1.

wrapped themselves round the columns, others hung from the statues, and some were half-visible through the windows and under the cornices: all of them, in their amazing zeal to watch, were disregarding the danger to their own safety. Then public officers led me like a sacrificial victim along the middle of the stage and stood me in the centre of the orchestra.

3 Next there was a loud shout of summons from the crier, and an elderly man stood up as speaker for the prosecution. In order to time his speech, water was poured into a small jar which had been finely pierced like a colander to let the water flow out drop by drop.[1] Here is his address to the people:

"The case before us is no small matter, but one which mightily affects the peace of the entire city and which will serve as an important precedent, my god-fearing fellow citizens.[2] Therefore it all the more behoves you, one and all, on behalf of the city's reputation, to see to it that this wicked killer does not go unpunished for his bloodily perpetrated butchery of multiple murders. And do not think that I have been stimulated by private grievances to rage in personal animosity, for I am commander of the night-watch, and up to this very day I am confident that no one can fault my constantly wakeful vigilance.

"I shall now, therefore, faithfully and fully report the facts about what happened last night. About

scrupulosa diligentia cunctae civitatis ostiatim singula considerans circumirem, conspicio istum crudelissimum iuvenem mucrone destricto passim caedibus operantem, iamque tres numero saevitia eius interemptos ante pedes ipsius spirantes adhuc, corporibus in multo sanguine palpitantibus.[1] Et ipse quidem conscientia tanti facinoris merito permotus statim profugit et in domum quandam praesidio tenebrarum elapsus perpetem noctem delituit. Sed providentia deum, quae nihil impunitum nocentibus permittit, priusquam iste clandestinis itineribus elaberetur, mane praestolatus ad gravissimum iudicii vestri sacramentum eum curavi perducere. Habetis itaque reum tot caedibus impiatum, reum coram deprensum, reum peregrinum. Constanter itaque in hominem alienum ferte sententias de eo crimine quod etiam in vestrum civem severiter vindicaretis."

4 Sic profatus accusator acerrimus immanem vocem repressit. Ac me statim praeco, siquid ad ea respondere vellem, iubebat incipere. At ego nihil tunc temporis amplius quam flere poteram, non tam hercules truculentam accusationem intuens quam meam miseram conscientiam. Sed tamen oborta divinitus audacia sic ad illa:

[1] F *palpitantes*, but perhaps *spirantes* should be changed to *spirantibus* instead.

midnight, as I was making my rounds, examining everything door by door throughout the entire town with minute care, I caught sight of this excessively cruel young man here with his sword drawn, wreaking wide-spread slaughter. Then I saw one, two, three men already murdered by his savagery, lying at his feet still breathing, their bodies quivering in pools of blood. But he himself, rightly disturbed by awareness of the enormity of his crime, quickly fled and slipped under cover of darkness into some house, where he lay hidden all night. But by the Providence of the gods, which never allows the guilty to go unpunished, before he could slip away by some secret route I was ready early in the morning, and I saw to it that he was brought before the awesome jurisdiction of your court. So you have before you a defendant defiled by manifold murders, a defendant caught in the act, a defendant who is a stranger. Be firm and pass sentence on a foreigner for a crime which you would severely punish even in the case of one of your fellow-citizens."

With these words my relentless accuser halted his dreadful speech. The crier immediately ordered me to begin whatever defence I might wish to make against these charges; but at that point I could do no more than weep—less, by Hercules, in view of that ferocious speech for the prosecution than in consideration of my own wretched conscience. Nonetheless heaven sent me the boldness to make the following defence:

"Nec ipse ignoro quam sit arduum, trinis civium corporibus expositis, eum qui caedis arguatur, quamvis vera dicat et de facto confiteatur ultro, tamen tantae multitudini quod sit innocens persuadere. Sed si paulisper audientiam publicam[1] mihi tribuerit humanitas, facile vos edocebo me discrimen capitis non meo merito, sed rationabilis indignationis eventu fortuito tantam criminis invidiam frustra sustinere.

5 "Nam cum a cena me serius aliquanto reciperem, potulentus alioquin, quod plane verum crimen meum non diffitebor, ante ipsas fores hospitii—ad bonum autem Milonem civem vestrum deverto—video quosdam saevissimos latrones aditum temptantes et domus ianuas cardinibus obtortis evellere gestientes, claustrisque omnibus, quae accuratissime affixa fuerant, violenter evulsis, secum iam de inhabitantium exitio deliberantes. Unus denique et manu promptior et corpore vastior his affatibus et ceteros incitabat:

"'Heus pueri, quam maribus animis et viribus alacribus dormientes aggrediamur. Omnis cunctatio, ignavia omnis facessat e pectore. Stricto mucrone per totam domum caedes ambulet. Qui

[1] Often emended to *publica*.

"I am not unaware how difficult it is, in the full display of the corpses of three citizens, for him who is accused of their murder, even though he speak the truth and voluntarily admit to the facts themselves, to persuade so large an audience that he is innocent. But if your kindness will briefly grant me a public hearing, I shall easily convince you that I am not on trial for my life through any fault of my own, but rather, I am groundlessly suffering the great odium of the accusation as an accidental outcome of reasonable indignation.

5 "You see, I was returning home rather late from supper in a drunken condition. That part of the accusation against me is quite true and I will not deny it. Right in front of my host's house—I am staying with your good fellow-citizen Milo—I saw some extremely fierce robbers trying to force an entrance and attempting to wrench off the hinges and rip the doors from the house. All the bolts, which had been very carefully fastened in place, had been violently torn loose and the men were now plotting among themselves to destroy the people inside. One of them, readier for action and more enormous in bulk than the others, was arousing the rest with the following speech.

"'Hey, boys!' he exclaimed. 'Let us use all our masculine courage and vigorous strength to attack them while they are sleeping. All hesitation, all cowardice be gone from your hearts. Let Murder draw her sword and stalk through the whole house.

sopitus iacebit trucidetur; qui repugnare temptaverit feriatur. Sic salvi recedemus, si salvum in domo neminem reliquerimus.'

"Fateor, Quirites, extremos latrones—boni civis officium arbitratus, simul et eximie metuens et hospitibus meis et mihi—gladiolo, qui me propter huius modi pericula comitabatur, armatus fugare atque proterrere eos aggressus sum. At illi barbari prorsus et immanes homines neque fugam capessunt et, cum me viderent in ferro, tamen audaciter resistunt.

6 "Dirigitur proeliaris acies. Ipse denique dux et signifer ceterorum validis me viribus aggressus ilico manibus ambabus capillo arreptum ac retro reflexum effligere lapide gestit. Quem dum sibi porrigi flagitat, certa manu percussum feliciter prosterno. Ac mox alium pedibus meis mordicus inhaerentem per scapulas ictu temperato tertiumque improvide occurrentem pectore offenso peremo.

"Sic pace vindicata domoque hospitum ac salute communi protecta, non tam impunem me, verum etiam laudabilem publice credebam fore, qui ne tantillo quidem umquam crimine postulatus, sed probe spectatus apud meos semper innocentiam commodis

Slaughter anyone who lies asleep and strike down anyone who tries to resist. We will get out alive only if we leave no one alive in the house.'

"I confess, worthy citizens, that I approached those desperate robbers—considering it the duty of a good citizen and also being extremely afraid for my hosts and myself—armed as I was with the little sword which accompanies me for dangers of this sort, and I tried to put them to flight and frighten them away. But they were absolute barbarians and gigantic fellows: they did not take to their heels, and even though they saw me with a weapon they boldly stood their ground.

6 "The battle-lines were drawn. Their general and standard-bearer attacked me himself on the spot with might and main, snatched me by the hair with both hands, bent me backwards, and was preparing to slay me with a stone. While he was shouting for someone to hand him the stone, I struck him with unerring hand and luckily laid him low. The second had fastened his teeth into my legs, but I felled him with a nice blow between the shoulder-blades, while the third ran carelessly toward me and I killed him with a stroke straight through the chest.

"Having thus restored peace and protected my hosts' home and the public safety, I trusted that I would be not only guiltless but even praiseworthy in the public eye. I had never before been summoned to court on even the tiniest charge, but had always been highly respected among my own people,

cunctis antetuleram. Nec possum reperire cur iustae ultionis, qua contra latrones deterrimos commotus sum, nunc istum reatum sustineam, cum nemo possit monstrare vel proprias inter nos inimicitias praecessisse ac ne omnino mihi notos illos latrones usquam fuisse. Vel certe ulla praeda monstretur, cuius cupidine tantum flagitium credatur admissum."

7 Haec profatus, rursum lacrimis obortis porrectisque in preces manibus per publicam misericordiam, per pignorum caritatem maestus tunc hos tunc illos deprecabar. Cumque iam humanitate commotos, misericordia fletuum affectos omnes satis crederem, Solis et Iustitiae testatus oculum[1] casumque praesentem meum commendans deum providentiae, paulo altius aspectu relato conspicio prorsus totum populum—risu cachinnabili diffluebant[2]—nec secus illum bonum hospitem parentemque meum Milonem risu maximo dissolutum. At tunc sic tacitus mecum "En fides," inquam "en conscientia! Ego quidem pro hospitis salute et homicida sum et reus capitis inducor; at ille non contentus quod mihi nec assistendi solacium perhibuit, insuper exitium meum cachinnat."

8 Inter haec quaedam mulier per medium theatrum lacrimosa et flebilis, atra veste contecta,

[1] *oculos* is preferred by many editors.

[2] To avoid this parenthetical break in syntax, one should perhaps follow an early emendation and read *diffluentem*.

placing my own innocence above every advantage. Furthermore, since my motive was just vengeance against the lowest sort of thugs, I can find no reason why I should now have to undergo this trial, since no one can demonstrate that there was any preexisting enmity between us, nor indeed that those robbers were even known to me at all. At least let them prove some profit, which might make a credible motive for committing so monstrous a crime."

7 When I had finished this speech my tears welled up again and I stretched out my hands in supplication, sorrowfully begging now one group in the name of public mercy and now another for the love of their own dear children. When I felt sure that they had all been sufficiently stirred with human sympathy and moved by the pathos of my weeping, I called on the eye of the Sun and of Justice as witness and commended my present misfortune to the Providence of the gods. Then I raised my eyes a little and caught sight of the audience: absolutely the entire populace was dissolved in raucous laughter, and even my kind host and uncle, Milo, was broken up by a huge fit of laughing. At that point I said to myself, "This is loyalty and responsibility for you! To save my host's life I have become a killer and am being tried for a capital offence, while he, not satisfied with refusing me the comfort of being my advocate, is even laughing at my downfall."

8 In the midst of all this a woman came running down through the theatre, crying and weeping. She

parvulum quendam sinu tolerans decurrit, ac pone eam anus alia pannis horridis obsita paribusque maesta fletibus, ramos oleagineos utraeque quatientes. Quae circumfusae lectulum quo peremptorum cadavera contecta fuerant, plangore sublato se lugubriter eiulantes, "Per publicam misericordiam, per commune ius humanitatis," aiunt "miseremini indigne caesorum iuvenum, nostraeque viduitati ac solitudini de vindicta solacium date. Certe parvuli huius in primis annis destituti fortunis succurrite, et de latronis huius sanguine legibus vestris et disciplinae publicae litate."

Post haec magistratus qui natu maior assurgit, et ad populum talia: "De scelere quidem, quod serio vindicandum est, nec ipse qui commisit potest diffiteri. Sed una tantum subsiciva sollicitudo nobis relicta est, ut ceteros socios tanti facinoris requiramus. Nec enim veri simile est hominem solitarium tres tam validos evitasse iuvenes. Prohinc tormentis veritas eruenda. Nam et qui comitabatur eum puer clanculo profugit, et res ad hoc deducta est ut per quaestionem sceleris sui participes indicet, ut tam dirae factionis funditus formido perematur."

9 Nec mora cum ritu Graeciensi ignis et rota, cum[1]

[1] Usually emended to *tum*.

was draped in a black robe and carried a little child at her bosom. Behind her was another woman, an old lady covered with tattered rags and weeping just as mournfully. Both were waving olive branches. They draped themselves around the bier on which lay the covered corpses of the victims, and raised a loud lamentation, mournfully bewailing their lot. "In the name of public mercy," they cried, "in the name of the common rights of humanity, have pity on these unjustly slaughtered youths and grant us the solace of vengeance in our widowhood and bereavement. At least succour the fortunes of this poor little child, orphaned in his earliest years, and make atonement to your laws and public order with that cut-throat's blood."

After this the elder of the two magistrates arose and addressed the following remarks to the people: "As for the crime itself, which must be severely punished, not even its perpetrator can make any denial. But just one residual problem is left for us, to search out his confederates in this daring crime: for it is not likely that one man by himself took the lives of three such strong youngsters. The truth, therefore, must now be extracted by torture. The slave who was accompanying him has secretly escaped, and matters have reached the point where the accused must be interrogated in order to expose his confederates in this crime, so that the dread of so dire a gang may be utterly extinguished."

9 Instantly they brought in fire and the wheel, in

omne flagrorum[1] genus inferuntur. Augetur oppido, immo duplicatur, mihi maestitia, quod integro saltim mori non licuerit. Sed anus illa quae fletibus cuncta turbaverat "Prius," inquit "optimi cives, quam latronem istum miserorum pignorum meorum peremptorem cruci affigatis, permittite corpora necatorum revelari, ut et formae simul et aetatis contemplatione magis magisque ad iustam indignationem arrecti pro modo facinoris saeviatis."

His dictis applauditur, et ilico me magistratus ipsum iubet corpora, quae lectulo fuerant posita, mea manu detegere. Luctantem me ac diu renuentem praecedens facinus instaurare nova ostensione, lictores iussu magistratuum quam instantissime compellunt. Manum denique ipsam e regione lateris tundentes[2] in exitium suum super ipsa cadavera porrigunt. Evictus tandem necessitate succumbo et, ingratis licet, abrepto pallio retexi corpora.

Dii boni, quae facies rei! Quod monstrum! Quae fortunarum mearum repentina mutatio! Quamquam enim iam in peculio Proserpinae et Orci familia numeratus, subito in contrariam faciem obstupe-

[1] The manuscripts' *flagitiorum*—or *flagitiosum*—might possibly be defensible, in the sense "all sorts of shameful devices."

[2] Usually emended to *trudentes* "pushing".

---

[1] Daughter of Ceres, who was abducted by Pluto and became queen of the Underworld.

[2] Popular name for the personified figure of death.

accordance with Greek style, and all sorts of whips. My gloom was greatly increased, nay doubled, by the fact that I would not even be allowed to die in one piece. But the old woman who had thrown everything into a turmoil with her tears spoke up. "First, noble citizens," she said, "before you fasten that thieving murderer of my poor little darlings to the cross, permit the victims' bodies to be uncovered, so that by contemplating both their beauty and their youth you may be aroused to a higher and higher pitch of just indignation and match your cruelty to the crime."

Her words met with applause, and the magistrate immediately ordered me to uncover with my own hands the bodies laid out on the bier. For a long time I resisted and refused to reinforce my earlier deed with this new exhibition. But the lictors, under orders from the magistrates, were most insistent in forcing me. They finally knocked my hand away from my side and stretched it out over the corpses toward its own destruction. At last, overpowered by necessity, I succumbed and, albeit unwillingly, snatched away the pall and exposed the bodies.

Good gods, what a sight! What an apparition! What a swift transformation of my fortunes! Although I had already been inventoried among the property of Proserpina[1] and the household of Orcus,[2] suddenly appearance reversed itself, and I

factus haesi. Nec possum novae illius imaginis rationem idoneis verbis expedire. Nam cadavera illa iugulatorum hominum erant tres utres inflati variisque secti foraminibus et, ut vespertinum proelium meum recordabar, his locis hiantes quibus latrones illos vulneraveram.

10 Tunc ille quorundam astu paulisper cohibitus risus libere iam exarsit in plebem. Hi gaudii nimietate gratulari,[1] illi dolorem ventris manuum compressione sedare. Et certe laetitia delibuti meque respectantes cuncti theatro facessunt. At ego, ut primum illam laciniam prenderam, fixus in lapidem[2] steti gelidus nihil secus quam una de ceteris theatri statuis vel columnis. Nec prius ab inferis emersi quam Milon hospes accessit, et iniecta manu me renitentem[3] lacrimisque rursum promicantibus crebra singultientem clementi violentia secum attraxit. Et observatis viae solitudinibus per quosdam anfractus domum suam perduxit, maestumque me atque etiam tunc trepidum variis solatur affatibus. Nec tamen indignationem iniuriae, quae inhaeserat altius meo pectori, ullo modo permulcere quivit.

11 Ecce ilico etiam ipsi magistratus cum suis insignibus domum nostram ingressi talibus me monitis

[1] Recent editors have all adopted Armini's simple and attractive emendation *graculari* "to cackle". But the word is otherwise unattested and emendation is not necessary.

[2] F *lapide*.

[3] F *retinentem*.

stood there dumbfounded. I cannot find the right words to give a rational account of that new vision. The corpses of those murdered men, you see, were three inflated wine-skins slit with various gashes, and, as I recalled my battle of the previous night, the holes were in those places where I had wounded the robbers.

10 Then the laughter, which some people had guilefully repressed for a time, now broke out unrestrainedly among the entire mob. Some were rejoicing with excessive mirth, while others were pressing their stomachs with their hands to ease the pain. At any event they were all drenched in happiness, and they kept turning round to look at me as they made their way out of the theatre. As for me, from the moment I had pulled back that cloth I stood stock still, frozen into stone just like one of the other statues or columns in the theatre. And I did not rise from the dead until my host Milo came up to me and took hold of me. I resisted; my tears were spurting out again and I was sobbing repeatedly, but he used gentle force to draw me along with him and led me to his home by a circuitous route, taking care to avoid people in the streets. I was downhearted and even then still shaking with fear. He tried to console me with various remarks, but found no way to soothe the indignation I felt at the wrong I had suffered, which had entered so deeply into my heart.

11 Suddenly, clad in all the insignia of their office, the magistrates themselves entered our house and

delenire gestiunt: "Neque tuae dignitatis vel etiam prosapiae tuorum ignari sumus, Luci domine. Nam et provinciam totam inclutae vestrae familiae nobilitas complectitur. Ac ne istud quod vehementer ingemescis contumeliae causa perpessus es. Omnem itaque de tuo pectore praesentem tristitudinem mitte et angorem animi depelle. Nam lusus iste, quem publice gratissimo deo Risui per annua reverticula sollemniter celebramus, semper commenti novitate florescit. Iste deus auctorem et actorem[1] suum propitius ubique comitabitur amanter, nec umquam patietur ut ex animo doleas, sed frontem tuam serena venustate laetabit assidue. At tibi civitas omnis pro ista gratia honores egregios obtulit; nam et patronum scripsit et ut in aere staret[2] imago tua decrevit."

Ad haec dicta sermonis vicem refero. "Tibi quidem," inquam "splendidissima et unica Thessaliae civitas, honorum talium parem gratiam memini, verum statuas et imagines dignioribus meique[3] maioribus reservare suadeo."

12 Sic pudenter allocutus et paulisper hilaro vultu renidens, quantumque poteram laetiorem me

[1] A very likely correction for F's *auctorem et torem.*

[2] Or *in aere stet.* F's original reading is uncertain.

[3] F *meisque.*

tried to calm me with the following observations: "We are not unaware, master Lucius, of either your high position or your family's origins. Indeed the high repute of your famous family embraces the entire province. And that experience you suffered, which you are so vehemently bemoaning, was not meant as an insult. So rid your heart completely of your present melancholy and shed your mental anguish. You see, the public holiday which we regularly celebrate after the passage of a year in honour of Laughter, the most pleasing of gods, always blossoms with some novel invention. That god will propitiously and lovingly accompany the man who has been both his producer and his performer, wherever he may go. He will never let your mind feel grief, but will constantly make your face smile in cloudless loveliness. And the city has unanimously offered you special honours in gratitude for what you have done. It has inscribed you as its patron and decreed that your likeness be preserved in bronze."

In response I made a speech in my turn: "Yours is the most brilliant city in Thessaly; it is unparallelled. I thank you greatly for these great honours. But I urge you to reserve statues and portraits for worthier and greater men than I."[1]

12 After this modest address I put on a cheerful look and smiled for a bit, pretending as best I could to be

[1] Apuleius tells us in the *Florida* (XVI) that several cities had honoured him with statues.

refingens, comiter abeuntes magistratus appello.

Et ecce quidam intro currens famulus "Rogat te" ait "tua parens Byrrhena, et convivii cui te sero desponderas iam appropinquantis admonet."

Ad haec ego, formidans et procul perhorrescens etiam ipsam domum eius, "Quam vellem," inquam "parens, iussis tuis obsequium commodare, si per fidem liceret id facere. Hospes enim meus Milon per hodierni diei praesentissimum numen adiurans effecit ut eius hodiernae cenae pignerarer, nec ipse discedit nec me digredi patitur. Prohinc epulare vadimonium differamus."

Haec adhuc me loquente, manu firmiter iniecta Milon, iussis balnearibus assequi, producit ad lavacrum proximum. At ego vitans oculos omnium, et quem ipse fabricaveram risum obviorum declinans, lateri eius adambulabam obtectus. Nec qui laverim, qui terserim, qui domum rursum reverterim, prae rubore memini: sic omnium oculis nutibus ac denique manibus denotatus impos animi stupebam.

13 Raptim denique paupertina Milonis cenula perfunctus, causatusque capitis acrem dolorem quem mihi lacrimarum assiduitas incusserat, cubitum venia facile tributa concedo. Et abiectus in lectulo

happier; and I bade the magistrates a courteous farewell as they left.

Just then a servant came running in. "Your aunt Byrrhena," he said, "invites your presence, and reminds you that the party you promised last night to attend will soon be starting."

I was frightened and terrified even at a distance by the mere thought of her house. "How I wish, dear aunt," I answered, "that I could arrange to comply with your bidding, if I could honourably do so. But my host Milo, swearing in the name of today's most manifest deity, made me pledge myself to his table today. He will neither leave me nor permit me to depart. Let us therefore grant a postponement for my appearance at a banquet."

While I was still talking, Milo firmly took hold of me and, ordering someone to follow with bathing paraphernalia, led the way to the baths nearby. To avoid everyone's stares and escape the laughter of the people we passed—laughter which I myself had manufactured—I walked close to his side, trying to conceal myself. Because of my embarrassment I have no recollection of how I washed, how I dried, how I returned home again. I was out of my mind, stunned from the branding of everyone's stares and nods and pointed fingers.

13 Ravenously I consumed Milo's poor little supper, and when I alleged a sharp headache induced by my constant weeping, I was readily excused and retired to bed. I threw myself down on my cot and lay there

meo, quae gesta fuerant singula maestus recordabar, quoad tandem Photis mea, dominae suae cubitu procurato, sui longe dissimilis advenit. Non enim[1] laeta facie nec sermone dicaculo, sed vultuosam frontem rugis insurgentibus asseverabat.

Cunctanter ac timide denique sermone prolato, "Ego" inquit "ipsa, confiteor ultro, ego origo[2] tibi huius molestiae fui." Et cum dicto lorum quempiam sinu suo depromit mihique porrigens, "Cape," inquit "oro te, et de[3] perfida muliere vindictam, immo vero licet maius quodvis supplicium sume. Nec tamen me putes, oro, sponte angorem istum tibi concinnasse. Dii mihi melius quam ut mei causa vel tantillum scrupulum patiare. Ac siquid adversi tuum caput respicit, id omne protinus meo luatur sanguine. Sed quod alterius rei causa facere iussa sum, mala quadam mea sorte in tuam recidit iniuriam."

14 Tunc ego familiaris curiositatis admonitus factique causam delitiscentem nudari gestiens suscipio: "Omnium quidem nequissimus audacissimusque lorus iste, quem tibi verberandae destinasti, prius a me concisus atque laceratus interibit ipse quam tuam plumeam lacteamque contingat cutem. Sed mihi cum fide memora: quod tuum factum

[1] A probable correction for F's *nonens.*

[2] The addition of *origo* here is a paleographically attractive way of curing F's *ego tibi huius molestiae fui.* Some editors insert *causa.*

[3] F has no preposition.

gloomily retracing all that had happened to me, until at last my darling Photis came in, having taken care of putting her mistress to bed. She was very different from her usual self: no cheerful expression or witty talk, but there were wrinkles rising on her forehead and she looked serious and sombre.

Finally she began to speak, hesitantly and fearfully. "I was the one," she said, "I willingly confess it. I was the source of your trouble." With this she pulled out a leather strap from inside her clothes and handed it to me. "Here," she said, "I beg you, take vengeance on the traitress. Or inflict some worse punishment instead, whatever you wish. But please, you must not believe that I intentionally devised that torment for you. God forbid you should suffer even the tiniest difficulty because of me. And if any harm threatens you, may it all quickly be expiated with my blood. But it was something I was ordered to do for a different purpose, and through some bad luck of mine it rebounded against you and hurt you."

4 Now, urged on by my usual curiosity, I was eager for the hidden cause of that event to be laid bare. "That is the wickedest and most audacious strap in the world," I said to her, "which you intended for your own lashing, but it will sooner perish, cut up and slashed by me, than touch your downy milk-white skin. But tell me truly. What was that deed of yours which subsequent bad luck converted to my

scaevitas[1] consecuta in meum convertit exitium? Adiuro enim tuum mihi carissimum caput nulli me prorsus ac ne tibi quidem ipsi asseveranti posse credere quod tu quicquam in meam cogitaveris perniciem. Porro meditatus innoxios casus incertus vel etiam adversus culpae non potest addicere."

Cum isto fine sermonis oculos Photidis meae, udos ac tremulos et prona libidine marcidos iamiamque semiadopertulos, adnixis et sorbillantibus saviis sitienter hauriebam.

Sic illa laetitia recreata "Patere," inquit "oro, prius fores cubiculi diligenter occludam, ne sermonis elapsi profana petulantia committam grande flagitium." Et cum dicto pessulis iniectis et uncino firmiter immisso, sic ad me reversa colloque meo manibus ambabus implexa, voce tenui et admodum minuta "Paveo" inquit "et formido solide domus huius operta detegere et arcana dominae meae revelare secreta. Sed melius de te doctrinaque tua praesumo, qui praeter generosam natalium dignitatem, praeter sublime ingenium, sacris pluribus initiatus profecto nosti sanctam silentii fidem. Quaecumque itaque commisero huius religiosi pectoris tui penetralibus, semper haec intra consaeptum clausa custodias, oro, et simplicitatem relationis meae tenacitate taciturnitatis tuae remunerare. Nam me, quae sola mortalium novi, amor is quo tibi

[1] Most editors unnecessarily add *Fortunae* or something similar before *scaevitas*.

destruction? For I swear on your head, the dearest thing I know, that no one could make me believe—even if you yourself asserted it—that you ever planned to destroy me. Furthermore, a chance or even adverse issue cannot make a crime of innocent intentions."

At the end of this speech my Photis' eyes were moist and trembling, languid with ready passion, and now prettily half-closed, and I tasted them thirstily with pressing, sipping kisses.

15 Her cheerfulness revived. "Please," she said, "first let me carefully lock the doors to the room, lest with the wanton profanity of an indiscreet tongue I perpetrate a monstrous crime." She immediately shoved in the bolts and firmly inserted the hook. Then she came back to me, folded both arms around my neck, and spoke in a soft and very tiny voice. "I am afraid," she said. "I am terribly frightened to uncover the secrets of this house and unveil my mistress's hidden mysteries. But I assume better things from you and your learning. Besides the inherited nobility of your birth, besides your lofty character, you have been initiated into many cults and you certainly understand the sacred trust of silence. Whatever knowledge, then, I shall entrust to the inner temple of your god-fearing heart, keep always locked within that precinct, I beg you, and repay my ingenuous disclosure with your stubborn silence. There are things which I alone know, and the love which binds me to you compels me to reveal

teneor indicare compellit. Iam scies omnem domus nostrae statum, iam scies erae meae miranda secreta, quibus obaudiunt manes, turbantur sidera, coguntur numina, serviunt elementa. Nec umquam magis artis huius violentia nititur quam cum scitulae formulae iuvenem quempiam libenter aspexit, quod quidem ei solet crebriter evenire.

16 "Nunc etiam adulescentem quendam Boeotium summe decorum efflictim deperit totasque artis manus, machinas omnes ardenter exercet. Audivi vesperi—meis his, inquam, auribus audivi—quod non celerius Sol caelo ruisset noctique ad exercendas illecebras magiae maturius cessisset, ipsi Soli nubilam caliginem et perpetuas tenebras comminantem. Hunc iuvenem, cum e balneis rediret ipsa, tonstrinae residentem hesterna die forte conspexit, ac me capillos eius, qui iam caede cultrorum desecti humi iacebant,[1] clanculo praecipit auferre. Quos me sedulo furtimque colligentem tonsor invenit et, quod alioquin publicitus maleficae disciplinae perinfames sumus, arreptam inclementer increpat: 'Tune, ultima, non cessas subinde lectorum iuvenum capillamenta surripere? Quod scelus nisi tandem desines, magistratibus te con-

[1] F *humidi iacebant.* The correct reading may well be *humi diiacebant*, depite the fact that the compound verb is otherwise unattested.

them. Now you will learn everything about our house. Now you will learn about my mistress's amazing secret powers, by which ghosts are made obedient, stars are thrown into turmoil, deities are coerced, and the elements enslaved. And never does she depend more upon the force of this art than when she has looked lustfully at some young man with a pretty figure—which indeed happens to her frequently.

16 "At present she is desperately in love with an extremely handsome Boeotian boy and is passionately employing all the resources of her art and all its devices. I heard her this evening—with my very own ears, I say, I heard her: because the Sun had not rushed down more quickly from heaven and yielded earlier to night, so that she could exercise her magic charms, she was threatening the Sun himself with cloudy darkness and perpetual gloom. When she was coming back from the baths yesterday, she happened to catch sight of her young man sitting at a barber's shop, and so she ordered me to pilfer some of his hair, which had been snipped off by the shears and was lying on the ground. I was gathering some with furtive care when the barber spotted me. We have a very bad reputation in town anyway for practising the black arts, and so he grabbed me and shouted mercilessly at me.

"'You good-for-nothing!' he screamed. 'Will you never stop this constant stealing of young gentlemen's hair! If you do not finally cease this

stanter obiciam.' Et verbum facto secutus, immissa manu scrutatus e mediis papillis meis iam capillos absconditos iratus abripit. Quo gesto graviter affecta mecumque reputans dominae meae mores, quod huius modi repulsa satis acriter commoveri meque verberare saevissime consuevit, iam de fuga consilium tenebam, sed istud quidem tui contemplatione abieci statim.

17 "Verum cum tristis inde discederem, ne prorsus vacuis manibus redirem, conspicor[1] quendam forficulis attondentem caprinos utres. Quos cum probe constrictos inflatosque et iam pendentes cernerem, capillos eorum humi iacentes, flavos ac per hoc illi Boeotio iuveni consimiles, plusculos aufero eosque dominae meae dissimulata veritate trado. Sic noctis initio, priusquam cena te reciperes, Pamphile mea iam vecors animi tectum scandulare conscendit, quod altrinsecus aedium patore perflabili nudatum, ad omnes orientales ceterosque aspectus[2] pervium, maxime his artibus suis commodatum secreto colit. Priusque apparatu solito instruit

[1] Or *conspicio*, for F's *conspico*.

[2] This prepositional phrase has been regularly, and variously, emended by transposing or adding words.

criminal behaviour I will hand you over to the magistrates at once.'[1] He followed words with action, thrust his hand down into my bosom, searched around, and angrily pulled out the strands of hair which I had already hidden there. This incident upset me terribly. Considering my mistress's temper, how she reacts quite violently to this sort of failure and beats me with the utmost savagery, I was planning to run away. But I thought of you and rejected that idea immediately.

17 "But as I was walking dejectedly away, afraid to come home completely empty-handed, I noticed someone trimming goatskin bags with scissors. I observed that they were nicely tied and inflated and already hung up, and their hair was lying on the ground. It was blonde, and therefore very much like the young Boeotian's; and so I picked up a handful and brought it to my mistress, concealing the truth. Then at nightfall, before you had returned from dinner, my mistress Pamphile, who was by now quite out of her mind, climbed up on to the shingled roof. There is a place on the other side of the house, exposed to every breeze that blows and providing an open view toward all eastern and other directions, which she secretly employs as the fittest workshop for those arts of hers. First she arranged her deadly laboratory with its customary apparatus, setting

[1] The practice of magic was a criminal offence in Roman law.

feralem officinam, omne genus aromatis et ignorabiliter laminis litteratis et infelicium avium[1] durantibus damnis, defletorum sepultorum etiam cadaverum expositis multis admodum membris: hic nares et digiti, illic carnosi clavi pendentium, alibi trucidatorum servatus cruor et extorta dentibus ferarum trunca calvaria.

18 "Tunc decantatis spirantibus fibris litat vario latice, nunc rore fontano, nunc lacte vaccino, nunc melle montano; litat et mulsa. Sic illos capillos in mutuos nexus obditos atque nodatos cum multis odoribus dat vivis carbonibus adolendos. Tunc protinus inexpugnabili magicae disciplinae potestate et caeca numinum coactorum violentia illa corpora, quorum fumabant stridentes capilli, spiritum mutuantur humanum et sentiunt et audiunt et ambulant, et qua nidor suarum ducebat exuviarum veniunt, et pro illo iuvene Boeotio aditum gestientes fores insiliunt; cum ecce crapula madens et improvidae Noctis deceptus caligine audacter mucrone destricto in insani modum Aiacis armatus, non ut ille vivis pecoribus infestus tota laniavit armenta, sed

[1] F *navium.*

out spices of all sorts, unintelligibly lettered metal plaques, the surviving remains of ill-omened birds, and numerous pieces of mourned and even buried corpses: here noses and fingers, there flesh-covered spikes from crucified bodies, elsewhere the preserved gore of murder victims and mutilated skulls wrenched from the teeth of wild beasts.

18 "Then she recited a charm over some pulsating entrails and made offerings with various liquids: now spring-water, now cow's milk, now mountain honey; she also made an offering of mead. Next she bound and knotted those hairs together in interlocking braids and put them to burn on live coals along with several kinds of incense. Suddenly, by the invincible strength of the magical arts and the invisible power of divine forces constrained to her will, the bodies whose hairs were smoking and sizzling borrowed human breath and began to feel and hear and walk, and they came where the stench from their shed hair was drawing them. Instead of that young Boeotian, it was they who kicked at our doors in their desire to get in the house. Then you came along, sodden with drink and deceived by the blackness of unforeseeing Night. So you boldly drew your sword, armed like mad Ajax[1]: he turned his anger against live sheep and slaughtered whole

[1] After Achilles' arms had been awarded to Ulysses, Ajax attempted to take vengeance on the Greek leaders, but in his madness slaughtered a flock of sheep instead.

longe[1] fortius qui tres inflatos caprinos utres exanimasti, ut ego te prostratis hostibus sine macula sanguinis non homicidam nunc, sed utricidam amplecterer."

19 Exarsi[2] lepido sermone Photidis et in vicem cavillatus, "Ergo igitur iam et ipse possum" inquam "mihi primam istam virtutis adoriam[3] ad exemplum duodeni laboris Herculei numerare, vel trigemino corpori Geryonis vel triplici formae Cerberi totidem peremptos utres coaequando. Sed ut ex animo tibi volens omne delictum quo me tantis angoribus implicasti remittam, praesta quod summis votis expostulo, et dominam tuam, cum aliquid huius divinae disciplinae molitur, ostende, cum deos invocat, certe cum reformatur[4] videam. Sum namque coram magiae noscendae ardentissimus cupitor, quamquam mihi nec ipsa tu videare rerum[5] rudis vel expers. Scio istud et plane sentio, cum semper alioquin spretorem matronalium amplexuum sic tuis istis micantibus oculis et rubentibus bucculis et renidentibus crinibus et hiantibus osculis et

[1] *tu* should perhaps be inserted to repair the syntax.

[2] F *amplecteres. At si.* The beginning of Lucius' reaction is lost beyond recovery. A sampling of conjectures offers laughter (*adrisi*), applause (*at ego plausi*), excitement (*erectus satis*), and renewal (*recreatus*).

[3] F *adorsam.*

[4] F probably wrote *cum reformatu.* The sentence seems clumsy. Perhaps a full stop should be read after *ostende*; or *ut* or *ut eam* may have been lost before *videam.*

[5] Some adjective modifying *rerum* may have been lost.

flocks, but you were much braver and drove the life's breath out of three inflated goatskin bags. Thus the enemy was felled without the stain of blood, and I may now embrace, not a manslayer, but a bag-slayer."

19 I caught the spark of Photis' clever speech and capped her jest. "All right, then," I said, "I can also count this first glorious deed in my heroic career like one of Hercules' twelve labors, comparing either the threefold body of Geryon[1] or the tripled shape of Cerberus[2] with the same number of slain wineskins. But if you want me to forgive you freely and entirely for that offence by which you entangled me in so much anguish, grant me something I clamour for with all my heart. Show me your mistress when she is working at some project of this supernatural discipline, and let me see her when she is invoking the gods, or at least when she is undergoing a transformation. I have the most passionate desire to know magic at first hand, although you yourself seem to me to be no unskilled or inexperienced practitioner of the art. I know that clearly enough from my own experience: although I have always disdained ladies' embraces, you, with your flashing eyes and reddening cheeks and glistening hair and parted lips and

[1] See II 32 and note.

[2] The three-headed dog who guards the entrance to the Underworld. Hercules chained him and dragged him up to earth.

fraglantibus papillis in servilem modum addictum atque mancipatum teneas volentem. Iam denique nec larem requiro nec domuitionem paro et nocte ista nihil antepono."

20 "Quam vellem" respondit[1] illa "praestare tibi, Luci, quod cupis, sed praeter invidos mores in solitudinem semper abstrusa et omnium praesentia viduata solet huius modi secreta perficere. Sed tuum postulatum praeponam periculo meo idque observatis opportunis temporibus sedulo perficiam; modo, ut initio praefata sum, rei tantae fidem silentiumque tribue."

Sic nobis garrientibus libido mutua et animos simul et membra suscitat. Omnibus abiectis amiculis, hactenus[2] denique intecti atque nudati bacchamur in Venerem, cum quidem mihi iam fatigato de propria liberalitate Photis puerile[3] obtulit corollarium; iamque luminibus nostris vigilia marcidis infusus sopor etiam in altum[4] diem nos attinuit.

21 Ad hunc modum transactis voluptarie paucis noctibus, quadam die percita Photis ac satis trepida me accurrit indicatque dominam suam, quod nihil etiam tunc in suos amores ceteris artibus promoveret, nocte proxima in avem sese plumaturam

[1] Before *respondit* F has *inquit*, which I have followed most editors in deleting, although it could be emended to *inquieta* "disturbed".

[2] If retained, *hactenus* (F *actenus*) will have the meaning "completely" or "hence" (as in VI 18).

[3] F *puerilis*. [4] F *alium*.

fragrant breasts, have taken possession of me, bought and bound over like a slave, and a willing one. In fact I do not miss my home any more and I am not preparing to return there, and nothing is more important to me than spending the night with you."

20 "How I wish," she replied, "that I could get you what you desire, Lucius. But, besides her nasty disposition, she always performs secret acts of this sort in seclusion and divorced from all company. Still, I will put your request ahead of my personal danger; I will watch for an opportune occasion and try very hard to accomplish what you want. Only, as I told you at the beginning, give me your promise and your silence about so serious a matter."

As we chattered so, mutual desire excited our emotions and bodies alike. We threw off all our clothes and then, completely uncovered and naked, performed an orgy to Venus. When I was tired, Photis of her own generosity played the boy's part with me as a bonus. Finally, when our eyes were drooping from lack of sleep, slumber flowed into them and held us fast until full daylight.

21 We spent a few more nights in similar pleasure. Then one day Photis came rushing up to me all excited and trembling, and informed me that her mistress, since she had still made no progress in her love affair with her other devices, intended that very night to feather herself up into a bird and so fly

atque ad suum cupitum sic devolaturam; proin memet ad rei tantae speculam caute praepararem. Iamque circa primam noctis vigiliam ad illud superius cubiculum suspenso et insono vestigio me perducit ipsa, perque rimam ostiorum quampiam iubet arbitrari, quae sic gesta sunt.

Iam primum omnibus laciniis se devestit Pamphile et arcula quadam reclusa pyxides plusculas inde depromit, de quis unius operculo remoto atque indidem egesta unguedine diuque palmulis suis affricta ab imis unguibus sese totam adusque summos capillos perlinit, multumque cum lucerna secreto collocuta, membra tremulo succussu quatit. Quis leniter fluctuantibus promicant molles plumulae, crescunt et fortes pinnulae; duratur nasus incurvus, coguntur ungues adunci. Fit bubo Pamphile. Sic edito stridore querulo iam sui periclitabunda paulatim terra resultat; mox in altum sublimata forinsecus totis alis evolat.

22 Et illa quidem magnis[1] suis artibus volens reformatur. At ego nullo decantatus carmine, praesentis tantum facti stupore defixus, quidvis aliud magis videbar esse quam Lucius. Sic exterminatus animi, attonitus in amentiam vigilans somniabar. Defrictis adeo diu pupulis, an vigilarem scire

[1] Almost universally emended to *magicis.*

away to the object of her desire. Accordingly I was to prepare myself cautiously for a glimpse of this feat. Later, about the first watch of night, Photis herself led me quietly on tiptoe up to that upstairs room and invited me to inspect, through a crack in the door, the events which occurred next.

First Pamphile took off all her clothes. Then she opened a box and removed several small jars from it. She took the cover off one of these and scooped out some ointment, which she massaged for some time between her palms and then smeared all over her body from the tips of her toenails to the top of her hair. After a long secret conversation with her lamp she began to shake her limbs in a quivering tremor. While her body undulated smoothly, soft down sprouted up through her skin, and strong wing-feathers grew out; her nose hardened and curved, and her toenails bent into hooks. Pamphile had become an owl. So she let out a plaintive screech and began testing herself by jumping off the ground a little at a time. Soon she soared aloft and flew out of the house on full wing.

22 Whereas hers was a willing metamorphosis brought about by her powerful arts, I, who had not been enchanted by any spell, yet was so transfixed with awe at the occurrence that I seemed to be something other than Lucius. I was outside the limits of my own mind, amazed to the point of madness, dreaming while awake. I rubbed my eyes again and again to try to discover if I were really awake.

quaerebam. Tandem denique reversus ad sensum praesentium arrepta manu Photidis et admota meis luminibus, "Patere, oro te," inquam "dum dictat occasio, magno et singulari me affectionis tuae fructu perfrui, et impertire nobis unctulum indidem per istas tuas papillas,[1] mea mellitula; tuumque mancipium irremunerabili beneficio sic tibi perpetuo pignera, ac iam perfice ut meae Veneri Cupido pinnatus assistam tibi."

"Ain," inquit "vulpinaris, amasio, meque sponte asceam cruribus meis illidere compellis? Sic inermem vix a lupulis conservo Thessalis. Hunc alitem factum ubi quaeram, videbo quando?"

23 "At mihi scelus istud depellant caelites" inquam "ut ego, quamvis ipsius aquilae sublimis volatibus toto caelo pervius et supremi Iovis certus nuntius vel laetus armiger, tamen non ad meum nidulum post illam pinnarum dignitatem subinde devolem? Adiuro per dulcem istum capilli tui nodulum, quo meum vinxisti spiritum, me nullam aliam meae Photidi malle. Tunc etiam istud meis cogitationibus occurrit, cum semel avem talem perunctus induero, domus omnes procul me vitare debere. Quam pulchro enim quamque festivo matronae perfruentur amatore bubone! Quid quod istas nocturnas aves,

[1] Some editors prefer to have him swear by her eyes, reading *pupillas.*

Finally, when I had returned to an awareness of present reality, I seized Photis' hand and pressed it to my eyes. "I beg you," I said, "while the opportunity prompts, let me enjoy a great and unique proof of your affection. Get me a little ointment from that same jar. I beg you by these pretty breasts of yours, my little honey. Bind me as your slave for ever by a favour I can never repay, and make me stand beside you now, a winged Cupid next to my Venus."

"What! You sly fox!" she cried. "Are you trying to force me, my love, to lay the axe to my own legs? I can scarcely keep you safe from the Thessalian bitches, unarmed as you are. If you get wings, where will I ever find you and when will I see you again?"

23 "May the heavenly gods preserve me from such a crime," I said. "Even if I could traverse the entire sky in the lofty flight of the eagle himself, even if I were the unerring messenger and happy weapon-bearer of almighty Jupiter, don't you think I would still fly right back down to my little nest after so nobly employing my wings? I swear by that sweet knot of your hair with which you have bound my soul that there is no other woman I prefer to my Photis. Then there is something else that has occurred to me: once I have anointed myself and costumed myself in that species of bird, I will have to stay far away from all houses. What a handsome and jolly lover housewives are going to enjoy in an owl! Aren't those nocturnal birds carefully caught

cum penetraverint larem quempiam, sollicite prehensas foribus videmus affigi, ut quod infaustis volatibus familiae minantur exitium suis luant cruciatibus? Sed, quod sciscitari paene praeterivi, quo dicto factove rursum exutis pinnulis illis ad meum redibo Lucium?"

"Bono animo es, quod ad huius rei curam pertinet" ait. "Nam mihi domina singula monstravit quae possunt rursus in facies hominum tales figuras reformare. Nec istud factum putes ulla benivolentia, sed ut ei redeunti medela salubri possem subsistere. Specta denique quam parvis quamque futtilibus tanta res procuretur herbulis[1]: anethi modicum cum lauri foliis immissum rori[2] fontano datur lavacrum et poculum."

24 Haec identidem asseverans summa cum trepidatione irrepit cubiculum et pyxidem depromit arcula. Quam ego amplexus ac deosculatus prius, utque mihi prosperis faveret volatibus deprecatus, abiectis propere laciniis totis, avide manus immersi et haurito plusculo cuncta[3] corporis mei membra perfricui. Iamque alternis conatibus libratis bracchiis in avem similem[4] gestiebam. Nec ullae plumulae nec

[1] F *herculis. herbusculis* is an alternative emendation.

[2] F *rore.* Alternatively emend the participle to *immistum* (or *immixtum*) "mixed in".

[3] F originally wrote *uncta*, then changed to *uncto*, which is printed by modern editors, although it makes neither good sense nor sound. *Unctus* or *unctu* are possible, but

whenever they get inside a home, and don't we see them nailed up on the door to expiate with their own sufferings the disaster threatened against the family by their ill-omened flight? But I almost forgot to ask: what have I to say or do in order to strip off those feathers and return to my old self again?"

"As far as that is concerned, you need have no fear," she replied. "My mistress has shown me in detail what can transmute all these shapes back into human form. But do not think she did this out of kindness. No, it was so that I could help her with restorative medicine when she comes home. Just look what small and cheap little herbs it takes to produce so mighty an effect: 'Suspend a pinch of anise and laurel leaves in spring water; administer as lotion and potion.'"

24 After repeating this recipe several times, she crept very nervously into the room and removed a jar from the box. First I embraced and kissed the jar and prayed to it to bless me with a lucky flight. Then I hastily threw off all my clothes, greedily plunged my hand into the jar, pulled out a largish daub, and rubbed my body all over. Next I spread out my arms and pumped them alternately, trying hard to become a bird like Pamphile. No down

less attractive, emendations.

[4] Should perhaps be emended to *similis*: "I made gestures like a bird."

usquam pinnulae, sed plane pili mei crassantur in setas, et cutis tenella duratur in corium, et in extimis palmulis perdito numero toti digiti coguntur in singulas ungulas, et de spinae meae termino grandis cauda procedit. Iam facies enormis et os prolixum et nares hiantes et labiae pendulae; sic et aures immodicis horripilant auctibus. Nec ullum miserae reformationis video solacium, nisi quod mihi iam nequeunti tenere Photidem natura crescebat. Ac dum salutis inopia cuncta corporis mei considerans non avem me sed asinum video, querens de facto Photidis, sed iam humano gestu simul et voce privatus, quod solum poteram, postrema deiecta labia, umidis tamen oculis obliquum respiciens ad illam tacitus expostulabam.

Quae ubi primum me talem aspexit, percussit faciem suam manibus infestis et "Occisa sum misera!" clamavit. "Me trepidatio simul et festinatio fefellit et pyxidum similitudo decepit. Sed bene quod facilior reformationis huius medela suppeditat. Nam rosis tantum demorsicatis exibis asinum statimque in meum Lucium postliminio redibis. Atque utinam vesperi de more nobis parassem corollas aliquas, ne moram talem patereris vel noctis

appeared, not a single feather. Instead my body hair was thickening into bristles and my soft skin hardening into hide. At the ends of my palms my fingers were losing their number and being all compressed together into single hoofs, and from the end of my spine came forth a great tail. My face was immense now, mouth spread, nostrils gaping, lips sagging. My ears too grew immoderately long and bristly. I saw no consolation in my wretched metamorphosis except for the fact that, although I could not now embrace Photis, my generative organ was growing.

25 Helplessly I examined every part of my body and saw that I was not a bird, but an ass. I wanted to complain about what Photis had done, but I lacked human gestures as well as words. Still, I did the only thing I could: I hung my lower lip, looked askance at her with moist eyes, and berated her in silence.

Her first reaction when she saw my condition was to strike her face violently with her hands and scream, "I am lost and done for! My nervousness and haste misled me, and the similarity of the jars fooled me. But luckily a very easy cure is available for this metamorphosis. All you have to do is take a bite of roses and you will depart from the ass and immediately return to be my own Lucius once again. I only wish I had fixed some garlands for us this evening as I usually do, and then you would not have to endure waiting even one night like this. But

unius. Sed primo diluculo remedium festinabitur tibi."

26 Sic illa maerebat. Ego vero, quamquam perfectus asinus et pro Lucio iumentum, sensum tamen retinebam humanum. Diu denique ac multum mecum ipse deliberavi an nequissimam facinerosissimamque illam feminam spissis calcibus feriens et mordicus appetens necare deberem. Sed ab incepto temerario melior me sententia revocavit, ne morte multata Photide salutares mihi suppetias rursus exstinguerem. Deiecto itaque et quassanti capite ac demussata temporali contumelia, durissimo casui meo serviens ad equum[1] illum vectorem meum probissimum in stabulum concedo, ubi alium etiam Milonis quondam hospitis mei asinum stabulantem inveni. Atque ego rebar, si quod inesset mutis animalibus tacitum ac naturale sacramentum, agnitione ac miseratione quadam inductum equum illum meum hospitium ac loca lautia mihi praebiturum. Sed pro Iuppiter hospitalis et Fidei secreta

[1] *equum* should perhaps be deleted as a gloss on the following phrase.

the remedy will be rushed to you at the first light of dawn."

26 So she lamented. For my part, although I was a complete ass and a beast of burden instead of Lucius, I still retained my human intelligence; and so I held a long, earnest debate[1] with myself concerning that utterly worthless and criminal woman. Should I kick her repeatedly with my hoofs, assault her with my teeth, and kill her? But that was a rash idea and better thinking brought me back to my senses, lest, by punishing Photis with death, I also destroy the assistance I needed for recovery. So, lowering and shaking my head, I silently swallowed my temporary humiliation, and accommodating myself to my harsh misfortune, I went off to the stable to join my horse, my most excellent mount. I discovered another ass stabled there too, belonging to Milo, who used to be my host. I assumed that, if any unspoken natural bond of allegiance existed among dumb animals, my horse would be moved by recognition and a feeling of pity to offer me hospitality and privileged treatment.[2] But—O thou guest-god Jupiter[3]! O ye invisible deities of Loyalty!—

[1] The debate reminds one of Odysseus' debate with himself when he ponders the problem of escape from the Cyclops' cave (Homer, *Odyssey* IX 298–305).

[2] A technical phrase for the marks of honour offered to foreign ambassadors by the Roman senate.

[3] Jupiter, and even more his Greek counterpart Zeus, was regarded as the special protector of guests.

numina! Praeclarus ille vector meus cum asino capita conferunt in meamque perniciem ilico consentiunt et, verentes scilicet cibariis suis, vix me praesepio videre proximantem: deiectis auribus iam furentes infestis calcibus insequuntur, et abigor quam procul ab hordeo, quod apposueram vesperi meis manibus illi gratissimo famulo.

27 Sic affectus atque in solitudinem relegatus angulo stabuli concesseram. Dumque de insolentia collegarum meorum mecum cogito, atque in alterum diem auxilio rosario Lucius denuo futurus equi perfidi vindictam meditor, respicio pilae mediae, quae stabuli trabes sustinebat, in ipso fere meditullio Eponae deae simulacrum residens aediculae, quod accurate corollis roseis equidem recentibus fuerat ornatum. Denique agnito salutari praesidio pronus spei, quantum extensis prioribus pedibus adniti poteram insurgo valide, et cervice prolixa nimiumque porrectis labiis, quanto maxime nisu poteram corollas appetebam. Quod me pessima scilicet sorte conantem servulus meus, cui semper equi cura mandata fuerat, repente conspiciens, indignatus exsurgit, et "Quo usque tandem" inquit

[1] Patron goddess of horses and mules, probably of Celtic origin.

that noble mount of mine and the ass put their heads together and immediately agreed on my destruction. No doubt they were afraid for their own rations: the moment they saw me getting close to the manger they lowered their ears and attacked me furiously with hostile kicks. I was driven far away from the barley which with my very own hands I had set before this fine, grateful servant of mine that evening.

27 Thus ill-treated and condemned to solitude, I withdrew into a corner of the stable. While I was pondering the effrontery of my colleagues and plotting the revenge I would take on my treacherous horse the next day, when I became Lucius again with the aid of roses, I caught sight of a statue of the goddess Epona[1] seated in a little shrine at almost the exact midpoint of the central pillar supporting the stable's roofbeams. The statue had been carefully decorated with garlands of roses, fresh roses. I recognised this as an instrument of salvation, and with eager anticipation, straining as hard as I could, I stretched out my front feet and stood powerfully upright; with my neck extended and my lips thrust forward, I summoned all the effort I could and tried to reach the garlands. But as I was making the attempt—this was bad luck, of course—my slave, who had always been in charge of caring for my horse, noticed me immediately. He stood up angrily and exclaimed: "How long, pray, shall we put up

"cantherium patiemur istum paulo ante cibariis iumentorum, nunc etiam simulacris deorum infestum? Quin iam ego istum sacrilegum debilem claudumque reddam." Et statim telum aliquod quaeritans temere fascem lignorum positum offendit, rimatusque frondosum fustem cunctis vastiorem, non prius miserum me tundere desiit quam, sonitu vehementi et largo strepitu percussis ianuis, trepido etiam rumore viciniae conclamatis[1] latronibus profugit territus.

28 Nec mora cum vi patefactis aedibus globus latronum invadit omnia, et singula domus membra cingit armata factio, et auxiliis hinc inde convolantibus obsistit discursus hostilis. Cuncti gladiis et facibus instructi noctem illuminant; coruscat in modum ortivi solis ignis et mucro. Tunc horreum quoddam satis validis claustris obsaeptum obseratumque, quod mediis aedibus constitutum gazis Milonis fuerat refertum, securibus validis aggressi diffindunt. Quo passim recluso totas opes vehunt raptimque constrictis sarcinis singuli partiuntur, sed gestaminum modus numerum gerulorum excedit. Tunc opulentiae nimiae nimio ad extremas incitas deducti, nos duos asinos et equum meum

[1] F *vicinae conclamantis.*

---

[1] The slave begins like Cicero in his first oration against Catiline: "How long, pray, will you abuse our patience, Catiline?"

with this old gelding who attacks first the animals' food and now even the gods' statues?[1] No, I shall now maim and cripple that temple-robber!" And as he quickly began to look round for some weapon, he stumbled on a bundle of sticks which happened to be lying there. Hunting out a leafy branch for a club, the thickest of them all, he began to beat me unceasingly, stopping only when he heard a crashing noise and the loud din of doors being battered, along with nearby cries of alarm and shouts of "Thieves! Thieves!" At this he fled in terror.

28 Instantly the doors were forced open and a troop of robbers invaded the whole place, an armed band occupied every part of the house, and some of the marauders blocked off the help that came swarming up from every direction. Then men, all armed with swords and torches, lit up the night; the fire and steel flashed like the rising sun. A storeroom in the middle of the house, closed and locked with very heavy bolts, had been stuffed full of Milo's treasures; they attacked it with large axes and broke their way through and when they had opened up the room they carried out all the valuables through the breaches created on every side, hastily tied them into bundles and divided the shares. But the volume of loads exceeded the number of load-carriers. At this turn, having been brought to a stalemate by the excess of their excessive riches, they led us two asses and my horse out of the stable,

productos e stabulo quantum potest gravioribus sarcinis onerant, et domo iam vacua minantes baculis exigunt, unoque de sociis ad speculandum, qui de facinoris inquisitione nuntiaret, relicto, nos crebra tundentes per avia montium ducunt concitos.

29 Iamque rerum tantarum pondere et montis ardui vertice et prolixo satis itinere nihil a mortuo differebam. Sed mihi sero quidem, serio tamen, subvenit ad auxilium civile decurrere et interposito venerabili principis nomine tot aerumnis me liberare. Cum denique iam luce clarissima vicum quempiam frequentem et nundinis celebrem praeteriremus, inter ipsas turbelas Graecorum genuino sermone nomen augustum Caesaris invocare temptavi. Et "O" quidem tantum disertum ac validum clamitavi, reliquum autem Caesaris nomen enuntiare non potui. Aspernati latrones clamorem absonum meum, caedentes hinc inde miserum corium nec cribris iam idoneum relinquunt.

Sed tandem mihi inopinatam salutem Iuppiter ille tribuit. Nam cum multas villulas et casas amplas praeterimus, hortulum quendam prospexi satis amoenum, in quo praeter ceteras gratas herbulas rosae virgines matutino rore florebant. His inhians et spe salutis alacer ac laetus propius accessi,

---

[1] The word-play *sero . . . serio* cannot be reproduced in English.

loaded us with the heaviest possible burdens, and drove us away from the now empty house, threatening us with sticks. They left one of their fellows behind as a spy to report what investigation was made of the crime. The others, beating us constantly, took us through the trackless mountains at full speed.

29 With the weight of all those goods and the height of the steep mountain and the extreme length of the march, I was as good as dead. But the idea came to me, late but seriously[1] for all that, of having recourse to the civil authorities for help, of freeing myself from all my tribulations by calling on the holy name of the Emperor. So when finally, in broad daylight now, we passed through a busy village thronged on market-day, I tried amidst those crowds of Greeks to invoke the august name of Caesar in my native tongue. And indeed I shouted the "O" by itself eloquently and vigorously, but I could not pronounce the rest of Caesar's name. The robbers disdained my discordant outcry and lashed my miserable hide right and left, leaving it not even fit to make sieves with.

At long last, however, Jupiter on high offered me an unexpected chance of salvation. After we had passed a number of little villas and large farmhouses, I suddenly caught sight of a very pleasant little garden, where among other lovely plants virgin roses were blooming in the morning dew. I gazed at them longingly; in my eagerness

dumque iam labiis undantibus affecto, consilium me subit longe salubrius, ne, si rursum asino remoto prodirem in Lucium, evidens[1] exitium inter manus latronum offenderem vel artis magicae suspectione vel indicii futuri criminatione. Tunc igitur a rosis et quidem necessario temperavi et casum praesentem tolerans in asini faciem faena rodebam.

[1] F *luciliu me videns.*

and joy at the hope of being saved, I walked closer to them and was on the point of touching them with quivering lips when a far safer plan of action occurred to me: I must not get rid of the ass and appear as Lucius, because I would obviously meet my death at the hands of the robbers, either from the suspicion of practicing magic or because of the accusation I would bring against them as an informer. I therefore refrained from eating the roses at that time out of necessity, and, bearing up under my present misfortune, I continued to munch hay in the likeness of an ass.

LIBER IV

1 Diem ferme circa medium, cum iam flagrantia solis caleretur, in pago quodam apud notos ac familiares latronibus senes devertimus. Sic enim primus aditus et sermo prolixus et oscula mutua quamvis asino sentire praestabant. Nam et rebus eos quibusdam dorso meo depromptis munerabantur, et secretis gannitibus quod essent latrocinio partae videbantur indicare. Iamque nos omni sarcina levatos[1] in pratum proximum passim libero pastui tradidere. Nec me cum asino vel equo meo compascuus coetus attinere potuit, adhuc insolitum alioquin prandere faenum; sed plane pone stabulum prospectum hortulum iam fame perditus fidenter invado, et quamvis crudis holeribus affatim tamen ventrem sagino, deosque comprecatus omnes cuncta prospectabam loca, sicubi forte conterminis in hortulis candens reperirem rosarium. Nam et ipsa solitudo iam mihi bonam fiduciam tribuebat, si devius

[1] Or *levigatos*, which F wrote first.

BOOK IV

1 Sometime around midday, when the sun's heat was already scorching, we stopped in a village at the house of some old men. They were friends and acquaintances of the robbers, as even an ass could understand from their initial reception, their lengthy conversation, and their exchange of kisses. They even took some of the objects off my back and gave them to the old men as presents, and in hushed whispers seemed to be indicating that the articles had been acquired in a robbery. Then they relieved us of all the baggage and put us out to wander and graze freely in a field next to the house. A pasturing partnership, however, with the ass or my horse held no appeal for me, since in any case I was as yet unaccustomed to dining on hay. But I caught a clear glimpse of a garden behind the stable and confidently marched in, dying from hunger by now. I stuffed my belly full of vegetables, raw though they were; and then with a prayer to all the gods I began to survey the whole area to see if perhaps I could spot a rose-bed gleaming among the neighbouring gardens. My isolation, you see, gave me confidence now, as long as I could eat the remedy in

et frutectis,[1] absconditus, sumpto remedio, de iumenti quadripedis incurvo gradu rursum erectus in hominem inspectante nullo resurgerem.

2 Ergo igitur cum in isto cogitationis salo fluctuarem, aliquanto longius video frondosi nemoris convallem umbrosam, cuius inter varias herbulas et laetissima virecta fulgentium rosarum mineus color renidebat. Iamque apud mea non usquequaque ferina praecordia Veneris et Gratiarum lucum illum arbitrabar, cuius inter opaca secreta floris genialis regius nitor relucebat. Tunc invocato hilaro atque prospero Eventu, cursu me concito proripio, ut hercule ipse sentirem non asinum me, verum etiam equum currulem nimio velocitatis effectum.[2] Sed agilis atque praeclarus ille conatus Fortunae meae scaevitatem anteire non potuit. Iam enim loco proximus non illas rosas teneras et amoenas, madidas divini roris et nectaris, quas rubi felices, beatae spinae generant, ac ne convallem quidem usquam nisi tantum ripae fluvialis marginem densis arboribus saeptam video. Hae arbores in lauri faciem prolixe foliatae pariunt in odori modum floris[3] porrectos caliculos modice punicantes, quos equidem fraglantis minime rures-

[1] F *protectus.*

[2] F *velocitati refectum.*

[3] F *in modum floris inodori.* The word-order here is Robertson's suggestion. Others read *in modum floris odori.*

private; and away from the road and hidden by the bushes, I could rise once more from the bent gait of a four-footed beast of burden to stand erect as a man, with no one watching.

2 Therefore, as I tossed upon this sea of thought, a little distance away I saw a leafy wood in a shady vale; in the midst of its various plants and flourishing greenery shone the crimson colour of glistening roses. In my not totally animal heart I judged that this must be a grove of Venus and the Graces, within whose dark recesses gleamed the royal splendour of the festal flower. Then, with a prayer to joyous and prosperous Success,[1] I hurled myself forward at such an accelerated pace that, by Hercules, I felt I was no longer an ass, but had been transformed by my extreme speed into a racehorse. Yet my nimble and noble effort could not outrun the perversity of my Fortune, for when I came close to the place I no longer saw those delicate, charming roses, wet with divine dew and nectar, such as spring up amid happy brambles and blessed briars; nor did I even see a vale at all, but only the edge of a river-bank hedged in with thick-set trees which have copious foliage resembling the laurel and produce long, pale red, cup-shaped blossoms like the fragrant flower: although these have no scent at all, uneducated folk call them by the rural name "laurel

[1] Eventus (often Bonus Eventus) was a Roman god of cult, with shrines and altars.

tri vocabulo vulgus indoctum rosas laureas appellant, quarumque cuncto pecori cibus letalis est.

3 Talibus fatis implicitus etiam ipsam salutem recusans sponte illud venenum rosarium sumere gestiebam. Sed dum cunctanter accedo decerpere, iuvenis quidam, ut mihi videbatur, hortulanus cuius omnia prorsus holera vastaveram, tanto damno cognito cum grandi baculo furens decurrit, adreptumque[1] me totum plagis obtundit adusque vitae ipsius periculum, nisi tandem sapienter alioquin ipse mihi tulissem auxilium. Nam lumbis elevatis in altum, pedum posteriorum[2] calcibus iactatis in eum crebriter, iam mulcato graviter atque iacente contra proclive montis attigui fuga me liberavi. Sed ilico mulier quaepiam, uxor eius scilicet, simul eum prostratum et semianimem ex edito despexit, ululabili cum plangore ad eum statim prosilit, ut sui videlicet miseratione mihi praesens crearet exitium. Cuncti enim pagani fletibus eius exciti statim conclamant canes, atque ad me laniandum rabie perciti ferrent impetum passim cohortantur.

Tunc igitur procul dubio iam morti proximus, cum viderem canes, et modo magnos et numero mul-

[1] F *abreptumque.*
[2] F *posterioribus.*

---

[1] The oleander, called "rose-laurel" (*rhododaphne*) in Greek.

roses",[1] and they are deadly poisonous to all grazing animals.

3 Such were the threads of fate in which I was entangled that I even disregarded my own safety and voluntarily made ready to consume that rosy poison. But as I hesitantly approached the flowers to pluck them, a young man came running furiously toward me with a huge stick. I supposed that he was the gardener whose vegetables I had thoroughly plundered and that he was now aware of his total loss. When he had caught me, he began pounding and beating me all over until I was actually in danger of my life, if I had not eventually had the sense to come to my own aid. I raised my rump in the air and kicked him with my rear hoofs again and again, until he lay seriously wounded against the adjacent hillside. Then I broke free and fled. Just then, however, some woman, evidently his wife, looked down from the hill and saw him stretched out half-dead. She instantly sprang down toward him with shrieks of woe obviously intending my immediate destruction by arousing pity for herself. In fact all the villagers were incited by her weeping and instantly called their dogs and sicked them on me from every side, provoking them to attack me in their furious rage and tear me to shreds.

At that point, then, I was beyond doubt at death's door, as I beheld those dogs who had been collected and roused against me: large in size, many in

tos et ursis ac leonibus ad compugnandum idoneos, in me convocatos exasperari, e re nata capto consilio fugam desino ac me retrorsus celeri gradu rursum in stabulum quo deverteramus recipio. At illi, canibus iam aegre cohibitis, arreptum me loro quam valido ad ansulam quandam destinatum rursum caedendo confecissent profecto, nisi dolore plagarum alvus artata, crudisque illis oleribus abundans et lubrico fluxu saucia, fimo fistulatim excusso, quosdam extremi liquoris aspergine, alios putore nidoris faetidi a meis iam quassis scapulis abegisset.

4 Nec mora cum, iam in meridiem prono iubare, rursum nos ac praecipue me longe gravius onustum producunt illi latrones stabulo. Iamque confecta bona parte itineris, et viae spatio defectus et sarcinae pondere depressus, ictibusque fustium fatigatus atque etiam ungulis extritis iam claudus et titubans, rivulum quendam serpentis leniter aquae propter insistens, subtilem occasionem feliciter nactus, cogitabam totum memet flexis scite cruribus pronum abicere, certus atque obstinatus nullis verberibus ad ingrediundum exsurgere, immo etiam paratus non fusti tantum, sed machaera perfossus occumbere. Rebar enim iam me prorsus exanima-

number, and fit to fight bears and lions. Taking my cue from the circumstances, I gave up my escape, reversed my course, and headed at a quick run back into the stable where we had turned in. But the men, after having with some difficulty controlled their dogs, caught me and tied me to a hook with a very strong strap. They began to beat me again, and would certainly have killed me if it had not been for my belly, which was constricted by the pain of the blows, crammed full with those raw vegetables, and weakened with slippery diarrhoea: it sent forth ordure in a jet and drove the men away from my poor beaten haunches, some with the spray of the foul liquid, others by the stink of the putrid stench.

4 Soon afterward, as the sun's radiance was now turning down toward afternoon, the robbers took us out of the stable and gave me specially a much heavier load. When we had completed a good part of our day's march and I was fatigued from the length of the route, depressed by the weight of my load, wearied by the blows of the clubs, and lamely staggering on worn-down hoofs, I halted beside a creek with quietly winding water. I happily seized on this fine opportunity and formed a plan: I would skilfully bend my knees and throw myself flat to the ground, bound and determined not to get up and walk for all the beatings in the world—yes, prepared to lie there even if they dug into me not just with a club but with a sword. I assumed that, since I was now totally exhausted and feeble, I

tum ac debilem mereri causariam missionem; certe latrones partim impatientia morae, partim studio festinatae fugae dorsi mei sarcinam duobus ceteris iumentis distributuros meque in altioris vindictae vicem lupis et vulturiis praedam relicturos.

5 Sed tam bellum consilium meum praevertit sors deterrima. Namque ille alius asinus, divinato et antecapto meo cogitatu, statim se mentita lassitudine cum rebus totis offudit,[1] iacensque in mortuum[2] non fustibus, non stimulis, ac ne cauda et auribus cruribusque undique versum elevatis, temptavit exsurgere, quoad tandem postumae spei fatigati secumque collocuti, ne tam diu mortuo, immo vero lapideo asino servientes fugam morarentur, sarcinis eius mihi equoque distributis, destricto gladio poplites eius totos amputant, ac paululum a via retractum per altissimum praeceps in vallem proximam etiam nunc spirantem praecipitant. Tunc ego miseri commilitonis fortunam cogitans statui iam dolis abiectis et fraudibus asinum me bonae frugi dominis exhibere. Nam et secum eos animadverteram colloquentes, quod in proximo nobis esset habenda mansio et totius viae finis quieta eorumque esset sedes illa et habitatio. Clementi denique transmisso clivulo pervenimus ad

[1] F *offuditur.* Alternatively *offunditur* can be read and the *se* at the beginning of the clause emended to *scilicet.*

[2] F *in mortui*, later corrected to *in mortuum.* Some editors read *in modum mortui.*

would earn a medical discharge: surely the robbers, partly from intolerance of delay and partly from eagerness for a swift getaway, would distribute the load from my back between the two other pack-animals and then, in lieu of any more serious punishment, would leave me behind as prey for wolves and vultures.

5 This fine plan of mine, however, was foiled by a wretched piece of luck. The other ass guessed and anticipated my scheme: at once he pretended exhaustion and threw himself down with all his baggage. He lay there like a corpse and, despite sticks and goads and despite their efforts to pull him up by his tail and ears and legs from every side, he made no attempt to rise. Finally the robbers, tired of waiting for posthumous success, agreed among themselves not to delay their flight too long by bondage to a dead—or rather petrified—ass. So they divided his load between me and the horse, pulled out their swords and hamstrung all his legs, dragged him a little way from the road, and hurled him, still breathing, off a high, steep precipice down into the next valley. At that point, considering the Fortune of my poor comrade-in-arms, I decided to abandon all schemes and tricks and show my masters that I could be a model ass. I had also gathered from their conversation that we would shortly be making a halt and taking a rest after the end of the journey, and that their headquarters and residence were there. We then climbed a gentle slope and

locum destinatum, ubi rebus totis exsolutis atque intus conditis iam pondere liberatus lassitudinem vice lavacri pulvereis[1] volutatibus digerebam.

6 Res ac tempus ipsum locorum speluncaeque illius quam[2] latrones inhabitant[3] descriptionem exponere flagitat. Nam et meum simul periclitabor ingenium, et faxo vos quoque an mente etiam sensuque fuerim asinus sedulo sentiatis.

Mons horridus silvestribusque frondibus umbrosus et in primis altus fuit. Huius perobliqua devexa, qua saxis asperrimis et ob id inaccessis cingitur, convalles lacunosae cavaeque nimium spinetis aggeratae et quaqua versus repositae naturalem tutelam praebentes ambiebant. De summo vertice fons affluens bullis ingentibus scaturribat, perque prona delapsus evomebat undas argenteas, iamque rivulis pluribus dispersus ac valles illas agminibus stagnantibus irrigans in modum stipati maris vel ignavi fluminis cuncta cohibebat. Insurgit speluncae, qua margines montanae desinunt, turris ardua. Caulae firmae[4] solidis cratibus ovili stabulationi commodae[5] porrectis undique lateribus ante fores exigui tramitis[6] vice structi parietis attenduntur. Ea tu bono certe meo periculo latronum dixeris atria. Nec iuxta quic-

[1] F *pulveris.*

[2] *quam* is not in F. Another possible supplement is *ubi.*

[3] Usually emended to the imperfect *inhabitabant.*

arrived at our destination. Once there, after all the goods had been unpacked and stashed away and I was freed from my burden, in place of a bath I dissipated my weariness by rolling in the dust.

6 The subject and the occasion itself demand that I produce a description of the region and the cave inhabited by the robbers, for thus I shall both put my talent to the test and also let you effectively perceive whether in intelligence and perception I was the ass that I appeared to be.

The mountain was wild, shaded with forest foliage, and pre-eminently high. Its precipitous slopes, where it was ringed with jagged and hence inaccessible rocks, were encircled by pitted, hollow gullies, well fortified by thick thorn-bushes and isolated on every side, furnishing a natural defence. From the mountain-top a flowing spring gushed out in giant bubbles and rushed down the steep sides, sending out a cascade of silvery waves; then separating into several streams and flooding the gorges with stagnant pools it filled the entire area like a lagoon or a sluggish river. Above the cave, where the edges of the mountain give out, rises a steep tower. Strong fencing of solid wickerwork of a sort suitable for confining sheep, flanked the door on either side and ran like a narrow path formed by masonry walls. You can take my word for it that here was the atrium of a band of

---

[4] F *caule firmas.*

[5] F *stabulatione commoda*

[6] F *tramites.*

quam quam parva casula cannulis temere contecta, quo speculatores e numero latronum, ut postea comperi, sorte ducti noctibus excubabant.

7 Ibi cum singuli derepsissent[1] stipatis artubus, nobis ante ipsas fores loro valido destinatis, anum quandam curvatam gravi senio, cui soli salus atque tutela tot numero iuvenum commissa videbatur, sic infesti compellant: "Etiamne tu, busti cadaver extremum et vitae dedecus primum et Orci fastidium solum, sic nobis otiosa domi residens lusitabis, nec nostris tam magnis tamque periculosis laboribus solacium de tam sera refectione tribues? Quae diebus ac noctibus nil quicquam rei quam merum saevienti ventri tuo soles aviditer ingurgitare."

Tremens ad haec et stridenti vocula pavida sic anus: "At vobis, fortissimi fidelissimique mei sospitatores[2] iuvenes, affatim cuncta suavi sapore percocta pulmenta praesto sunt, panis numerosus, vinum probe calicibus ecfricatis affluenter immissum, et ex more calida tumultuario lavacro vestro praeparata."

In fine sermonis huius statim sese devestiunt, nudatique et flammae largissimae vapore recreati calidaque perfusi et oleo peruncti mensas dapibus

[1] F *direpsissent.*
[2] F *hospitatores.*

robbers. There was nothing nearby except a tiny hut carelessly thatched with cane, where, as I later learned, lookouts chosen by lot from among the robbers kept watch at night.

7 Now they stooped and crept down into the cave one at a time, after tying us up right in front of the entrance with a strong strap. There was an old woman, bent with extreme age, who alone, it appeared, was responsible for the health and upkeep of that large band of young men. They accosted her with insults: "You last corpse on the funeral pyre, life's foremost disgrace and Orcus'[1] sole reject! Are you just going to sit idly amusing yourself at home all day, and not offer us some late-evening refreshment after all our dangerous labours? Day and night all you do is greedily pour strong drink into your insatiable belly."

Trembling and frightened, the old woman answered in a high-pitched voice. "But," she said, "my brave and trusty young saviours, there is plenty of stew all cooked and ready for you, tender and delicious. There is lots of bread, the cups have been nicely rubbed clean and filled to the brim with wine, and, as usual, hot water is ready for a quick bath."

When she finished speaking, they hastily took off their clothes; after they had stripped, warmed themselves in the heat from a huge fire, poured hot water over themselves, and rubbed themselves down with

[1] See note at III 9.

largiter instructas accumbunt.

8 Commodum cubuerant et ecce quidam longe plures numero iuvenes adveniunt alii, quos incunctanter adaeque latrones arbitrarere. Nam et ipsi praedas aureorum argentariorum[1] nummorum ac vasculorum vestisque sericae et intextae filis aureis invehebant. Hi simili lavacro refoti inter toros sociorum sese reponunt. Tunc sorte ducti ministerium faciunt. Estur ac potatur incondite, pulmentis acervatim, panibus aggeratim, poculis agminatim ingestis. Clamore ludunt, strepitu cantilant, conviciis iocantur, ac iam cetera semiferis Lapithis Centaurisque[2] similia.

Tunc inter eos unus, qui robore ceteros antistabat, "Nos quidem" inquit "Milonis Hypatini domum fortiter expugnavimus. Praeter tantam fortunae copiam, quam nostra virtute nacti sumus, et incolumi numero castra nostra petivimus[3] et, si quid ad rem facit, octo pedibus auctiores remeavimus. At vos, qui Boeotias urbes appetistis, ipso duce vestro

[1] Usually emended to *argentariorumque.*

[2] F has *tebcinibus* before *Centaurisque.* Several imaginative attempts have been made to recover the word: e.g. *cenantibus*, *bibonibus*, *euantibus*, *semihominibus*, *titubantibus.* Apuleius may have written any or none of these.

[3] Should perhaps be emended to *repetivimus.*

oil, they lay down to tables lavishly heaped with food.

8 They had just taken their places when up came another much larger group of young men, whom you would unhesitatingly judge to be robbers also, since they too were bringing in loot: gold and silver—coins and vessels—and silk cloth embroidered with gold thread. When, like the others, they had warmed themselves with a bath, they took their places on the couches beside their comrades. Then they determined by lot who would do the serving. They ate and drank in utter disorder, swallowing meat by the heap, bread by the stack, and cups by the legion. They played raucously, sang deafeningly, and joked abusively, and in every other respect behaved just like those half-beasts, the Lapiths and Centaurs.[1]

Then one who surpassed all the others in brawn spoke up. "We have stormed the house of Milo of Hypata, a fine job! Beside the great quantity of fortune we acquired by our courage, we not only returned to camp with our company intact, but even—if it means anything—augmented our forces by eight feet. But you, who attacked the cities of Boeotia, brought your company back weakened by the loss of your general himself, the valiant

[1] At the wedding of Pirithous, king of the Lapiths (a Thessalian tribe), a drunken brawl broke out between the Lapiths and their guests the Centaurs, who were half man and half horse.

fortissimo Lamacho deminuti debilem numerum reduxistis, cuius salutem merito sarcinis istis quas advexistis omnibus antetulerim. Sed illum quidem utcumque nimia virtus sua peremit, inter inclutos reges ac duces proeliorum tanti viri memoria celebrabitur. Enim vos bonae frugi latrones inter furta parva atque servilia timidule per balneas et aniles cellulas reptantes scrutariam facitis."

9 Suscipit unus ex illo posteriore numero. "Tune solus ignoras longe faciliores ad expugnandum domus esse maiores? Quippe quod, licet numerosa familia latis deversetur aedibus, tamen quisque magis suae saluti quam domini consulat opibus. Frugi autem et solitarii homines fortunam parvam vel certe satis amplam dissimulanter obtectam protegunt acrius et sanguinis sui periculo muniunt. Res ipsa denique fidem sermoni meo dabit.

"Vix enim Thebas heptapylos accessimus; quod est huic disciplinae primarium studium, sedum sedulo fortunas inquirebamus popularium.[1] Nec nos denique latuit Chryseros quidam nummularius copiosae pecuniae dominus, qui metu officiorum ac munerum publicorum magnis artibus magnam dis-

[1] F *sed dum . . . popularium.* Most editors bracket *sed dum* as an unerased scribal error of dittography, and read *popularis* to modify *fortunas.*

---

[1] A famous Athenian general with this name (which means "fighter for the people") in the fifth century B.C. was killed during the ill-fated Sicilian expedition.

Lamachus,[1] whose life I would rate, with good reason, above all those bundles you brought in. In his case, however, it was his fearless courage that destroyed him, and this great hero's memory will live in the company of renowned kings and generals. But you, honest robbers, with your petty, slavish pilferings, are just junk-dealers creeping timidly through baths and old ladies' apartments."

9 One of the second gang answered him. "Any fool knows," he said, "that larger houses are much easier to break into. That is because, although a spacious mansion may have a large staff living in it, each of them looks out more for his own safety than for his master's property. But simple men who live alone keep their little fortunes—or for that matter large ones—cunningly hidden, and protect them more fiercely and guard them at the risk of their own lives. The facts themselves will confirm what I say.

"Immediately after arriving at seven-gated[2] Thebes, in accordance with the first principle of our professional training we made careful inquiries about the fortunes of the local residences. We thus discovered that a certain Chryseros,[3] a banker and master of considerable cash, concealed his great wealth with great skill, for fear of civic duties and

[2] The Homeric epithet for Thebes.

[3] His name means "Lovegold."

simulabat opulentiam. Denique solus ac solitarius, parva sed satis munita domuncula contentus, pannosus alioquin ac sordidus, aureos folles incubabat. Ergo placuit ad hunc primum ferremus aditum, ut contempta pugna manus unicae nullo negotio cunctis opibus otiose potiremur.

10 "Nec mora cum noctis initio foribus eius praestolamur, quas neque sublevare neque dimovere ac ne perfringere quidem nobis videbatur, ne valvarum sonus cunctam viciniam nostro suscitaret exitio. Tunc itaque sublimis ille vexillarius noster Lamachus spectatae[1] virtutis suae fiducia, qua clavis immittendae foramen patebat sensim immissa manu, claustrum evellere gestiebat. Sed dudum scilicet omnium bipedum nequissimus Chryseros vigilans et singula rerum sentiens, lenem gradum et obnixum silentium tolerans paulatim arrepit, grandique clavo manum ducis nostri repente nisu fortissimo ad ostii tabulam offigit. Et exitiabili nexu patibulatum[2] relinquens, gurgustioli sui tectum ascendit, atque inde contentissima voce clamitans rogansque[3] vicinos et unum quemque

[1] F *spectate*; *spectata* might also be read, modifying *fiducia*.

[2] F *patibulum*.

[3] *corrogansque* is an attractive emendation.

liturgies.[1] Alone and solitary, content with a tiny but well-protected house, dressed in rags and living in squalor, he sat brooding over bags of gold. We decided, therefore, to attack him first: we thought nothing of battling a single opponent and assumed we could at our leisure lay our hands on all his wealth without any trouble.

10 "We lost no time, and by nightfall we were ready at his front doors. We decided not to remove or force them apart or break them down, for fear that the noise would arouse the whole neighbourhood and ruin us. And so our noble standard-bearer Lamachus, with all the confidence of his tried valour, gradually slipped his hand through the hole for inserting the key and attempted to dislodge the bolt. But that vilest of two-legged creatures, Chryseros, must have been keeping watch for a long time and observing everything that happened. Stepping softly and keeping absolute silence, he slowly crept up and suddenly with a mighty blow nailed our leader's hand to the panel of the door with a large spike. Then, leaving him fatally ensnared as it were on a cross, he climbed up to the roof of his hut and shouted at the top of his lungs, calling the neighbours and summoning them one by

[1] Wealthy citizens were required to perform various public functions (liturgies) for the city at their own expense (e.g. maintain and repair public buildings, streets, and markets).

proprio nomine ciens et salutis communis admonens, diffamat incendio repentino domum suam possideri. Sic unus quisque proximi periculi confinio territus suppetiatum decurrunt anxii.

11 "Tunc nos in ancipiti periculo constituti vel opprimendi nostri vel deserendi socii, remedium e re nata validum eo volente comminiscimus. Antesignani nostri partem qua manus umerum subit ictu per articulum medium temperato prorsus abscidimus, atque ibi bracchio relicto, multis laciniis offulto vulnere ne stillae sanguinis vestigium proderent, ceterum Lamachum raptim reportamus. Ac dum trepidi regionis[1] urguemur gravi tumultu et instantis periculi metu terremur ad fugam, nec vel sequi propere vel remanere tuto potest, vir sublimis animi virtutisque praecipuus multis nos affatibus multisque precibus querens adhortatur per dexteram Martis, per fidem sacramenti, bonum commilitonem cruciatu simul et captivitate liberaremus. Cur enim manui, quae rapere et iugulare sola posset, fortem latronem supervivere? Sat se beatum, qui manu socia volens occumberet. Cumque nulli nostrum spontale parricidium suadens persuadere posset, manu reliqua sumptum gladium suum diuque deosculatum per medium pectus ictu fortissimo transadigit. Tunc

[1] F *religionis.*

one, each by his own name; reminding them of the common safety, he spread the story that his house was being attacked by a sudden fire. So each one, frightened by his own proximity to the danger next door, came anxiously running to help.

11 "Trapped in the dilemma of either getting caught or deserting our comrade, we devised with his consent a drastic remedy for the situation. We forthwith amputated the limb of our front-line commander, with a stroke straight through the middle of the joint where the arm joins the shoulder. Leaving the arm where it was and staunching the wound with lots of rags lest drops of blood should betray our tracks, we hastily took the rest of Lamachus away with us. In some agitation we were beset by the loud outcry in the vicinity and frightened into flight by the terror of imminent danger—but he could neither speedily follow us nor safely remain behind. Our hero of lofty spirit and pre-eminent valour plaintively exhorted us with many an appeal and many a prayer. 'By Mars' right hand,' he pleaded, 'and by the loyalty of your oath, free a good fellow-soldier from torture and capture alike. Why should a brave robber outlive that hand of his which alone can steal and murder? Happy is the man who can choose to die by a comrade's hand!' When he had failed to persuade any of us to slay the willing victim, he drew his sword with his remaining hand, kissed it again and again and drove it with a mighty stroke through the middle of his chest. We then

nos magnanimi ducis vigore venerato corpus reliquum veste[1] lintea diligenter convolutum mari celandum commisimus. Et nunc iacet noster Lamachus elemento toto sepultus.

12 "Et ille quidem dignum virtutibus suis vitae terminum posuit. Enimvero Alcimus sollertibus coeptis consonum[2] Fortunae nutum non potuit adducere. Qui, cum dormientis anus perfracto tuguriolo conscendisset cubiculum superius iamque protinus oblisis faucibus interstinguere eam debuisset, prius maluit rerum singula per latiorem fenestram forinsecus, nobis scilicet rapienda, dispergere. Cumque iam cuncta rerum naviter emolitus nec toro quidem aniculae quiescentis parcere vellet, eaque lectulo suo devoluta vestem stragulam subductam scilicet iactare similiter destinaret, genibus eius profusa sic nequissima illa deprecatur: 'Quid, oro, fili, paupertinas pannosasque resculas miserrimae anus donas vicinis divitibus, quorum haec fenestra domum prospicit?'

Quo sermone callido deceptus astu et vera quae dicta sunt credens Alcimus, verens scilicet ne et ea quae prius miserat quaeque postea missurus foret,

[1] F *vestite.*
[2] F *eūseuū.*

paid homage to the strength of our stout-hearted general, carefully wrapped what was left of his body in a linen cloth, and committed it to the concealment of the sea. Now lies our Lamachus with an entire element for his grave.

12 "Whereas he put an end to his life in a manner worthy of his qualities, Alcimus,[1] despite his cautious plans, could not attract the approving nod of Fortune. He had broken into the cottage of an old woman who was asleep, and had gone to the bedroom upstairs. Although he should have squeezed her throat and strangled her to death at once, he chose first to toss her possessions out through a fairly wide window, item by item—for us to pick up, of course. He had already diligently heaved out everything else, but he was unwilling to pass up even the bed on which the poor old lady was sleeping; so he rolled her off the cot and pulled out the bedclothes, evidently planning to throw them out the window too. But the wicked woman grovelled at his knees and pleaded with him. 'Please, my son,' she said, 'why are you giving a miserable old lady's poor shabby junk to her rich neighbours, whose house is outside that window?'

"That clever speech cunningly deceived Alcimus, who believed that she was telling the truth. He was doubtless afraid that what he had already thrown out and what he was going to throw out later would

[1] The name means "stout".

non sociis suis, sed in alienos lares iam certus erroris abiceret, suspendit se fenestra sagaciter perspecturus omnia, praesertim domus attiguae, quam dixerat illa, fortunas arbitraturus. Quod eum strenue quidem et satis improvide conantem senile illud facinus, quamquam invalido, repentino tamen et inopinato pulsu nutantem ac pendulum et in prospectu alioquin attonitum praeceps inegit. Qui praeter altitudinem nimiam super quendam etiam vastissimum lapidem propter iacentem decidens, perfracta diffusaque crate costarum rivos sanguinis vomens imitus, narratisque nobis quae gesta sunt, non diu cruciatus vitam evasit. Quem prioris exemplo sepulturae traditum bonum secutorem Lamacho dedimus.

13 "Tunc orbitatis duplici plaga petiti iamque Thebanis conatibus abnuentes, Plataeas proximam conscendimus civitatem. Ibi famam celebrem super quodam Demochare munus edituro gladiatorium deprehendimus. Nam vir et genere primarius et opibus plurimus et liberalitate praecipuus digno fortunae suae splendore publicas voluptates instruebat. Quis tantus ingenii, quis facundiae, qui singulas species apparatus multiiugi verbis idoneis posset explicare? Gladiatores isti famosae manus, venatores illi probatae pernicitatis, alibi noxii perdita securitate suis epulis bestiarum saginas

[1] His name means "People-pleaser".

be a gift to someone else's household and not his comrades, since he was now convinced of his mistake. Therefore he leaned out of the window in order to take a careful survey of the situation, and especially to estimate the fortunes of that house next door which she had mentioned. As he was making this energetic and not very prudent attempt, that old sinner gave him a shove; although it was weak, it caught him suddenly and unexpectedly, while he hung balanced there and was preoccupied with his spying. She sent him head over heels. Not to mention the considerable altitude, he fell on to a huge rock lying beside the house, shattering and scattering his ribcage. Vomiting streams of blood from deep within, he told us what had happened and then departed from life without much suffering. We buried him as we had our other comrade, and so gave Lamachus a worthy squire.

13 "Struck by this double blow of bereavement, we now abandoned our Theban efforts and moved on to the next city, Plataea. There we picked up the current talk about a certain Demochares[1] who was about to produce a gladiatorial show. A man of high birth, great wealth and liberality, he was preparing a public entertainment of a brilliance to match his fortune. Who has enough talent, enough eloquence, to find the right words to describe each item of the elaborate show? There were gladiators of renowned strength, animal-hunters of proven agility, and criminals, too, without hope of reprieve, who were to

instruentes. Confixilis machinae sublicae, turres tabularum[1] nexibus ad instar circumforaneae domus, floridae picturae, decora futurae venationis receptacula. Qui praeterea numerus, quae facies ferarum! Nam praecipuo studio foris[2] etiam advexerat generosa illa damnatorum capitum funera. Sed praeter ceteram speciosi muneris supellectilem totis utcumque patrimonii viribus immanis ursae comparabat numerum copiosum. Nam praeter domesticis venationibus captas, praeter largis emptionibus partas, amicorum etiam donationibus variis certatim oblatas tutela sumptuosa sollicite nutriebat.[3]

14 "Nec ille tam clarus tamque splendidus publicae voluptatis apparatus Invidiae noxios effugit oculos. Nam diutina captivitate fatigatae simul et aestiva flagrantia maceratae, pigra etiam sessione languidae, repentina correptae pestilentia paene ad nullum redivere numerum. Passim per plateas plurimas cerneres iacere semivivorum corporum ferina naufragia. Tunc vulgus ignobile, quos inculta pau-

[1] F *stabularum.* This sentence is difficult (though not necessarily corrupt) and has engendered much emendation in addition to the necessary restoration of *tabularum.*

[2] Or *forinsecus*, for F's *forensis.*

[3] F *oblata . . . nutriebant.* Possibly *oblatae . . . nutriebantur.*

provide a banquet of themselves to fatten the beasts. There was also an articulated contrivance made of wood, towers formed of scaffolding rather like houses on wheels, coloured with gay paintings, ornamental cages for the beasts to be hunted.[1] And oh the quantity and fine appearance of the wild beasts! For he had taken great pains and had even imported from abroad these noble sepulchres for the condemned men. Beside the other furnishings for this showy spectacle, he employed the total resources of his inheritance to collect a large band of enormous bears. In addition to those hunted and captured by his own staff and those acquired by expensive purchases, others had been presented to him by friends vying with one another in their various gifts. He lavishly tended and fed all those bears with the utmost care.

14 "But such grand and splendid preparations for the public's pleasure did not escape the baleful eyes of Envy. The bears, exhausted by their lengthy captivity, emaciated from the burning summer heat, and listless from their sedentary inactivity, were attacked by a sudden epidemic and had their numbers reduced almost to nothing. You could see the animal wreckage of their moribund carcases lying scattered in most of the streets. Then the common people, who are forced by ignorant poverty

[1] Some sort of movable stage-machinery is being described, but the exact interpretation is very uncertain.

peries sine dilectu[1] ciborum tenuato ventri cogit sordentia supplementa et dapes gratuitas conquirere, passim iacentes epulas accurrunt. Tunc e re nata subtile consilium ego et iste Babulus[2] tale comminiscimur. Unam, quae ceteris sarcina corporis praevalebat, quasi cibo parandam portamus ad nostrum receptaculum, eiusque probe nudatum carnibus corium, servatis sollerter totis unguibus, ipso etiam bestiae capite adusque confinium cervicis solido relicto, tergus omne rasura studiosa tenuamus et minuto cinere perspersum soli siccandum tradimus. Ac dum caelestis vaporis flammis examurgatur, nos interdum pulpis eius valenter saginantes sic instanti militiae disponimus sacramentum, ut unus e numero nostro, non qui corporis adeo, sed animi robore ceteris antistaret, atque is in primis voluntarius, pelle illa contectus ursae subiret effigiem, domumque Democharis illatus per opportuna noctis silentia nobis ianuae faciles praestaret aditus.

15 "Nec paucos fortissimi collegii sollers species ad munus obeundum arrexerat. Quorum prae ceteris Thrasyleon factionis optione delectus ancipitis machinae subivit aleam, iamque habili corio et

[1] F *delictu.*

[2] Bursian's *Eubulus* "Good Adviser" is an attractive conjecture.

---

[1] If correct, his name means "Babbler"; but see textual note.

[2] His name means "bold lion."

with no taste in their choice of food to seek the filthiest supplements and free meals for their shrunken bellies, came running up to these banquets lying strewn about. Taking advantage of the situation, Babulus[1] here and I devised an ingenious scheme. We picked the bear with the greatest bulk of body and carried it off to our hideout, as if we were going to prepare it for eating. There we neatly stripped the meat from the hide, taking care to preserve all the claws. We also left the beast's head intact all the way down to where it joins the neck. Then by hard scraping we thinned down the entire skin, sprinkled it with fine ashes, and laid it in the sun to dry out. While it was being dehydrated by the flames of celestial heat, we stuffed ourselves valiantly with its flesh and assigned duties for the ensuing campaign as follows: one of our company, who should outrank his fellows in courage even more than in physical strength, and above all be a volunteer, was to conceal himself in that skin and take on the likeness of a bear; after he had been brought into Demochares' house, he was to take advantage of the still of night and provide us with an easy entrance through the door.

15 "This clever disguise prompted several of our courageous company to volunteer for the post. By the troop's choice Thrasyleon[2] was selected over the others and undertook the hazard of this dangerous stratagem. With cheerful demeanour he hid himself inside the skin, now fitting easily with flexible soft-

mollitie tractabili vultu sereno sese recondit. Tunc tenui sarcimine summas oras eius adaequamus, et iuncturae rimam, licet gracilem, setae circumfluentis densitate saepimus. Ad ipsum confinium gulae, qua cervix bestiae fuerat exsecta, Thrasyleonis caput subire cogimus, parvisque respiratui circa nares et oculos datis foraminibus, fortissimum socium nostrum prorsus bestiam factum immittimus caveae modico praedestinatae[1] pretio, quam constanti vigore festinus irrepsit ipse.

"Ad hunc modum prioribus incohatis sic ad[2] reli-
16 qua fallaciae pergimus. Sciscitati nomen cuiusdam Nicanoris, qui genere Thracio proditus ius amicitiae summum cum illo Demochare colebat, litteras affingimus, ut venationis suae primitias bonus amicus videretur ornando muneri dedicasse. Iamque provecta vespera abusi praesidio tenebrarum, Thrasyleonis caveam Demochari cum litteris illis adulterinis offerimus. Qui miratus bestiae magnitudinem suique contubernalis opportuna liberalitate laetatus, iubet nobis protinus gaudii sui gerulis, ut ipse habebat,[3] decem aureos e suis loculis

[1] Should perhaps be emended to either *praestinatae* or *destinatae*.

[2] F omits *ad*.

[3] *ut ipse habebat* occurs in F after *aureos*, where it yields no sense. If the phrase is correctly transmitted, it probably means "as he thought", "or so he, at any rate, thought", and it should be transposed to a context it will fit. The text adopted here is possible, although hardly to be regarded with great confidence.

ness. Then we joined the edges smoothly with a fine stitch and, although the gap was tiny, we covered the seam with the thick-flowing hair around it. We forced Thrasyleon's head right up to the edge of the beast's throat through the hollowed-out neck, gave him some small holes around his nose and eyes for breathing, and put our dauntless comrade—totally turned beast—in a cage, which we had purchased beforehand fairly cheap. With resolute vigour he eagerly ambled into it unaided.

"Having thus begun the preliminaries, we pro-
16 ceeded to the remainder of our ruse. We found out the name of a certain Nicanor,[1] a man of Thracian origin who cultivated the very closest bonds of friendship with Demochares. We forged a letter to make it appear that he, as a good friend, had dedicated the first fruits of his hunt to embellish the show. Then, late in the evening, taking advantage of the protection of darkness, we presented Thrasyleon's cage to Democharles along with the counterfeit letter. He was so amazed at the size of the beast and delighted by the timely generosity of his comrade that he immediately had ten gold pieces counted out of his strongbox for us, the bearers of

[1] His name means "man of victory."

annumerari. Tunc, ut novitas consuevit ad repentinas visiones animos hominum pellere, multi numero mirabundi bestiam confluebant, quorum satis callenter curiosos aspectus Thrasyleon noster impetu minaci frequenter inhibebat. Consonaque civium voce satis felix ac beatus Demochares ille saepe celebratus, quod post tantam cladem ferarum novo proventu quoquo modo Fortunae resisteret, iubet novalibus suis confestim bestiam ire, iubet[1] summa cum diligentia reportari.

17 "Sed suscipiens ego, 'Caveas,' inquam 'domine, flagrantia solis et itineris spatio fatigatam coetui multarum et, ut audio, non recte valentium committere ferarum. Quin potius domus tuae patulum ac perflabilem locum, immo et lacu aliquo conterminum refrigerantemque prospicis? An ignoras hoc genus bestiae lucos consitos et specus roridos et fontes amoenos semper incubare?'

"Talibus monitis Demochares perterritus numerumque perditorum[2] secum recensens non difficulter assensus, ut ex arbitrio nostro caveam locaremus facile permisit. 'Sed et nos' inquam 'ipsi parati sumus hic ibidem pro cavea ista excubare noctes, ut aestus et vexationis incommodo bestiae

[1] Most editors delete *ire* and the second *iubet*.

[2] Usually emended to *perditarum* "lost bears".

his happiness, as he thought. Then, since a novelty always arouses men's desires to see it at once, a great throng came streaming up to admire the beast. But our Thrasyleon quite shrewdly hindered their inquisitive stares with repeated menacing attacks. By the unanimous voice of the citizenry Demochares was more than once pronounced very lucky and blessed because, after so great a disaster to his animals, with this new arrival he had somehow managed to thwart Fortune. He ordered the animal to go at once to his park, and he ordered the greatest precaution to be taken in its removal.

17 "But I intervened. 'Be careful, sir,' I said, 'not to take a bear who is tired from the hot sun and a long journey and entrust it to the company of a lot of other animals who are not, as I have heard, in the best of health. Instead why not look around your house for an open, well-ventilated area? Better yet a place next to some pool, which would be cooling. Or don't you know that this type of beast always has its lair in thick groves and moist caves and near pleasant springs?'

"Frightened by this warning and mentally calculating the number of his losses, he had no difficulty in agreeing and readily permitted us to position the cage where we thought best. 'You know,' I offered, 'we are quite willing to camp out right here in front of the cage at night. The animal is worn out from the inconvenience of the heat and movement of the journey, and we shall see that he is given the food

fatigatae et cibum tempestivum et potum solitum accuratius offeramus.'

"'Nihil indigemus labore isto vestro' respondit ille. 'Iam paene tota familia per diutinam consuetudinem nutriendis ursis exercitata est.'

18 "Post haec valefacto discessimus, et portam civitatis egressi monumentum quoddam conspicamur procul a via remoto et abdito loco positum. Ibi capulos carie et vetustate semitectos, quis inhabitabant pulverei et iam cinerosi mortui, passim ad futurae praedae receptacula reseramus. Et ex disciplina sectae servato noctis illunio tempore, quo somnus obvius impetu primo corda mortalium validius invadit ac premit, cohortem nostram gladiis armatam ante ipsas fores Democharis velut expilationis vadimonium sistimus. Nec setius Thrasyleon examussim capto noctis latrocinali momento prorepit cavea, statimque custodes, qui propter sopiti quiescebant, omnes ad unum, mox etiam ianitorem ipsum gladio conficit; clavique subtracta fores ianuae repandit, nobisque prompte convolantibus et domus alveo receptis demonstrat horreum ubi vespera sagaciter argentum copiosum recondi viderat. Quo protinus perfracto confertae manus violentia, iubeo singulos commilitonum asportare quantum quisque poterat auri vel argenti, et in illis

and drink he is accustomed to at exactly the right time.'

"'There is no need for you to take that trouble,' he answered. 'By now nearly all my staff have had plenty of practice in feeding bears.'

18 "After that we said farewell and left. We walked outside the town gate and sighted a tomb located in a remote and hidden spot far from the road. The coffins where the dusty and now ashen dead resided were half covered with decay and age, and we opened up several at random to serve as storage bins for our expected loot. Then, following the rules of our profession, we watched for that moonless time of night when sleep comes strongest with its first attack to invade and subdue mortal hearts. It was then that we stationed our cohort, armed with swords, before the very doors of Demochares' house, as a guarantee of our intention to plunder it. Thrasyleon with equal precision picked the robber's moment of the night, crawled out of his cage, immediately used a sword to do away with the guards, who lay asleep nearby, to the last man, and then killed the doorkeeper, from whom he lifted the key and opened the doors of the gate. We promptly rushed in and were received into the interior of the house. There he pointed out the storeroom where he had keenly observed a great quantity of silver being stored that evening. We broke into it at once, using the force of a packed formation. I ordered each of my fellow-soldiers to carry off as much gold and

aedibus fidelissimorum mortuorum occultare propere, rursumque concito gradu recurrentes sarcinas iterare. Quod enim ex usu foret omnium, me solum resistentem pro domus limine cuncta rerum exploraturum sollicite, dum redirent. Nam et facies ursae mediis aedibus discurrentis ad proterrendos, siqui de familia forte vigilassent, videbatur opportuna. Quis enim, quamvis fortis et intrepidus, immani forma tantae bestiae noctu praesertim visitata, non se ad fugam statim concitaret, non obdito cellae pessulo pavens et trepidus sese cohiberet?

19 "His omnibus salubri consilio recte dispositis occurrit scaevus Eventus. Namque dum reduces socios nostros suspensus opperior, quidam servulus strepitu[1] scilicet divinitus inquietus proserpit leniter, visaque bestia, quae libere discurrens totis aedibus commeabat, premens obnixum silentium vestigium suum replicat et utcumque cunctis in domo visa pronuntiat. Nec mora cum numerosae familiae frequentia domus tota completur. Taedis, lucernis, cereis, sebaciis, et ceteris nocturni luminis instrumentis clarescunt tenebrae. Nec inermis quisquam de tanta copia processit, sed singuli fustibus, lanceis, destrictis denique gladiis armati muniunt aditus. Nec secus[2] canes etiam venaticos

[1] F *servulum strepitus.*

[2] Or the comparative *setius*, for F's *sedus.*

silver as he could and hide it hastily in those houses of the dead—the most trustworthy guardians—and then come running back again at the double for a second load. For everyone's benefit I would wait alone in front of the entrance and keep a careful lookout on all sides until they returned. Likewise the figure of a bear running around in the middle of the yard seemed a good idea, to frighten off any members of the household who might have awakened. Who, no matter how strong and fearless, on seeing the monstrous shape of such a huge animal, especially at night, would not take to his heels immediately, slam the bolt of his bedroom door, and stay there quaking and trembling?

19 "Everything had been soundly planned and properly organised, but Bad Luck intervened. While I was anxiously awaiting our comrades' return, one of the slaves, restless from the noise—by divine inspiration, no doubt—crept softly out and saw the animal running loose and wandering all around the yard. In absolute silence he retraced his steps and somehow or other announced what he had seen to everyone in the building. In no time the entire house was filled with a multitude of servants. The darkness was illuminated by torches, lamps, wax tapers, tallow-candles, and every other device for lighting the dark. No one in that large force came forth unarmed, but each held a club or spear or drawn sword as they guarded the approaches. They also called the hunting dogs—the long-eared kind

auritos illos et horricomes ad comprimendam bestiam cohortantur.

20 "Tunc ego sensim, gliscente adhuc illo tumultu, retrogradi fuga domo facesso, sed plane Thrasyleonem mire canibus repugnantem latens pone ianuam ipse prospicio. Quamquam enim vitae metas ultimas obiret, non tamen sui nostrique vel pristinae virtutis oblitus, iam faucibus ipsis hiantis Cerberi reluctabat. Scaenam denique, quam sponte sumpserat, cum anima retinens, nunc fugiens, nunc resistens variis corporis sui schemis ac motibus, tandem domo prolapsus est. Nec tamen, quamvis publica potitus libertate, salutem fuga quaerere potuit. Quippe cuncti canes de proximo angiportu satis feri satisque copiosi venaticis illis, qui commodum domo similiter[1] insequentes processerant, se ommiscent agminatim. Miserum funestumque spectamen aspexi, Thrasyleonem nostrum catervis canum saevientium cinctum atque obsessum multisque numero morsibus laniatum.

"Denique tanti doloris impatiens populi circumfluentis turbelis immisceor et, in quo solo poteram celatum auxilium bono ferre commilitoni, sic indaginis principes dehortabar: 'O grande' inquam 'et extremum flagitium! Magnam et vere pretiosam perdimus bestiam.'

[1] F *civiliter*.

---

[1] See note at III 19.

with bristling hair—and sicked them on the beast to subdue him.

20 "While the uproar was still increasing, I slowly made off from the house in a backward retreat. Hiding behind the door, however, I got a good view of Thrasyleon marvellously defending himself against those dogs. Although he was near the end of life, he never forgot himself or us or his courage of old as he wrestled now against the gaping jaws of Cerberus[1] himself. As long as he hung on to life, he hung on to the role he had volunteered to play. Sometimes retreating, sometimes making a stand, varying the postures and movements of his body, he finally slipped out of the house. But even though he had gained the freedom of the public streets, he could no longer find a safe escape, since all the dogs from the neighboring alley, as fierce as they were numerous, joined formation with the hunting dogs who had also come bounding out of the house in pursuit. I witnessed a pitiable and ghastly spectacle: our Thrasyleon surrounded and besieged by packs of savage dogs, and lacerated by their countless bites.

"Finally I could endure the torment no longer. I mingled with the crowds of people surging around and covertly tried to help a good fellow-soldier in the only way I could, by trying to dissuade the leaders of the hunt. 'Shame!' I cried. 'It's a monstrous crime! We are destroying a large and really expensive animal.'

21 "Nec tamen nostri sermonis artes infelicissimo profuerunt iuveni. Quippe quidam procurrens e domo procerus et validus incunctanter lanceam mediis iniecit ursae praecordiis, nec secus alius; et ecce plurimi, iam timore discusso, certatim gladios etiam de proximo congerunt. Enimvero Thrasyleon, egregium decus nostrae factionis, tandem immortalitate digno illo spiritu expugnato magis quam patientia, neque clamore ac ne ululatu quidem fidem sacramenti prodidit, sed iam morsibus laceratus ferroque laniatus, obnixo mugitu et ferino fremitu praesentem casum generoso vigore tolerans gloriam sibi reservavit, vitam fato reddidit. Tanto tamen terrore tantaque formidine coetum illum turbaverat, ut usque diluculum, immo et in multum diem nemo quisquam fuerit ausus, quamvis iacentem, bestiam vel digito contingere, nisi tandem pigre ac timide quidam lanius paulo fidentior, utero bestiae resecto, ursae magnificum despoliavit latronem. Sic etiam Thrasyleon nobis perivit, sed a gloria non perivit.[1]

"Confestim itaque constrictis sarcinis illis, quas nobis servaverant fideles mortui, Plataeae terminos concito gradu deserentes, istud apud nostros animos identidem reputabamus: merito nullam fidem in

[1] Or Apuleius may have written the future, *peribit.* Interchange of *b* and *v* is frequent in F.

21 "But my rhetorical skills were of no help to the poor unfortunate youth: a tall, strong fellow came running out of the house and without a moment's hesitation hurled a spear straight into the bear's midriff. Then another did the same; and suddenly several others, now that their fear was dispelled, were even vying with one another to lay on with swords at close quarters. Thrasyleon's spirit, which deserved immortality, was finally overcome, but not his endurance. That illustrious pride of our band never betrayed his soldier's oath by crying out or even screaming. Though torn by teeth and ripped with steel, he continued to growl and roar like an animal, as he bore his present misfortune with noble constancy. He won eternal glory for himself, although he surrendered his life to Fate. He had thrown that crowd into such a tumult of terror and fright that until dawn—no, even until full daylight—no one dared so much as to touch the beast with his finger, lying still as he was, until finally, gingerly and timidly, a butcher with a little more confidence approached and cut open the animal's belly, stripping the magnificent robber of his bearskin. Thus Thrasyleon too was lost to us, but not lost to the annals of glory.

"Hastily, then, we gathered up those bundles which the trustworthy dead had guarded for us, and, as we were deserting the boundaries of Plataea on the double, we pondered again and again in our minds the following thought: it is with good reason

vita nostra reperiri, quod ad manes iam et mortuos odio perfidiae nostrae demigrarit. Sic onere vecturae simul et asperae[1] viae toti fatigati, tribus comitum desideratis, istas quas videtis praedas adveximus."

22 Post istum sermonis terminum poculis aureis memoriae defunctorum commilitonum vino mero libant. Dehinc canticis quibusdam Marti deo blanditi paululum conquiescunt. Enim nobis anus illa recens hordeum affatim et sine ulla mensura largita est, ut equus quidem meus tanta copia et quidem solus potitus saliares esse cenas crederet. Ego vero, numquam alias hordeo cibatus nisi tunsum minutatim et diutina coquitatione iurulentum semper esset, rimatus[2] angulum, quo panes reliquiae totius multitudinis congestae fuerant, fauces diutina fame saucias et araneantes valenter exerceo.

Et ecce nocte promota latrones expergiti castra commovent, instructique varie, partim gladiis armati, partim[3] in Lemures reformati, concito se gradu proripiunt. Nec me tamen instanter ac for-

[1] Usually emended to *asperitate.*

[2] The end of the previous sentence and the beginning of this one (*saliares . . . rimatus*) are badly maimed in F. Although the meaning is beyond doubt, printed texts differ greatly in detail.

[3] F *armatim.*

that loyalty is nowhere to be found in this life, because she has gone to live among the ghosts now and the dead, out of disgust at our disloyalty. And so, thoroughly wearied by the burden of our luggage and the rough road, and missing three of our comrades, we brought in the booty which you see before you."

22 That was the end of his story. The robbers poured a libation of unmixed wine from golden cups to the memory of their deceased comrades-in-arms, sang some hymns to flatter the god Mars, and then went to sleep for a while. As for us, the old woman gave us generous, immeasurable quantities of fresh barley, so that my horse, at least, having got hold of such abundance all by himself, thought that this must be a feast of the Salian priests.[1] But I had never eaten barley before, unless it had been finely pounded and cooked for a long time to make a porridge, and so I searched around and found the corner where they had piled the bread left over by the whole mob. My jaws were hurting and full of cobwebs from their long starvation, and I proceeded to give them a hard workout.

Then suddenly, well into the night, the robbers woke up and decamped. Variously equipped—some armed with swords and others disguised as goblins—they rushed off at the double. Meanwhile,

[1] A select Roman brotherhood of priests of Mars, whose banquets were notoriously luxurious.

titer manducantem vel somnus imminens impedire potuit. Et quamquam prius, cum essem Lucius, unico vel secundo pane contentus mensa decederem, tunc ventri tam profundo serviens iam ferme tertium qualum rumigabam. Huic me operi attonitum clara lux oppressit.

23 Tandem itaque asinali verecundia ductus, aegerrime tamen digrediens rivulo proximo sitim lenio. Nec mora cum latrones ultra[1] anxii atque solliciti remeant, nullam quidem prorsus sarcinam vel omnino, licet vilem, laciniam ferentes, sed tantum gladiis,[2] totis manibus, immo factionis suae cunctis viribus unicam virginem, filo liberalem et, ut matronatus eius indicabat, summatem regionis,[3] puellam mehercules et asino tali concupiscendam, maerentem et crines cum veste sua lacerantem, advehebant. Eam simul intra speluncam[4] verbisque quae dolebat minora facientes, sic alloquuntur:

"Tu quidem salutis et pudicitiae secura brevem patientiam nostro compendio tribue, quos ad istam sectam paupertatis necessitas adegit. Parentes autem tui de tanto suarum divitiarum cumulo, quamquam satis cupidi, tamen sine mora parabunt

[1] Often emended, sometimes by adding *modum*.

[2] Another *totis* should probably be supplied after *gladiis* (so Lōfstedt), and this has been translated.

[3] F *religionis*.

[4] Most editors emend this phrase to supply a verb.

I kept aggressively and bravely chewing away: even impending sleep could not hinder me. Although previously, when I was Lucius, I would leave the table satisfied after one or perhaps two pieces of bread, I now had such a vast belly to serve that I was already masticating nearly my third basketful. The clear light of dawn caught me still intent upon this task.

23 At long last, moved by an ass's sense of shame but still with considerable reluctance, I walked away and began to slake my thirst in the stream nearby. At this instant the robbers returned, very nervous and preoccupied, carrying not a single piece of baggage, not even a rag, however worthless. With all their swords and all their manpower, indeed with the full strength of their band, the only thing they brought with them was one poor maiden, of refined qualities and, as her ladylike bearing showed, from one of the district's foremost families. She was a very desirable girl, by Hercules, even to an ass like me. She was grieving and tearing her hair and clothes, and as soon as she was inside the cave they tried to lighten her worries by talking to her.

"You need have no fear for your life or your honour," they said. "Just have a little patience with our desire for profit, for we are men whom the constraint of poverty has driven into this profession. Surely your parents, no matter how greedy they are, will not hesitate to pay an appropriate ransom from their great pile of riches, since it is for their own

scilicet idoneam sui sanguinis redemptionem."

24 His et his similibus blateratis nequicquam dolor sedatur puellae—quidni?—quae inter genua sua deposito capite sine modo flebat. At illi intro vocatae anui praecipiunt assidens eam blando quantum posset solaretur alloquio, seque ad sectae sueta conferunt. Nec tamen puella quivit ullis aniculae sermonibus ab inceptis fletibus avocari, sed altius eiulans sese et assiduis singultibus ilia quatiens mihi etiam lacrimas excussit.

Ac sic "An ego" inquit "misera tali domo, tanta familia, tam caris vernulis, tam sanctis parentibus desolata, et infelicis rapinae praeda et mancipium effecta, inque isto saxeo carcere serviliter clausa, et omnibus deliciis quis innata atque innutrita sum privata, sub incerta salutis et carnificinae laniena[1] inter tot ac tales latrones et horrendum gladiatorum populum vel fletum desinere vel omnino vivere potero?"

Lamentata sic et animi dolore et faucium tendore[2] et corporis lassitudine iam fatigata, mar-
25 centes oculos demisit ad soporem. At[3] commodum coniverat, nec diu cum repente lymphatico ritu somno recussa longeque[4] vehementius afflictare

[1] Although the phrase *sub ... laniena* may seem strained, the various emendations proposed are no less so.

[2] Or *tundore* "beating." Neither word is otherwise attested. [3] F *an.*

[4] Editors unwilling to interpret *recussa* as a finite verb without the copula have proposed various emendations.

flesh and blood."

24 The girl's grief was not at all soothed by this sort of blathering—how could it be? She kept her head down between her knees and wept uncontrollably. So they called the old woman inside and instructed her to sit down beside the girl and console her as best she could with soothing words, while they carried on with their customary professional activities. The girl, however, could not be dissuaded from her tears by anything the old woman said. She only bewailed her fate all the louder and her sides heaved with incessant sobs, to the point that she even forced tears out of me.

"Poor me," she cried, "torn from a wonderful home, my big household, my dear dear servants, and my honourable parents; a piece of booty from an unfortunate robbery, turned into a slave and locked up like a slave in this rocky prison, and deprived of all the pleasures I was born and raised to; tortured by uncertainty whether I will live or be butchered in the midst of all these terrible robbers and this horrible gang of gladiators—how can I either stop crying or even go on living at all?"

So ran her lamentation. Then, tired out by the pain in her heart and the strain on her throat and the fatigue in her body, she let fall her drooping eyes
25 in sleep. But she had just shut her eyes for a few moments when suddenly, like a woman possessed, she started up from sleep and began to torment herself much more violently, beating her breast with

sese et pectus etiam palmis infestis tundere et faciem illam luculentam verberare incipit. Et aniculae quamquam instantissime causas novi et instaurati maeroris requirenti sic assuspirans altius infit: "Em nunc certe, nunc maxime funditus perii, nunc spei salutiferae renuntiavi. Laqueus aut gladius aut certe praecipitium procul dubio capessendum est."

Ad haec anus iratior dicere eam saeviore iam vultu iubebat quid, malum, fleret, vel quid repente postliminio pressae quietis lamentationes licentiosas refricaret. "Nimirum" inquit "tanto compendio tuae redemptionis defraudare iuvenes meos destinas? Quod si pergis ulterius, iam faxo lacrimis istis, quas parvi pendere latrones consuerunt, insuper habitis viva exurare."

26 Tali puella sermone deterrita manuque[1] eius exosculata, "Parce," inquit "mi parens, et durissimo casui meo pietatis humanae memor subsiste paululum. Nec enim, ut reor, aevo longiore maturae tibi in ista sancta canitie miseratio prorsus exaruit. Specta denique scaenam meae calamitatis.

"Speciosus adulescens inter suos principalis, quem filium publicum omnis sibi civitas cooptavit, meus alioquin consobrinus, tantulo triennio maior in aetate, qui mecum primis ab annis nutritus et adultus individuo contubernio domusculae, immo

[1] Usually emended to *manusque* to avoid making *exosculata* passive; but cf. XI 17.

hostile hands, and striking that pretty face of hers. Although the old woman earnestly asked her the reasons for this fresh outburst of grief, she only heaved a deeper sigh and exclaimed, "Oh! Now it is certain. Now I am totally and utterly done for. Now I have lost all hope of rescue. Without a doubt I must take up a noose, or a sword, or at least a suicide leap."

At this the old woman grew quite angry and asked her with a scowl to say what the hell she was crying about and what had suddenly brought her back from a sound sleep and provoked that unrestrained wailing again. "Doubtless," she said, "you intend to cheat my young men of their large profit from your ransom? But if you keep this up any longer, I will see to it that they ignore your tears—robbers do not usually pay much attention to them anyway—and burn you alive."

26 Terrified by her words, the girl kissed the old woman's hands. "Forgive me, dear mother," she begged, "and show some human kindness; help me a little in my harsh misfortune. You have had much experience in your long life and I do not think pity has totally dried up in that honourable grey head of yours. Just listen to the story of my calamity.

"There is a handsome young man, first among his peers, whom the city has unanimously elected their common son. He is my cousin. A bare three years older than I, he was raised and grew up with me from earliest childhood. We were inseparable play-

vero cubiculi torique, sanctae caritatis affectione mutuo mihi pigneratus, votisque nuptialibus pacto iugali pridem destinatus, consensu parentum tabulis etiam maritus nuncupatus, ad nuptias officio frequenti cognatorum et affinium stipatus, templis et aedibus publicis victimas immolabat. Domus tota lauris obsita, taedis lucida, constrepebat hymenaeum. Tunc me gremio suo mater infelix tolerans mundo nuptiali decenter ornabat, mellitisque saviis crebriter ingestis iam spem futuram liberorum votis anxiis propagabat, cum irruptionis subitae gladiatorum impetus ad belli faciem saeviens, nudis et infestis[1] mucronibus coruscans, non caedi, non rapinae manus afferunt, sed denso conglobatoque cuneo cubiculum nostrum invadunt protinus. Nec ullo de familiaribus nostris repugnante ac ne tantillum quidem resistente, miseram,[2] exanimem saevo pavore, trepido de medio matris gremio rapuere. Sic ad instar Attidis vel Protesilai dispectae disturbataeque nuptiae.

27 "Sed ecce saevissimo somnio mihi nunc etiam

[1] F *infertis.*

[2] F *misera.* Other emendations and punctuations have also been proposed.

---

[1] Attis was the youthful consort of the goddess Cybele. According to one version, she prevented his marriage to another by castrating him. Protesilaus was the first

mates in our little house, sharing even bedroom and bed. He was mutually plighted to me through the affection of hallowed love, long since engaged in a marriage contract with promises to wed, and even registered in documents as husband by the parents' consent. In preparation for the wedding he sacrificed victims at the public temple and shrines, accompanied by a ceremonious throng of kinsmen and in-laws. Our whole house was planted with laurels and alight with torches, and was blaring out the wedding hymn. At that time my poor unhappy mother was holding me in her lap and prettily decorating me with wedding finery. She was pressing honey-sweet kisses on my lips, planting now with anxious prayers the hope of children to come, when suddenly a gang of gladiators came bursting in, fierce with the look of war, brandishing their bared and hostile blades. They turned their hands neither to murder nor to plunder, but marched in dense and close-ranked formation straight into our room. No one in our household fought back, or even offered the slightest resistance, as they snatched me, miserable and fainting from cruel fear, right from my mother's trembling arms. Thus our wedding, like that of Attis or Protesilaus,[1] was interrupted and broken up.

27 "But just now the cruelest dream renewed—no,

Greek to lose his life in the Trojan War, having left home immediately after his marriage to Laodamia.

redintegratur, immo vero cumulatur, infortunium meum. Nam visa sum mihi de domo, de thalamo, de cubiculo, de toro denique ipso violenter extracta, per solitudines avias infortunatissimi mariti nomen invocare, eumque, ut primum meis amplexibus viduatus est, adhuc unguentis madidum, coronis floridum, consequi vestigio me pedibus fugientem alienis. Utque clamore percito formosae raptum uxoris conquerens populi testatur auxilium, quidam de latronibus, importunae persecutionis indignatione permotus, saxo grandi pro pedibus arrepto, misellum iuvenem maritum meum percussum interemit. Talis aspectus atrocitate perterrita somno funesto pavens excussa sum."

Tunc fletibus eius assuspirans anus sic incipit: "Bono animo esto, mi erilis, nec vanis somniorum figmentis terreare. Nam praeter quod diurnae quietis imagines falsae perhibentur, tunc etiam nocturnae visiones contrarios eventus nonnumquam pronuntiant. Denique flere et vapulare et nonnumquam iugulari lucrosum prosperumque proventum nuntiant; contra ridere et mellitis dulciolis ventrem saginare vel in voluptatem Veneriam convenire tristitie animi, languore corporis, damnisque ceteris vexatum iri praedicabunt.[1] Sed ego te narrationibus

[1] F *tristitiae animi languori corporis damnique ceteris vel axatum iri praedicabant.* The restoration is far from certain, although the meaning seems clear.

crowned—my misfortune. I saw myself, after I had been dragged violently from my house, my bridal apartment, my room, my very bed, calling my poor luckless husband's name through the trackless wilds. And I saw him, the moment he was widowed of my embraces, still wet with perfumes and garlanded with flowers, following my tracks as I fled on others' feet. As with pitiful cries he lamented his lovely wife's kidnapping and called on the populace for aid, one of the robbers, furious at his annoying pursuit, picked up a huge stone at his feet, struck my unhappy young husband, and killed him. It was this hideous vision that terrified me and shook me out of my deathly sleep."

The old woman heaved a sigh at the girl's tears and began to speak. "Cheer up, my mistress," she said, "and do not be frightened by the empty fictions of dreams. In the first place, the visions which come with naps during the day are said to be false. And furthermore, even dreams at night sometimes predict opposite outcomes. For instance, weeping and being beaten and occasionally having your throat cut announce some lucrative and profitable outcome. Conversely, laughing and stuffing the belly with honey-sweet pastries or joining in Venus' pleasure will foretell that one is going to be harassed by mental depression and physical weakness and every other sort of loss. But right now I

lepidis anilibusque fabulis protinus avocabo." Et incipit:

28 "Erant in quadam civitate rex et regina. Hi tres numero filias forma conspicuas habuere. Sed maiores quidem natu, quamvis gratissima specie, idonee tamen celebrari posse laudibus humanis credebantur. At vero puellae iunioris tam praecipua, tam praeclara pulchritudo nec exprimi ac ne sufficienter quidem laudari sermonis humani penuria poterat. Multi denique civium et advenae copiosi, quos eximii spectaculi rumor studiosa celebritate congregabat, inaccessae formositatis admiratione stupidi et admoventes oribus suis dexteram, primore digito in erectum pollicem residente,[1] ut ipsam prorsus deam Venerem venerabantur[2] religiosis adorationibus. Iamque proximas civitates et attiguas regiones fama pervaserat deam quam caerulum profundum pelagi peperit et ros spumantium fluctuum educavit iam numinis sui passim tributa venia in mediis conversari populi coetibus, vel certe rursum novo caelestium stillarum germine non maria, sed terras, Venerem

[1] F *residentem. eam* should perhaps be supplied before *ut.*

[2] F has no verb. Most editors prefer to insert *venerabantur* somewhere, but *religiosis adorabant orationibus* has also been suggested.

shall divert you with a pretty story and an old wife's tale." And she began.

28 "Once upon a time in a certain city there lived a king and queen. They had three daughters of remarkable beauty. Yet the older two, although of very pleasing appearance, could still, it was thought, be worthily celebrated with mortal praise. But the youngest girl's beauty was so dazzling and glorious that it could not be described nor even adequately praised for the sheer poverty of human speech. Many citizens, as well as multitudes of visitors, whom the rumour of an extraordinary spectacle was attracting in eager throngs, were dumbfounded in their wonderment at her unapproachable loveliness and would move their right hands to their lips, forefinger resting upon outstretched thumb,[1] and venerate her with pious prayers as if she were the very goddess Venus herself. Soon the report had spread through nearby cities and neighbouring lands that the goddess born of the blue depths of the sea and brought forth of the spray of the foaming waves was now distributing her deity's grace far and wide and mingling amid human gatherings; or, if that was not so, that in a new germination of skyborn drops, not the ocean[2] but the earth had sprouted another Venus, this one endowed with the

[1] A common gesture of admiration.

[2] The name of Venus' Greek counterpart, Aphrodite, was believed to derive from *aphros* "foam."

aliam virginali flore praeditam pullulasse.

29 "Sic immensum procedit in dies opinio; sic insulas iam proximas et terrae plusculum provinciasque plurimas fama porrecta pervagatur. Iam multi mortalium longis itineribus atque altissimis maris meatibus ad saeculi specimen gloriosum confluebant. Paphon nemo, Cnidon nemo, ac ne ipsa quidem Cythera ad conspectum deae Veneris navigabant. Sacra differuntur,[1] templa deformantur,[2] pulvinaria perteruntur,[3] caerimoniae negleguntur; incoronata simulacra et arae viduae frigido cinere foedatae. Puellae supplicatur et in humanis vultibus deae tantae numina placantur; et in matutino progressu virginis victimis et epulis Veneris absentis nomen propitiatur; iamque per plateas commeantem populi frequenter floribus sertis et solutis apprecantur.

"Haec honorum caelestium ad puellae mortalis cultum immodica translatio verae Veneris vehementer incendit animos, et impatiens indignationis capite quassanti fremens altius sic secum disserit:

30 "'En rerum naturae prisca parens, en elementorum origo initialis, en orbis totius alma Venus,

[1] F *die praeferuntur.* Editors have offered many different variations with approximately the same meaning.

[2] F *deformant.*

[3] F *perferuntur.* Other suggestions include *proteruntur*, *proferuntur* ("postponed" or "carried out of the shrine"), and *perforantur* ("perforated").

bloom of virginity.

29 "Day by day the story spread by leaps and bounds, and her fame stretched out and ranged through the nearby islands and much of the mainland and most of the provinces. Many mortals travelled far by land and journeyed over the deep seas, flocking together to see the famous sight of the age. No one sailed to Paphos or Cnidos or even Cythera[1] to behold the goddess Venus. Her rites were postponed, her temples fell into disrepair, her cushions were trodden under foot, her ceremonies neglected, her statues ungarlanded, and her abandoned altars marred by cold ashes. It was the girl that people worshipped: they sought to appease the mighty goddess's power in a human face. When the maiden walked out in the morning, people would invoke the name of the absent Venus with feast and sacrifice, and when she walked through the streets, crowds would worship her with garlands and flowers.

"This extravagant transfer of heavenly honours to the cult of a mortal girl inflamed the real Venus to violent wrath. In uncontrolled indignation she shook her head, gave forth a deep groan, and thus she spoke with herself:

30 "'Look at me, the primal mother of all that exists, the original source of the elements, the bountiful

[1] Sites of the most famous shrines of Venus in antiquity. Paphos is on Cyprus, Cnidos on the coast of Asia Minor, and Cythera an island south of the Peloponnese.

quae cum mortali puella partiario maiestatis honore tractor! Et nomen meum caelo conditum terrenis sordibus profanatur! Nimirum communi numinis piamento vicariae venerationis incertum sustinebo, et imaginem meam circumferet puella moritura. Frustra me pastor ille, cuius iustitiam fidemque magnus comprobavit Iuppiter, ob eximiam speciem tantis praetulit deabus. Sed non adeo gaudens ista, quaecumque est, meos honores usurpaverit[1]: iam faxo huius etiam ipsius illicitae formositatis paeniteat.'[2]

"Et vocat confestim puerum suum pinnatum illum et satis temerarium, qui malis suis moribus contempta disciplina publica, flammis et sagittis armatus, per alienas domos nocte discurrens et omnium matrimonia corrumpens, impune committit tanta flagitia et nihil prorsus boni facit. Hunc, quamquam genuina licentia procacem, verbis quoque insuper stimulat et perducit ad illam civitatem et Psychen—hoc enim nomine puella nuncupabatur—coram ostendit. Et tota illa perlata de formositatis aemulatione fabula, gemens ac fremens

[1] F *usurpavit.*
[2] *eam* is usually added somewhere in this sentence.

---

[1] Perhaps a reference to Lucretius I 2.
[2] Paris.
[3] His Latin name is either Cupido or Amor, his Greek name Eros; all are also common nouns meaning "erotic passion" or "desire".

mother of the whole world,[1] driven to divide my majesty's honors with a mortal girl! My name, which is founded in heaven, is being profaned with earthly pollution. Am I to endure the uncertain position of vicarious veneration by sharing our deity's worship, and is a girl subject to death to walk around bearing my likeness? So it meant nothing when that shepherd,[2] whose justice and trustworthiness were confirmed by great Jupiter, preferred me for my surpassing beauty to such mighty goddesses. But, whoever she is, she will certainly get no joy out of having usurped my honours: I will soon make her regret that illegitimate beauty of hers!'

"She quickly sent for her son, that winged and headstrong boy who, with his bad character and his disdain for law and order, goes running about at night through other folk's houses armed with flames and arrows, ruining everyone's marriages, and commits the most shameful acts with impunity and accomplishes absolutely no good.[3] Even though he was naturally unrestrained and impudent, Venus verbally goaded him on even further. She took him to that city and showed him Psyche[4] in person—that was the girl's name—and related the whole tale of her rival's loveliness, moaning and groaning

[4] Greek for "soul". The Latin word is *anima*, and the story which follows is full of word-play on the names of the two principal characters, Psyche and Cupid.

31 indignatione, 'Per ego te' inquit 'maternae caritatis foedera deprecor, per tuae sagittae dulcia vulnera, per flammae istius mellitas uredines, vindictam tuae parenti sed plenam tribue, et in pulchritudinem contumacem severiter[1] vindica; idque unum et pro omnibus unicum volens effice: virgo ista amore flagrantissimo teneatur hominis extremi, quem et dignitatis et patrimonii simul et incolumitatis ipsius Fortuna damnavit, tamque infimi,[2] ut per totum orbem non inveniat miseriae suae comparem.'

"Sic effata et osculis hiantibus filium diu ac pressule saviata, proximas oras reflui litoris petit, plantisque roseis vibrantium fluctuum summo rore calcato, ecce iam profundi[3] maris sudo resedit vertice. Et ipsum quod incipit velle et statim,[4] quasi pridem praeceperit—non moratur marinum obsequium. Adsunt Nerei filiae chorum canentes, et Portunus caerulis barbis hispidus, et gravis piscoso sinu Salacia, et auriga parvulus delphini Palaemon. Iam passim maria persultantes Tritonum catervae: hic concha sonaci leniter bucinat, ille serico tegmine flagrantiae solis obsistit inimici, alius sub oculis dominae speculum progerit, curru biiuges alii subnatant. Talis ad Oceanum pergentem Venerem

[1] F *reverenter.*

[2] F *infirmi.*

[3] Often emended to *profundum*, which is then taken as subject of *resedit.*

[4] The first part of this sentence is frequently and variously emended.

31 with indignation. 'I beseech you,' she said, 'by the bonds of maternal love, by your arrows' sweet wounds, by your flame's honey-sweet scorchings, avenge your mother and avenge her totally, and exact condign punishment from defiant beauty. Accomplish this one act with a good will and it will take care of everything: let that girl be gripped with a violent, flaming passion for the meanest man, a man whom Fortune has condemned to lack rank, wealth, and even health, a man so lowly that he could not find his equal in misery in the whole world.'

"So saying she kissed her son long and intensely with parted lips. Then she sought the nearest beach on the tide-swept shore, stepped out with rosy feet over the topmost foam of the quivering waves, and—lo!—she sat down upon the clear surface of the deep sea. What she began to desire happened at once, as if she had given orders in advance: the instant obeisance of the seas. Nereus' daughters came singing a choral song, and shaggy Portunus with his sea-green beard, and Salacia with her womb teeming with fish, and Palaemon the little dolphin-charioteer. Now troops of Tritons bounded helter-skelter through the sea-water: one blew gently on a tuneful conch shell; another shielded her from the hostile sun's blaze with a silken awning; another carried a mirror before his mistress's eyes; others swam along yoked in pairs to the chariot. Such was the army escorting Venus as she moved

comitatur exercitus.

32 "Interea Psyche cum sua sibi perspicua pulchritudine nullum decoris sui fructum percipit. Spectatur ab omnibus, laudatur ab omnibus, nec quisquam, non rex, non regius, nec de plebe saltem cupiens eius nuptiarum petitor accedit. Mirantur quidem divinam speciem, sed ut simulacrum fabre politum mirantur omnes. Olim duae maiores sorores, quarum temperatam formositatem nulli diffamarant populi, procis regibus desponsae iam beatas nuptias adeptae. Sed Psyche virgo vidua domi residens deflet desertam suam solitudinem, aegra corporis, animi saucia,[1] et quamvis gentibus totis complacitam odit in se suam formositatem. Sic infortunatissimae filiae miserrimus pater, suspectatis caelestibus odiis et irae superum metuens, dei Milesii vetustissimum percontatur oraculum, et a[2] tanto numine precibus et victimis ingratae virgini petit nuptias et maritum. Sed Apollo, quamquam Graecus et Ionicus, propter Milesiae conditorem sic Latina sorte respondit:

[1] F *animis audacia.*

[2] F has no preposition. Some larger change may well be preferable, e.g. inserting *venerato* after *victimis.*

out toward Ocean.

32 "Meanwhile Psyche, for all her manifest beauty, reaped no profit from her charms. Everyone gazed at her, everyone praised her, but no one, neither king nor prince nor even commoner, desired to marry her and came to seek her hand. They admired her heavenly beauty, of course, but as people admire an exquisitely finished statue. Long ago her two older sisters, whose more moderate beauty had not been broadcast throughout the world, had been engaged to royal suitors and had already made fine marriages. But Psyche stayed at home, a husbandless virgin, weeping over her forlorn loneliness, sick in body and wounded in heart. She hated in herself that beauty of hers which the world found so pleasing.

"The unfortunate girl's wretched father, suspecting divine hostility and fearing the gods' anger, consulted the ancient oracle of the Milesian god.[1] With prayers and sacrifice he asked the powerful deity for a marriage and a husband for the slighted maiden. Apollo, although a Greek and an Ionic Greek at that, answered with an oracle in Latin to show favour to the author of this Milesian tale.[2]

[1] At Didyma near Miletus.

[2] I.e. Apuleius.

33 "'Montis in excelsi scopulo, rex, siste[1] puellam
ornatam mundo funerei thalami.
Nec speres generum mortali stirpe creatum,
sed saevum atque ferum vipereumque malum,
quod pinnis volitans super aethera cuncta fatigat,
flammaque et ferro singula debilitat,
quod tremit ipse Iovis, quo numina terrificantur
fluminaque horrescunt et Stygiae tenebrae.'

"Rex olim beatus, affatu sanctae vaticinationis accepto, piger[2] tristisque retro domum pergit, suaeque coniugi praecepta sortis enodat infaustae. Maeretur, fletur, lamentatur diebus plusculis. Sed dirae sortis iam urget taeter effectus. Iam feralium nuptiarum miserrimae virgini choragium struitur, iam taedae lumen atrae fuliginis cinere marcescit; et sonus tibiae zygiae mutatur in querulum Ludii modum, cantusque laetus hymenaei lugubri finitur ululatu; et puella nuptura deterget lacrimas ipso suo flammeo. Sic affectae domus triste fatum cuncta etiam civitas congemebat, luctuque publico confestim congruens edicitur iustitium.

34 "Sed monitis caelestibus parendi necessitas misellam Psychen ad destinatam poenam efflagitabat. Perfectis igitur feralis thalami cum summo maerore sollemnibus, toto prosequente

[1] The letters between *scopulo* and *siste* in F are obscured by a later correction. *rex* is likely but not certain.

[2] Or *pigens*.

33 "'Set out thy daughter, king, on a lofty mountain crag,
Decked out in finery for a funereal wedding.
Hope not for a son-in-law born of mortal stock,
But a cruel and wild and snaky monster,
That flies on wings above the ether and vexes all,
And harries the world with fire and sword,
Makes Jove himself quake and the gods tremble,
And rivers shudder and the shades of Styx.'

"The king, once a fortunate man, upon hearing the holy prophecy's pronouncement returned home slowly and sorrowfully, and unravelled for his wife the ill-omened oracle's instructions. For several days they moaned and wept and wailed. But soon the hideous execution of this dreadful lot approached. Now the scene was set for the wretched maiden's funereal wedding. Now the light of the wedding torch grew dim with black, sooty ashes. Now the tune of the conjugal flute changed into the plaintive Lydian mode and the happy song of the marriage-hymn ended in a mournful wail. The bride-to-be was wiping tears away with her own flame-red bridal veil. The whole city joined in grief over the harsh fate of the afflicted house, and business was at once suspended as an appropriate show of public mourning.

34 "But the obligation to obey the divine injunction demanded poor Psyche for her appointed punishment. Therefore, the ceremonial preparations for this funereal marriage were completed in utmost

populo vivum producitur funus, et lacrimosa Psyche comitatur non nuptias sed exsequias suas. Ac dum maesti parentes et tanto malo perciti nefarium facinus perficere cunctantur, ipsa illa filia talibus eos adhortatur vocibus:

"'Quid infelicem senectam fletu diutino cruciatis? Quid spiritum vestrum, qui magis meus est, crebris eiulatibus fatigatis? Quid lacrimis inefficacibus ora mihi veneranda foedatis? Quid laceratis in vestris oculis mea lumina? Quid canitiem scinditis? Quid pectora, quid ubera sancta tunditis? haec erunt vobis egregiae formositatis meae praeclara praemia. Invidiae nefariae letali plaga percussi sero sentitis. Cum gentes et populi celebrarent nos divinis honoribus, cum novam me Venerem ore consono nuncuparent, tunc dolere, tunc flere, tunc me iam quasi peremptam lugere debuistis. Iam sentio, iam video solo me nomine Veneris perisse. Ducite me et cui sors addixit scopulo sistite. Festino felices istas nuptias obire, festino generosum illum maritum meum videre. Quid differo, quid detrecto venientem, qui totius orbis exitio natus est?'

grief, the living corpse was led from the house accompanied by the entire populace, and a tearful Psyche marched along, not in her wedding procession but in her own funeral cortège. Her parents, dejected and overwrought by this great misfortune, hesitated to perform the heinous deed, but their daughter herself urged them on.

"'Why,' she asked, 'are you torturing your unhappy old age with prolonged weeping? Why are you exhausting your life's breath—really my own—with constant wailing? Why are you marring with useless tears those features that I revere? Why do you wound my eyes in wounding your own? Why are you tearing your grey hair? Why are you beating your bosoms and the breasts that fed me? Are these sufferings to be your glorious reward for my outstanding beauty? Too late you realise that the blow which destroys you is dealt by wicked Envy. When countries and peoples were giving me divine honours, when with a single voice they were all calling me a new Venus, that is when you should have grieved, that is when you should have wept, that is when you should have mourned me as if I were already dead. Now I understand. Now I see that it is Venus' name alone that has destroyed me. Take me and put me on the cliff appointed by the oracle. I hasten to enter into this happy marriage, I hasten to see this high-born husband of mine. Why should I postpone and shun the coming of him who was born for the whole world's ruin?'

35 "Sic profata virgo conticuit ingressuque iam valido pompae populi prosequentis sese miscuit. Itur ad constitutum scopulum montis ardui, cuius in summo cacumine statutam puellam cuncti deserunt, taedasque nuptiales quibus praeluxerant ibidem lacrimis suis exstinctas relinquentes, deiectis capitibus domuitionem parant. Et miseri quidem parentes eius tanta clade defessi, clausae domus abstrusi tenebris, perpetuae nocti sese dedidere.

"Psychen autem, paventem ac trepidam et in ipso scopuli vertice deflentem, mitis aura molliter spirantis Zephyri vibratis hinc inde laciniis et reflato sinu sensim levatam suo tranquillo spiritu vehens paulatim per devexa rupis excelsae, vallis subditae florentis caespitis gremio leniter delapsam reclinat.

35 "After this pronouncement the maiden fell silent, and with firm step joined the procession of escorting citizens. They came to the appointed crag of the steep mountain and placed the girl, as decreed, on its very summit, where they abandoned her one and all. The bridal torches, with which they had lighted the way, now extinguished by their tears, they left behind; and with heads bent low they began their homeward journey. Her unhappy parents, shattered by this great catastrophe, shut themselves up in the darkness of their house, resigning themselves to perpetual night.

"Psyche, meanwhile, frightened, trembling and weeping at the very top of the cliff, was slowly lifted by a gentle breeze from the softly-blowing Zephyr, which stirred her raiment on this side and on that, and caused her dress to billow. With its tranquil breath it gradually carried her down the slopes of the high cliff, and in the valley deep below laid her tenderly on the lap of the flowery turf.

LIBER V

1 "Psyche teneris et herbosis locis in ipso toro roscidi graminis suave recubans, tanta mentis perturbatione sedata, dulce conquievit. Iamque sufficienti recreata somno, placido resurgit animo. Videt lucum proceris et vastis arboribus consitum, videt fontem vitreo latice perlucidum.

"Medio luci meditullio prope fontis allapsum domus regia est, aedificata non humanis manibus, sed divinis artibus. Iam scies ab introitu primo dei cuiuspiam luculentum et amoenum videre te diversorium. Nam summa laquearia citro et ebore curiose cavata subeunt aureae columnae; parietes omnes argenteo caelamine conteguntur, haediis et id genus pecudibus occurrentibus ob os introeuntium. Mirus prorsum [magnae artis][1] homo, immo semideus vel certe deus, qui magnae artis subtilitate tantum efferavit argentum. Enimvero pavimenta ipsa lapide pretioso caesim deminuto in varia picturae genera discriminantur. Vehementer iterum ac saepius beatos illos qui super gemmas et

[1] The repetition of *magnae artis* here and in the next line is probably a scribal error.

BOOK V

1 "As Psyche lay pleasantly reclining in the soft lawn on her bed of dew-covered grass, her great mental distress was relieved and she fell peacefully asleep. When she had been restored by enough slumber, she arose feeling calm. She saw a grove planted with huge, tall trees; she saw a glistening spring of crystal water.

"At the midmost center of the grove beside the gliding stream is a royal palace, constructed not with human hands but by divine skills. You will know from the moment you enter that you are looking at the resplendent and charming residence of some god. High coffered ceilings, exquisitely carved from citron-wood and ivory, are supported on golden columns. All the walls are covered with silver reliefs, with wild beasts and herds of that kind meeting your gaze as you enter. It was indeed a miraculous man, or rather a demigod or even a god, who used the refinement of great art to make animals out of so much silver. Even the floors are zoned into different sorts of pictures made from precious stones cut in tiny pieces. Truly blessed—twice so and even more—are those who tread upon

monilia calcant! Iam ceterae partes longe lateque dispositae domus sine pretio pretiosae, totique parietes solidati massis aureis splendore proprio coruscant, ut diem suum sibi domus faciat[1] licet sole nolente: sic cubicula, sic porticus, sic ipsae valvae[2] fulgurant. Nec setius opes ceterae maiestati domus respondent, ut equidem illud recte videatur ad conversationem humanam magno Iovi fabricatum caeleste palatium.

2 "Invitata Psyche talium locorum oblectatione propius accessit et paulo fidentior intra limen sese facit. Mox prolectante studio pulcherrimae visionis rimatur singula, et altrinsecus aedium horrea sublimi fabrica perfecta magnisque congesta gazis conspicit. Nec est quicquam quod ibi non est. Sed praeter ceteram tantarum divitiarum admirationem hoc erat praecipue mirificum, quod nullo vinculo, nullo claustro, nullo custode totius orbis thesaurus ille muniebatur. Haec ei summa cum voluptate visenti offert sese vox quaedam corporis sui nuda, et 'Quid,' inquit 'domina, tantis obstupescis opibus? Tua sunt haec omnia. Prohinc cubiculo te refer, et lectulo lassitudinem refove, et ex arbitrio lavacrum pete. Nos, quarum voces accipis,

[1] F *faciant.*
[2] F *valneae.*

gems and jewellery! All the other quarters of the house throughout its length and breadth are likewise precious beyond price, and all the walls are constructed of solid gold masonry and sparkle with their own brilliance, so that the house creates its own daylight even though the sun deny his rays. The rooms, the colonnades, even the doors flash lightning. Every other luxury too is equally matched with the house's magnificence, so that you may quite correctly think it a heavenly palace constructed for great Jupiter's use in his human visitations.

2 "Psyche, attracted by the allurement of this beautiful place, came closer, and as she gained a little more confidence, crossed the threshold. Soon her eagerness to look at such beautiful things drew her on to examine every object, and on the other side of the palace she spotted storerooms built with lofty craftsmanship and heaped high with vast treasures. Nothing exists which is not there. But beyond her wonderment at the enormous quantity of wealth, she found it especially amazing that there was not a single chain or lock or guard protecting this treasure-house of all the world. As she was gazing at all this with rapturous pleasure, a voice without a body came to her. 'Mistress,' it said, 'why are you so astounded at this great wealth? All this belongs to you. So retire to your room and soothe your weariness upon a bed, and when you wish, take a bath. We whose voices you hear are your servants who

tuae famulae sedulo tibi praeministrabimus, nec corporis curatae tibi regales epulae morabuntur.'

3 "Sensit Psyche divinae providentiae beatitudinem, monitusque vocis informis audiens et prius somno et mox lavacro fatigationem sui diluit; visoque statim proximo semirotundo suggestu, propter instrumentum cenatorium rata refectui suo commodum, libens accumbit. Et ilico vini nectarei eduliumque variorum fercula copiosa nullo serviente, sed tantum spiritu quodam impulsa sumministrantur. Nec quemquam tamen illa videre poterat, sed verba tantum audiebat excidentia et solas voces famulas habebat. Post opimas dapes quidam introcessit et cantavit invisus, et alius citharam pulsavit, quae videbatur nec ipsa. Tunc modulatae multitudinis conferta[1] vox aures eius affertur, ut, quamvis hominum nemo pareret, chorus tamen esse pateret.

4 "Finitis voluptatibus, vespera suadente concedit Psyche cubitum. Iamque provecta nocte clemens[2] quidam sonus aures eius accedit. Tunc virginitati suae pro tanta solitudine metuens, et pavet et horrescit et quovis malo plus timet quod ignorat. Iamque aderat ignobilis maritus, et torum inscenderat, et uxorem sibi Psychen fecerat, et ante lucis

[1] *conserta* "blended" is a plausible emendation.

[2] F *demens.*

will wait on you diligently, and when your body is refreshed you shall straightway have a royal feast.'

3 "Psyche felt the blessing of divine Providence, and she obeyed the suggestions of the disembodied voice, washing away her weariness first with sleep and then with a bath. And suddenly she saw near her a raised semicircular platform, and judging from the dinner setting that it was meant for her own refreshment, she promptly reclined there. Instantly trays loaded with nectarous wine and various foods appeared, with no one serving; it was only some breath of air[1] that wafted them and placed them before her. She could see no one, but merely heard words emanating from somewhere; her servants were only voices. After her sumptuous dinner someone unseen came in and sang, and someone else played a lyre, which was invisible too. Then the compact sound of a large melodious group came to her ears; although no human being appeared, it was obviously a choir.

4 "When the pleasures were over, at the evening star's urging Psyche retired to bed. Then, when night was well advanced, a dulcet sound impinged upon her ears. Now being all alone she feared for her virginity. She trembles and shudders, and fears worse than anything the thing she is ignorant of. Now her unknown husband had arrived, had mounted the bed, had made Psyche his wife, and

[1] The Latin *spiritu* might possibly be translated "spirit".

exortum propere discesserat. Statim voces cubiculo praestolatae novam nuptam interfectae virginitatis curant. Haec diutino tempore sic agebantur. Atque, ut est natura redditum, novitas per assiduam consuetudinem delectationem ei commendarat, et sonus vocis incertae solitudinis erat solacium.

"Interea parentes eius indefesso luctu atque maerore consenescebant, latiusque porrecta fama sorores illae maiores cuncta cognorant, propereque maestae atque lugubres deserto lare certatim ad parentum suorum conspectum affatumque perrexerant.

5 "Ea nocte ad suam Psychen sic infit maritus—namque praeter oculos et manibus et auribus nihilominus[1] sentiebatur:

"'Psyche dulcissima et cara uxor, exitiabile tibi periculum minatur Fortuna saevior, quod observandum pressiore cautela censeo. Sorores iam tuae mortis opinione turbatae tuumque vestigium requirentes scopulum istum protinus aderunt. Quarum si quas forte lamentationes acceperis, neque respondeas, immo nec prospicias omnino. Ceterum mihi quidem gravissimum dolorem, tibi vero summum creabis exitium.'

"Annuit et ex arbitrio mariti se facturam spopondit. Sed eo simul cum nocte dilapso diem totum lacrimis ac plangoribus misella consumit, se nunc

[1] F *ius nichil*. I have simply provided a minimal stopgap. None of the dozens of proposed emendations is convincing enough to print.

had quickly departed before the rising of daylight. At once voices-in-waiting in the bedchamber cared for the new bride whose virginity was ended. This happened thus for a long time, and, as nature provides, her new condition through constant habituation won her over to its pleasure, and the sound of a mysterious voice gave comfort to her loneliness.

"In the meantime her parents were growing old in their tireless mourning and grief. The story had spread widely, and when her older sisters learned all that had happened, in sorrow and mourning they hastily deserted their own homes and vied with each other in their rush to see and console their parents.

5 "That very night Psyche's husband spoke to her: though she could not see him, he was none the less sensible both to her hands and to her ears.

"'My dearest Psyche,' he said, 'my darling wife, cruel Fortune is threatening you with a deadly danger, which I advise you to guard against with the utmost caution. Your sisters are now upset by the belief that you are dead, and in searching for some trace of you they will very soon come to that cliff. If you should happen to hear any of their laments, do not answer; no, do not even look in their direction. Otherwise you will cause me the most bitter pain, and yourself utter destruction.'

"She nodded assent and promised to behave as her husband wished. But when he and the night had both slipped away, she spent the whole day miserably weeping and lamenting, saying repeat-

maxime prorsus perisse iterans, quae beati carceris custodia saepta et humanae conversationis colloquio viduata, nec sororibus quidem suis de se maerentibus opem salutarem ferre ac ne videre eas quidem omnino posset. Nec lavacro nec cibo nec ulla denique refectione recreata, flens ubertim decessit
6 ad somnum. Nec mora cum paulo maturius lectum maritus accubans, eamque etiam nunc lacrimantem complexus sic expostulat:

"'Haecine mihi pollicebare, Psyche mea? Quid iam de te tuus maritus exspecto, quid spero? Et perdia et pernox nec inter amplexus coniugales desinis cruciatum. Age iam nunc ut voles, et animo tuo damnosa poscenti pareto! Tantum memineris meae seriae monitionis, cum coeperis sero paenitere.'

"Tunc illa precibus et dum se morituram comminatur extorquet a marito cupitis annuat, ut sorores videat, luctus mulceat, ora conferat. Sic ille novae nuptae precibus veniam tribuit, et insuper quibuscumque vellet eas auri vel monilium donare concessit. Sed identidem monuit ac saepe terruit, ne quando sororum pernicioso consilio suasa de forma mariti quaerat, neve se sacrilega curiositate de tanto fortunarum suggestu pessum deiciat nec

edly that now she really was utterly dead: fenced in by the confinement of her luxurious prison, and bereft of human company and conversation, she could not even help to save her own sisters in their mourning for her; and worse, she could not even see them at all. With neither bath nor food nor any other refreshment to restore her, she retired to sleep
5 weeping profusely. In no time her husband came to bed, a little earlier than usual, and finding her still crying as he took her in his arms, he scolded her.

"'Is this what you promised me, my Psyche?' he asked. 'What am I, your husband, to expect of you now? What am I to hope from you? All day and all night you never stop torturing yourself, even in the midst of love-making. Very well, do as you like and obey your heart's ruinous demands. Only remember my earnest warning, when you begin to repent too late.'

"Then she pleaded with him and threatened to die until she wrenched from her husband his consent to her wishes: to see her sisters, to soothe their grief, and to converse with them. Thus he gave in to his new bride's entreaties, and in addition he permitted her to present them with whatever gold or jewellery she might wish. But he warned her time and again, often with threats, never to yield to her sisters' pernicious advice to investigate her husband's appearance. Otherwise, through her sacrilegious curiosity, she would cast herself down from the exalted height of her fortunes and never after-

suum postea contingat amplexum.

"Gratias egit marito, iamque laetior animo 'Sed prius' inquit 'centies moriar quam tuo isto dulcissimo conubio caream. Amo enim et efflictim te, quicumque es, diligo aeque ut meum spiritum, nec ipsi Cupidini comparo. Sed istud etiam meis precibus, oro, largire, et illi tuo famulo Zephyro praecipe simili vectura sorores hic mihi sistat.' Et imprimens oscula suasoria et ingerens verba mulcentia et inserens[1] membra cogentia[2] haec etiam blanditiis astruit: 'Mi mellite, mi marite, tuae Psychae dulcis anima.' Vi ac potestate Venerii susurrus[3] invitus succubuit maritus et cuncta se facturum spopondit, atque etiam luce proximante de manibus uxoris evanuit.

7 "At illae sorores, percontatae scopulum locumque illum quo fuerat Psyche deserta, festinanter adveniunt, ibique difflebant[4] oculos et plangebant ubera, quoad crebris earum eiulatibus saxa cautesque parilem sonum resultarent. Iamque nomine proprio sororem miseram ciebant, quoad sono penetrabili vocis ululabilis per prona delapso, amens et trepida Psyche procurrit e domo.

[1] F *ingerens.*
[2] Or *cohibentia*, a correction in F.
[3] F *veneris usurus.*
[4] F *deflebant.*

wards enjoy his embrace.

"She thanked her husband and, feeling happier now, said, 'I would rather die a hundred times than be robbed of your sweet caresses. For I love and adore you passionately, whoever you are, as much as my own life's breath, and I would not even compare Cupid[1] himself with you. But please grant me this favour also, I beg you: instruct your servant Zephyr to bring my sisters here to me the same way he carried me. And she began to press persuasive kisses upon him and pile on caressing words and entwine him with her irresistible limbs, adding to her charms expressions like 'My honey-sweet,' 'My husband,' 'Sweet soul of your Psyche.' Her husband reluctantly succumbed to the force and power of her alluring whispers and promised he would do everything. Then as daylight drew near he vanished from his wife's embrace.

7 "Meanwhile her sisters, having ascertained the location of the cliff where Psyche had been abandoned, hurried there and began to weep their eyes out and beat their breasts until the rocks and crags reverberated with the echo of their repeated howls. Then they started summoning their poor sister by her own name until, as the penetrating sound of their wailing voices slipped down over the slopes, Psyche came running out of her house, distraught and trembling.

[1] The first mention of his name in the story.

"Et 'Quid' inquit 'vos miseris lamentationibus necquicquam effligitis? Quam lugetis adsum. Lugubres voces desinite et diutinis lacrimis madentes genas siccate tandem, quippe cum iam possitis quam plangebatis amplecti.'

"Tunc vocatum Zephyrum praecepti maritalis admonet. Nec mora cum ille parens imperio statim clementissimis flatibus innoxia vectura deportat illas. Iam mutuis amplexibus et festinantibus saviis sese perfruuntur, et illae sedatae lacrimae postliminio redeunt prolectante gaudio.

"'Sed et tectum' inquit 'et larem nostrum laetae succedite, et afflictas animas cum Psyche vestra recreate.'

8 "Sic allocuta, summas opes domus aureae vocumque[1] servientium populosam familiam demonstrat auribus earum, lavacroque pulcherrimo et inhumanae mensae lautitiis eas opipare reficit, ut illarum prorsus caelestium divitiarum copiis affluentibus satiatae iam praecordiis penitus nutrirent invidiam. Denique altera earum satis scrupulose curioseque percontari non desinit, quis illarum caelestium

[1] F *locumque.*

"'Why needlessly destroy yourselves,' she cried, 'with pitiful lamentation? I, whom you are mourning, am here. Stop those mournful sounds and at last dry your cheeks soaked so long in tears, for you can now embrace the girl for whom you were grieving.'

"Then she called Zephyr and reminded him of her husband's instructions. Instantly he obeyed the command and immediately, with a harmless ride on the gentlest of breezes, they were carried down to their destination. First the sisters took their delight in mutual embraces and eager kisses, and the tears that had been allayed came back again at joy's urging.

"'But come under our roof,' Psyche said, 'enter our home in happiness, and refresh your troubled souls together with your Psyche.'

8 "After this welcome she pointed out the supreme riches of the golden house[1] and showed their ears the large staff of voices-in-waiting. She refreshed them luxuriously with a beautiful bath and the delicacies of her unearthly table; with the result that, glutted with the abundant plenty of this truly heavenly wealth, they began to nourish envy deep in their hearts. One of them then began to interrogate her minutely and inquisitively without stopping. Who was the owner of these heavenly

[1] Nero's luxurious palace in Rome had also been called the "Golden House" (Suetonius, *Nero* 31).

rerum dominus, quisve vel qualis ipsius sit maritus. Nec tamen Psyche coniugale illud praeceptum ullo pacto temerat vel pectoris arcanis exigit, sed e re nata confingit esse iuvenem quendam et speciosum, commodum lanoso barbitio genas inumbrantem, plerumque rurestribus ac montanis venatibus occupatum. Et ne qua sermonis procedentis labe consilium tacitum proderetur, auro facto gemmosisque monilibus onustas eas statim vocato Zephyro tradit reportandas.

9 "Quo protinus perpetrato, sorores egregiae domum redeuntes iamque gliscentis invidiae felle flagrantes[1] multa secum sermonibus mutuis perstrepebant. Sic denique infit altera:

"'En orba et saeva et iniqua Fortuna! Hocine tibi complacuit, ut utroque parente prognatae[2] diversam sortem sustineremus? Et nos quidem, quae natu maiores sumus, maritis advenis ancillae deditae, extorres et lare et ipsa patria degamus longe parentum velut exulantes, haec autem novissima, quam fetu satiante postremus partus effudit, tantis opibus et deo marito potita sit? Quae nec uti recte tanta bonorum copia novit. Vidisti, soror, quanta in domo iacent et qualia monilia, quae praenitent vestes, quae splendicant gemmae, quantum praeterea pas-

[1] F *fraglantes. Flagro* "burn" and *fragro* (or *fraglo*) "smell" are frequently (and understandably) confused in the manuscripts — and perhaps even by Apuleius.

[2] Usually emended by some addition to emphasise that they are full sisters, e.g. *eodem, germanae.*

objects? Who was her husband? What sort of man was he? But Psyche did not in the least violate her husband's command nor banish it from her heart's secret keeping; but extemporising she pretended that he was a young and handsome man, just beginning the shadow of a downy beard on his cheeks, and that he spent much of his time hunting in the fields and on the mountains. But afraid that, if the conversation continued, with some slip she might betray her counsel of silence, she loaded them with wrought gold and jewelled necklaces, quickly summoned Zephyr, and handed them over to his charge for transport back.

9 "This was accomplished right away. Now returning home those worthy sisters were consumed with the gall of swelling Envy and complained loud and long to each other.

"'O blind, cruel, unjust fortune!' began the one. 'Was that your pleasure, then, for us daughters of the same two parents to suffer such a different lot? Indeed, are we, the older, surrendered as slaves to foreign husbands and banished from home and country too, to live like exiles far from our parents; while she, the youngest, the last product of our mother's weary womb, has acquired all that wealth and a god for a husband? Why, she does not even know how to use all those possessions properly. Did you see, sister, how much jewellery was lying around in her house, and how fine it was? Did you see those shining clothes and sparkling gems, and

sim calcatur aurum? Quodsi maritum etiam tam formosum tenet, ut affirmat, nulla nunc in orbe toto felicior vivit. Fortassis tamen procedente consuetudine et affectione roborata deam quoque illam deus maritus efficiet. Sic est hercules, sic se gerebat ferebatque. Iam iam sursum respicit et deam spirat mulier, quae voces ancillas habet et ventis ipsis imperitat.[1] At ego misera primum patre meo seniorem maritum sortita sum, dein cucurbita calviorem et quovis puero pusilliorem, cunctam domum seris et catenis obditam custodientem.'

10 "Suscipit alia: 'Ego vero maritum articulari etiam morbo complicatum curvatumque ac per hoc rarissimo Venerem meam recolentem sustineo, plerumque detortos et duratos in lapidem digitos eius perfricans, fomentis olidis et pannis sordidis et foetidis cataplasmatibus manus tam delicatas istas adurens, nec uxoris officiosam faciem, sed medicae laboriosam personam sustinens. Et tu quidem, soror, videris quam patienti vel potius servili—dicam enim libere quod sentio—haec perferas animo. Enimvero ego nequeo sustinere ulterius tam beatam fortunam allapsam[2] indignae. Recordare enim quam superbe, quam arroganter nobiscum egerit, et ipsa iactatione immodicae ostentationis

[1] Or *imperat*, a correction in F.

[2] F *conlapsam*; *collatam* is also possible.

all that gold under foot everywhere? And if she has and holds such a handsome husband, as she says, there is not a luckier woman now alive in the whole world. But maybe, as their familiarity continues and their affection increases, her divine husband will make her a goddess too. That's it, by Hercules! That is the way she was acting and behaving. The woman is already looking skywards and aspiring to godhead, the way she has voices for maids and gives orders even to the winds. But look at poor me! In the first place I drew a husband older than my father, and besides he is balder than a pumpkin and punier than any child, and he keeps the whole house locked up with bolts and chains.'

10 "The other sister took over. 'As for me, I have to put up with a husband who is even doubled over and bent with arthritis, and therefore hardly ever pays homage to my Venus. I am forever rubbing his twisted and petrified fingers and burning these delicate hands of mine with smelly fomentations and dirty bandages and stinking poultices. Instead of playing the dutiful part of a wife, I have to endure the laborious role of a doctor. You, sister, may decide for yourself with what attitude of patience and servility—I shall say frankly what I feel—you may tolerate this situation. But as for me, I can no longer endure the fact that so blessed a fortune befell an undeserving girl. Just remember how haughtily, how arrogantly she dealt with us; and how she revealed her swollen pride by the very

tumentem suum prodiderit animum, deque tantis divitiis exigua nobis invita proiecerit, confestimque praesentia nostra gravata propelli et efflari exsibilarique nos iusserit. Nec sum mulier nec omnino spiro, nisi eam pessum de tantis opibus deiecero. Ac si tibi etiam, ut par est, inacuit nostra contumelia, consilium validum requiramus ambae. Iamque ista quae ferimus non parentibus nostris ac nec ulli monstremus alii, immo nec omnino quicquam de eius salute norimus. Sat est quod ipsae vidimus quae vidisse paenituit, nedum[1] ut genitoribus et omnibus populis tam beatum eius differamus praeconium. Nec sunt enim beati quorum divitias nemo novit. Sciet se non ancillas, sed sorores habere maiores. Et nunc quidem concedamus ad maritos, et lares pauperes nostros sed plane sobrios revisamus, diuque cogitationibus pressioribus instructae, ad superbiam poeniendam firmiores redeamus.'

11 "Placet pro bono duabus malis malum consilium. Totisque illis tam pretiosis muneribus absconditis, comam trahentes et proinde ut merebantur ora lacerantes, simulatos redintegrant fletus. Ac sic parentes quoque redulcerato prorsum dolore raptim deterrentes vesania turgidae domus suas contendunt, dolum scelestum, immo vero parricidium, struentes contra sororem insontem.

[1] F *necdum.*

boastfulness of her immoderate display; and how she reluctantly tossed us a few little things from all that treasure; and then, burdened by our presence, she hastily ordered us to be driven out, blown off, and whistled away. I am no woman, I have no breath in me at all, if I do not cast her down from that pile of wealth. And if you too, as you ought, have felt the sting of this insult to us, let us devise some effective plan of action together. Let us not show our parents or anyone else these things that we are bringing back—no, let us not even be aware that she is alive. It is enough that we ourselves saw things that we regretted seeing, let alone that we should proclaim such glorious tidings of her to her parents and to all the world. They are not glorious whose riches nobody knows. She will discover that she does not have maids, but older sisters. And so now let us go back to our husbands and return to our poor but respectable hearths. Then, after we have fortified ourselves with deep deliberation, let us return in greater strength to punish her pride.'

11 "This wicked plan seemed a good idea to the two wicked women. They hid all their costly gifts; then, tearing their hair and scratching their cheeks—precisely as they deserved—began renewing their mock lamentations. Thus they quickly frightened their parents by reopening the wound of their grief too. Then, swollen with madness, they hastened to their own homes to plot some heinous crime—even murder—against their innocent sister.

"Interea Psychen maritus ille, quem nescit, rursum suis illis nocturnis sermonibus sic commonet: 'Videsne quantum tibi periculum? Velitatur Fortuna eminus, ac nisi longe firmiter praecaves, mox comminus congredietur. Perfidae lupulae magnis conatibus nefarias insidias tibi comparant, quarum summa est ut te suadeant meos explorare vultus, quos, ut tibi saepe praedixi, non videbis si videris. Ergo igitur si posthac pessimae illae lamiae noxiis animis armatae venerint—venient autem, scio—neque omnino sermonem conferas; et si id tolerare pro genuina simplicitate proque animi tui teneritudine non potueris, certe de marito nil quicquam vel audias vel respondeas. Nam et familiam nostram iam propagabimus et hic adhuc infantilis uterus gestat nobis infantem alium, si texeris nostra secreta silentio, divinum, si profanaveris, mortalem.'

12 "Nuntio Psyche laeta florebat, et divinae subolis solacio plaudebat, et futuri pignoris gloria gestiebat, et materni nominis dignitate gaudebat. Crescentes dies et menses exeuntes anxia numerat, et sarcinae nesciae rudimento miratur de brevi punctulo tantum incrementulum locupletis uteri.

"Sed iam pestes illae taeterrimaeque Furiae

---

[1] See note at I 19.

"Meanwhile Psyche was again being warned by her unknown husband in his nightly talks with her. 'Do you see how much danger you are in?' he asked. 'Fortune is now firing at long range, and unless you take very strong precautionary measures, she will soon attack at close quarters. Those deceitful bitches are making great efforts to execute a villainous plot against you, the gist of which is to persuade you to examine my face. As I have often told you before, if you see it, you will never see it again. Therefore, if those horrible harpies armed with their pernicious thoughts come again—and they will come, I know—you must not talk to them at all. And if you cannot bear that because of your simple innocence and tenderheartedness, then at least, if they talk about your husband, neither listen nor answer. You see, we are now about to increase our family, and your womb, still a child's, bears another child for us, who will be a god if you guard our secret in silence, but a mortal if you profane it.'

12 "Psyche blossomed with happiness at the news, hailed the comfort of a divine child, exulted in the glory of the baby to be born and rejoiced in the honour of the name of mother. She anxiously counted the growing days and the departing months, and, being a new recruit who knew naught of the pack she bore, she was amazed at such a pretty swelling of her fertile womb from just a tiny pinprick.

"But already those pests and foulest of Furies[1]

anhelantes vipereum virus et festinantes impia celeritate navigabant. Tunc sic iterum momentarius maritus suam Psychen admonet: 'Dies ultima et casus extremus et sexus infestus et sanguis inimicus iam sumpsit arma et castra commovit et aciem direxit et classicum personavit. Iam mucrone destricto iugulum tuum nefariae tuae sorores petunt. Heu quantis urguemur cladibus, Psyche dulcissima! Tui nostrique miserere, religiosaque continentia domum, maritum, teque et istum parvulum nostrum imminentis ruinae infortunio libera. Nec illas scelestas feminas, quas tibi post internecivum odium et calcata sanguinis foedera sorores appellare non licet, vel videas vel audias, cum in morem Sirenum scopulo prominentes funestis vocibus saxa personabunt.'

13 "Suscipit Psyche singultu lacrimoso sermonem incertans: 'Iam dudum, quod sciam, fidei atque parciloquio meo perpendisti documenta, nec eo setius approbabitur tibi nunc etiam firmitas animi mei. Tu modo Zephyro nostro rursum praecipe, fungatur obsequio,[1] et in vicem denegatae sacrosanctae imaginis tuae redde saltem conspectum sororum.

[1] F *obsequia.*

had set sail, breathing viperous poison and hastening with impious speed. Then for a second time her transient husband warned his Psyche. 'The critical day,' he said, 'the ultimate peril, the malice of your sex, and your blood in hatred have now taken arms against you: they have struck camp, are arrayed for battle, and have sounded the charge. Now your wicked sisters have drawn the sword and are attacking your throat. O my sweetest Psyche, what disasters are upon us! Have mercy on yourself and me. By resolute self-restraint free your home, your husband, yourself, and our little one from the catastrophe of ruin which threatens. Those vile women—you cannot call them sisters after their murderous hatred and their trampling on the ties of blood—do not look at them or listen to them when they lean out over the cliff like Sirens[1] and make the rocks resound with their fatal songs.'

13 "Psyche answered, making her words indistinct through her tearful sobbing. 'Some time ago, I think, you assayed proofs of my loyalty and discretion; now too you will no less approve the resolution of my mind. Just give your servant Zephyr his orders again. Let him perform his duty. To compensate for forbidding me a sight of your holy face, at least grant me a look at my sisters. I beg you, by

[1] Half women, half birds, who lured sailors to their death with enchanting songs (cf. Homer, *Odyssey* XII 165–200).

Per istos cinnameos et undique pendulos crines tuos, per teneras et teretes et mei similes genas, per pectus nescio quo calore fervidum, sic in hoc saltem parvulo cognoscam faciem tuam: supplicis anxiae piis precibus erogatus, germani complexus indulge fructum, et tibi devotae dicataeque Psychae animam gaudio recrea. Nec quicquam amplius in tuo vultu requiro. Iam nil officiunt mihi nec ipsae nocturnae tenebrae: teneo te, meum lumen.'

"His verbis et amplexibus mollibus decantatus maritus lacrimasque eius suis crinibus detergens facturum spopondit, et praevertit statim lumen nascentis diei.

14 "Iugum sororium consponsae factionis, ne parentibus quidem visis, recta de navibus scopulum petunt illum praecipiti cum velocitate, nec venti ferentis oppertae praesentiam, licentiosa cum temeritate prosiliunt in altum. Nec immemor Zephyrus regalis edicti, quamvis invitus, susceptas eas gremio spirantis aurae solo reddidit. At illae incunctatae statim conferto vestigio domum penetrant, complexaeque praedam suam sorores nomine mentientes, thesaurumque penitus abditae fraudis vultu laeto tegentes, sic adulant:

"'Psyche, non ita ut pridem parvula, et ipsa iam

those cinnamon-scented curls hanging around your head, by those soft round cheeks so like my own, by your breast so wonderfully aflame with heat: please, as I hope to know your looks at least in my unborn babe's, be conquered by the loving prayers of an anxious suppliant and grant me the enjoyment of a sisterly embrace. Revive with joy the soul of your devout and dedicated Psyche. I shall ask no further about your appearance. Not even the night's darkness hurts me now, because I have you in my arms, my light.'

"Bewitched by her words and soft caresses, her husband dried her tears with his hair and promised assent; and then instantly departed ahead of the light of the newborn day.

14 "Yoked in a conspiratorial faction, the two sisters never stopped to visit their parents but headed straight from the ships to the cliff at breakneck speed. Nor did they await the arrival of a carrying wind, but with unbridled recklessness leapt out into the chasm. Zephyr, mindful of the royal edict, caught them, albeit with reluctance, in the bosom of his airy breeze and deposited them on the ground. With no hesitation they instantly penetrated the house side by side and embraced their prey, falsely calling themselves sisters. Masking the storehouse of their deeply hidden treachery behind cheerful faces, they began to flatter her.

"'O Psyche,' they said, 'you are not the tiny little Psyche you used to be, but you are now yourself a

mater es. Quantum, putas, boni nobis in ista geris perula! Quantis gaudiis totam domum nostram hilarabis! O nos beatas, quas infantis aurei nutrimenta laetabunt! Qui si parentum, ut oportet, pulchritudini responderit, prorsus Cupido nascetur.'

15 "Sic affectione simulata paulatim sororis invadunt animum. Statimque eas, lassitudine viae sedilibus refotas et balnearum vaporosis fontibus curatas, pulcherrime triclinio mirisque illis et beatis edulibus atque tuccetis oblectat. Iubet citharam loqui, psallitur; tibias agere, sonatur; choros canere, cantatur. Quae cuncta nullo praesente dulcissimis modulis animos audientium remulcebant. Nec tamen scelestarum feminarum nequitia vel illa mellita cantus dulcedine mollita conquievit, sed ad destinatam fraudium pedicam sermonem conferentes, dissimulanter occipiunt sciscitari qualis ei maritus et unde natalium, secta cuia[1] proveniret. Tunc illa simplicitate nimia pristini sermonis oblita novum commentum instruit, aitque maritum suum de provincia proxima magnis pecuniis negotiantem iam medium cursum aetatis agere, interspersum rara canitie. Nec in sermone isto tantillum morata,

[1] F *sectacula.*

mother! Think what a good thing for us you are carrying in your purse! With what pleasure you will gladden our whole house! O how lucky we are! How much joy we will have bringing up that golden baby! If he resembles his parents—as he ought to—in beauty, he will be born an absolute Cupid!'

5 "Thus with their pretended affection they gradually invaded their sister's heart. As soon as they had been relieved of their travel-weariness by resting and refreshed by the steamy waters of the baths, she feasted them most beautifully in her dining room with those marvellous rich foods and sausages. She commanded a lyre to speak and there was strumming; flutes to perform and there was piping; choirs to sing and there was singing. All those sounds with no one present caressed the listeners' spirits with the most delightful melodies. But the wickedness of the accursed women was not mollified even by the mellifluous sweetness of the music. They turned the conversation to the deceitful trap they had plotted, and casually began to enquire about her husband: what sort of man he was, what his origins were, what sort of background he came from. In her excessive simplicity Psyche forgot her earlier story and invented a different fiction. She said that her husband came from the next province, was a merchant dealing in large sums, and was now middle-aged with a sprinkling of grey in his hair. Without lingering a moment longer in the conversation, she loaded them down once

rursum opiparis muneribus eas onustas ventoso vehiculo reddidit.

16 "Sed dum Zephyri tranquillo spiritu sublimatae domum redeunt, sic secum altercantes: 'Quid, soror, dicimus de tam monstruoso fatuae illius mendacio? Tunc adulescens modo florenti lanugine barbam instruens, nunc aetate media candenti canitie lucidus. Quis ille, quem temporis modici spatium repentina senecta reformavit? Nil aliud reperies, mi soror, quam vel mendacia[1] istam pessimam feminam confingere vel formam mariti sui nescire; quorum utrum verum est, opibus istis quam primum exterminanda est. Quodsi viri sui faciem ignorat, deo profecto denupsit et deum nobis praegnatione ista gerit. Certe si divini puelli—quod absit—haec mater audierit, statim me laqueo nexili suspendam. Ergo interim ad parentes nostros redeamus et exordio sermonis huius quam concolores fallacias attexamus.'

17 "Sic inflammatae, parentibus fastidienter appellatis et nocte turbatis vigiliis, perditae[2] matutino scopulum pervolant, et inde solito venti praesidio vehementer devolant, lacrimisque pressura palpebrarum coactis hoc astu puellam appellant: 'Tu quidem felix et ipsa tanti mali ignorantia beata

[1] F *mendacio.*

[2] The words *et . . . perditae* have been variously emended and punctuated.

more with lavish gifts and sent them back by their aerial conveyance.

6 "While they were returning home, raised aloft on Zephyr's gentle breath, they angrily discussed the situation. 'Well, sister, what do we say about that silly girl's monstrous lie? First he was a young man just growing a beard of soft down; next he is middle-aged, distinguished by silvery white hair. Who can he be who is suddenly transformed by such a short space of time into an old man? The only answer, my sister, is that the wicked woman is either telling us a string of lies or she does not know what her husband looks like. Whichever is the case, she must be dislodged as quickly as possible from her riches. If she is ignorant of her husband's appearance, then surely she must have married a god, and is carrying a god for us in that pregnancy of hers. Well, if—god forbid—she becomes known as the mother of a divine child, I shall immediately knot a noose and hang myself. In the meantime, then, let us go back to our parents and weave a woof of guile to match the colour of our discussion's warp.'

7 "Enflamed as they were, they greeted their parents haughtily and spent a disturbed and wakeful night. Early in the morning those damned women flew to the cliff, and thence with the wind's customary help swooped violently downward. Having pressed their eyelids to force tears, they greeted the girl with their display of guile: 'Here you sit, happy and fortunate in your very ignorance of

sedes incuriosa periculi tui. Nos autem, quae pervigili cura rebus tuis excubamus, cladibus tuis misere cruciamur. Pro vero namque comperimus, nec te, sociae scilicet doloris casusque tui, celare possumus, immanem colubrum multinodis voluminibus serpentem, veneno noxio colla sanguinantem hiantemque ingluvie profunda, tecum noctibus latenter acquiescere. Nunc recordare sortis Pythicae, quae te trucis bestiae nuptiis destinatam esse clamavit. Et multi coloni quique circumsecus venantur et accolae plurimi viderunt eum vespera redeuntem
18 e pastu proximique fluminis vadis innatantem. Nec diu blandis alimoniarum obsequiis te saginaturum omnes affirmant, sed, cum primum praegnationem tuam plenus maturaverit uterus, opimiore fructu praeditam devoraturum. Ad haec iam tua est existimatio, utrum sororibus pro tua cara salute sollicitis assentiri velis et declinata morte nobiscum secura periculi vivere, an saevissimae bestiae sepeliri visceribus. Quodsi te ruris huius vocalis solitudo, vel clandestinae Veneris foetidi periculo-

your great misfortune. You are not even curious about the danger you are in, while we have been awake all night in sleepless concern over your situation, pitifully tortured by your calamities. We now know the truth, you see, and since of course we share your pain and plight, we cannot conceal it from you. It is a monstrous snake gliding with many-knotted coils, its bloody neck oozing noxious poison and its deep maw gaping wide, that sleeps beside you hidden in the night. Remember now Apollo's[1] oracle, which proclaimed that you were destined to marry a savage beast. Moreover, several farmers and people who hunt hereabouts and many residents of the neighbourhood have seen him coming home from feeding in the evening, and swim-
8 ming in the shallows of the river nearby. They all say that he will not long continue to fatten you with the charming indulgences of nourishment, but as soon as a full womb brings your pregnancy to completion and endowed you with more luscious fruit, he will eat you up. Given these facts, it is now your decision. Are you willing to listen to your sisters in their concern for your dear safety and avoid death and live with us free from peril? Or do you prefer to be buried in the bowels of a ferocious beast? If you really enjoy the voiceful loneliness of this country place, or the stinking and perilous copulations of

[1] The Latin says "Pythian", i.e. "Delphic", but in fact (cf. IV 32) the oracle was given at Miletus, not Delphi.

sique concubitus et venenati serpentis amplexus delectant, certe piae sorores nostrum fecerimus.'

"Tunc Psyche misella, utpote simplex et animi tenella, rapitur verborum tam tristium formidine. Extra terminum mentis suae posita prorsus omnium mariti monitionum suarumque promissionum memoriam effudit, et in profundum calamitatis sese praecipitavit, tremensque et exsangui colore lurida, tertiata verba semihianti voce substrepens, sic ad illas ait:

19 "'Vos quidem, carissimae sorores, ut par erat, in officio vestrae pietatis permanetis, verum et illi, qui talia vobis affirmant, non videntur mihi mendacium fingere. Nec enim umquam viri mei vidi faciem, vel omnino cuiatis sit novi, sed tantum nocturnis subaudiens vocibus maritum incerti status et prorsus lucifugam tolero, bestiamque aliquam recte dicentibus vobis merito[1] consentio. Meque magnopere semper a suis terret aspectibus malumque grande de vultus curiositate praeminatur. Nunc si quam salutarem opem periclitanti sorori vestrae potestis afferre, iam nunc subsistite. Ceterum incuria sequens prioris providentiae beneficia corrumpet.'

"Tunc[2] nanctae iam portis patentibus nudatum sororis animum facinerosae mulieres, omissis tectae

[1] F *marito.* Possibly Apuleius wrote *maritum merito.*
[2] F *hunc.*

furtive love and the embraces of a poisonous snake —at least we will have done our duty as loving sisters.'

"Then poor little Psyche, artless and tender-hearted as she was, was seized with terror at their grim words. Driven beyond the limits of her own mind, she completely shed the memory of all her husband's warnings and her own promises, and hurled herself headlong into an abyss of disaster. Trembling, pallid, the blood drained from her face, barely able to stammer her words through half-open lips, she answered them as follows.

19 "'You, my dearest sisters, as was only right, are being true and firm in your family loyalty. And I do not think that the people who told you these stories are telling a lie. In fact I have never seen my husband's face, and I have no knowledge at all where he comes from. I only barely hear his talking at night, and I must endure a husband of unknown standing who totally shuns the light. You must be right when you say he is some beast, I agree. He is always intimidating me from looking at him, and threatening some great punishment for any curiosity about his features. If now you can bring some salvation to your sister in her danger, help me right now. Otherwise, your subsequent neglect will undo all the benefits of your concern thus far.'

"The gates were open now, and those vicious women, having reached their sister's defenceless mind, quit the concealment of their covered artil-

machinae latibulis, destrictis gladiis fraudium simplicis puellae paventes cogitationes invadunt.

20 "Sic denique altera: 'Quoniam nos originis nexus pro tua incolumitate ne[1] periculum quidem ullum ante oculos habere compellit, viam quae sola deducit iter[2] ad salutem diu diuque cogitatam monstrabimus tibi. Novaculam praeacutam, appulsu etiam palmulae lenientis exasperatam, tori qua parte cubare consuesti latenter absconde, lucernamque concinnem, completam oleo, claro lumine praemicantem, subde aliquo claudentis aululae tegmine. Omnique isto apparatu tenacissime dissimulato, postquam sulcatos[3] intrahens gressus cubile solitum conscenderit, iamque porrectus et exordio somni prementis implicitus altum soporem flare coeperit, toro delapsa nudoque vestigio pensilem gradum paullulatim[4] minuens, caecae tenebrae custodio liberata lucerna, praeclari tui facinoris opportunitatem de luminis consilio mutuare, et ancipiti telo illo audaciter, prius dextera sursum elata, nisu quam valido noxii serpentis nodum cervicis et capitis abscide.[5] Nec nostrum tibi deerit subsidium; sed cum primum illius morte salutem tibi feceris, anxie praestolatae advolabimus,[6] cunctisque istis ocius[7] tecum relatis, votivis nuptiis hominem te

[1] F omits *ne*. [2] The strangeness of *via deducit iter* has induced various emendations.

[3] F *sulcato*. [4] F *pullulatim*. [5] F *abscinde*.

[6] F *anxiae praestolabimus*. [7] F *sociis*.

lery, unsheathed the swords of their deception, and assaulted the timorous thoughts of the guileless girl.

20 "One of them said, 'Since the bond of our common origin compels us to disregard all possible danger when your life is at stake, we shall show you the only way which promises a path to salvation, which we have been planning for a long, long time. Take a very sharp razor, whet it with the application of your soft stroking palm, and secretly conceal it on that side of the bed where you usually lie. Then get a lamp, trimmed and filled with oil and burning with a clear light, and hide it beneath the cover of a little pot. Dissemble all this preparation very carefully; and then, after he has drawn along his furrowing gait and mounted the bed as usual, when he is stretched out entangled in the first threads of oppressing sleep and begins to breathe deep slumber, slip off the couch, and, with bare feet lessening little by little your airy tread, free the lamp from the prison of its blind darkness. From the light's good counsel borrow the occasion for a glorious deed of your own: boldly grasping your double-edged weapon, first raise your right hand high; then, with as strong a stroke as you can, sever the knot that joins the poisonous serpent's neck and head. We shall not fail to support you, but as soon as you have won safety by his death we shall be anxiously waiting to fly to your side; and after bringing back along with you all this treasure, we will make a

iungemus homini.'

21 "Tali verborum incendio flammata viscera sororis iam prorsus ardentis deserentes ipsae[1] protinus, tanti mali confinium sibi etiam eximie metuentes, flatus alitis impulsu solito porrectae super scopulum, ilico pernici se[2] fuga proripiunt, statimque conscensis navibus abeunt.

"At Psyche relicta sola, nisi quod infestis Furiis agitata sola non est, aestu pelagi simile maerendo fluctuat, et, quamvis statuto consilio et obstinato animo, iam tamen facinori manus admovens, adhuc incerta consilii titubat multisque calamitatis suae distrahitur affectibus. Festinat differt, audet trepidat, diffidit irascitur; et, quod est ultimum, in eodem corpore odit bestiam, diligit maritum. Vespera tamen iam noctem trahente, praecipiti festinatione nefarii sceleris instruit apparatum. Nox aderat et maritus aderat priusque[3] Veneris proeliis velitatus altum in[4] soporem descenderat.

22 "Tunc Psyche, et corporis et animi alioquin infirma, fati tamen saevitia sumministrante viribus roboratur, et prolata lucerna et arrepta novacula sexum audacia mutatur.[5] Sed cum primum luminis oblatione tori secreta claruerunt, videt omnium

[1] F *ipsa.*

[2] F *perniciosae.*

[3] F *primusque.*

[4] F has no preposition.

[5] F *mutavit*, although the last three letters are a later correction.

desirable marriage for you, human to human.'

21 "With this blaze of words they inflamed their sister's burning heart, for in truth it was already on fire, and then straightway left her, for they were greatly afraid even to be in the neighbourhood of such an evil deed. As usual they were carried to the top of the cliff by the wafting of the winged breeze and rushed away at once in rapid retreat; they boarded their ships at once and were gone.

"Psyche was left alone, except that a woman driven by hostile furies is not alone. In her grief she ebbed and flowed like the billows of the sea. Although she had determined her plan and her mind was made up, nevertheless, as she turned her hands toward the act itself, she still wavered irresolutely, torn apart by the many emotions raised by her dilemma. She felt haste and procrastination, daring and fear, despair and anger; and worst of all, in the same body she loathed the beast but loved the husband. But as evening began to bring on the night, she prepared the apparatus for her abominable crime with frantic haste. Night came, and her husband came, and after skirmishing in love's warfare he dropped into a deep sleep.

22 "Then Psyche, though naturally weak in both body and spirit, was fed with strength by the cruelty of Fate. She brought out the lamp, seized the razor, and in her boldness changed her sex. But as soon as the bed's mysteries were illumined as the lamp was brought near, she beheld that wild creature who is

ferarum mitissimam dulcissimamque bestiam, ipsum illum Cupidinem formosum deum formose cubantem. Cuius aspectu lucernae quoque lumen hilaratum increbruit et acuminis sacrilegi novaculam paenitebat.[1] At vero Psyche tanto aspectu deterrita et impos animi, marcido pallore defecta tremensque desedit in imos poplites et ferrum quaerit abscondere, sed in suo pectore. Quod profecto fecisset, nisi ferrum timore tanti flagitii manibus temerariis delapsum evolasset. Iamque lassa, salute defecta, dum saepius divini vultus intuetur pulchritudinem, recreatur animi.

"Videt capitis aurei genialem caesariem ambrosia temulentam, cervices lacteas genasque purpureas pererrantes crinium globos decoriter impeditos, alios antependulos, alios retropendulos, quorum splendore nimio fulgurante iam et ipsum lumen lucernae vacillabat. Per umeros volatilis dei pinnae roscidae micanti flore candicant, et quamvis alis quiescentibus extimae plumulae tenellae ac delicatae tremule resultantes inquieta lasciviunt. Ceterum corpus glabellum atque luculentum et quale peperisse Venerem non paeniteret. Ante lectuli pedes iacebat arcus et pharetra et sagittae, magni dei propitia tela.

[1] F *novacula praenitebat.*

the gentlest and sweetest beast of all, Cupid himself, the beautiful god beautifully sleeping. At the sight of him even the light of the lamp quickened in joy, and the razor repented its sacrilegious sharpness. But Psyche was terrified at this marvellous sight and put out of her mind; overcome with the pallor of exhaustion she sank faint and trembling to her knees. She tried to hide the weapon—in her own heart. And she would certainly have done so, had not the blade slipped out and flown away from her reckless hands in its horror of so atrocious a deed. She was now weary and overcome by the sense of being safe, but as she gazed repeatedly at the beauty of that divine countenance her spirit began to revive.

"On his golden head she saw the glorious hair drenched with ambrosia: wandering over his milky neck and rosy cheeks were the neatly shackled ringlets of his locks, some prettily hanging in front, others behind; the lightning of their great brilliance made even the lamp's light flicker. Along the shoulders of the winged god white feathers glistened like flowers in the morning dew; and although his wings were at rest, soft and delicate little plumes along their edges quivered restlessly in wanton play. The rest of his body was hairless and resplendent, such as to cause Venus no regrets for having borne this child. By the feet of the bed lay a bow and quiver and arrows, gracious weapons of the mighty god.

23 "Quae dum insatiabili animo Psyche, satis et curiosa, rimatur atque pertrectat et mariti sui miratur arma, depromit unam de pharetra sagittam et puncto pollicis extremam aciem periclitabunda trementis etiam nunc articuli nisu fortiore pupugit altius, ut per summam cutem roraverint parvulae sanguinis rosei guttae. Sic ignara Psyche sponte in Amoris incidit amorem. Tunc magis magisque cupidine flagrans Cupidinis, prona in eum efflictim inhians, patulis ac petulantibus saviis festinanter ingestis, de somni mensura metuebat. Sed dum bono tanto percita saucia mente fluctuat, lucerna illa sive perfidia pessima sive invidia noxia sive quod tale corpus contingere et quasi basiare et ipsa gestiebat, evomuit de summa luminis sui stillam ferventis olei super umerum dei dexterum. Hem audax et temeraria lucerna et Amoris vile ministerium, ipsum ignis totius deum[1] aduris, cum te scilicet amator aliquis, ut diutius cupitis etiam nocte potiretur, primus invenerit. Sic inustus exsiluit deus visaque detectae fidei colluvie protinus ex osculis[2] et manibus infelicissimae coniugis tacitus avolavit.

[1] Or perhaps *dominum*.
[2] F *prorsus ex oculis*.

23 "Insatiably, and with some curiosity, Psyche scrutinised and handled and marvelled at her husband's arms. She drew one of the arrows from the quiver and tested the point against the tip of her thumb; but her hand was still trembling and she pushed a little too hard and pricked too deep, so that tiny drops of rose-red blood moistened the surface of her skin. Thus without knowing it Psyche of her own accord fell in love with Love. Then more and more enflamed with desire for Cupid[1] she leaned over him, panting desperately for him. She eagerly covered him with impassioned and impetuous kisses till she feared about the depth of his slumber. But while her wounded heart was swirling under the excitement of so much bliss, the lamp—either from wicked treachery or malicious jealousy or simply because it too longed to touch and, in its way, kiss such a beautiful body—sputtered forth from the top of its flame a drop of boiling oil on to the god's right shoulder. O bold and reckless lamp, worthless servant of Love, to scorch the very god of all fire, when it must have been some lover who first invented you that even by night he might the longer enjoy the object of his desire! Thus burnt the god jumped up, and seeing the ruin of betrayed trust, straightway flew up from the kisses and embraces of his poor unhappy wife without a word.

[1] The Latin for "desire" is *cupido*. For his names, see note at IV 30.

24 "At Psyche, statim resurgentis eius crure dextero manibus ambabus arrepto, sublimis evectionis appendix miseranda et per nubilas plagas penduli comitatus extrema consequia, tandem fessa delabitur solo. Nec deus amator humi iacentem deserens, involavit proximam cupressum, deque eius alto cacumine sic eam graviter commotus affatur:

"'Ego quidem, simplicissima Psyche, parentis meae Veneris praeceptorum immemor, quae te miseri extremique hominis devinctam cupidine infimo matrimonio addici iusserat, ipse potius amator advolavi tibi. Sed hoc feci leviter, scio, et praeclarus ille sagittarius ipse me telo meo percussi teque coniugem meam feci, ut bestia scilicet tibi viderer et ferro caput excideres meum, quod istos amatores tuos oculos gerit. Haec tibi identidem semper cavenda censebam, haec benivole remonebam. Sed illae quidem consiliatrices egregiae tuae tam perniciosi magisterii dabunt actutum mihi poenas; te vero tantum fuga mea punivero.' Et cum termino sermonis pinnis in altum se proripuit.

25 "Psyche vero, humi prostrata et quantum visu[1] poterat volatus mariti prospiciens, extremis affligebat lamentationibus animum. Sed ubi remi-

[1] F *visi.*

24 "But as he rose Psyche quickly grasped his right leg with both hands, forming a pitiable appendage to his soaring flight and a trailing attachment in dangling companionship through the cloudy regions. At last, exhausted, she fell to the ground. Her divine lover did not desert her as she lay on the ground, but flew to a cypress nearby, from whose high summit he spoke to her in deep distress.

"'My poor naive Psyche!' he said. 'I in fact disobeyed the orders of my mother Venus, who had commanded me to chain you with passion for some wretched and worthless man and sentence you to the lowest sort of marriage. Instead I flew to you myself as your lover. But that was a frivolous thing to do, I know. Illustrious archer that I am, I shot myself with my own weapon and made you my wife, for the pleasure, it seems, of having you think me a wild beast and cut off my head with a sword, the head that holds these eyes which are your lovers! I told you time and time again that you must always be on your guard against this, and I kept warning you about it for your own good. As for those excellent advisers of yours, I shall soon be revenged on them for their disastrous instructions. But I shall punish you merely by leaving.'

"And as his words ended he took wing and soared into the sky.

25 "Psyche lay flat upon the ground and watched her husband's flight as far as her sight enabled her, tormenting her soul with the most piteous lamenta-

gio plumae raptum maritum proceritas spatii fecerat alienum, per proximi fluminis marginem praecipitem sese dedit. Sed mitis fluvius, in honorem dei scilicet, qui et ipsas aquas urere consuevit, metuens sibi, confestim eam innoxio volumine super ripam florentem herbis exposuit. Tunc forte Pan deus rusticus iuxta supercilium amnis sedebat, complexus Echo montanam[1] deam eamque voculas omnimodas[2] edocens recinere. Proxime ripam vago pastu lasciviunt comam fluvii tondentes capellae. Hircuosus deus sauciam Psychen atque defectam, utcumque casus eius non inscius, clementer ad se vocatam sic permulcet verbis lenientibus:

"'Puella scitula, sum quidem rusticanus et upilio, sed senectutis prolixae beneficio multis experimentis instructus. Verum si recte coniecto, quod profecto prudentes viri divinationem autumant, ab isto titubante et saepius vacillante vestigio deque nimio pallore corporis et assiduo suspiritu, immo et ipsis maerentibus[3] oculis tuis, amore nimio laboras. Ergo mihi ausculta, nec te rursus praecipitio vel ullo mortis accersitae[4] genere perimas. Luctum desine et pone maerorem, precibusque potius Cupidinem deorum maximum percole, et utpote adulescentem delicatum luxuriosumque blandis obsequiis

[1] F *haec homo canam*, for *Echo montanam.*

[2] F *omninedas.*

[3] Should perhaps be emended to *marcentibus* "pining".

[4] F *accersito.*

tions. But after her husband, speeding on his oarage of wings, had been removed from her view by vastness of distance she threw herself over the edge of a nearby river. The gentle stream, however, no doubt respecting the god who can kindle even water but also apprehensive for himself, quickly caught her in his harmless current and deposited her on a bank deep in grass. At that moment the rustic god Pan happened to be sitting beside the stream's brow, embracing the mountain goddess Echo and teaching her to sing back to him all kinds of tunes. Near the bank wandering she-goats grazed and frolicked as they cropped the river's hair. The goat-like god saw Psyche sad and weary, and being not unaware of her misfortune, he called her gently over to him and calmed her with soothing words.

"'Pretty maiden,' said he, 'although I am a country fellow and a herdsman, by benefit of an advanced old age I have been schooled by much experience. Now if I guess rightly—though wise men call it not guessing but divination—from your weak and oft tottering footsteps, your extremely pale complexion, your constant sighing, and still more by your sad eyes, you are suffering from an overdose of love. Listen to me, therefore, and do not try to kill yourself again by a fatal leap or any other sort of suicide. Stop your mourning and put away your grief. Instead pray to Cupid, the greatest of the gods, and worship him and earn his favour with flattering deference, since he is a pleasure-loving

promerere.'

26 "Sic locuto deo pastore nulloque sermone reddito sed adorato tantum numine salutari, Psyche pergit ire. Sed cum[1] aliquam multum viae laboranti vestigio pererrasset, inscio[2] quodam tramite iam die labente[3] accedit quandam civitatem, in qua regnum maritus unius sororis eius obtinebat. Qua re cognita Psyche nuntiari praesentiam suam sorori desiderat. Mox inducta, mutuis amplexibus alternae salutationis expletis, percontanti causas adventus sui sic incipit:

"'Meministi consilium vestrum scilicet quo mihi suasistis ut bestiam, quae mariti mentito nomine mecum quiescebat, priusquam ingluvie voraci me misellam hauriret, ancipiti novacula peremerem. Sed cum primum, ut aeque placuerat, conscio lumine vultus eius aspexi, video mirum divinumque prorsus spectaculum, ipsum illum deae Veneris filium, ipsum inquam Cupidinem, leni quiete sopitum. Ac dum tanti boni spectaculo percita et nimia voluptatis[4] copia turbata fruendi laborarem inopia, casu scilicet pessimo lucerna fervens oleum rebullivit in eius umerum. Quo dolore statim somno recussus, ubi me ferro et igni conspexit armatam,

[1] *cum* is not in F.

[2] Often emended to *inscia*, to modify Psyche in its usual active sense of "unknowing".

[3] F *delabente*, for *die labente.*

[4] F *voluntatis.*

and soft-hearted youth.'

26 "When the shepherd god had finished speaking, Psyche did not reply, but merely gestured reverently to the beneficent deity and went her way. After she had wandered a rather long way in her weary walking, she took an unfamiliar road, and as daylight was fading she came to a city where the husband of one of her sisters was king. When she discovered this, Psyche asked that her presence be announced to her sister. She was soon invited in, and when they had had their fill of embracing and greeting each other, her sister enquired into the reasons for her coming. Psyche began:

"'You remember that advice of yours: I mean when the two of you persuaded me to take a double-edged razor and kill the beast who was sleeping with me under the false name of husband, before my wretched body was swallowed in his greedy maw. Well, as soon as I had taken the light as my accomplice—in which I concurred with your advice—and looked at his face, I saw an amazing and utterly divine spectacle: the goddess Venus' son in person, I mean Cupid himself, lying peacefully asleep. Excited by the spectacle of so much bliss and confused by an overabundance of delight, I was feeling distress at my inability to enjoy it fully when, obviously through some terrible misfortune, a drop of burning oil spurted on to his shoulder. Immediately the pain jolted him from sleep, and when he saw me armed with fire and sword he declared: "On

"Tu quidem" inquit "ob istud tam dirum facinus confestim toro meo divorte, tibique res tuas habeto. Ego vero sororem tuam"—et nomen quo tu censeris aiebat—"iam mihi confarreatis[1] nuptiis coniugabo." Et statim Zephyro praecipit ultra terminos me domus eius efflaret.'

27 "Necdum sermonem Psyche finierat; illa[2] vesanae libidinis et invidiae noxiae stimulis agitata, e re concinnato mendacio fallens maritum, quasi de morte parentum aliquid comperisset, statim navem ascendit et ad illum scopulum protinus pergit. Et quamvis alio flante vento, caeca spe tamen inhians, 'Accipe me,' dicens 'Cupido, dignam te coniugem, et tu, Zephyre, suscipe dominam,' saltu se maximo praecipitem dedit. Nec tamen ad illum locum vel saltem mortua pervenire potuit. Nam per saxa cautium membris iactatis atque dissipatis et proinde ut merebatur laceratis visceribus suis, alitibus bestiisque obvium ferens pabulum interiit.

"Nec vindictae sequentis poena tardavit. Nam Psyche rursus errabundo gradu pervenit ad civitatem aliam, in qua pari modo soror morabatur alia. Nec setius et ipsa fallacie germanitatis inducta et in

[1] F *confestim arreat his,* erroneously repeating *confestim* from the previous sentence.

[2] *et* or *at* may have fallen out before *illa.*

account of your dreadful crime, you are forthwith to depart from my couch and take what is yours with you. I shall now wed your sister in holy matrimony"[1]—and he spoke your full name. Then at once he commanded Zephyr to waft me beyond the boundaries of his house.'

27 "Psyche had not even finished talking before her sister, goaded by the spurs of insane passion and poisonous jealousy, contrived on the spot a lie to deceive her husband, pretending that she had just heard the news of her parents' death, then instantly boarded a ship and went straight to the cliff. Although a different wind was blowing, in the blind hope of her desire she cried out, 'Take me, Cupid, a wife worthy of you! And you, Zephyr, catch your mistress!' and made a great leap. She plunged downward, but even in death she could not reach that destination: her body was tossed and torn apart by the crag's jutting rocks, and, just as she deserved, with entrails ripped open her corpse provided a ready meal for bird and beast.

"Nor was the infliction of the second punishment slow in coming, for resuming her wandering steps Psyche arrived at another city, in which that other sister was living in similar style. She too, likewise led on by her sister's false story, and an eager claimant for the wicked possession of her sister's

[1] *Tibi res tuas habeto* was the customary formula for divorce, and *confarreatio* the most ancient and solemn form of marriage among the Romans.

sororis sceleratas nuptias aemula, festinavit ad scopulum inque simile mortis exitium cecidit.

28 "Interim dum Psyche quaesitioni Cupidinis intenta populos circumibat, at ille vulnere lucernae dolens in ipso thalamo matris iacens ingemebat. Tunc avis peralba illa gavia, quae super fluctus marinos pinnis natat, demergit sese propere ad Oceani profundum gremium. Ibi commodum Venerem lavantem natantemque propter assistens, indicat adustum filium eius, gravi vulneris dolore maerentem, dubium salutis iacere; iamque per cunctorum ora populorum rumoribus conviciisque variis omnem Veneris familiam male audire, quod ille quidem montano scortatu, tu vero marino natatu secesseritis, ac per hoc non voluptas ulla, non gratia, non lepos, sed incompta et agrestia et horrida cuncta sint, non nuptiae coniugales, non amicitiae sociales, non liberum caritates, sed enormis colluvies[1] et squalentium foederum insuave fastidium. Haec illa verbosa et satis curiosa avis in auribus Veneris fili[2] lacerans existimationem ganniebat.

"At Venus irata solidum exclamat repente: 'Ergo iam ille bonus filius meus habet amicam aliquam? Prome agedum, quae sola mihi servis amanter,

[1] F *gluvies.*
[2] F *filium.*

marriage, hastened to the cliff and fell to the selfsame deadly doom.

28 "Psyche meanwhile, intent on her search for Cupid, was travelling about the country, while he lay groaning in pain from the lamp's wound, in his mother's own bedchamber. At this point a bird, the white seagull who swims on wings above the waves, dived hurriedly down deep into Ocean's bosom, where she at once found Venus as she bathed and swam. The bird stood beside her and informed her that her son had been burned, that he was in grievous pain from the wound, that he had taken to his bed, and that his recovery was uncertain. 'Furthermore,' she said, 'because of various rumours and reproaches circulating by word of mouth throughout the whole world, Venus' entire household is getting a bad reputation. They are saying that the two of you have gone off on vacation, he to his mountainside whoring, you to swimming in the sea; and so there is no joy any more, no grace, no charm. Everything is unkempt and boorish and harsh. Weddings and social intercourse and the love of children are gone, leaving only a monstrous mess and an unpleasant disregard for anything as squalid as the bonds of marriage.' Thus did that talkative and altogether interfering bird cackle into Venus' ear, tearing her son's reputation to shreds.

"Venus was furious and burst out: 'So now that virtuous son of mine has a girlfriend, has he? Come on, then, my only loyal servant, and tell me the

nomen eius, quae puerum ingenuum et investem sollicitavit, sive illa de Nympharum populo seu de Horarum numero seu de Musarum choro vel de mearum Gratiarum ministerio.'

"Nec loquax illa conticuit avis, sed 'Nescio,' inquit 'domina. Puto, puellam[1]—si probe memini, Psyches nomine— dicitur efflicte cupere.'

"Tunc indignata Venus exclamavit vel maxime: 'Psychen illam[2] meae formae succubam, mei nominis aemulam vere diligit? Nimirum illud incrementum lenam me putavit, cuius monstratu puellam illam cognosceret.'

29 "Haec quiritans properiter emergit e mari suumque protinus aureum thalamum petit, et reperto sicut audierat aegroto puero, iam inde a foribus quam maxime boans, 'Honesta' inquit 'haec et natalibus nostris bonaeque tuae frugi congruentia, ut primum quidem tuae parentis—immo dominae—praecepta calcares, nec sordidis amoribus inimicam meam cruciares, verum etiam hoc aetatis puer tuis licentiosis et immaturis iungeres amplexibus, ut ego nurum scilicet tolerarem inimicam. Sed utique praesumis, nugo et corruptor et inamabilis, te solum generosum, nec me iam per aetatem posse concipere. Velim ergo

[1] F *puella.*
[2] F *illae.*

name of the creature who seduced that simple and innocent boy. Is she one of the tribe of Nymphs, or the band of Hours, or the choir of Muses, or my own company of Graces?'

"The loquacious bird did not hold her tongue. 'I do not know, mistress. But I think that he is desperately in love with a girl, who is known, if I remember correctly, by the name of Psyche.'

"Then Venus indignantly screamed at the top of her voice: 'Psyche! Is it really Psyche he loves, that whorish rival of my beauty, that pretender to my name? The young imp must have thought I was a madam who was showing him the girl so that he could get to know her.'

29 "With these loud plaints she speedily surfaced from the sea and headed immediately for her golden bedroom, where she found her ailing boy, just as she had heard. From the doorway she bellowed at him for all she was worth. 'What fine behaviour! And how appropriate to your parentage and your virtuous character! First you trample underfoot your mother's commands—your queen's I should say—and fail to torture my enemy with some low-class passion. And furthermore at your age, a mere boy, you couple with her in your unrestrained, immature lovemaking, evidently supposing that I would tolerate as a daughter-in-law a woman I hate. You must presume, you good-for-nothing, unlovable seducer, that you alone are the prince and that I am too old to conceive. Well, I want you to know that I

scias multo te meliorem filium alium genituram, immo ut contumeliam magis sentias, aliquem de meis adoptaturam vernulis eique donaturam istas pinnas et flammas et arcum et ipsas sagittas et omnem meam supellectilem, quam tibi non ad hos usus dederam. Nec enim de patris tui bonis ad instructionem istam quicquam concessum est. Sed male prima pueritia inductus es et acutas manus habes et maiores tuos irreverenter pulsasti totiens, et ipsam matrem tuam, me inquam ipsam, parricida denudas cotidie et percussisti saepius et quasi viduam utique contemnis, nec vitricum tuum fortissimum illum maximumque bellatorem metuis—quidni?—cui saepius in angorem mei paelicatus puellas propinare consuesti. Sed iam faxo te lusus huius paeniteat et sentias acidas et amaras istas nuptias.

"'Sed nunc irrisui habita quid agam? Quo me conferam? Quibus modis stelionem istum cohibeam? Petamne auxilium ab inimica mea Sobrietate, quam propter huius ipsius luxuriam offendi saepius? At rusticae squalentisque feminae colloquium prorsus [adhibendum est][1] horresco. Nec

[1] So F: a faulty anticipation of *adhibenda est*.

will produce another son much better than you.
Indeed, in order to make you feel the insult all the
more I will adopt one of my young slaves and make
over to him those wings of yours and torches, your
bow and arrows, and the rest of my equipment,
which I did not give you to use that way.
Remember, there was no allowance granted from
30 your father's property for outfitting you. But you
were badly trained as a baby, and you have sharp
hands, and you disrespectfully strike your elders all
the time, and you expose me your mother to shame
every day, you monstrous son! You have beaten me
several times and you scorn me as if I were a widow
and you have no respect for your stepfather, who is
the world's strongest and greatest warrior.[1] Why
should you, when you are always supplying him
with girls to torment me with his adultery? But
now I will make you sorry for mocking me, and that
marriage of yours will taste sour and bitter.

"'But now that I have been made a laughing-stock, what am I to do? Where can I turn? How am I going to repress this reptile? should I ask for help from my enemy Temperance, whom I have so often offended precisely because of my son's extravagance? But I shudder at the thought of talking to that crude and dirty woman. Still the consolation of

[1] Mars. Venus here legitimises their relationship, which is usually not presented as marriage; similarly at the end of chapter 29 she represents herself as divorced from Cupid's father Vulcan.

tamen vindictae solacium undeunde spernendum est. Illa mihi prorsus adhibenda est nec ulla alia, quae castiget asperrime nugonem istum, pharetram explicet et sagittas dearmet, arcum enodet, taedam deflammet, immo et ipsum corpus eius acrioribus remediis coerceat. Tunc iniuriae meae litatum crediderim, cum eius comas, quas istis manibus meis subinde aureo nitore perstrinxi, deraserit, pinnas, quas meo gremio nectarei fontis infeci, praetotonderit.'

31 "Sic effata foras sese proripit infesta et stomachata biles Venerias. Sed eam protinus Ceres et Iuno continantur, visamque vultu tumido[1] quaesiere cur truci supercilio tantam venustatem micantium oculorum coerceret. At illa 'Opportune' inquit 'ardenti prorsus isto meo pectori violentiam[2] scilicet perpetraturae venitis. Sed totis, oro, vestris viribus Psychen illam fugitivam volaticam mihi requirite. Nec enim vos utique domus meae famosa fabula et non dicendi filii mei facta latuerunt.'

"Tunc illae, non ignarae[3] quae gesta sunt, palpare Veneris iram saevientem sic adortae: 'Quid tale, domina, deliquit tuus filius, ut animo pervicaci voluptates illius impugnes et quam ille diligit tu quoque perdere gestias? Quod autem, oramus, isti crimen, si puellae lepidae libenter arrisit? An ignoras eum masculum et iuvenem esse, vel certe

[1] F *timido.*

[2] Often emended to *volentiam.*

[3] F omits *non.*

revenge is not to be rejected, whatever the source. I really must employ her and her alone to give the harshest possible punishment to that good-for-nothing, dismantle his quiver and disarm his arrows, unknot his bow, defuse his torch, yes and even curb his body with harsher medicines. I shall not consider my humiliation atoned for until she has shaved off his hair, which I with my own hands have often brushed to a golden sheen, and clipped his wings, which I have dyed in my bosom's fount of nectar.'

31 "So saying, she rushed out of doors, furious and angry with passion's own bitterness. Ceres and Juno came up to her at that very moment, and when they saw her wrathful countenance asked why she spoiled the charm of her flashing eyes with such a sullen frown. 'How opportune!' she replied. 'My heart is quite on fire, and I suppose you have come to coerce me to desist. But please use all your powers to help me hunt out Psyche, my elusive runaway. I assume that the notorious tale about my family and the exploits of my unspeakable son have not escaped your notice.'

"Not unaware what had happened they tried to soothe Venus' savage anger. 'My lady,' they asked, 'what fault did your son commit so grave as to make you attack his pleasures so determinedly and also be so keen to destroy the girl he loves? What crime is that, we ask you, if he likes smiling at a pretty girl? Or are you not aware that he is male, and a

iam quot sit annorum oblita es? An, quod aetatem portat bellule, puer tibi semper videtur? Mater autem tu et praeterea cordata mulier filii tui lusus semper explorabis curiose, et in eo luxuriem culpabis et amores revinces, et tuas artes tuasque delicias in formoso filio reprehendes? Quis autem te deum, quis hominum patietur passim cupidines populis disseminantem, cum tuae domus amores amare coerceas et vitiorum muliebrium publicam praecludas officinam?'

"Sic illae metu sagittarum patrocinio gratioso Cupidini, quamvis absenti, blandiebantur. Sed Venus indignata ridicule tractari suas iniurias praeversis illis alterorsus[1] concito gradu pelago viam capessit.

[1] F *alte rursus.*

young man at that? Or perhaps you have forgotten how old he is now? Just because he carries his years prettily, do you think of him as being for ever a child? Now, you are a mother, and a sensible woman besides. Will you never stop spying inquisitively into your son's pastimes, blaming self-indulgence in him, scolding him for his love-affairs, and, in short, finding fault with your own talents and your own delights in the case of your handsome son? What god, what human will tolerate your scattering the seeds of desire all over the world while in your own house you bitterly restrict love-affairs and close down the factory in which the natural faults of women are made?'

"Thus, in fear of his arrows they flattered Cupid with an obliging defence, although he was not in the courtroom. But Venus, offended that her wrongs were being treated with ridicule, swept past them on the other side and set out quickly toward the sea.

LIBER VI

1 "Interea Psyche variis iactabatur discursibus dies noctesque mariti vestigationibus inquieta animo, tanto cupidior iratum licet, si non uxoriis[1] blanditiis lenire, certe servilibus precibus propitiare. Et prospecto templo quodam in ardui montis vertice, 'Unde autem' inquit 'scio an istic meus degat dominus?' Et ilico dirigit citatum gradum, quem defectum prorsus assiduis laboribus spes incitabat et votum. Iamque naviter emensis celsioribus iugis pulvinaribus sese proximam intulit. Videt spicas frumentarias in acervo et alias flexiles in corona, et spicas hordei videt. Erant et falces et operae messoriae mundus omnis, sed cuncta passim iacentia et incuria confusa et ut solet aestu laborantium manibus proiecta. Haec singula Psyche curiose dividit et discretim semota[2] rite componit, rata scilicet nullius dei fana ac[3] caerimonias neglegere se debere, sed omnium benivolam misericordiam corrogare.

[1] F *uxoris.*
[2] F *remota.*
[3] F omits *ac.*

BOOK VI

"Meanwhile Psyche wandered this way and that, restlessly tracking her husband day and night, so eager was she, even if she could not soften his anger with a wife's allurements, at least to try to appease him with a slave's prayers. When she spotted a temple at the top of a high mountain, she said, 'How do I know if perhaps that is not where my master lives?' At once she began to walk rapidly toward it; although she was very weary from continuous effort, hope and desire quickened her pace. When she had valiantly climbed the lofty ridge, she went in and stood near the holy couch. There she saw ears of grain in a heap and others woven into wreaths, and ears of barley. There were sickles too, and all the implements of harvest work, but everything was lying scattered about and in careless disorder, as if tossed from the labourers' hands in the summer heat. Psyche carefully separated all these objects one by one and arranged them properly in distinct piles, evidently believing that she ought not to neglect any god's shrines and rituals, but appeal to the benevolence and pity of them all.

2 "Haec eam sollicite seduloque curantem Ceres alma deprehendit, et longum exclamat protinus: 'Ain, Psyche miseranda? Totum per orbem Venus anxia disquisitione tuum vestigium furens animi requirit, teque ad extremum supplicium expetit et totis numinis sui viribus ultionem flagitat. Tu vero rerum mearum tutelam nunc geris et aliud quicquam cogitas nisi de tua salute?'

"Tunc Psyche pedes eius advoluta et uberi fletu rigans deae vestigia humumque verrens crinibus suis, multiiugis precibus editis veniam postulabat. 'Per ego te frugiferam tuam dexteram istam deprecor, per laetificas messium caerimonias, per tacita secreta cistarum, et per famulorum tuorum draconum pinnata curricula, et glebae Siculae sulcamina, et currum rapacem et terram tenacem, et illuminarum Proserpinae nuptiarum demeacula et luminosarum filiae inventionum remeacula, et cetera quae silentio tegit Eleusinis Atticae sacrarium: miserandae Psyches animae, supplicis tuae, subsiste. Inter istam spicarum congeriem patere vel pauculos dies delitescam, quoad deae

---

[1] Ceres (the Greek Demeter) was a goddess of agriculture. Her daughter Proserpina was abducted in Sicily by Pluto and removed to the underworld, and her mother's grief brought infertility upon the world: a compromise was reached whereby the daughter would spend part of the year above ground and part below. Her most famous cult-centre was at Eleusis, near Athens,

2 "When bountiful Ceres discovered her attentively and diligently taking care of her shrine, she instantly exclaimed from afar: 'What's this, pitiable Psyche? All over the world Venus is making an intense investigation to track you down, raging in her heart. She seeks to inflict condign punishment upon you and demands vengeance with all the power of her godhead. But here you are, acting as caretaker of my property. How can you be thinking about anything except your own safety?'

"Then Psyche fell before her, drenching the goddess's feet with a flood of tears and sweeping the ground with her hair. She uttered manifold entreaties as she sought to win her favour. 'I beseech you by your fertile right hand, by the fructifying rites of the harvest, by the silent mysteries of the sacred baskets; and by the winged course of your dragon-servants, the furrows of the Sicilian soil, the ravisher's chariot and the grasping ground, Proserpina's descent to a lightless wedding and your daughter's lamplit discovery and ascent; and by all other secrets which the sanctuary of Attic Eleusis cloaks in silence[1]: succour the pitiable soul of Psyche, your suppliant. Let me hide here for a few days at least, among your stores of grain, until the

where mysteries were celebrated involving death and resurrection. Sacred objects in her cult were concealed in a basket (*cista*), and Ceres is sometimes represented as travelling in a dragon-drawn chariot. See Ovid, *Metamorphoses* V 341–661.

tantae saeviens ira spatio temporis mitigetur, vel certe meae vires diutino labore fessae quietis intervallo leniantur.'

3 "Suscipit Ceres: 'Tuis quidem lacrimosis precibus et commoveor et opitulari cupio, sed cognatae meae, cum qua etiam foedus antiquum amicitiae colo, bonae praeterea feminae, malam gratiam subire nequeo. Decede itaque istis aedibus protinus, et quod a me retenta custoditaque non fueris, optimi consule.'

"Contra spem suam repulsa Psyche et afflicta duplici maestitia, iter retrorsum porrigens, inter subsitae convallis sublucidum lucum prospicit fanum sollerti fabrica structum. Nec ullam vel dubiam spei melioris viam volens omittere, sed adire cuiuscumque dei veniam, sacratis foribus proximat. Videt dona pretiosa et[1] lacinias auro litteratas ramis arborum postibusque suffixas, quae cum gratia facti nomen deae cui fuerant dicata testabantur. Tunc genu nixa et manibus aram tepentem amplexa, detersis ante lacrimis sic apprecatur:

4 "'Magni Iovis germana et coniuga, sive tu Sami, quae sola[2] partu vagituque et alimonia tua gloriatur, tenes vetusta delubra; sive celsae Carthaginis,

[1] F *haec.*

[2] A certain correction for F's *quaerola.*

powerful goddess's raging anger is softened by the passing of time, or at least until my strength, which is exhausted from my long toil, is soothed by an interval of rest.'

3 "Ceres replied, 'Your tearful prayers move me deeply and I long to come to your aid, but Venus is my relative and we have old ties of friendship. Besides she is a good woman, and I cannot risk causing bad feelings between us. So depart from this house at once, and count yourself lucky that I did not detain you as my prisoner.'

"Driven out, disappointed in her hopes, and doubly afflicted with grief, Psyche retraced her steps. In a valley below, in the middle of a faintly lighted grove, she caught sight of an artfully constructed shrine. Unwilling to omit any possible path, however doubtful, toward improved hopes, and willing to seek favour from any divinity, she approached the consecrated doors. She saw costly offerings and ribbons lettered in gold attached to the tree-branches and doorposts, which bore witness to the name of the goddess to whom they had been dedicated, along with thanks for her deed. Psyche knelt and embraced in her arms the altar still warm with sacrifice, dried her tears, and then prayed.

4 "'O sister and consort of great Jupiter—whether you dwell in the ancient sanctuary of Samos, which alone glories in your birth and infant wails and nursing; or whether you frequent the blessed site of lofty Carthage, which worships you as a virgin who

quae te virginem vectura leonis caelo commeantem percolit, beatas sedes frequentas; seu[1] prope ripas Inachi, qui te iam nuptam Tonantis et reginam dearum memorat, inclutis Argivorum praesides moenibus; quam cunctus oriens Zygiam veneratur et omnis occidens Lucinam appellat: sis meis extremis casibus Iuno Sospita, meque in tantis exanclatis laboribus defessam imminentis periculi metu libera. Quod sciam, soles praegnatibus periclitantibus ultro subvenire.'

"Ad istum modum supplicanti statim sese Iuno cum totius sui numinis augusta dignitate praesentat, et protinus 'Quam vellem' inquit 'per fidem nutum meum precibus tuis accommodare. Sed contra voluntatem Veneris, nurus meae, quam filiae semper dilexi loco, praestare me pudor non sinit. Tunc etiam legibus quae servos alienos perfugas[2] invitis dominis vetant suscipi prohibeor.'

[1] F *seues.*
[2] Sometimes emended to *profugos.*

---

[1] Juno (the Greek Hera) is here learnedly and accurately invoked by Psyche with a syncretistic mixture of references to Greek, Roman, and Punic cult-centres, titles and functions. Samos is an island in the eastern Aegean. At Carthage, the Romans assimilated the Punic goddess Tanit, calling her Juno Caelestis. Argos was a city-state in the Peloponnese; its personified river Inachus was the father of Io, whom Jupiter raped and Juno

travels through the sky on the back of a lion; or whether you protect the renowned walls of the Argives beside the banks of Inachus, who proclaims you now the Thunderer's bride and queen of goddesses—you whom all the East adores as "Yoker" and all the West calls "Bringer into Light"—be you Juno Savioulress to me in my uttermost misfortunes.[1] I am so weary from enduring great toils. Free me from fear of the danger threatening me, for I know you are wont to come freely to the aid of pregnant women in peril.'

"While she was making this supplication Juno suddenly appeared to her in all the august majesty of her godhead. 'In faith, how I wish,' she said at once, 'that I could accommodate my will to your petitions. But I would be ashamed to set myself against the will of my daughter-in-law Venus,[2] whom I have always loved as a daughter. And besides I am prevented by laws forbidding anyone to harbour the fugitive slaves of others without their masters' consent.'[3]

mercilessly persecuted. The titles Zygia (Greek) and Lucina (Latin) refer to Juno's primary function in the Greco-Roman world, that of woman's protector in marriage and childbirth.

[2] Vulcan was Juno's son.

[3] E.g. *Codex Iustinianus* VI i 4: "Whoever shall harbour a runaway slave in his house or on his land without the owner's knowledge shall return him, together with another slave of equal value or twenty solidi."

5 "Isto quoque Fortunae naufragio Psyche perterrita, nec indipisci iam maritum volatilem quiens, tota spe salutis deposita, sic ipsa suas cogitationes consuluit:

"'Iam quae possunt alia meis aerumnis temptari vel adhiberi subsidia, cui nec dearum quidem, quamquam volentium, potuerunt prodesse suffragia? Quo rursum itaque tantis laqueis inclusa vestigium porrigam, quibusque tectis vel etiam tenebris abscondita magnae Veneris inevitabiles oculos effugiam? Quin igitur masculum tandem sumis animum et cassae speculae renuntias fortiter, et ultroneam te dominae tuae reddis et vel sera modestia saevientes impetus eius mitigas? Qui scias an etiam, quem diu quaeritas, illuc in domo matris reperies?' Sic ad dubium obsequium, immo ad certum exitium praeparata, principium futurae secum meditabatur obsecrationis.

6 "At Venus terrenis remediis inquisitionis abnuens caelum petit. Iubet instrui[1] currum, quem ei Vulcanus aurifex subtili fabrica studiose poliverat et ante thalami rudimentum nuptiale munus obtulerat, limae tenuantis detrimento conspicuum et ipsius auri damno pretiosum. De multis, quae circa

[1] F *construi.*

5 "Terrified by this second shipwreck of her fortunes, and now unable to reach her winged husband, Psyche gave up all hope of being saved and took counsel with her own thoughts.

"'What more can I try now? What other aids can be applied to my tribulations, since even the votes of the goddesses, favourable as they are, could not help me? Where else can I turn my steps, caught as I am in such a powerful noose? What roof or darkness can I hide beneath to evade the inescapable eyes of mighty Venus? So why not finally take courage like a man and bravely abandon your vain hopes? Hand yourself over voluntarily to your mistress and soften her furious attacks by submission, late though it be. Besides, who knows but what you will actually find the one you have long been searching for, there in his mother's house?'

In this way, prepared to risk the uncertain consequences of compliance—or rather sure destruction—she pondered how she should begin her coming appeal.

6 "Venus, meanwhile, had abandoned her attempts to track her down on earth and was making for heaven. She ordered her chariot fitted out, the one that Vulcan the goldsmith had carefully embellished with refined craftsmanship and offered her as a wedding gift before their first experience of marriage. It shone more brightly for what had been rubbed away by the refining file, and had become more valuable from the very loss of gold. From the

cubiculum dominae stabulant, procedunt quattuor candidae columbae, et hilaris incessibus picta colla torquentes iugum gemmeum subeunt, susceptaque domina laetae subvolant. Currum deae prosequentes gannitu constrepenti lasciviunt passeres, et ceterae quae dulce cantitant aves melleis modulis suave resonantes adventum deae pronuntiant. Cedunt nubes et Caelum filiae panditur et summus aether cum gaudio suscipit deam, nec obvias aquilas vel accipitres rapaces pertimescit magnae Veneris canora familia.

7 "Tunc se protinus ad Iovis regias arces dirigit, et petitu superbo Mercuri, dei vocalis, operae necessariam usuram postulat. Nec renuit Iovis caerulum supercilium. Tunc ovans ilico, comitante etiam Mercurio, Venus caelo demeat eique sollicite serit verba:

"'Frater Arcadi, scis nempe sororem tuam Venerem sine Mercuri praesentia nil umquam fecisse, nec te praeterit utique quanto iam tempore delitescentem ancillam nequiverim reperire. Nil ergo superest quam tuo praeconio praemium investigationis publicitus edicere. Fac ergo mandatum matures meum et indicia qui possit agnosci manifeste designes, ne, si quis occultationis illicitae

---

[1] See note at IV 28.

[2] In epic, Mercury functions as messenger between gods and men.

flock stabled round their mistress's bedroom, four white doves step forward and with joyful gait twist their painted necks and walk beneath the jewelled yoke, then lift their mistress and happily take flight. Sparrows follow in the train of the goddess's chariot, frisking about with merry chirping; and all the other kinds of songbird too proclaim the goddess's approach by delightfully sounding their sweet melodies. The clouds make way and Heaven opens up to its daughter[1] and the topmost ether receives the goddess in gladness. Nor is great Venus' song-filled retinue afraid of swooping eagles or preying hawks along their path.

7 "Then she went straight to the royal citadel of Jupiter and declared in a haughty petition that she urgently required to borrow the services of Mercury, the herald god.[2] Nor did Jupiter's cerulean brow nod nay. At once Venus triumphantly descended from heaven, with Mercury too in her train, to whom she spoke the following earnest words:

"'Arcadian brother, you know full well that your sister Venus has never accomplished anything without Mercury's presence, and it has surely not escaped your notice that I have long been vainly trying to find my runaway slave-girl. Nothing else is left then but for you to proclaim publicly a reward for whoever finds her. So see to it that you execute my commission quickly, and clearly describe the features by which she can be recognised. I do not want anyone who may be faced with the charge of

crimen subierit, ignorantiae se possit excusatione defendere.' Et simul dicens libellum ei porrigit, ubi Psyches nomen continebatur et cetera. Quo facto protinus domum secessit.

8 "Nec Mercurius omisit obsequium. Nam per omnium ora populorum passim discurrens, sic mandatae praedicationis munus exsequebatur: 'Si quis a fuga retrahere vel occultam demonstrare poterit fugitivam regis filiam, Veneris ancillam, nomine Psychen, conveniat retro metas Murtias Mercurium praedicatorem, accepturus indicivae[1] nomine ab ipsa Venere septem savia suavia et unum blandientis appulsu linguae longe mellitum.'

"Ad hunc modum pronuntiante Mercurio tanti praemii cupido certatim omnium mortalium studium arrexerat. Quae res nunc vel maxime sustulit Psyches omnem cunctationem. Iamque fores eius dominae proximanti occurrit una de famulitione Veneris nomine Consuetudo, statimque quantum maxime potuit exclamat: 'Tandem, ancilla nequissima, dominam habere te scire coepisti? An pro cetera morum tuorum temeritate istud quoque nescire te fingis, quantos labores circa tuas inquisitiones sustinuerimus? Sed bene quod meas

[1] F *indiciviae.*

illegal concealment to be able to defend himself with a plea of ignorance.' With these words she handed him a handbill containing Psyche's name and all other particulars, and immediately departed home.

8 "Mercury did not fail to comply, but ran from person to person everywhere, fulfilling his assigned responsibility with the following proclamation: 'If anyone can arrest the flight or reveal the whereabouts of a runaway princess, a slave-girl of Venus, known as Psyche, he should meet this announcer, Mercury, behind the Murcian turning-post.[1] There as a reward for his information he will receive from Venus herself seven delicious kisses plus one more, deeply sweetened by the touch of her caressing tongue.'

"At this proclamation from Mercury, the lust for so splendid a reward aroused the competitive zeal of every mortal man. This circumstance more than all else put an end to Psyche's hesitation. As she was approaching her mistress's door, one of Venus' domestic staff, named Habit, ran towards her and instantly began shouting at the top of her voice. 'So you have finally come to recognise that you have a mistress, you worthless hussy! This would be just like your usual thoughtless behaviour, pretending not to know how much trouble we have had to suffer in our search for you. But it's a good job that I'm the

[1] A spot in the Circus Maximus at Rome, where there was a shrine of Venus Murcia. The passage suggests that Apuleius was writing at Rome for a Roman audience.

potissimum manus incidisti et inter Orci cancros iam ipsos haesisti datura scilicet actutum tantae contumaciae poenas.'

9 "Et audaciter in capillos eius immissa manu trahebat eam nequaquam renitentem.[1] Quam ubi primum inductam oblatamque sibi conspexit Venus, laetissimum cachinnum extollit et qualem solent furenter irati, caputque quatiens et ascalpens aurem dexteram, 'Tandem' inquit 'dignata es socrum tuam salutare? An potius maritum, qui tuo vulnere periclitatur, intervisere venisti? Sed esto secura; iam enim excipiam te, ut bonam nurum condecet.' Et 'Ubi sunt' inquit 'Sollicitudo atque Tristities, ancillae meae?'

"Quibus intro vocatis torquendam tradidit eam. At illae sequentes erile praeceptum Psychen misellam flagellis afflictam et ceteris tormentis excruciatam iterum dominae conspectui reddunt. Tunc rursus sublato risu Venus 'Et ecce' inquit 'nobis turgidi ventris sui lenocinio commovet miserationem, unde me praeclara subole aviam beatam scilicet faciat. Felix vero ego, quae in ipso aetatis meae flore vocabor avia, et vilis ancillae filius nepos Veneris audiet. Quamquam inepta ego frustra filium

[1] F *retinentem.*

---

[1] Literally "the crabs of Orcus": the expression is puzzling, for we expect *fauces*, "jaws", as at VII 7 *mediis Orci faucibus.*

one into whose hands you have fallen, for now you are caught in the very clutches of Death[1] and you will certainly pay the penalty without delay for your gross insubordination.'

9 "With that she boldly seized her by the hair and dragged her inside. Psyche offered no resistance, and was brought in and presented to Venus. The instant the goddess caught sight of her, she burst out in wild laughter, as men are wont to do in rage. Then shaking her head and scratching at her right ear, she exclaimed: 'So, you have finally deigned to call on your mother-in-law, have you? Or have you come rather to visit your husband, who is in critical condition from that wound you gave him? But don't you worry: I shall receive you now in the proper way for a good daughter-in-law.' And she called out, 'Where are my servants Trouble and Sadness?'

"When they had been summoned in, she handed Psyche over to them for torture. Following their mistress's orders they scourged poor Psyche with whips and tortured her with every other sort of device, and brought her back to Venus' presence. Then Venus burst out laughing again. 'Look at her!' she said. 'She is moving us to pity with that alluring swollen belly of hers. With that illustrious progeny she no doubt means to make me a happy grandmother. Lucky me! In the very flower of my youth I shall be called grandmother; and the son of a cheap slave-girl will be known as Venus' grandson. But how foolish I am to misuse the word "son", since the

dicam. Impares enim nuptiae et praeterea in villa sine testibus et patre non consentiente factae legitimae non possunt videri, ac per hoc spurius iste nascetur, si tamen partum omnino perferre te patiemur.'

10 "His editis involat eam vestemque plurifariam diloricat, capilloque discisso et capite conquassato graviter affligit. Et accepto frumento et hordeo et milio et papavere et cicere et lente et faba commixtisque acervatim confusis in unum grumulum, sic ad illam: 'Videris enim mihi tam deformis ancilla nullo alio sed tantum sedulo ministerio amatores tuos promereri. Iam ergo et ipsa[1] frugem tuam periclitabor. Discerne[2] seminum istorum passivam congeriem, singulisque granis rite dispositis atque seiugatis ante istam vesperam opus expeditum approbato mihi.'

"Sic assignato tantorum seminum cumulo ipsa cenae nuptiali[3] concessit. Nec Psyche manus admolitur inconditae illi et inextricabili moli, sed immanitate praecepti consternata silens obstupescit. Tunc formicula illa parvula atque ruricola, certa[4] difficultatis tantae laborisque, miserta contuber-

[1] F *ipsam.*

[2] F *discernere.*

[3] F *nuptialis.*

[4] F *certati* corrected to *certata.*

marriage was between unequals[1]; besides, it took place in a country house without witnesses and without the father's consent. Hence it cannot be regarded as legal and therefore your child will be born illegitimate—if indeed we allow you to go through with the birth at all.'

10 "Having delivered this tirade Venus flew at her, ripped her dress into several pieces, tore her hair, and beat her head, hurting her sorely. Next she took some wheat and barley and millet and poppy-seed and chickpeas and lentils and beans, jumbled them up by the heapful and poured them together in a single mound. Then she turned to Psyche. 'You are such a hideous slave,' she said, 'that I do not think you can attract lovers by anything except hard work. Therefore I shall now test your worth myself. Sort out that motley mass of seeds and put each grain properly in its own separate pile. Finish the job before this evening and show it to me for my approval.'

"After assigning her this mountain of seeds, she herself went off to a wedding dinner. Psyche, instead of applying her hands to that disordered and unresolvable mass, sat silently dumbfounded and dismayed by the enormity of the task. Then an ant—the little country ant—recognising the great difficulty and toil involved, pitied the bride of the

[1] Under Roman law marriage could not take place between parties of widely different social position (e.g. free and servile).

nalis magni dei socrusque saevitiam exsecrata, discurrens naviter convocat corrogatque cunctam formicarum accolarum classem. 'Miseremini, Terrae omniparentis agiles alumnae, miseremini, et Amoris uxori, puellae lepidae, periclitanti prompta velocitate succurrite.' Ruunt aliae superque aliae sepedum populorum undae, summoque studio singulae granatim totum digerunt acervum, separatimque distributis dissitisque generibus, e conspectu perniciter abeunt.

11 "Sed initio noctis e convivio nuptiali, vino madens et fraglans balsama, Venus remeat totumque revincta corpus rosis micantibus, visaque diligentia miri laboris, 'Non tuum,' inquit 'nequissima, nec tuarum manuum istud opus, sed illius cui tuo, immo et ipsius, malo placuisti.' Et frusto cibarii panis ei proiecto cubitum facessit.

"Interim Cupido solus interioris domus unici cubiculi custodia clausus coercebatur acriter, partim ne petulanti luxurie vulnus gravaret, partim ne cum sua cupita conveniret. Sic ergo distentis et sub uno tecto separatis amatoribus taetra nox exanclata.

"Sed Aurora commodum inequitante, vocatae

great god and abominated the cruelty of her mother-in-law. Running strenuously this way and that, it convoked and assembled an entire squadron of neighborhood ants, shouting, 'Have pity, ye nimble nurselings of Earth, the mother of all, have pity, and be prompt and quick to aid Love's wife, a pretty girl in peril.' Wave after wave of the six-footed folk came rushing up. With indefatigable industry they individually took the entire heap apart, grain by grain, distributed and sorted the different kinds in separate piles, and then speedily disappeared from sight.

11 "At nightfall Venus returned from her wedding banquet, soaked in wine and smelling of balsam, her whole body wreathed in glistening roses. When she saw the wonderful industry with which the task had been performed, she exclaimed: 'This is not your work, vile creature, nor the accomplishment of those hands of yours, but rather his, the boy who fell in love with you, to your misfortune, and his too.' Then she tossed her a piece of bread for her supper and went off to bed.

"In the meantime Cupid was being kept under close guard, locked up in solitary confinement in one room in the inner part of the house, partly for fear that he would aggravate his wound by wanton self-indulgence, and partly to keep him from meeting his beloved. Thus, sundered and separated under one roof, the lovers dragged out an anguished night.

"Just as Dawn came riding in, Venus summoned

Psychae Venus infit talia: 'Videsne illud nemus, quod fluvio praeterluenti ripisque longis attenditur, cuius invii frutices[1] vicinum fontem despiciunt? Oves ibi nitentis auri vero decore[2] florentes incustodito pastu vagantur. Inde de coma pretiosi velleris floccum mihi confestim quoquo modo quaesitum afferas censeo.'

12 "Perrexit Psyche volenter non obsequium quidem illa functura, sed requiem malorum praecipitio fluvialis rupis habitura. Sed inde de fluvio musicae suavis nutricula, leni crepitu dulcis aurae divinitus inspirata, sic vaticinatur harundo viridis: 'Psyche, tantis aerumnis exercita, neque tua miserrima morte meas sanctas aquas polluas, nec vero istud horae[3] contra formidabiles oves feras aditum, quoad de solis flagrantia mutuatae[4] calorem truci rabie solent efferri,[5] cornuque acuto et fronte saxea et nonnunquam venenatis morsibus in exitium saevire mortalium. Sed dum meridies solis sedaverit vaporem et pecua[6] spiritus fluvialis serenitate conquieverint, poteris sub illa procerissima platano, quae mecum simul unum fluentum bibit, latenter abscondere. Et cum primum mitigata furia laxaverint oves animum, percussis frondibus attigui nemoris lanosum aurum reperies, quod passim stirpibus convexis obhaerescit.'

[1] F *imi gurgites.* [2] F *nitentes auri .. cole.*
[3] F *istius ore.* [4] F *mutuata.*
[5] *efferari* is an attractive emendation.
[6] F *pecula.*

Psyche and addressed her. 'Do you see those woods that fringe the long banks of the river flowing past, where dense thickets look down upon a nearby spring? Sheep whose fleeces shine with the pure hue of gold wander there and graze unguarded. Procure a hank of their fleece of precious wool in any way you please, and bring it to me at once. That is my decree.'

12 "Psyche set out with a will, not indeed to fulfil the assignment but to find rest from her ills by throwing herself off the cliff into the river. But, there from the stream, a green reed, nurse of melodious music, divinely inspired by the gentle stirring of a sweet breeze, prophesied as follows. 'Poor Psyche, you are assailed by so many sorrows. Do not pollute my sacred waters with your pitiful suicide. And do not approach those fearsome wild sheep at this time of day, when they borrow heat from the burning sun and often break out in fierce madness, venting their fury in the destruction of men with their sharp horns and rock-like foreheads, and sometimes even with poisonous bites. But until the afternoon allays the sun's heat and the flock settles down under the calming influence of the river breeze, you can hide in concealment under this tall plane-tree which drinks from the same current as I. And then as soon as the flock's madness is assuaged and their spirit relaxed, if you shake the foliage in the adjacent woods, you will find some of the woolly gold clinging here and there to the bent branches.'

13 "Sic harundo simplex et humana Psychen aegerrimam salutem suam docebat. Nec auscultatu impaenitendo[1] diligenter instructa illa cessavit, sed observatis omnibus furatrina facili flaventis auri mollitie congestum gremium Veneri reportat. Nec tamen apud dominam saltem secundi laboris periculum secundum testimonium meruit, sed contortis superciliis surridens amarum sic inquit: 'Nec me praeterit huius quoque facti auctor adulterinus. Sed iam nunc ego sedulo periclitabor an oppido forti animo singularique prudentia sis praedita. Videsne insistentem celsissimae illi rupi montis ardui verticem, de quo fontis atri fuscae defluunt undae proximaeque conceptaculo vallis inclusae Stygias irrigant paludes et rauca[2] Cocyti fluenta nutriunt? Indidem mihi de summi fontis penita scaturrigine rorem rigentem hauritum ista confestim defers urnula.'[3] Sic aiens crystallo dedolatum vasculum, insuper ei graviora comminata, tradidit.

14 "At illa studiose gradum celerans montis extremum petit cumulum, certe vel illic inventura vitae[4] pessimae finem. Sed cum primum praedicti iugi conterminos locos appulit, videt rei vastae letalem difficultatem. Namque saxum immani mag-

[1] F *paenitendo.*

[2] F *pauca.*

[3] F *defer surnula.*

[4] F *invitae* for *inventura vitae.*

13 "Thus a kind and simple reed taught suffering Psyche how to save herself. Once she had been carefully instructed she never faltered or had reason to regret obeying. She heeded all the advice, and with facile thievery filled the folds of her dress with the softness of yellow gold and brought it back to Venus. But, in her mistress's eyes at least, the danger of her second labour earned her no favourable commendation. Venus knitted her eyebrows and said with a bitter smile, 'I am well aware of the illicit prompter of this accomplishment too! But I shall now seriously put you to the test to find out if you really are endowed with courageous spirit and singular intelligence. Do you see that steep mountain-peak standing above the towering cliff? Dark waves flow down from a black spring on that peak and are enclosed by the reservoir formed by the valley nearby, to water the swamps of Styx and feed the rasping currents of Cocytus. Draw me some of the freezing liquid from there, from the innermost bubbling at the top of the spring, and bring it to me quickly in this phial.' With that she handed her a small vessel hewn out of crystal, and added some harsher threats for good measure.

14 "Psyche eagerly and speedily began walking toward the top of that mountain-peak, determined there at least to end her wretched life. But when she reached the area adjacent to the aforementioned ridge, she saw at once the deadly difficulty of her enormous task. A towering rock of monstrous size,

nitudine procerum et inaccessa salebritate lubricum mediis e faucibus lapidis fontes horridos evomebat, qui statim proni foraminis lacunis editi perque proclive delapsi et angusti canalis exarato[1] contecti tramite proximam convallem latenter incidebant. Dextra laevaque cautibus cavatis proserpunt ecce[2] longa colla porrecti saevi dracones, inconivae vigiliae luminibus addictis et in perpetuam lucem pupulis excubantibus. Iamque et ipsae semet muniebant vocales aquae. Nam et 'Discede!' et 'Quid facis? Vide!' et 'Quid agis? Cave!' et 'Fuge!' et 'Peribis!' subinde clamant. Sic impossibilitate ipsa mutata in lapidem Psyche, quamvis praesenti corpore, sensibus tamen aberat, et inextricabilis periculi mole prorsus obruta lacrimarum etiam extremo solacio carebat.

15 "Nec Providentiae bonae graves oculos innocentis animae latuit aerumna. Nam supremi[3] Iovis regalis ales illa repente propansis utrimque pinnis affuit, rapax aquila, memorque veteris obsequii, quo ductu Cupidinis Iovi pocillatorem Phrygium sustulerat, opportunam ferens opem deique numen in uxoris laboribus percolens, alti culminis diales vias

[1] F *exarto.*
[2] F *et.*
[3] F *primi.*

---

[1] Ganymede.

precariously jagged and inaccessible, belched from its stony jaws hideous streams, which issuing immediately from the chinks of a vertical opening flowed down over the slopes. Then, concealed in the path of a narrow channel that it had furrowed out for itself, the water slipped unseen down into the neighbouring valley. To right and left fierce snakes crawled out of the pitted crags, snakes which stretched out long necks, their eyes pledged to unblinking wakefulness and their pupils keeping nightwatch in ceaseless vision. And now even the water was defending itself, for it could talk, and it repeatedly cried out: 'Go away!' 'What are you doing? Look out!' 'What are you up to? Be careful!' 'Run!' 'You will die!' In her utter helplessness Psyche was transformed into stone. Although present in the body, she had taken leave of her senses, and, completely overwhelmed by the magnitude of her inescapable danger,she lacked even the last solace of tears.

15 "But the serious eyes of good Providence did not miss the tribulation of an innocent soul. Almighty Jupiter's royal bird, both wings outstretched, was there to help her: the rapacious eagle recalled that old service he had performed, when under Cupid's command he carried the Phrygian cupbearer[1] up to Jupiter; now he was bringing timely assistance and honouring the god's claim on him during his wife's ordeal. He abandoned the bright paths of heaven's

deserit et ob os puellae praevolans incipit:

"'At tu, simplex alioquin et expers rerum talium, sperasne[1] te sanctissimi nec minus truculenti fontis vel unam stillam posse furari vel omnino contingere? Diis etiam ipsique Iovi formidabiles aquas istas Stygias vel fando comperisti, quodque vos deieratis per numina deorum, deos per Stygis maiestatem solere? Sed cedo istam urnulam.'

"Et[2] protinus arreptam completum aquae[3] festinat, libratisque pinnarum nutantium molibus inter genas saevientium dentium et trisulca vibramina draconum remigium dextra laevaque porrigens, nolentes aquas et ut abiret innoxius praeminantes excipit, commentus ob iussum Veneris petere eique se praeministrare, quare paulo facilior adeundi fuit copia.

16 "Sic acceptam cum gaudio plenam urnulam Psyche Veneri citata rettulit. Nec tamen nutum deae saevientis vel tunc expiare potuit. Nam sic eam maiora atque peiora flagitia comminans appellat renidens exitiabile: 'Iam tu quidem magna videris quaedam mihi et alta prorsus malefica, quae talibus praeceptis meis obtemperasti naviter. Sed adhuc istud, mea pupula, ministrare debebis. Sume

[1] F *sperasque.*

[2] F *sed.*

[3] F *adreptam completamque.*

high summit and swooped down in front of the girl's face.

"'Do you,' he began, 'naive and inexperienced as you are in such matters, really expect to be able to steal, or even touch, a single drop from that holiest—and cruelest—of springs? Even the gods and Jupiter himself are frightened of these Stygian waters. You must know that, at least by hearsay, and that, as you swear by the powers of the gods, so the gods always swear by the majesty of the Styx. But here, give me that phial!'

"He snatched it out of her hands and hurried off to fill it with the water. Balancing his massive waving pinions he flew between the serpents' jaws, with their savage teeth and three-furrowed flickering tongues, plying his oars both right and left. The water resisted and threatened to harm him if he did not depart, but he took some, alleging that he was making his petition at Venus' orders and acting as her agent, on which account he was granted somewhat easier access.

16 "So Psyche joyfully took the full pitcher and speedily brought it back to Venus. But even then she still could not appease the cruel goddess's will. Menacing her with stronger and more terrible threats, Venus said to her with a baleful smile: 'I am convinced now that you must be some sort of great and mighty sorceress, seeing how thoroughly you have carried out these difficult tasks of mine. But there is still one more service you must perform, my

istam pyxidem et de die[1] protinus usque ad inferos et ipsius Orci ferales penates te derige. Tunc conferens[2] pyxidem Proserpinae, "Petit de te Venus" dicito "modicum de tua mittas ei formositate vel ad unam saltem dieculam sufficiens. Nam quod habuit, dum filium curat aegrotum consumpsit atque contrivit omne." Sed haud immaturius redito, quia me necesse est indidem delitam theatrum deorum frequentare.'

17 "Tunc Psyche vel maxime sensit ultimas fortunas suas, et velamento reiecto ad promptum exitium sese compelli manifeste comperit—quidni?—quae suis pedibus ultro ad Tartarum manesque commeare cogeretur. Nec cunctata diutius pergit ad quampiam turrim praealtam, indidem sese datura[3] praecipitem. Sic enim rebatur ad inferos recte atque pulcherrime se posse descendere. Sed turris prorumpit in vocem subitam, et 'Quid te' inquit 'praecipitio, misella, quaeris exstinguere? Quidque iam novissimo periculo laborique isto temere succumbis? Nam si spiritus corpore tuo semel fuerit seiugatus, ibis quidem profecto ad imum Tartarum,
18 sed inde nullo pacto redire poteris. Mihi ausculta.

[1] F *et dedit.*
[2] F *conferes.*
[3] F *sesedaturam.*

pet. Take this jar and go straight down from the daylight to the underworld and Orcus' own dismal abode. Then hand the jar to Proserpina and say: "Venus requests that you send her a little of your beauty, just enough to last her one brief day, because she has used up and exhausted all she had while caring for her sick son." But do not be too late coming back, because I have to rub some of it on before I go to attend the congress of the gods.'

17 "Then Psyche felt more than ever that her fortunes had reached the end: the veil had been drawn aside, and she realised clearly that she was being driven to immediate destruction—obviously, since she was being compelled to take a voluntary trip on her own two feet to Tartarus[1] and the shades of the dead. Without further delay she headed towards a very high tower, with the intention of jumping off it, since she thought this was the most direct and decorous route by which she could descend to the underworld.[2] But the tower suddenly broke into speech: 'Why, unhappy girl, do you want to destroy yourself in a suicide-leap? And why rashly succumb now to this task, which is the last of your labours? Once your breath is separated from your body, you will indeed go straight down to the bottom of Tartarus, but in no way will you be able to return from
18 there. Listen to my advice. The famous Achaean

[1] The underworld.

[2] Cf. Aristophanes, *Frogs* 117–33, where this is the jesting advice of Heracles to Dionysus.

Lacedaemo, Achaiae nobilis civitas, non longe sita est. Huius conterminam deviis abditam locis quaere Taenarum. Inibi spiraculum Ditis, et per portas hiantes monstratur iter invium, cui[1] te limine transmeato simul commiseris, iam canale directo perges ad ipsam Orci regiam. Sed non hactenus vacua debebis per illas tenebras incedere, sed offas polentae mulso concretas ambabus gestare manibus, at in ipso ore duas ferre stipes. Iamque confecta bona parte mortiferae viae, continaberis claudum asinum lignorum gerulum cum agasone simili, qui te rogabit decidentis[2] sarcinae fusticulos aliquos porrigas ei; sed tu nulla voce deprompta tacita praeterito. Nec mora cum ad flumen mortuum venies, cui praefectus Charon, protinus expetens portorium, sic ad ripam ulteriorem sutili cumba deducit commeantes. Ergo et inter mortuos avaritia vivit, nec Charon ille Ditis exactor[3] tantus deus quicquam gratuito facit. Sed moriens pauper viaticum debet quaerere, et aes si forte prae manu

[1] F *cuius.*
[2] F *decidenti.*
[3] F *Ditis et pater.*

---

[1] The Roman province Achaea included Lacedaemon (Sparta) and Cape Taenarus, where there was a temple and cave traditionally considered an entrance to the underworld. [2] The expression comes from Vergil,

city Lacedaemon is not far from here. Ask for Taenarus, hidden in a remote area bordering Lacedaemon.[1] There is Dis's breathing-vent,[2] and through wide-gaping doors one is shown a dead-end road. Once you cross the threshold and commit yourself to this road, you will continue by a direct track to Orcus' palace. But you must not go forward into that shadowy region empty-handed. In each hand you must carry a barley-cake soaked in mead, and hold two coins in your mouth.[3] Now, when you have completed a good part of your deathly journey you will meet a lame ass carrying wood, with a driver lame as well, who will ask you to hand him some twigs that have fallen off his load. But you must not utter a single word and must pass by him in silence. Very soon you will come to the river of the dead,[4] where the administrator Charon immediately demands the toll and then ferries travellers to the farther bank in his patched skiff. We see that greed is alive even among the dead; and Charon, Dis's tax-gatherer, great god that he is, does nothing unpaid. A poor man who is dying must find his passage-money, and unless a copper happens to be

Aeneid VII 568, and in this and the following chapter there are several other echoes of the poet.

[3] The dead were often buried with a small coin in the mouth to pay the ferryman Charon.

[4] Or "the dead river", if *mortuum* is read as neuter accusative singular instead of genitive plural.

non fuerit, nemo eum exspirare patietur. Huic squalido seni dabis nauli nomine de stipibus quas feres alteram, sic tamen ut ipse sua manu de tuo sumat ore. Nec setius tibi pigrum fluentum transmeanti quidam supernatans senex mortuus putres attollens manus orabit ut eum intra navigium trahas[1]; nec tu tamen illicita afflectare pietate.
19 Transito fluvio modicum te progressam[2] textrices orabunt anus telam struentes, manus paulisper accommodes; nec id tamen tibi contingere fas est. Nam haec omnia tibi et multa alia de Veneris insidiis orientur, ut vel unam de manibus omittas offulam. Nec putes futile istud polentacium damnum leve: altera enim perdita, lux haec tibi prorsus denegabitur. Canis namque praegrandis, teriugo et satis amplo capite praeditus, immanis et formidabilis, tonantibus[3] oblatrans faucibus mortuos, quibus iam nil mali potest facere, frustra territando, ante ipsum limen et atra atria Proserpinae semper excubans servat vacuam Ditis domum. Hunc offrenatum unius offulae praeda facile praeteribis ad ipsamque protinus Proserpinam introibis, quae te comiter excipiet ac benigne, ut et molliter assidere et prandium opipare suadeat sumere. Sed tu et humi

[1] F *tradas*. [2] F *progressa*.
[3] F *conantibus*.

---

[1] An allusion to the trick practised on Theseus, by which

on hand no one will let him breathe his last breath. For your fare you will give that filthy old man one of the coins you are carrying; but make him take it out of your mouth with his own hand. Likewise, while you are crossing that sluggish steam a dead old man, floating on the surface, will lift up his rotting hands and beg you to pull him into the boat. But be
19 not swayed by unlawful pity. After you have crossed the river and gone on a little farther, some old women weaving at a loom will ask you to lend a hand for a moment. But you must not touch this either. All this and much more will arise from traps for you laid by Venus, to make you let at least one cake out of your hands. Do not suppose that this paltry loss of a barley-cake is of no consequence: if you lose either cake you will never see the daylight again. For there is a huge dog with a triple head of vast size, a monstrous, fearsome creature who barks with thundering jaws, trying in vain to frighten the dead, to whom he can do no harm now. He lies in constant watch in front of the threshold outside Proserpina's black halls, guarding the insubstantial house of Dis. If you restrain him with one cake for prey, you will easily get by him and pass directly into Proserpina's presence. She will receive you courteously and kindly and try to persuade you to sit down comfortably beside her and eat a sumptuous supper.[1] But you must sit on the floor and ask

he was compelled to sit there for ever (see *Aeneid* VI 617–618).

reside et panem sordidum petitum esto; deinde nuntiato quid adveneris, susceptoque quod offeretur[1] rursus remeans canis saevitiam offula reliqua redime; ac deinde, avaro navitae data quam reservaveras stipe transitoque eius fluvio, recolens[2] priora vestigia ad istum caelestium siderum redies chorum. Sed inter omnia hoc observandum praecipue tibi censeo, ne velis aperire vel inspicere illam quam feres pyxidem, vel omnino divinae formositatis abditum arbitrari[3] curiosius thesaurum.'

20 "Sic turris illa prospicua vaticinationis munus explicuit. nec morata Psyche pergit Taenarum, sumptisque rite stipibus illis et offulis, infernum decurrit meatum. Transitoque per silentium asinario debili et amnica stipe vectori data, neglecto supernatantis mortui desiderio et spretis textricum subdolis precibus et offulae cibo sopita canis horrenda rabie, domum Proserpinae penetrat. Nec offerentis hospitae sedile delicatum vel cibum beatum amplexa, sed ante pedes eius residens humilis cibario pane contenta, Veneriam pertulit legationem. Statimque secreto repletam conclusamque pyxidem suscipit, et offulae sequentis fraude caninis latratibus obseratis residuaque navitae reddita stipe, longe vegetior ab inferis recurrit.

[1] F *efferetur*.

[2] Or perhaps *recalcans* "retreading".

[3] *arbitrari* is supplied by conjecture. Some infinitive seems to be needed: other suggestions are *scrutari*, *temptare*, *rimari*.

for common bread and eat that. Then announce why you have come, take what is put before you, and return, buying off the dog's cruelty with the remaining cake. Then give the greedy sailor the coin you have kept in reserve, cross his river, and by retracing your earlier steps you will return to this choir of heavenly stars. But above all else, I advise you to be especially careful not to open or look into the jar that you will be carrying, and in fact do not even think too inquisitively about the hidden treasure of divine beauty.'

20 "Thus that far-seeing tower performed its service of revelation. Without delay Psyche went to Taenarus, and when she had duly acquired the coins and cakes, she raced down the path to the underworld. She passed by the crippled ass-driver in silence, gave river-toll to the ferry-man, ignored the pleas of the floating corpse, spurned the cunning requests of the weaver-women, drugged the dog's terrifying madness by feeding him a cake, and penetrated the house of Proserpina. She embraced neither the luxurious seat nor the rich food which her hostess offered, but sitting on the ground at her feet and contenting herself with ordinary bread, she carried out Venus' commission. Quickly the jar was filled and closed in secret, and Psyche took it. She silenced the dog's barking with the trick of the second cake, paid her remaining coin to the sailor, and ran even more nimbly back from the underworld. When she had returned to the bright

Et repetita atque adorata candida ista luce, quamquam festinans obsequium terminare, mentem capitur temeraria curiositate. Et 'Ecce' inquit 'inepta ego divinae formositatis gerula, quae nec tantillum quidem indidem mihi delibo, vel sic illi amatori meo formoso placitura.'

21 "Et cum dicto reserat pyxidem; nec quicquam ibi rerum nec formositas ulla, sed infernus somnus ac vere Stygius, qui statim coperculo revelatus invadit eam crassaque soporis nebula cunctis eius membris perfunditur, et in ipso vestigio ipsaque semita collapsam possidet. Et iacebat immobilis et nihil aliud quam dormiens cadaver.

"Sed Cupido iam cicatrice solida revalescens, nec diutinam suae Psyches absentiam tolerans, per altissimam cubiculi quo cohibebatur elapsus fenestram, refectisque pinnis aliquanta quiete longe velocius provolans, Psychen accurrit suam; detersoque somno curiose et rursum in pristinam pyxidis sedem recondito, Psychen innoxio punctulo sagittae suae suscitat. Et 'Ecce' inquit 'rursum perieras, misella, simili curiositate. Sed interim quidem tu provinciam, quae tibi matris meae praecepto mandata est, exsequere naviter; cetera egomet videro.' His dictis amator levis in pinnas se dedit. Psyche vero

daylight and worshipfully saluted it, despite her haste to be finished with her term of service, her mind was overcome by rash curiosity. 'Look,' she said to herself, 'I am a fool to be a porter of divine beauty and not take out a tiny drop of it for myself. It might even enable me to please my beautiful lover.'

21 "No sooner said than done. She opened the jar, but there was nothing there, not a drop of beauty, just sleep—deathlike and truly Stygian sleep. Revealed when the cover was removed, it attacked her instantly, enveloping her entire body in a dense cloud of slumber. She collapsed on the path where she stood and the sleep took possession of her. She lay there motionless, no better than a sleeping corpse.

"But Cupid, recovering now that his scar had healed, could no longer endure the long absence of his beloved Psyche, and slipped out of the high window in the bedroom where he was confined. Since his wings had been restored by a period of rest, he flew much more rapidly; he rushed to his Psyche's side, carefully wiped off the sleep, and returned it to its original place in the jar. Then he roused her with a harmless prick of his arrow. 'See,' he said, 'you almost destroyed yourself again, poor girl, by your incurable curiosity. But now be quick and complete the commission assigned you by my mother's orders. I will take care of everything else.' With these words her lover lightly took to his wings. For her

confestim Veneri munus reportat Proserpinae.

22 "Interea Cupido amore nimio peresus et aegra facie matris suae repentinam sobrietatem pertimescens, ad armillum redit, alisque pernicibus caeli penetrato vertice, magno Iovi supplicat suamque causam probat. Tunc Iuppiter, prehensa Cupidinis buccula manuque ad os suum relata consaviat, atque sic ad illum 'Licet tu,' inquit 'domine fili, numquam mihi concessu deum decretum servaris honorem, sed istud pectus meum, quo leges elementorum et vices siderum disponuntur, convulneraris assiduis ictibus, crebrisque terrenae libidinis foedaveris casibus, contraque leges et ipsam Iuliam disciplinamque publicam turpibus adulteriis existimationem famamque meam laeseris, in serpentes, in ignes,[1] in feras, in aves, et gregalia pecua serenos vultus meos sordide reformando, at tamen modestiae meae memor quodque inter istas meas manus creveris, cuncta perficiam, dum tamen scias aemulos tuos cavere, ac si qua nunc in terris puella praepollet pulchritudine, praesentis beneficii vicem per

[1] Jahn has proposed *imbres*, referring to the seduction of Danaë, whom we expect to be mentioned; the two words are often confused.

---

[1] Literally "went back to the wine-jug", a proverbial phrase.

[2] The Lex Julia *de adulteriis*, of about 18 B.C., in which Augustus prescribed the penalties for adultery.

part, Psyche speedily carried Proserpina's gift back to Venus.

22 "Cupid, meanwhile, consumed with uncontrollable love and pale of face, was apprehensive of his mother's sudden austerity and so turned back to his old tricks.[1] On rapid wings he penetrated heaven's summit, where he knelt before great Jupiter and tried to win support for his case. Jupiter, pinching Cupid's cheek and raising his hand to his lips, kissed it, and then replied. 'My lord son,' he said, 'despite the fact that you have never preserved the respect decreed to me by the gods' permission, but have wounded my heart with repeated blows and shamed it with frequent failings of terrestrial passion, who ordain the laws of the elements and the orbits of the stars; and despite the fact that, in defiance of the laws—including the Julian decree itself[2]—and of public order, you have injured my good name and reputation through scandalous adulteries by vile transformations of my serene countenance into snakes, flames, beasts, birds, and herd-cattle[3]; nevertheless, mindful of my moderate disposition and the fact that you grew up in my own arms, I shall do everything you ask; but only on the condition that you know how to take precautions against your competitors, and also, if there is now on the earth a girl of outstanding beauty, you must give me

[3] In his seductions Jupiter employed many disguises: e.g. snake (Proserpina), flame (Aegina), swan (Leda), bull (Europa). See Ovid, *Metamorphoses* VI 103–114.

eam mihi repensare te debere.'

23 "Sic fatus iubet Mercurium deos omnes ad contionem protinus convocare ac, si qui coetu caelestium defuisset, in poenam decem milium nummum conventum iri pronuntiare. Quo metu statim completo caelesti theatro, pro sede sublimi sedens procerus Iuppiter sic enuntiat:

"'Dei conscripti Musarum albo, adulescentem istum quod manibus meis alumnatus sim profecto scitis omnes. Cuius primae iuventutis caloratos impetus freno quodam coercendos existimavi. Sat est cotidianis eum fabulis ob adulteria cunctasque corruptelas infamatum. Tollenda est omnis occasio, et luxuria puerilis nuptialibus pedicis alliganda. Puellam elegit et virginitate privavit. Teneat, possideat, amplexus Psychen semper suis amoribus perfruatur.'

"Et ad Venerem collata facie, 'Nec tu,' inquit 'filia, quicquam contristere, nec prosapiae tantae tuae statuque de matrimonio mortali metuas. Iam faxo nuptias non impares, sed legitimas et iure civili congruas.'

"Et ilico per Mercurium arripi Psychen et in caelum perduci iubet. Porrecto ambrosiae poculo, 'Sume,' inquit 'Psyche, et immortalis esto. Nec umquam digredietur a tuo nexu Cupido, sed istae vobis erunt perpetuae nuptiae.'

her as repayment for my present favor.'

23 "So saying he ordered Mercury to summon an immediate assembly of all the gods, announcing that anyone who absented himself from the meeting of the celestial citizens would be fined ten thousand sesterces. At this threat the celestial assembly-theatre was filled at once. Tall Jupiter, seated in his throne on high, made the following pronouncement:

"'O gods enrolled in the Muses' register, you all surely know that I raised this boy with my own hands. I have decided that the hot-blooded impulses of his early youth must be restrained by some bridle. There has been enough scandal from the daily tales of his adulteries and all sorts of immoralities. We must remove every opportunity, and chain his boyish self-indulgence with the shackles of matrimony. He has selected a girl and robbed her of her maidenhood: let him keep her to have and to hold, and in Psyche's arms let him indulge his passion forever.'

"Then he added, turning to Venus, 'Now, my daughter, do not be so gloomy and do not be afraid for your excellent pedigree and your status because of a mortal marriage. I will make the wedding no longer uneven, but legitimate and in accordance with civil law.'

"He immediately ordered Mercury to take hold of Psyche and bring her to heaven. Then he handed her a cup of ambrosia, saying, 'Drink this, Psyche, and you will be immortal. Cupid will never leave your embrace, and your marriage will last for ever.'

24 "Nec mora cum cena nuptialis affluens exhibetur. Accumbebat summum torum maritus, Psychen gremio suo complexus. Sic et cum sua Iunone Iuppiter ac deinde per ordinem toti dei. Tunc poculum nectaris, quod vinum deorum est, Iovi quidem suus pocillator, ille rusticus puer, ceteris vero Liber ministrabat; Vulcanus cenam coquebat, Horae rosis et ceteris floribus purpurabant omnia, Gratiae spargebant balsama, Musae quoque canora personabant. Apollo cantavit ad citharam,[1] Venus suavi musicae superingressa formosa saltavit, scaena sibi sic concinnata ut Musae quidem chorum canerent, tibias inflaret Saturus, et Paniscus ad fistulam diceret.[2]

"Sic rite Psyche convenit in manum Cupidinis; et nascitur illis maturo partu filia, quam Voluptatem nominamus."

25 Sic captivae puellae delira et temulenta illa narrabat anicula. Sed astans ego non procul dolebam mehercules quod pugillares et stilum non habebam qui tam bellam fabellam praenotarem.

Ecce confecto nescio quo gravi proelio latrones

[1] F *chiteram.*
[2] F *inflarent . . . dicerent.*

---

[1] Ganymede (cf. VI 15).
[2] Bacchus (the Greek Dionysus), god of the vintage.
[3] In his capacity as god of fire.

24 "Instantly there appeared a rich wedding-banquet. The bridegroom reclined on the couch of honour, clasping Psyche in his arms. Jupiter with his wife Juno were similarly placed, and then all the gods in order of rank. Jupiter was served a cup of nectar—the wine of the gods—by his shepherd cupbearer[1]; and the others were served by Liber.[2] Vulcan was cooking the dinner,[3] the Hours were colouring everything with roses and all the other flowers, the Graces were sprinkling balsam, and the Muses too were there, singing melodiously. Apollo chanted to the accompaniment of his lyre,[4] and Venus danced gorgeously, stepping to the tune of the lovely music. She had arranged the stage so that the Muses were singing in chorus, a Satyr blew the flute, and a Paniscus[5] played on the reed-pipes.

"Thus in proper form Psyche was given in marriage to Cupid. And when her time was come, a daughter was born to them, whom we call by the name Pleasure."

25 So ran the story told to the captive girl by that crazy, drunken old woman. I was standing not far off, and by Hercules I was upset not to have tablets and stilus to write down such a pretty tale.

Suddenly the robbers returned, after the conclu-

[4] He was associated with music and poetry, and is often portrayed holding a lyre.

[5] A type of woodland creature who were associated with Pan and shared some of his goat-like qualities.

adveniunt onusti. Non nulli tamen, immo promptiores, vulneratis domi relictis et plagas recurantibus, ipsi ad reliquas occultatas in quadam spelunca sarcinas, ut aiebant, proficisci gestiunt. Prandioque raptim tuburcinato, me et equum vectores rerum illarum futuros fustibus exinde tundentes producunt in viam, multisque clivis et anfractibus fatigatos prope ipsam vesperam perducunt ad quampiam speluncam, unde multis onustos rebus rursum ne breviculo quidem tempore refectos ociter[1] reducunt. Tantaque trepidatione festinabant, ut me plagis multis obtundentes propellentesque super lapidem propter viam positum deicerent, unde crebris aeque ingestis ictibus crure dextero et ungula sinistra me debilitatum aegre ad exsurgendum compellunt.

26 Et unus "Quo usque" inquit "ruptum istum asellum, nunc etiam claudum, frustra pascemus?" Et alius, "Quid quod et pessimo pede domum nostram accessit, nec quicquam idonei lucri exinde cepimus, sed vulnera et fortissimorum occisiones?" Alius iterum, "Certe ego, cum primum sarcinas istas quamquam invitus pertulerit, protinus eum vulturiis gratissimum pabulum futurum praecipitabo."

Dum secum mitissimi homines altercant de mea

[1] F *obiter.*

sion of some heavy fighting. They were loaded down, but some of them—the more enterprising, I mean—were eager to leave the injured at home to heal their wounds and start out again after the rest of the sacks, which they had hidden in a cave, as I heard them say. Hastily bolting down their dinner, they took me and the horse out on the road as future conveyors of the goods, beating us constantly with sticks. Finally toward evening, when we were exhausted from many a hill and winding dale, they brought us to a cave, loaded us with quantities of loot, and, not even allowing us a brief moment to regain our strength, started us back again with all speed. They were so agitated and in such a hurry that with their frequent battering and shoving they made me fall over a rock at the side of the road. They continued none the less to rain blows on me, eventually forcing me to get up, though I found it difficult, for I had gone lame in my right leg and left hoof.

26 "How long," said one of them, "are we going to waste food on this worn-out ass? Now he has gone lame as well." "Yes," said another, "his arrival brought our house bad luck, and since then we have not made any decent profit, but have suffered wounds and the loss of our bravest." "As for me," added a third, "as soon as he has finished, however unwillingly, carrying these sacks, I will throw him right over the cliff as a nice meal for the vultures."

While these gentle souls were still discussing my

nece, iam et domum perveneramus, nam timor ungulas mihi alas fecerat. Tum quae ferebamus amoliti properiter, nulla salutis nostrae cura ac ne meae quidem necis habita, comitibus ascitis qui vulnerati remanserant dudum, recurrunt reliqua ipsi[1] laturi taedio, ut aiebant, nostrae tarditatis.

Nec me tamen mediocris carpebat scrupulus contemplatione comminatae mihi mortis. Et ipse mecum: "Quid stas, Luci, vel quid iam novissimum exspectas? Mors, et haec acerbissima, decreto latronum tibi comparata est. Nec magno conatu res indiget. Vides istas rupinas proximas et praeacutas in his prominentes silices, quae te penetrantes antequam[2] decideris membratim dissipabunt? Nam et illa ipsa praeclara magia tua vultum laboresque tibi tantum asini, verum corium non asini crassum, sed hirudinis[3] tenue membranulum circumdedit. Quin igitur masculum tandem sumis animum tuaeque saluti, dum licet, consulis? Habes summam opportunitatem fugae, dum latrones absunt. An custodiam anus semimortuae formidabis, quam licet claudi pedis tui calce unica finire poteris? Sed quo gentium capessetur fuga, vel hospitium quis dabit? Haec quidem inepta et prorsus asinina cogi-

[1] F omits *-liqua ipsi.*
[2] A probable correction for F's *penetrante quam.*
[3] F *hirundinis.*

---

[1] Lucius quotes Psyche's words in VI 5.

death, we had already reached home, for fear had turned my hoofs into wings. They speedily unloaded the things we were carrying and, with no concern for our welfare or, for that matter, for my execution, they summoned the injured companions who had previously stayed behind and ran back to fetch the rest of the booty themselves, out of impatience, as they said, at our slowness.

I was racked by considerable anxiety as I contemplated the threat of death that hung over me. I thought to myself, "What are you standing around for, Lucius? Why are you waiting for the final act? Your death—and a very cruel death, too—has already been arranged by decree of the robbers. And its execution does not require much effort. Do you see that chasm over there, and those sharp rocks jutting out into it, which will impale you before you hit the bottom and tear you limb from limb? That wonderful magic of yours only gave you the appearance and burdens of an ass, but instead of an ass's thick hide it wrapped you in skin as delicate as a leech's. Well then, why not now display courage like a man[1] and seek your safety while you can? You have an excellent chance of escape while the robbers are away. Or are you afraid of that half-dead old hag guarding you? You can finish her off with just one kick of your foot, even if it is lame. But whither in the world shall your flight be directed? And who will provide sanctuary for you? Now that is a silly and totally asinine line of reason-

tatio. Quis enim viantium vectorem suum non libenter auferat secum?"

27 Et alacri statim nisu lorum quo fueram destinatus abrumpo meque quadripedi cursu proripio. Nec tamen astutulae anus milvinos oculos effugere potui. Nam ubi me conspexit absolutum, capta super sexum et aetatem audacia lorum prehendit ac me deducere ac revocare contendit. Nec tamen ego, memor exitiabilis propositi latronum, pietate ulla commoveor, sed incussis in eam posteriorum pedum calcibus protinus applaudo terrae. At illa, quamvis humi prostrata, loro tamen tenaciter inhaerebat, ut me procurrentem aliquantisper tractu sui sequeretur. Et occipit statim clamosis ululatibus auxilium validioris manus implorare. Sed frustra fletibus cassum tumultum commovebat, quippe cum nullus afforet qui suppetias ei ferre posset, nisi sola illa virgo captiva. Quae vocis excitu procurrens videt hercules memorandi spectaculi scaenam, non tauro, sed asino dependentem Dircen aniculam, sumptaque constantia virili facinus audet pulcherrimum. Extorto etenim loro manibus eius, me placidis gannitibus ab impetu revocatum naviter inscendit et sic ad cursum rursum incitat.

28 Ego simul voluntariae fugae voto et liberandae

---

[1] The wife of Lycus, king of Thebes. The sons of Antiope punished her for mistreating their mother by tying her to the horns of a bull, who tore her to pieces.

ing: what traveller would not be glad to take his means of transport with him?"

27 And so with a sudden brisk tug I broke the strap by which I had been hitched and darted forward on my four-footed course. But I still could not escape the hawk-like eyes of that vigilant old hag. When she saw that I had broken loose, with more boldness than one would expect of her sex and years she grabbed the strap and strove to pull me round and bring me back. But remembering the robbers' murderous intentions, I felt no pity for her but kicked at her with my hind feet and knocked her to the ground. But though she was lying flat she still clung stubbornly to the strap, so that for some distance, while I was running forward, she pursued me even as she was dragged along. At once she began to scream noisily, imploring the help of some stronger hand, but the feeble furore she caused with her crying was all in vain, because there was no one to come to her aid save only the captive maiden. She ran out in response to the cries and saw before her, by Hercules, a scene from a memorable show: an aged Dirce[1] dangling from an ass instead of a bull. The girl summoned up a man's courage and performed a bold and beautiful feat: she twisted the strap out of the old woman's hands, recalled me from my headlong flight with coaxing chatter, nimbly mounted my back, and then spurred me to a gallop once more.

28 I was moved not only by desire to effect my own

virginis studio, sed et plagarum suasu, quae me saepicule commonebant,[1] equestri celeritate quadripedi cursu solum replaudens, virgini[2] delicatas voculas adhinnire temptabam. Sed et scabendi dorsi mei simulatione nonnumquam obliquata cervice, pedes decoros puellae basiabam.

Tunc illa suspirans[3] altius caelumque sollicito nutu petens, "Vos," inquit "superi, tandem meis supremis periculis opem facite, et tu, Fortuna durior, iam saevire desiste. Sat tibi miseris istis cruciatibus meis litatum est. Tuque, praesidium meae libertatis meaeque salutis, si me domum pervexeris incolumem parentibusque et formoso proco reddideris, quas tibi gratias perhibebo, quos honores habebo, quos cibos exhibebo! Iam primum iubam istam tuam probe pectinatam meis virginalibus monilibus adornabo, frontem vero crispatam prius decoriter discriminabo, caudaeque setas incuria lavacri congestas et horridas prompta[4] diligentia perpolibo, bullisque te multis aureis inoculatum velut stellis sidereis relucentem et gaudiis popularium pomparum ovantem, sinu serico progestans nucleos et[5] edulia mitiora, te meum sospitatorem
29 cotidie saginabo. Sed nec inter cibos delicatos et otium profundum vitaeque totius beatitudinem deerit tibi dignitas gloriosa. Nam memoriam

[1] F *commovebant.*
[2] F *virginis.*
[3] F *spirans.*
[4] F (after correction) *compta.*
[5] *et* is an editorial addition.

self-chosen escape and eagerness to rescue the maiden, but also by the persuasion of the blows which admonished me from time to time; and so I smote the earth in a four-footed gallop with the speed of a racehorse. I tried to neigh soft sentences to the maiden, and sometimes, pretending to scratch my back, I bent my neck and kissed the girl's lovely feet.

Then she sighed deeply and turned her face anxiously toward heaven. "O gods above," she said, "help me at long last in my extreme peril. And you, cruel Fortune, now cease your fury. I have made you enough atonement with these pitiable torments I have suffered. And you, O guardian of my freedom and my life, if you carry me home safe and return me to my parents and my handsome suitor, how I shall thank you, and honour you, and provide you with food! First of all I will comb that mane of yours properly and adorn it with my girlhood jewellery. Next I will curl the hair on your forehead and part it gracefully. And the hair on your tail which now is matted and bristly from lack of washing I will disentangle with earnest attention. Spangled with many golden amulets and shining like the starry sky, you will march triumphantly in the people's joyous parades; in a silken apron I will bring you nuts and soft dainties, my saviour, and I will feed you full
29 every day. Yet in the midst of this fine food and the serene repose and complete happiness of your daily life, you will also enjoy this glorious honour. I will

praesentis fortunae meae divinaeque providentiae perpetua testatione signabo, et depictam in tabula fugae praesentis imaginem meae domus atrio dedicabo. Visetur et in fabulis audietur doctorumque stilis rudis perpetuabitur historia, 'Asino vectore virgo regia fugiens captivitatem.' Accedes antiquis et ipse miraculis, et iam credemus exemplo tuae veritatis et Phrixum arieti supernatasse et Arionem delphinum gubernasse et Europam tauro supercubasse. Quodsi vere Iuppiter mugivit in bovem, potest in asino meo latere aliqui vel vultus hominis vel facies deorum."

Dum haec identidem puella replicat votisque crebros intermiscet suspiratus, ad quoddam pervenimus trivium, unde me arrepto capistro dirigere dextrorsum magnopere gestiebat, quod ad parentes eius ea scilicet iretur via. Sed ego gnarus latrones illac ad reliquas commeasse praedas, renitebar firmiter atque sic in animo meo tacitus expostulabam: "Quid facis, infelix puella? Quid agis? Cur festinas ad Orcum? Quid meis pedibus facere contendis? Non enim te tantum verum etiam me perditum ibis." Sic nos diversa tendentes et in causa finali de proprietate soli, immo viae herciscundae

[1] Phrixus crossed the Hellespont on the ram with a golden fleece; the minstrel Arion was saved from drowning and carried to land by a dolphin (see Herodotus I 24); Europa was ferried across the sea by Jupiter in the form of a bull (see Ovid, *Metamorphoses* II 833–875).

put a seal on the memory of my present fortune and of divine providence by giving a lasting testimony, and I will have a panel painted with the picture of our present escape and enshrine it in the entrance-hall of my home. People will come to see this simple tale, and will hear about it when stories are told, and the pens of the learned will perpetuate it. 'A royal maiden flees captivity riding on an ass.' You yourself will be added to the ancient tales of wonder, and from the fact of your actual existence we will now believe that Phrixus swam the sea on a ram's back, that Arion piloted a dolphin, and that Europa rode on the back of a bull.[1] But if Jupiter truly bellowed with the throat of a bull, perhaps in this ass I am riding lurks the face of a man or the likeness of a god."

While the girl was repeating these sentiments again and again, mingling frequent sighs with her prayers, we arrived at a fork in the road. She seized my halter and tried hard to turn me to the right, because that was evidently the way to her parents'. But I knew that the robbers had gone along that road to fetch the rest of their loot, and so I stubbornly resisted, while objecting silently in my mind. "What are you doing, unhappy girl? What are you up to? Why are you hurrying so to the next world? Why do you insist on doing it on my feet? You are going to destroy not just yourself, but me too." And so there we were, straining in different directions, arguing a boundary dispute over possession of

contendentes, rapinis suis onusti coram deprehendunt ipsi latrones, et ad lunae splendorem iam inde longius cognitos risu maligno salutant.

30 Et unus e numero sic appellat: "Quorsum istam festinanti vestigio lucubratis viam, nec noctis intempestae manes larvasque formidatis? An tu, probissima puella, parentes tuos intervisere properas? Sed nos et solitudini tuae praesidium praestabimus et compendiosum ad tuos iter monstrabimus." Et verbum manu secutus prehenso loro retrorsum me circumtorquet, nec baculi nodosi quod gerebat suetis ictibus temperat. Tunc ingratis ad promptum recurrens exitium reminiscor doloris ungulae et occipio nutanti capite claudicare. Sed "Ecce" inquit ille qui me retraxerat "rursum titubas et vacillas, et putres isti tui pedes fugere possunt, ambulare nesciunt? At paulo ante pinnatam Pegasi vincebas celeritatem."

Dum sic mecum fustem quatiens benignus iocatur comes, iam domus eorum extremam loricam perveneramus. Et ecce de quodam ramo procerae cupressus induta laqueum anus illa pendebat. Quam quidem detractam protinus cum suo sibi funiculo devinctam dedere praecipitem, puellaque

---

[1] The winged horse ridden by Bellerophon when he slew the Chimaera.

property—or rather about a right of way—when we were caught in the open by the robbers loaded with their plunder. By the light of the moon they had recognised us from a long way off, and they greeted us with a malicious laugh.

30 One of the troop addressed us: "Where are you going at such a fast pace, travelling by night like this? Aren't you afraid of ghosts and demons in the deep of the night? Are you in a hurry to visit your parents, my dutiful girl? So then, we will provide you with a convoy for your loneliness, and show you a shortcut to your family." Suiting the action to the word, he grasped my rein and twisted me back round, nor did he spare me the usual beating with a knobby walking-stick that he was carrying. Then, as I was hastening unwillingly to a ready and waiting death, I became aware again of the pain in my hoof, and I began to nod my head and limp. "Well, well," said the fellow who had dragged me round, "you are staggering and wavering again. You mean those rotten feet of yours can run away but not walk? And yet just a little while ago you were surpassing the winged velocity of Pegasus."[1]

While my kindly comrade was jesting with me in these terms and brandishing his club, we had reached the outer defences of their home. And there, hanging from a branch of a tall cypress with a noose round her neck, was the old woman. They immediately pulled her down, tied her up with her own rope, and threw her over the cliff. Straightway

statim distenta vinculis, cenam, quam postuma diligentia praeparaverat infelix anicula, ferinis invadunt animis.

31 Ac dum avida voracitate cuncta contruncant, iam incipiunt de nostra poena suaque vindicta secum considerare. Et utpote in coetu turbulento variae fuere sententiae, ut primus vivam cremari censeret puellam, secundus bestiis obici suaderet, tertius patibulo suffigi iuberet, quartus tormentis excarnificari praeciperet. Certe calculo cunctorum utcumque mors ei fuerat destinata. Tunc unus omnium sedato tumultu placido sermone sic orsus est:

"Nec sectae collegii nec mansuetudini singulorum ac ne meae quidem modestiae congruit pati vos ultra modum delictique saevire terminum, nec feras nec cruces nec ignes nec tormenta ac ne mortis quidem maturatae festinas tenebras accersere. Meis itaque consiliis auscultantes vitam puellae, sed quam meretur, largimini. Nec vos memoria deseruit utique quid iam dudum decreveritis de isto asino semper pigro quidem, sed manducone summo, nunc etiam mendaci fictae debilitatis et virginalis fugae sequestro ministroque. Hunc igitur iugulare

they bound the girl in chains, and like ravenous animals attacked their dinner, which had been cooked for them by the wretched crone's posthumous diligence.

31 While bolting down all the food with voracious gluttony, they began to discuss among themselves our punishment and their revenge. As happens in a boisterous gathering, the opinions expressed were varied. One advised that the girl be burned alive; a second exhorted that she be thrown to the beasts; a third advocated that she be nailed to a cross; a fourth recommended that she be torn to pieces on the rack. But at least everyone voted that in any case she must die. Then one member of the group quieted the uproar and began calmly to deliver the following address:

"It is not in keeping with the principles of our guild," he said, "nor with the gentle disposition of each and all, nor indeed with my own sense of moderation, to allow you to indulge your fury beyond the limits of the crime. You ought not to invoke wild beasts or crosses or flames or racks—in short, a speedy extinction by a quick death. If you listen to my advice you will grant the girl her life, but the kind of life she deserves. Surely you have not forgotten your recent decree regarding that ass of ours, who is always lazy but a consummate glutton, and who is now besides a falsifier of counterfeit lameness and an aider and abettor of maidenly escape. You should vote, therefore, to slit his throat

crastino placeat, totisque vacuefacto praecordiis per mediam alvum nudam virginem, quam praetulit nobis, insuere, ut sola facie praeminente ceterum corpus puellae nexu ferino coerceat; tunc super aliquod saxum scruposum insiciatum[1] et fartilem asinum exponere et solis ardentis vaporibus tra-
32 dere. Sic enim cuncta, quae recte statuistis, ambo sustinebunt, et mortem asinus, quam pridem meruit, et illa morsus ferarum, cum vermes membra laniabunt, et ignis flagrantiam, cum sol nimiis caloribus inflammarit uterum, et patibuli cruciatum, cum canes et vultures intima protrahent viscera. Sed et ceteras eius aerumnas et tormenta numerate: mortuae bestiae ipsa vivens ventrem habitabit; tum faetore nimio nares aestuabit, et inediae[2] inediae diutinae letali fame tabescet, nec suis saltem liberis manibus mortem sibi fabricare poterit."

Talibus dictis non pedibus sed totis animis latrones in eius vadunt sententiam. Quam meis tam magnis auribus accipiens, quid aliud quam meum crastinum deflebam cadaver?

[1] F *insiticium.*
[2] F *nares aestuet inediae.*

in the morning, and then clean out all the guts. Strip the girl—whom he preferred to our company—and sew her up inside his belly so that only her face protrudes and he confines all the rest of her body with his beastly entwinement. Next set this ass crammed with stuffing upon the top of some rugged rock and let the heat of the burning sun take
32 over. By this means, you see, both of them will suffer all those punishments which you have quite properly determined for them: the ass will die, as he has long deserved; the girl will endure the bites of beasts when the worms lacerate her limbs, the scorching of fire when the sun scorches the ass's belly with its excessive heat, and the agony of the cross when the dogs and vultures draw out her very guts. And just count up all her other sufferings and torments too: she will be inhabiting while alive the inside of a dead animal; her nostrils will burn from the terrible stench; extended fasting will make her waste away with lethal starvation; even her hands will not be free to encompass her own death."

At the end of this speech the robbers assented to his proposal, not with their votes only[1] but with their whole hearts. As I listened to this with my long ears, what else could I do but bewail the corpse that I would be on the morrow?

[1] See note on II 7.